THE ONE YOU REALLY WANT

THE ONE YOU REALLY WANT

Jill Mansell

headline

First published in 2004
by HEADLINE BOOK PUBLISHING

10 9 8 7 6

Cataloguing in Publication Data is
available from the British Library

ISBN 0 7553 0486 1 (hardback)
ISBN 0 7553 0487 X (trade paperback)

Typeset in Times by Palimpsest Book Production Limited,
Polmont, Stirlingshire
Printed and bound in Great Britain by
Mackays of Chatham plc, Chatham Kent

HEADLINE BOOK PUBLISHING
A division of Hodder Headline
338 Euston Road
LONDON NW1 3BH
www.headline.co.uk
www.hodderheadline.com

To Gail Annan

And with many thanks to Jules for generously supporting Barts Cancer Centre of Excellence.

Chapter 1

'Go on, you can say it,' Nancy offered, because it was so obviously what Carmen was longing to blurt out down the phone. Five-year-olds had more self-control than Carmen.

Five hundred miles away in London, Carmen replied innocently, 'I wouldn't dream of saying I told you so. We all know what happens to best friends who do that. You're the one who married Jonathan, so it stands to reason you thought he was the bee's knees. If I'd told you then what part of a bee I thought he was, you'd have hated me. That's why I pretended to like him.'

Nancy smiled to herself, thinking that she really should be crying. 'And that's why you don't have a Bafta. You may have tried to pretend, but it didn't fool anyone.'

'Ah, but I didn't tell you I thought he was an idiot,' said Carmen, 'and that's the important thing. You didn't feel as if you had to stick up for him the whole time, you didn't always have to defend him, d'you see, because if I had told you, you wouldn't have taken a blind bit of notice anyway. And we'd have ended up falling out.'

'Would we?' Nancy couldn't imagine falling out with Carmen. They'd been inseparable since they were eight.

'It wouldn't have been easy. Anyway, that's why I didn't. Which is why we're still friends,' Carmen said cheerfully.

'You can still say I told you so if you want to.' Nancy was feeling generous.

'Thanks, but I'll wait until I've put the phone down. I'm polite like that.' More seriously, Carmen said, 'Are you sure you're all right?'

Was she? Who could tell? Nancy suspected that she was actually in a mild state of shock. It was Christmas morning, after all. Christmas was such a happy day, in her experience, that it was quite hard to take in what had happened. When you'd put so much effort into buying and wrapping presents, sending cards, choosing a tree and decorating the house – well, it assumed a momentum of its own. Actually holding up your hands and saying Stop! was easier said than done.

When you'd spent this long gearing up to Christmas, it was hard to imagine not . . . well, going ahead and having it.

'I'm great,' said Nancy, because the last thing she wanted was Carmen worrying about her. 'Mum's going to be here soon to give me a hand with lunch.'

'And you're really not going to tell her?'

Nancy closed her eyes. 'Completely ruin her Christmas, you mean?' Compared with the devastation this would cause, keeping the news to herself would be a doddle. 'You know how Mum feels about Jonathan. She'd be distraught.'

'OK, you're the boss.' Mischievously Carmen said, 'Off you go, back to peeling the parsnips like a good little wifey. Ever tried them poached in honey and arsenic?'

'If I had, I wouldn't be here to tell you, would I?'

'See? You always were the clever one. I'd better let you go. Keep in touch,' said Carmen. 'Give me a ring this evening.'

'OK. Thanks.' Belatedly, Nancy said, 'Are you all right?'

'Me? I'm wonderful.'

Nancy felt guilty, because if anyone deserved to have a big fuss made of them over the Christmas period, it was Carmen. When your husband had died three years ago – and, unlike herself and Jonathan, Carmen had been totally devoted to Spike – you were entitled to be depressed. 'Well, look after yourself. I'll call you tonight when I get a chance.'

'Can't wait. And don't forget,' Carmen said chirpily, 'the honey disguises the taste of the arsenic.'

Had it only happened this morning? Was it really less than three hours ago that her world had tilted and begun to crumble?

OK, maybe not her whole world, but certainly her marriage.

Nancy, her breath misting up the bedroom window of their four-bedroomed detached house, gazed out over the frosty garden, sparkling iridescent in the sunlight like one of those glitter-strewn Christmas cards her Auntie Mags was so fond of sending. The sky was cloudless and an unseasonal shade of duck-egg blue. In the distance, beyond Kilnachranan, the mountains rose up snow-peaked and dramatic. The garden itself, all three-quarters of an acre of it, was wreathed in a glittery whiteness and heartbreakingly beautiful.

And down there on the stiff white grass stood the cause of her current torment. Her Christmas present from Jonathan.

2

It was all thanks to this . . . *thing,* that her life was about to change in a pretty major way.

The card had arrived ten days ago, among half a dozen others, as Nancy had been upstairs cleaning the bath. Even the sound of Christmas cards *phflummping* through the letterbox onto the mat was a thrilling one. They definitely made a more exciting noise, she had thought happily, than boring old bills and circulars. Because you never knew who might have sent you a card, completely out of the blue and against all the odds. Prince William perhaps, or Bono from U2, or Michael Douglas and Catherine Zeta Jones . . .

Well, she couldn't help thinking it and getting that lovely squirly feeling in her stomach, the one she always used to get when she woke up on Christmas morning and saw the bulging pillowcase of presents from Santa at the foot of her bed.

And incredibly, this time, there *was* an intriguing-looking envelope amongst the rest, a heavy expensive cream one addressed in handwriting she didn't recognise. Incapable of saving it until last, Nancy cast aside the others – from Auntie Jane and Uncle Denis in Brighton, the boring Matthews family across the road, Jonathan's smug cousin Edgar in Dundee – and ripped open the mystery envelope. The picture on the front of the card was a snow scene of an Edinburgh street. The rank of shops depicted in the painting rang a vague bell. Cavendish Row, that was it. Opening the card, Nancy read the printed inscription inside.

Christmas and New Year greetings to a valued customer, from all at Rossiter and Co., Fine Jewellers.

To personalise it, there was a formless squiggle of a signature at the bottom, the kind a monkey might have made. Tuh, so much for being sent a card by someone exciting. This was from someone who was barely human.

What's more, Nancy thought crossly, Jonathan's surprise had now been ruined. He'd clearly paid a visit to Rossiter's on Cavendish Row and bought her something from there for Christmas. Bought her something expensive, more to the point, because they were unlikely to send classy greetings cards, with Valued Customer on them, to every Tom, Dick and Harry who needed a new watch battery and popped into the shop. Except it hadn't occurred to the not-so-clever people at Rossiter's that cards sent to the home of a married male customer stood a good chance of being opened, completely innocently, by his wife.

And since the whole point of Christmas presents was that they should be a fabulous surprise, her own Christmas morning was now spoiled.

Well, that was what she'd thought ten days ago. Gripping the window ledge, Nancy gazed down at her present. Having discreetly disposed of the greetings card in the dustbin, she'd spent ages practising her surprised-and-delighted face, because that was how she'd planned to react when she opened the satin-lined box containing whatever item of jewellery Jonathan had ended up choosing for her.

Instead he had steered her across the bedroom, instructed her to close her eyes, then pulled open the curtains with a triumphant flourish.

'Ta-daaa! You can open your eyes now,' Jonathan had proclaimed, and Nancy had obediently opened her eyes, mystified as to why he would have wanted to put the jewellery box containing her Christmas present out on the windowsill.

Except, of course, he hadn't.

'It's a lawnmower.' It had taken her a good few seconds to get the words out.

'The sit-on kind,' Jonathan informed her with pride.

'It's . . . it's . . .'

'You just wait, you won't know how you ever managed without one.' Jonathan was beaming now, incredibly pleased with himself. 'No more pushing and shoving that old petrol mower, this takes all the effort out of doing the grass. Trust me,' he slid his arms round Nancy's waist and kissed the back of her neck, 'you're going to love it.'

It took a little while for all the implications to sink in. When they finally did, Nancy felt like the slow girl at school, the very last one to get the punchline of a joke. If Jonathan hadn't bought some mystery item of jewellery from Rossiter's for her, then he must have bought it for someone else.

Hadn't he?

OK, OK, it was a mess, but not an entirely unexpected mess. If she was honest, there had been hints before now that Jonathan might be up to something, but never any that had been concrete enough to act upon. Nancy knew that girls who were overly possessive, jealous if their men so much as glanced in the direction of another girl, did themselves no favours at all. One of her old student flatmates, Doug, had got himself saddled with one of these. Having convinced herself that he was playing away, Ella had interrogated him endlessly, demanding to be kept informed of his every movement, even rummaging through his dirty laundry bag in order to go through Doug's tatty jeans pockets for phone numbers, and to sniff the collars of his shirts for traces of Other Women's Perfume. Nancy had caught her doing this once, at two o'clock in the morning. In a way, she'd felt sorry for Ella but at the same time she'd known the girl was making a terrible mistake. Everyone had laughed about her behind her back, and Doug had been embarrassed because, let's face it, looks-wise, he was no Johnny Depp. Girls weren't exactly falling over themselves to go out with him. If it had taken him six months to pluck up the courage to ask Ella out on a date, how likely was it that he'd be simultaneously seeing several other girls on the side?

Eventually the teasing had become too much to tolerate and Ella's inability to stop being jealous had taken its toll. Doug had finished with her and Ella had been inconsolable, begging Nancy to persuade him to see sense and take her back. All this had had a profound effect on Nancy, who had longed to say I told you so, I told you you'd drive him away in the end. Instead, she'd vowed never to be the jealous type, never to indulge in interrogation sessions – and never *ever* to accuse any man of hers of doing something he hadn't done.

Unless, of course, she knew he definitely had.

Nancy frowned. The thing was, did she know for sure? Could there still be an innocent explanation for what had happened, one that simply hadn't occurred to her? And if there was no innocent explanation, who in heaven's name could Jonathan be seeing?

Someone she knew? Someone from his office? Not his secretary, surely to God. The whole point of a mistress was getting one prettier and younger and bustier than your wife. Tania looked like a potato in a pashmina.

It couldn't be her, Nancy decided. To be honest, she'd be insulted if it was.

A car toot-tooted outside, bringing her back to earth. Rose, her mother, was rattling up the drive in her green Mini. Car, not skirt.

OK, forget the unfaithful husband and the all-but-over marriage. It was Christmas Day. On with the show.

'Darling!' Rose threw her arms round her beloved only daughter. 'You look beautiful! Merry Christmas!'

'You too, Mum.' Nancy hugged Rose in return, thinking how frail she felt. Her mother was only in her late sixties, but there was always the worry that this year might be her last. This was why she couldn't tell Rose about Jonathan's philandering – OK, alleged philandering. It would break her heart and ruin her Christmas. If it kills me, Nancy thought, I will protect Mum from that.

'Where's that lovely son-in-law of mine?' Rose was peering hopefully past Nancy into the house. 'I've got bags of presents here – they weigh an absolute ton.'

5

'Jonathan's gone down to the pub to meet Hamish and Pete. Pre-lunch drinks.' Nancy, who'd been delighted to be shot of Jonathan for an hour, said, 'You know how it is, all the men get together and compare Christmas sweaters, the one with the most horrible pattern wins a – um, not that Jonathan ever stands a chance of winning', she added hastily, 'but some people have families with terrible taste. Anyway, he'll be back by two o'clock. Let me carry the bags inside. Oh Mum, you are naughty, you've brought far too many presents.'

'Rubbish, I enjoy buying them.' Following Nancy inside, Rose heaved a sigh of pleasure. 'Such a gorgeous house. You're so lucky, darling. Can you believe how lucky you are?'

Nancy thought back to the times at the beginning of their marriage when she had thought she'd been lucky. Or before she'd begun to inwardly suspect that Jonathan might not turn out to be Mr Faithful-till-the-End-of-Time after all.

But this was her mother asking the question. This time last year Rose had bought Jonathan a mug with World's Best Son-in-Law! printed on it. Hastily changing the subject, Nancy said, 'The turkey's in the oven. I've done the potatoes and the bread sauce, but the rest of the vegetables are still—'

'How did I guess they would be?' Rose had been busily arranging the Christmas presents under the tree. Straightening, she beamed. 'Don't worry, darling, I'm here now. We can have a glass of sherry and a lovely chat while we're doing it all. You can tell me everything that's been going on.'

Nancy had to turn away so as not to let Rose see the tears in her eyes. Did other 28-year-olds tell their mothers everything that had been going on in their lives? Maybe they did. But Rose always saw the best in people; there was a kind of innocence about her. Nancy, feeling it was her duty to protect her mother from disappointment, had never been able to bring herself to tell Rose the truth.

'Now, parsnips. Carrots. Oh my word, asparagus – that must have cost a fortune, you are naughty.' Rose, surveying the contents of the vegetable basket, was torn between delight and terror at the thought of how much the bundles of fresh asparagus must have cost. 'Right, I'll make a start on the carrots.'

Swallowing the lump in her throat, Nancy watched her mother deftly peel and chop the carrots. Rose McAndrew, sixty-eight years old, four feet eleven inches tall and weighing less than seven stone with all her clothes on. Widowed thirteen years ago, she had never so much as looked at another man. She lived alone in a tiny, pin-neat, rented flat in Edinburgh, still worked part-time as a cleaner in an old people's home and was a prodigious knitter. Every spare second was spent producing, at lightning speed, soft knitted toys which she then donated to a charity shop supporting a children's hospice. Privately Nancy found it heartbreaking that her mother could spend eight hours knitting, sewing together and stuffing an intricately detailed clown complete with knitted tube of toothpaste, toothbrush and pyjamas, only for it to be sold in the shop for four pounds fifty. *Four pounds fifty.* She'd visited the shop and seen the price tags with her own eyes. So much work for so little return, yet Rose had exclaimed in delight at the amount of money she was raising for the poor sick children. It simply wouldn't occur to her to be offended, because that wasn't the kind of person she was.

There was no one better.

Turning, Rose said happily, 'And what did Jonathan get you for Christmas?'

Nancy swallowed. 'A lawnmower. The kind you sit on. It's out in the garden.'

'A sit-on lawnmower? Oh my word, how marvellous! I say, darling, you'll be able to ride around on it like the Queen. What fun!'

Forcing a smile, because she was unsure how often the Queen actually rode around on a lawnmower, Nancy said, 'I know.'

'That's Jonathan for you, isn't it? So original. He always knows exactly the right thing to buy.'

Other people might have mothers in whom they could confide every tiny detail of their lives, but Rose wasn't that kind of mother. She needed to be cosseted and protected from details that would only upset her.

Nancy knew she couldn't tell her the truth.

Chapter 2

It was six in the evening when Carmen Todd let herself back into her empty house. She'd been helping out at the shelter for the homeless in Paddington since ten o'clock, serving up plates of Christmas dinner and pouring endless mugs of steaming hot, conker-brown tea. Nobody at the shelter knew who she was, which suited Carmen just fine. Now, reaching her bedroom, she stripped off her bleached blue sweatshirt and old jeans and chucked them into the laundry basket. They'd been clean on this morning, but you never wanted to stay in the clothes you'd visited the shelter in.

In the bathroom, Carmen switched on the power shower and examined her face in the bathroom mirror while she waited for the water to heat up. Her short black hair was tousled and spiky, as if she'd spent ages faffing it about with gel and mousse – except she hadn't. Her dark brown eyes stood out against the pallor of her face and her slanted eyebrows were more like the ticks made by a teacher with a fat felt pen, in a hurry to finish marking. She knew she could look better than this, but no one at the shelter was all that bothered when it came to make-up. So long as she slipped them a few extra cigarettes, that was all they cared about.

Oh well, maybe next Christmas would be better for both them and herself.

The doorbell rang just as she was about to climb into the shower. Hesitating, Carmen wondered who on earth it could be at six o'clock on Christmas night. Not carol singers, surely. She certainly wasn't expecting any visitors.

But not answering the door – or at least speaking into the entryphone – was beyond her capabilities. Hurriedly wrapping a daffodil-yellow towel round herself – not that anyone could see her, but old habits died hard – Carmen padded through to the hallway and pressed the button on the speaker.

'Yes?'

'Carmen Todd, this is the police. Open the door please, we have a warrant to search the premises.'

Breathless with disbelief, Carmen said cautiously, 'Rennie? Is that you?'

'Of course it's me! Open the door this minute, woman, before my feet freeze to the pavement. And you'd better put some clothes on before I get there.'

Startled, Carmen leapt back from the entryphone. 'How d'you know I'm not dressed?'

'I'm a man. It's my job to know these things. Superman isn't the only one with X-ray vision, let me tell you.' Rennie cleared his throat with characteristic impatience. 'By the way, I wasn't kidding about it being bloody cold out here.'

'Oh, sorry!' Hastily Carmen buzzed him in, before racing through to the bedroom to swap her bath towel for a parrot-blue velour dressing gown. By the time she'd finished fastening the belt – tied with a double knot in case Rennie got boisterous – he'd arrived at her front door.

'It's really you! I can't believe you're here.' Thrilled to see him, she hurled herself into his arms. 'I thought you were in Alabama or Mississippi or somewhere . . .'

'Somewhere with lots of vowels,' said Rennie, hugging her hard in return. 'I know, we were. Well, Illinois, same difference. They had to cancel the rest of the tour. Dave's been hitting the bottle again and Andy's snorting coke like a human Dyson. Neither of them were capable of doing their stuff on stage, and seeing as there was a drying-out clinic handy, Ed packed them both off there. So that's it, I flew back last night. Thought I'd come and see how you're doing. Now, stand back and let me take a good look at you.'

Ditto. Smiling, Carmen took in the almost shoulder-length dark hair, the deep tan, a wicked grin and those glittering dark-green eyes that always looked as though they were ringed with eyeliner – except they weren't, that was just Rennie's impossibly thick eyelashes. He was wearing a tan leather jacket, crumpled cream jeans, a faded brown polo shirt and the kind of hideous brass-buckled belt that only a cowboy would wear. But he was looking lean and fit, as ever. For as long as Carmen had known him, he'd exuded an air of health. The whites of his eyes were a clear blue-white, his tongue raspberry pink, his stomach washboard flat. The cowboy belt let the overall effect down badly, but Rennie wouldn't allow that to bother him. If he liked something, he wore it, and that was that.

'Stunning as ever,' he pronounced at last, his brown hands on Carmen's shoulders. 'Anyway, I thought this was a respectable street.'

'It's a dressing gown! It's completely done up,' Carmen protested.

'I'm not talking about you, I'm talking about the street. I thought it was supposed to be dead posh around here.'

What with his touring commitments, combined with the fact that he'd spent the majority of the last three years out of the country, Carmen forgave him. Just.

'Actually, it is dead posh.'

'Sorry, it's gone right downhill since I was here last. Rear Admirals, QCs, the silver spoon brigade – more pompous gits than you could shake a stick at in the good old days. Call the police as soon as look at you, they would. Answer the door to a stranger? Good grief, you must be joking.'

Patiently Carmen said, 'Is there a point to this, or is it just a general off-the-cuff rant?'

'Sweetheart, of course there's a point.' Heading through to the kitchen, Rennie opened the fridge and seized a bottle of Veuve Cliquot. 'OK to open this?'

She hesitated. The bottle had been there for over two years. She'd bought it on the first anniversary of Spike's death, along with several packets of paracetamol and Nurofen. The plan had been to spend the night at home alone, just for a change, and give herself until midnight to carefully think things through. If, when the clock chimed twelve, she decided there was no point in carrying on, she would finish the bottle of champagne then swallow the painkillers.

At eleven o'clock, with the bottle chilling nicely in the fridge, she had opened a writing pad and begun to compose a suicide note.

By midnight the wastepaper bin was piled high with scrunched-up sheets of paper. Mortified, Carmen had discovered that suicide notes weren't as easy to write as she'd recklessly imagined. Everything she put down sounded ridiculous when she tried reading it aloud, like one of those really bad plays in the Morecambe and Wise shows Spike had so loved to watch on cable TV. Increasingly self-conscious and frustrated, Carmen realised how embarrassed she would be to leave behind the kind of suicide note people might secretly snigger at.

Furious with herself, she'd ended up putting the unopened bottle back into the fridge and making herself a cup of tea instead. Since flushing the painkillers down the loo would have been nothing but a criminal waste of painkillers, she'd stacked them in the bathroom cabinet to use in the recommended dose when her next period arrived.

Waste not, want not.

Well, if she was going to carry on living, she'd need them.

The champagne she'd left there in the fridge, however, as a salutary reminder.

What the hell. Carmen gestured at the bottle. 'Good idea. You open it, I'll get the glasses.'

'And I'll get back to my point,' said Rennie, 'which is that I arrived here two hours ago. You were out.'

'I was at the shelter.'

'That explains the smell.' Rennie had never been one to keep his innermost thoughts to himself. Catching the look on Carmen's face he grinned and said, 'OK, OK, and it's very noble of you to do your bit, but I'm just telling you, you do smell.'

The trouble was, she knew he was right. Exasperated, Carmen headed for the bathroom. 'Open the bottle. I'll be back in five minutes.'

Helpfully Rennie said, 'Want a hand?'

'You're hilarious. Go and sit down in the living room. And don't eat all my Thornton's truffles.'

As she shampooed her hair and soaped her body in the steaming shower, Carmen marvelled at Rennie's attitude to life. He had more energy than anyone she'd ever known, working hard and playing harder, always joking, incapable of not flirting with practically any girl who happened to cross his path. And, being Rennie, an awful lot crossed his path.

Rennie Todd, her brother-in-law. Spike's younger brother. Apart from their smiles, no two brothers could have been less alike. Closing her eyes as rivers of shampoo cascaded down over her face, Carmen pictured Spike, her beloved husband, with his sparkling grey eyes, dark blond hair and tendency towards pudginess. Whereas Rennie crackled and fizzed with energy, Spike had always been the quieter, calmer member of the band, the couch potato physically. He'd thought more deeply about things, written songs with profoundly meaningful lyrics. Rennie, Carmen was fairly sure, had never had a profound meaningful thought in his life.

And he was still alive, that was another pretty significant difference between the pair of them. Rennie was dazzlingly alive and Spike was dead.

Chapter 3

Out of the shower, Carmen roughly towel-dried her hair and wrapped herself back up in her dressing gown. With a bit of luck she now smelled of Jo Malone tuberose rather than Eau de Shelter.

In the living room, predictably, Rennie had made himself entirely at home. Stretched out across the navy sofa, he was busy finishing off a tube of Pringles, flicking through TV channels and simultaneously chatting on his mobile. Grinning across at Carmen, he said into the phone, 'Sorry, darling, have to go now, the nurses are bringing my grandmother in to see me . . . hello, Granny, you're looking well . . . OK, I'll give you a ring, bye now.'

'Thanks a lot.' Reaching over, Carmen snatched the remote control from him, because Rennie could flick channels for England and it drove her insane.

'Sorry.' He grinned up at her, unrepentant. 'Her name's Nicole, but the lads call her Clingfilm. She was desperate to spend Christmas with me. I had to come up with a decent excuse.'

It wasn't only where TV programmes were concerned that Rennie had the attention span of a gnat.

'Couldn't you just have told her you were visiting your tragic old sister-in-law? Wouldn't that have been boring enough?'

'You're joking. Nicole was a huge Spike fan. She'd have wanted to come along and meet you,' said Rennie. 'That's why I invented a granny-in-a-nursing-home in Stockton-on-Tees. That's better.' He sniffed approvingly as Carmen shoved his feet to one side and sat down. 'Same stuff Spike used to buy you.'

'It's my favourite,' said Carmen. 'Unlike some people, I don't get bored of something after three days and rush off to try something new.'

'Touché. And if I wanted a big lecture I could have stayed in Illinois and listened to my manager. Anyway, it's Christmas and we mustn't bicker. Guess what I did this afternoon when I came here and discovered you were out?'

This was one of those completely unanswerable questions, so Carmen didn't even attempt to answer it. With a lazy shrug she said, 'Who knows?'

'Sat down on your front step.' Rennie raised his eyebrows at her, miming outrage. 'Now, bearing in mind that this *is* Fitzallen Square in the very *poshest* part of Chelsea, I'm sure you'll agree that this is an appalling thing to do. I fully expected to be harangued by retired brigadiers, ordered out of the square by SAS troops swinging down from helicopters – Jesus, I'll never understand why Spike wanted to live in a place like this.'

He did, though. It had been that very air of pompous gentility that had attracted Spike, the thought of shocking the residents and sending them into a blind panic at the prospect of sharing their elegant Georgian square with a member of a heavy rock band like Red Lizard. The sunny, seven-bedroomed property, arranged on four floors and immaculately renovated throughout, was the last place anyone had imagined they'd choose to settle.

It had appealed to Spike's sense of humour. He'd bought the five million pound house as a joke. But within a few months he and Carmen had both fallen in love with it.

'So the SAS swooped in,' said Carmen.

'No, they *didn't*. That's just it. One of your neighbours opened their front door and asked if they could help me.'

'Thinking you were about to launch into a spot of breaking and entering.'

'Absolutely. I told them you were out, and said I'd wait on the step until you came back. So they said I couldn't possibly wait outside and why didn't I come over and join them for a drink? Well, at this point, *obviously*, I thought I must be having some kind of hallucination,' said Rennie. 'What were these posh people thinking of, for crying out loud? Didn't they realise what they sounded like? Poor people, normal people, that's what. And here they were behaving as if they lived on a . . . a . . . council estate!'

'OK, calm down. In that case I'll hazard a guess that it wasn't the Brough-Badhams at number sixty-two.'

Brigadier Brough-Badham and his wife, the Hon. Marjorie, had been so horrified when they'd first heard four years earlier who their new neighbours were to be, that they had started a petition. Neither of them had ever spoken a word to their deeply undesirable residents; the Brigadier bristled his moustache and the Honourable Marjorie looked

13

down her anteater nose at Carmen whenever they passed each other in the square.

Actually, it was the thought of allowing the Brough-Badhams to think they'd won that had stopped her from moving away after Spike died.

'It was your other neighbour, the one on this side.' Rennie jerked his thumb to the right. 'Number fifty-eight.'

'Funny name for a neighbour.'

'Been reading Christmas cracker jokes again?' Digging her in the ribs, Rennie said, 'I can't believe you've never met him. What a great bloke. When he invited me in, I thought you must know each other but he says not. He reckons you've been hiding from him.'

'I have not,' Carmen protested with a fraction too much denial. 'He only moved in three months ago, then he was off again, then I was away for a fortnight when I took Mum to Cyprus. You know how it is around here,' she ploughed on. 'People are busy, out at work – our paths just haven't crossed, that's all. I haven't been hiding.'

This was true. More or less. Well, not counting the couple of times she'd seen her neighbour climbing out of his car and had ducked away from the window before he could catch a glimpse of her and wave.

'His name's Connor O'Shea,' said Rennie.

'Is it?'

'Then again, I thought you might have known that, after he pushed that note through your door inviting you to his house-warming party.'

Bugger. The blood rushed to Carmen's pale cheeks.

'So you see, it rather looks as if you have been hiding from him after all.'

'Don't start nagging,' she said self-consciously.

'Come on,' Rennie argued. 'Someone has to. Sweetheart, it's been three years now. The old Carmen would have jumped at the idea of a party.'

'But I'm not the old Carmen, am I? I'm the new Carmen now. And it's not as easy as you're making out.' She paused and watched him expertly remove the cork from the bottle of Veuve Cliquot – with a discreet hiss, just like a wine waiter. In the old days they'd opened bottles of champagne like racing drivers – it was a wonder there'd ever been any left to drink.

'Great new neighbour. Friendly invite to a house-warming. I don't see the problem.'

'Well, you wouldn't, would you? Because you're you.' Carmen sipped

14

the champagne she'd been saving for her suicide attempt. Actually, it was really nice. 'But I was married to Spike and now I'm not. He's gone and I'm the one that's left. The one nobody's interested in.'

'Oh, come on, that's—'

'Don't shout at me. I'm not fishing for compliments or going for the sympathy vote. It's just that whenever I meet new people and they find out who I am, all they want to talk about is Spike and what it was like being married to him. They think I'm lucky, because he left me every-thing in his will, which is pretty weird because I don't feel lucky. So that's why I didn't go to the house-warming party. And I know I should have at least replied to the invitation but I didn't and that's that. Sometimes I have the manners of a pig.'

'OK, now I get it,' said Rennie. 'That's why you spend all your time at that damn shelter. Nobody knows who you are, do they? Nobody there has any idea that you live in a place like this, that you were married to Spike Todd. They think you're just a normal girl in jeans and a sweat-shirt who travels there on the tube.'

'So? Is that so weird? They treat me like they treat anyone else,' said Carmen. 'It's nice.'

'You mean they're just as happy to pee on your shoes as anyone else's? I can see how nice that would be. If I came along with you, would they pee on my shoes too?'

'So what does he do? This neighbour of mine.' Carmen was keen to change the subject.

'You see? You're no different to anyone else. Connor O'Shea, big friendly Irish guy in his thirties – how has he managed to make enough money to live next door to you?'

Carmen punched him. 'That's not what I'm asking.'

'Of course it is. Admit it, you're dying to know. It's human nature,' said Rennie. 'He's just bought a house in Fitzallen Square. He drives a Bentley. He has an apartment in New York and a villa in the south of France. So what do you reckon, could he work in the paint department of B&Q? Behind the counter at the post office on Finchley High Street? School caretaker, perhaps? Or maybe he's a clerical officer in the civil service and he spends his day flicking paper clips at—'

'Right, that's it. I don't want to know,' said Carmen. 'So don't tell me.'

'Fine. Just making a point,' Rennie said innocently. 'Could be a bank robber, come to think of it. Someone big in the East End gangland under-world thingy. Did he look a bit shifty to you, when you were secretly peeping down at him from your bedroom window?'

Bugger, was this another of Rennie's inspired guesses or had that bloody neighbour of hers spotted her and let on to him?

'East End? I thought you said he was Irish.'

'Ah well, begorrah, of course he *said* he was Irish.' Rennie adopted the most appalling Dublin accent. 'But that could just be a cover, couldn't it? A front to steer people away from the truth. Rather like you, down at that shelter of yours.'

'You don't have to stay here, you know. You could always go back to your Irish Cockney gang leader and spend the rest of the evening there.'

'He's already invited us. He's got a house full of friends and family. We're welcome over there any time this evening,' said Rennie. 'Then tomorrow they're flying off to Barbados for a couple of weeks.'

'With their forged banknotes and sawn-off shotguns.'

'If we do go round there, look after me. Whatever you do, don't let me flirt with his girlfriend. She's a minx.' Rennie shuddered. 'I don't want to end up in the Thames wearing extra heavy boots. Not my idea of a Christmas present.'

Taking another sip of champagne, Carmen wondered whether this would be a good time to meet her mystery neighbour. Probably, with Rennie here, it was the ideal opportunity. She knew she should be making more of an effort. As he'd already pointed out, she never used to shy away from people and parties.

But in an odd way, Fitzallen Square's air of reserve – OK, downright unfriendliness – suited the way she'd been feeling. She was used to it now. Once you started smiling and saying hello to your neighbours you ran the risk of falling into conversation with them. After that, they started inviting you to boring residents' meetings or hideous cheese and wine parties. And from then on you really were on the slippery slope to getting entangled with the kind of people you really didn't want to be entangled with and knowing that all the time they were talking about you behind your back.

'Not tonight,' said Carmen. 'Maybe when they get back from holiday. I'd rather just stay here. What time do you have to leave?'

'Charming. Trying to get rid of me already?'

'No!' She hit him on the head with the empty Pringles tube. 'Just asking a perfectly normal question. You turn up out of the blue, you eat my Pringles – if you're hoping for a Christmas dinner, you're out of luck, because I didn't buy any proper f—'

'Hey, calm down, I'm not on the scrounge for a free meal. I came here to see you. And your Pringles obviously.'

16

'There's another tube out in the kitchen.' Carmen was glad to see him, glad he was here. Deep down, she'd been dreading spending Christmas evening on her own. She'd volunteered to stay on at the shelter but they had told her, kindly, firmly, that eight hours was enough.

Chapter 4

They spent the next couple of hours catching up on all the news, drinking, eating and intermittently flipping through the channels on TV. A festive re-run of *Fatal Attraction* prompted Carmen to tell Rennie the story of Nancy and the Christmas card from the jewellers.

Predictably, Rennie shook his head and tut-tutted. 'What an amateur. Number one rule when you're buying anything like that, always pay in cash. And always, *always* give a false address. Ouch.'

'It's not funny. You're single, he's married. Nancy is my best friend and that bastard's cheating on her, I just know he is.'

Looking around the living room, with its complete absence of Christmas decorations, Rennie said, 'If she's your best friend and you were going to be here on your own, why didn't she invite you up there for Christmas?'

'She did. I turned her down, said I couldn't miss my shift at the shelter.'

'And the real reason is?'

'You know what I'm like. I can get a bit mopey at this time of year. I didn't want to inflict my moods on other people, make them feel guilty for having fun and enjoying themselves.' Carmen wriggled herself into a more comfortable position on the sofa. 'Plus, I never did like Jonathan. The thought of having to pretend I did was more than I could stand.'

'You see? That's the difference between us. I never pretend to like people I don't like. Complete waste of time. Why can't everyone just say what they think?'

'Because world war would break out and everyone would end up dead.' Patiently, Carmen said, 'And how would that help?'

'But what if your friend Nancy's got it all wrong? I mean, I've never met her husband, and he does *sound* like a dickhead, but she doesn't know for sure that he's fooling around, does she? OK, just off the top of my head here,' Rennie raked his fingers impatiently through his tousled hair, 'he could have gone out a few weeks ago and bought her an emerald necklace for Christmas. Then a few days later, Nancy happens to mention in passing that she can't stand emerald necklaces. What's he going to do? Take it back to the shop. Buy her something else instead, like a sit-on lawnmower. But in the meantime his details have already gone into the computer. He's been added to their Christmas card list.'

'Jonathan would never have done that.' Carmen's voice dripped with scorn.

Rennie shrugged. 'Maybe not, but it's feasible. That'd be *my* excuse.'

The phone rang. Hastily swallowing a mouthful of Viennese truffle, Carmen snatched it up before Rennie could get in first and say something hideously embarrassing.

'Hi, it's me.' Nancy's voice was hushed and strained.

'And?' Carmen's heart went out to her.

'Mum's just gone up to bed. I don't want her to overhear me. God, what a day. All this pretending everything's fine is exhausting.'

Carmen, who knew all about putting on a brave face and pretending everything was fine, said, 'Where's Jonathan?'

'Out.'

'What? It's Christmas night!'

'I know. He came back from the pub at two o'clock and we had a nice afternoon. Well, nice for Mum,' Nancy amended. 'I mean, everything was like normal, as far as she was concerned. Then at eight o'clock Jonathan got a call on his mobile. He said it was his friend Hamish, having trouble getting his new computer fixed up. So off he went to help, but that was three hours ago and now his phone's switched off, and I'm a bit worried that when he does get home I might punch him.'

'OK, sshh,' Carmen said soothingly as Nancy's voice rose. 'How long is your mum staying with you?'

'Until tomorrow night. That's another thing,' Nancy burst out. 'This afternoon Jonathan told me we've been invited to a Boxing Day party at the pub. Well, I said no because I knew Mum wouldn't be too keen. Pubs aren't really her thing, and she wouldn't know anyone. So Jonathan said fine, me and Mum could stay at home if we liked, but he didn't see why he should miss out on a bloody good party. Oh God.' Nancy took a deep breath, steadying herself. 'It's just awful. What's Mum going to think if he disappears again?'

'Tell her,' said Carmen.

'I can't, I just can't. She'd be so upset.' Nancy sounded close to tears.

'She's your mother.'

'Exactly!'

'Take her home at lunchtime and go on to the party afterwards.'

'How can I do that?' Nancy let out a wail. 'She's all excited about staying with us until tomorrow night!'

'OK, so all three of you have to go to the party.' Carmen was fast running out of options.

'I know, I know we will. But I keep having this horrible thought,' said Nancy. 'What if Jonathan's girlfriend is there? That could be the reason he's so determined to go.'

'Well—'

'Hang on, I can hear a car!' There was the sound of a curtain being swished back, then Nancy hissed, 'It's Jonathan, he's home. I have to go.'

'OK, good luck . . .' but the line had already gone dead. 'She's all on her own,' Carmen said defensively, because her eyes were starting to glisten and Rennie was about to make fun of her for being such a girl.

'She's not on her own, she's got her mother and her husband there with her. I bet she wishes she was on her own.'

'You're all heart,' said Carmen.

'I'm not so bad.' Grinning across at her, Rennie said, 'I've got hidden depths.'

As he took out his mobile, Carmen eyed it suspiciously. 'Who are you ringing now?'

'Calling a cab.'

'Where are you going?' Her stomach contracted; she'd been perfectly all right on her own. But now that Rennie was here, she didn't want him to leave.

'The Savoy.'

'You can stay here if you want.' Carmen prayed she didn't sound as needy as she thought she sounded.

'I know.' Rennie winked to show he'd been teasing her. 'I am staying here. But I'm already booked into the Savoy. I need to get over there and pick up my stuff.'

'Here, cup of tea. Happy Boxing Day.'

Hmm? From the depths of sleep, Carmen heard the clink of china and smelled toothpaste and soap. Her eyes snapping open in disbelief, she saw that Rennie had brought her a cup of tea. Not only that, but it was still pitch black outside. He was even wearing aftershave.

'Oh my God,' squeaked Carmen, catching sight of the alarm clock. 'It's four o'clock in the morning!'

'I know, blame it on the jet lag. Now drink your tea,' Rennie said bossily, 'and chuck a few things into a case. Car's going to be here in half an hour.'

Was he hallucinating? Sleepwalking? Unbelievably drunk?

'What's going on?' Carmen eyed him with suspicion.

'I didn't bring you a Christmas present. So this is it. We're going on a little trip.'

The trouble with Rennie was he had absolutely no concept of the words little trip. Last night he'd been talking about Australia and she'd mentioned that it was somewhere she'd always wanted to visit.

Cautiously, Carmen said, 'How are we getting there?'

'Plane. Don't worry, I've already booked the tickets.'

Oh God, it was Australia!

'I don't know where my passport is.' She rubbed her eyes.

'Come on, where's your sense of adventure?'

'Gone walkabout.' Then Carmen saw that he was laughing at her.

'You don't trust me at all, do you? I wasn't actually planning to whisk you off to the Australian outback.'

'Where then?'

'Thought we might try the Edinburgh outback instead. See what Boxing Day parties are like up there.' Rennie ruffled her hair. 'Give your friend Nancy a bit of moral support.'

Chapter 5

Nancy nearly fainted when she answered the front door at ten thirty on Boxing Day morning and found Rennie Todd standing on the doorstep.

'Rennie? Good grief, what are you doing here?'

The last time she'd seen him had been at Spike's funeral. The time before that, at Spike and Carmen's wedding. He was her best friend's brother-in-law and she'd always found herself slightly at a loss for words in his presence.

And now here he was, looking even more like a rock star than ever in the out-of-context environment of her own front doorstep. His long hair gleamed, his diamond earring glittered in the sunlight and he was ridiculously tanned.

'I came up to see Carmen,' said Rennie.

'What? But she isn't here!'

He frowned. 'Yes she is.'

'Honestly, she isn't.' As Nancy shook her head, Jonathan came up behind her to find out what was going on.

'Who is it?'

'Carmen's brother-in-law.' Embarrassed to say his name, Nancy gestured awkwardly towards Rennie. 'He's looking for Carmen. I'm just explaining she isn't here.'

'Look, I'm sorry, but she is,' Rennie insisted, reaching over and yanking Carmen into view.

'Waaaahhhh,' shrieked Nancy, hugging her. 'I only spoke to you last night!'

'It was Rennie's idea. We caught the eight o'clock flight.'

'But you said you couldn't come up because you have to work!'

'I made her see sense. They already had plenty of volunteers for today.' Rennie grinned. 'Carmen isn't as indispensable as she likes to think. Hi, I'm Rennie.' He nodded at Jonathan, who was still standing behind Nancy. 'I've heard all about you.'

Oh God, thought Nancy, please don't.

'Actually we've met before.' Leaning past Nancy, Jonathan shook his hand. 'I was there at the wedding.' When Rennie looked blank, he added, 'Carmen's wedding . . . when she married your brother.'

'Oh, right. Sorry, I don't remember you. Never mind, we're here now.' Rennie flashed his dazzling smile. 'All the way up from London. You can invite us in if you like.'

'I can't believe it,' Nancy whispered when Jonathan had borne Rennie off. 'You're actually here. You don't know how much better that makes me feel.' Lowering her voice still further, she added, 'Does Rennie know?'

Nodding, Carmen said, 'It's OK, he won't say anything. We're on your side.'

'God, this makes all the difference in the world. Come through and say hello to Mum.' Happily Nancy dragged her through to the kitchen, where Rose flung herself at Carmen in delight.

'What a surprise! Oh my word, it's Christmas and I don't even have anything for you.' Rose loved to buy gifts for everyone; to be caught out like this clearly bothered her.

'You didn't know we were going to be here.' Carmen, who'd always been fond of Nancy's tiny, doll-sized mother, smiled and said, 'I didn't know we were going to be here. I didn't get anything for you either.'

But Rose was already dragging an enamelled bangle off her wrist. 'Here, pet, you have this. Pretty, isn't it? But it'll look so much better on you than on me . . . here, take it.'

'Rose, I couldn't possibly—'

'It's just a wee present. Don't offend me now,' Rose said anxiously, as she crammed the bangle over Carmen's left hand. 'Don't hurt my feelings by trying to give it back.'

There really was no answer to that. Rose would give you the shirt off her back if you wanted to polish your sunglasses. Whatever she offered, you knew her feelings would be hurt if you refused. Forced to give in gracefully, Carmen said, 'It's gorgeous, thank you so much,' and kissed Rose's soft powdered cheek. The powder smelled and tasted like powder from the olden days, which, seeing as Rose only ever wore it on very special occasions, it undoubtedly was.

'It's lovely to see you again.' Having patted Carmen's face, Rose turned and said, 'And you're Rennie. We haven't met before.'

Stepping forward to drop a kiss on each of her cheeks, Rennie grinned. 'If we had, I'd definitely have remembered. Mmm, you smell gorgeous, like a Hollywood goddess. It's like kissing Greta Garbo.'

23

He'd always known how to charm the opposite sex.

'Ah, get away with you!' Flushing with pleasure, Rose playfully slapped his hand. 'Greta Garbo's dead.'

'It's like kissing Greta Garbo at the height of her beauty.' Rennie was undeterred. 'When she starred in *Queen Christina*. That's one of my all-time favourite films.'

'Truly?' Rose's face lit up. 'Greta Garbo's my all-time favourite actress. I watched *Queen Christina* on the television just the other week. They were showing it on a Sunday afternoon—'

'I've got it on video,' said Rennie. 'And *Ninotchka*.'

'Oh, I just love *Ninotchka*!'

'And *Camille*,' Rennie pulled a face, 'but I don't love it as much as the others.'

'Well, who'd have thought it? You, another Garbo fan! And with hair like yours,' Rose marvelled. 'I mean, I know it's one of those music things, but does it really have to be that long?'

'*Rose*,' hissed Jonathan. 'He's our guest.'

'So's Rose,' Rennie said easily. 'Which means we can both say whatever we like. Now, we've sprung ourselves on you, so would you let me take you all out to lunch, to make up for it?'

'We can feed you!' Rose looked deeply offended; on the worktop behind her stood bowls of chopped carrots, potatoes and onions. 'There's more than enough for everyone.'

Under his breath Jonathan murmured, 'There's enough for everyone in Kilnachranan.'

'But wouldn't lunch out be more of a treat for you? How about the Kincaid Hotel in Edinburgh?' said Rennie. 'It's supposed to be fantastic. We could make a proper afternoon of it.'

Jonathan said, 'Bit short notice. I wouldn't think you'd get a table.'

'Oh, they'll find one for me. Suzy Kincaid's an old friend.'

Leaning against the worktop, Carmen wondered what it must be like to be Rennie, always able to do anything you wanted to do. In fairness, he'd been exactly the same before the band had known fame and fortune.

'That sounds great then.' Clearing his throat, Jonathan said, 'The thing is, we've been invited to a party this afternoon. Seems a bit rude to let your friends down because you've had a better offer. Maybe I should give the lunch a miss.'

He sounded torn. Carmen guessed that, much as he wanted to be down at the party with all his friends, he was reluctant to pass up the opportunity to boast to them that he had been taken out to lunch by Rennie Todd.

One thing was for sure, though. Jonathan really didn't want to miss out on this Boxing Day bash down at the Talbot Arms. Which was interesting, Carmen thought, and rather made you wonder why not.

'Right, better idea,' said Rennie. 'We'll have Rose's casserole for lunch and book a table at Kincaid's for dinner this evening. Then you lot can go to your party this afternoon.' He paused as if the thought had just occurred to him. 'Actually, would they mind if you brought along a couple of extra guests?'

'Great. No problem. Of course you can come along.' Jonathan nodded vigorously and Rose let out a little exclamation of pleasure.

'OK with you, Miss Garbo?' Rennie turned to her to double-check. 'You don't mind if we gatecrash?'

'I'd be delighted.' Beaming up at him, Rose said, 'And now I'll know somebody else there. Right, I've a turkey casserole that needs putting together.' In businesslike fashion she rolled up the sleeves of her blue-and-white Paisley printed shirt.

'Go on, you two.' Shooing Carmen and Nancy towards the kitchen door, Rennie said, 'I know you're dying for a proper gossip. I'll stay in here and let Queen Christina show me how to make a casserole.'

Rose, who hadn't grasped quite how famous her new pupil actually was, flicked at his rear end with a tea towel and said, 'Ah now, you're not to make fun of an old woman. Call me Rose and away with your nonsense.' Flicking him a second time as he sneaked a wedge of raw carrot, she added, 'And wash your hands before you start. That's how people end up in hospital.'

'Whatever you say, your majesty. Falling in love again . . .' sang Rennie, turning the kitchen tap on too fast and showering himself with water.

'That's Marlene Dietrich, you daft lad.' This time Rose had to use the towel to dab him dry.

'I know it's Marlene Dietrich. She's my second favourite actress. You know,' Rennie said cheerfully, 'if I didn't know myself better, I'd wonder if I was gay.'

Outside, bundled up in fleeces against the bitter cold, Nancy said, 'Who'd have thought it? My mum and Rennie Todd, getting on like a house on fire.'

'Ah well, that's Rennie for you. He has the knack. It's a good job Rose isn't twenty years younger.' Carmen's mouth twitched. 'You wouldn't risk leaving her alone with him in the kitchen – oh my God, here it is!'

They had rounded the side of the house. There, ahead of them on the frosted lawn, stood the shiny red lawnmower.

'Exhibit A, m'lud,' said Nancy. 'The vehicle the defendant was driving when she ran over her husband.'

'And mowed him to death, chopping him into a million pieces.' Carmen, arms outstretched and fingers wiggling, mimed little bits of Jonathan flying across the garden. 'Well, you wouldn't have to scatter his ashes. Cut out the middle man, that's what I say.'

This was how they had always dealt with emotional crises. Ever since their schooldays, they had learned that poking fun at their various predicaments – and at the members of the opposite sex who had invariably been the cause of them – was their coping mechanism of choice.

'It would make the garden grow,' said Nancy, her nose prickling with the cold.

'You could put it on his gravestone,' Carmen suggested. 'Lousy husband, great plant food.'

'Lousy husband, lousy lay, great plant food.'

'Really?'

'Not really. But imagine how cross he'd be, having to lie there with that carved on his headstone.' Nancy paused, then said, 'Thanks for coming up.'

'What are you going to do?'

'Get today over with, hope nothing awful happens at the party this afternoon. Once Mum's gone back to her flat, I can ask Jonathan what he's playing at. See what he has to say for himself.'

'And if he's seeing someone?' Carmen raised her slanting eyebrows. 'What then?'

'I leave him.'

'OK. And if he denies it?'

'I don't know.' Nancy felt a bit sick.

'Which would you prefer?'

'What?'

'Jonathan admitting he's guilty or denying everything?'

'I don't know.'

'You could stay,' said Carmen. 'Either way, you can put it behind you and forget anything ever happened. Plenty of wives do.'

Nancy looked at her. 'Why are you saying this? You don't even like him.'

'I know.' Carmen smiled and gave her arm a squeeze. 'But Rennie and I have rushed up here like the cavalry. Whatever you decide to do is up to you. This is your marriage. I don't want you to feel pressurised into doing something drastic, just because we're here. Because if you do, and you end up wishing you hadn't, you might blame me for ruining your life. You might end up hating me.'

Nancy was touched. It was a big thing she could be on the verge of doing, and thinking about it was deeply scary.

'Whatever happens, I won't hate you. I promise.' She patted Carmen's icy hand. 'It's just so ironic, isn't it? When you think back to a few years ago. Nobody gave your marriage a chance. Everyone was horrified when you and Spike got together. They were convinced you were making the biggest mistake of your life, they said it wouldn't last six months. And look how happy the two of you were.'

'Until he went and died and spoiled it all,' said Carmen.

'But if he hadn't, you know you'd still be together. Spike told me once that you and he were like a couple of swans,' Nancy remembered. 'He said you were mated for life.'

'We got such a kick out of proving everyone wrong.' Carmen smiled. 'Unlike you and Jonathan.'

'I know,' Nancy said wryly. 'Fairy-tale stuff. A dream come true. I was so lucky, Jonathan was such a catch, what had I ever done to deserve someone so handsome, so wealthy, with such a good job?'

'Oh yes, you were the one with the perfect man, the perfect marriage—'

'NANCY!' Above them, the bedroom window was flung open and Jonathan stuck his head out. 'Where's my blue Ralph Lauren shirt?'

Nancy tilted her face up. 'No idea. Hanging up in your wardrobe?'

'It isn't there. That's why I'm asking you what you've done with it.'

'Used it to mop the kitchen floor,' Nancy murmured under her breath. Raising her voice, she said, 'In your gym bag?'

'Shit.' Jonathan reappeared seconds later holding the offending shirt, every bit as damp and crumpled as if it had been used to mop the kitchen floor. 'I wanted to wear this this afternoon.' He looked hopeful. 'If you quickly washed it, couldn't you iron it dry?'

Honestly, it was like having a teenager in the house.

'Wear the white one,' said Nancy. 'That's washed and ironed.'

Heaving a sigh, Jonathan gave up and closed the bedroom window.

'You're a cruel and heartless woman.' Carmen tut-tutted. 'Fancy not rushing up there to wash and iron his shirt.'

'I know.' It had been the most minuscule gesture of defiance, but Nancy felt oddly liberated. 'Just plain selfish, that's me.'

27

Chapter 6

The Talbot Arms, on the outskirts of Kilnachranan, was lit up as they approached it, festooned with multicoloured Christmas lights and a flashing Santa on the roof. From the sound of things, a riotous party was already in progress.

'We needn't stay for long,' Nancy reassured her mother, because Rose wasn't used to parties. 'Just an hour or two.'

'Don't be such a spoilsport,' said Jonathan. 'It's Boxing Day. This lot will still be going at midnight.'

Nancy looked at him; a little hindsight was a dangerous thing. Now that she was fairly sure he was having an affair, everything he said or did seemed significant. The amount of effort he had put into his appearance could mean something. Was he secretly tweezing those stray hairs between his eyebrows? Why, after six years of wearing Eau Sauvage aftershave, had he recently switched to the new Calvin Klein? And was it to match his underpants?

'Will it be mainly young people?' wondered Rose.

'There's Nora who does the food. She's around your age,' said Jonathan. 'If you wanted, you could give her a hand in the kitchen.'

'Sorry,' said Rennie, putting his arm round Rose's shoulders as they made their way up to the front door of the pub, 'she won't have time for skivvying in the kitchen, she's going to be far too busy dancing with me.'

'Och, get away with you.' Rose dug him playfully in the ribs. 'I'm nothing but an old relic.'

'Don't knock yourself. I bet you've had a bit of a jive in your time.'

'There might be karaoke.' Nancy felt it only fair to warn Rennie. They were notoriously fond of a singalong down here at the Talbot Arms.

'No problem.' Rennie winked at her. 'Me and Rose would be delighted to show them how it's done. We'll sing a duet.'

Nancy was on edge, Carmen could tell. She was smiling and greeting people she knew, but there was a hint of brittleness to her smile and her knuckles, as she clutched her drink, were white. Luckily, nobody else was paying her much attention. Everyone was far more interested in nudging each other and whispering that that was Rennie Todd.

It was always amusing, watching other people's reactions to celebrities. Rennie, on his best behaviour for Nancy's sake, was handling the situation well. He was great at remembering people's names – just as well, seeing that Jonathan was currently proudly introducing him to Hamish, Pete and a whole host of drinking friends – and excellent at pretending to be interested when they all regaled him with stories of how they had once been in a band that could have made it, if only the record companies had had the sense to offer them a record deal.

Spike had hated the attention, but Rennie took it all in his stride. Listening, Carmen smiled to herself as she heard the plump one called Hamish saying, 'Ah, we were great, everyone said so, but you'd send out a load of demo tapes and never hear back. If you ask me, no one ever even bothered to listen to them. I'm telling you, we could have been *mega*.'

'It's a tough business,' Rennie agreed sympathetically. 'We spent a couple of years doing the pub circuit down south. One night we played to an audience of six, and two of them were passed out drunk on the floor.'

'Still, you got your lucky break in the end.' Hamish evidently still felt it was unfair.

'We did, we were lucky,' Rennie agreed good-naturedly. 'Hey, you've almost finished that one. Let me get you another drink. Rose, how about you? By the way, have you two met before? Hamish, this is Rose, my new girlfriend. Rose, say hello to Hamish.'

'And to think you were worried about your mother,' Carmen murmured an hour later.

'I know.' Nancy smiled, though her eyes continued to dart restlessly around the pub. 'D'you think that could be the one, over there?'

Jonathan was chatting easily to a girl in a red top and a short PVC miniskirt.

'Wouldn't have thought she was his type.' Then again, Carmen supposed, it was hard to know what kind of girl Jonathan might go for. Any one of them here could be a potential Other Woman. Plus, they could have got it all wrong and she wasn't here at all.

'I'm going to give Nora a hand with the food,' said Nancy. 'Have a chat with her, see if I think she knows anything.'

Carmen gave her hand a reassuring squeeze.

When Nancy had disappeared into the kitchen at the back of the pub, Carmen made her way over to the bar where Rose and Rennie were surrounded by a crowd of Jonathan's friends. Hamish was now quizzing Rennie about how it felt to play in front of an audience of forty thousand fans at Wembley. Rose, chatting away to a dark-haired woman in her late thirties, was admiring her dress.

'Monsoon,' Carmen heard the woman tell Rose. 'A few sequins always brightens things up, don't you think?'

'I've never had anything sparkly like this.' Rose was stroking the sleeve. 'Always too worried about the dry-cleaning bills, I suppose. I feel safer in things you can put in the washing machine. But this is beautiful. Oh my word, so is *that*.' Reverently she pointed to the brunette's right hand. 'Look at this ring!'

From where she was standing, Carmen saw three things. Firstly, despite being in mid-conversation at the time, Rennie stopped speaking for a moment.

Secondly, six feet away, Jonathan turned his head and glanced across at the brunette.

Third, and most damningly of all, the brunette dimpled with pleasure and proudly waggled her fingers so that the diamond glittered in the lights from the nearby Christmas tree. And for just a fraction of a second she met Jonathan's gaze and smiled at him.

'Haven't seen that before!' Grabbing her hand, Hamish bellowed, 'Bloody hell, Paula. Bit of a rock, isn't it? Where did that come from?'

'My Auntie May bought it for me for Christmas. It's not real,' said Paula. 'Cubic zirconium.'

'It never is.' Shaking her head in admiration, Rose said, 'Aren't people clever these days? You'd never know the difference.'

'Thought you'd got yourself a secret admirer,' said Hamish jovially. 'Right, who's for another drink?'

Having extricated himself from the crowd, Rennie said in a low voice, 'Is it a fake?'

Carmen's jaw was tight. 'How would I know? I'm no expert. But I saw the way she looked at Jonathan.'

'Right, don't say anything to Nancy just yet. Leave this to me.'

Within minutes, Rennie was doing what he did better than anything else in the world. Flirting with the brunette whose name was Paula. It was a talent he'd never needed to hone; flirting came as naturally to him as breathing. Aware that Nancy was still in the kitchen and Carmen was sitting on a stool over at the bar watching him, he found out that her name was Paula McKechnie and that she was thirty-five and divorced with no children. He also learned that she worked in an art gallery in Edinburgh, was currently single and adored Thai food.

'Tell me,' said Rennie confidentially, 'd'you ever get that thing where you meet a complete stranger out of the blue and just . . . click with them?'

Paula regarded him playfully. 'I suppose it's been known to happen. Why?'

Rennie pulled an apologetic face. 'The thing is, I think it may be happening now. What are you doing tomorrow night?'

'Um . . .' Clearly flattered and excited, Paula said, 'Why are you asking?'

'Well, I'm staying at the Kincaid Hotel for a few days. I've never been to Edinburgh before, so I don't know anywhere, but if you could suggest a good Thai restaurant, I thought maybe you and I could check it out. Or anywhere you like. I'd love to take you out to dinner, get to know you better.' Rennie paused, a hesitant smile on his lips, then shook his head and said self-deprecatingly, 'But it's OK if you don't want to. Just thought I'd ask. Nothing ventured, nothing gained.'

During the course of their conversation he had been aware of Jonathan standing a short distance away, talking about rugby with his friends but clearly paying close attention to what was going on in the vicinity. Paula, also aware of this, said 'Um, the thing is, it's a bit—'

'Sorry, forget I asked. No problem.' Holding up his hands, Rennie began to back away.

Paula, terrified that she was about to miss her chance, whispered in a frantic undertone, 'No, look, give me a call tomorrow.' Turning away from Jonathan, she scrabbled discreetly in her fake Louis Vuitton handbag for a card and thrust it into his hand. 'There's my number, but it's better if you don't tell anyone. You know what people can be like . . .'

As smooth as any pickpocket, Rennie slid the card out of sight.

'You'd rather keep it between us.' He nodded understandingly. 'It's OK, I do know what people can be like.'

There was no sign of Nancy. Carmen was still on her stool watching them intently. Beckoning her to join them, Rennie said cheerfully, 'Hey, Carmen, over here. Got something to show both of you.'

Paula giggled. 'What is it?'

'Bring the bottle with you,' Rennie added as Carmen slipped down from the stool.

Obediently Carmen picked up the almost empty bottle of Frascati.

'OK, little trick I learned.' Pushing up his sleeves in businesslike fashion, Rennie rubbed his hands together and waggled his fingers like Paul Daniels.

'Magic,' Paula exclaimed with delight. 'I love magic!'

Carmen, sensing something was up, said, 'Rennie's full of tricks.'

'If I can remember how to do it.' He paused, deep in thought, then nodded and held out his hand to Paula. 'Right, give me that ring of yours.'

Entranced, Paula slid it off her finger and passed it over. 'Don't make it disappear, will you? Auntie May'll go mad.'

'I won't make it disappear,' Rennie promised. Taking the Frascati bottle in one hand and carefully eyeing the level of the wine, Rennie held up Paula's ring and said, 'OK, now concentrate. I can only do this once.' He exhaled slowly. 'Ready?'

Carmen was narrowing her eyes at him, warning him not to mess about, to get on with whatever it was he was about to do.

'Ready,' Paula said breathlessly.

'Right, here goes.' Gripping the ring between his fingers Rennie raked it down the side of the bottle.

The scratch in the glass was clearly visible.

'Is that it?' said Paula.

'Better tell Auntie May to take your ring back to the shop and complain. This isn't cubic zirconium,' said Rennie. 'They've only gone and sold her one with a real diamond in it instead.'

'OK.' Paula leaned forward confidingly and lowered her voice. 'Someone gave me the ring for Christmas. I know it's a real diamond. I just didn't want everyone else to know. You have no idea what it's like, living in a place like Kilnachranan.'

'Having an affair with a married man, making sure his wife doesn't find out,' said Rennie. 'Can't be easy.'

Paula's jaw tightened. She looked at him for a couple of seconds then briefly shook her head. 'It isn't. Can I have my ring back now?'

But Rennie was studying it. 'Know what Jonathan bought Nancy for Christmas? A lawnmower.'

He watched the colour drain from Paula's face, her breathing become fast and shallow.

'Did he?' Her voice was neutral.

Carmen said, 'Rennie, I—'

'I'd say you got the better deal,' Rennie continued. Maybe this wasn't how they'd planned it but he was buggered if he'd stop now. 'It's Jonathan, isn't it?'

Paula now looked as if she'd stopped breathing completely. '*What?*'

'Come on, don't give me that. You're having an affair with Jonathan Adams, right under his wife's nose, and now you've been caught out—'

'Rennie,' hissed Carmen, jabbing him hard in the ribs, and this time he did stop. But it was too late. Turning, he saw Rose standing behind him holding a tray of baked potatoes and a bowl of prawns in mayonnaise. Shit, shit. From the expression on her face, she'd heard everything.

Rennie mentally braced himself for the crash of the metal tray dropping to the ground. Shit, of all the people to have come up behind him at that moment.

'Is this true?' whispered Rose.

'Sorry.' Shaking his head, Rennie put a hand on her arm. 'Rose, I'm so sorry.'

Ignoring him, Rose stared at Paula. Still clutching the tray, she repeated, *'Is it true?'*

Chapter 7

Around them, the party was carrying on in full swing. Literally, in the case of the local curling team in their kilts, recklessly dancing along as Jon Bon Jovi blared from the jukebox.

Paralysed with horror, Paula tried to take a step back. She glanced helplessly across at Jonathan, but he was too busy laughing at the antics of the curling team to notice.

'Outside,' Rose hissed.

'Wh-what?'

'Outside. Now.' Passing the tray of baked potatoes over to Carmen, Rose nodded at the door. 'Without drawing attention to yourself.'

At that moment one of the kilted dancers lost his balance and stumbled backwards, landing on his backside on the dance floor and creating a handy diversion. As his audience screamed with delight upon discovering he was a true Scot, Rose prodded Paula, like a small ferocious bouncer, out of the pub.

Rennie looked at Carmen. 'Bloody hell.'

Carmen put down the tray. 'Nancy's going to kill you.'

'That's if her mother doesn't kill Paula first.'

They followed Paula and Rose out through the front door of the pub. It was four o'clock, already dark outside, and snow had begun to fall. Illuminated by the misty orange glow of the street lights, with snowflakes already gathering in her hair, Rose McAndrew was giving the trembling younger woman a piece of her mind.

'. . . you're going to listen to me and pay attention. My daughter's a good girl. She deserves so much *better* than this. Her husband may be a despicable idiot, but for some reason, God only knows why, Nancy worships him. She loves that man and I won't have her hurt. If you think it's clever to steal a married man away from his wife, well, then you're as stupid as he is. Men like that aren't worth stealing, trust me. And I'm certainly not going to stand by and see you hurt my daughter.'

'But—' began Paula.

'No buts,' Rose interjected icily. 'It's over. You aren't going to see Jonathan again and Nancy is never going to find out what her pathetic apology for a husband has been up to behind her back.'

'Actually, it's OK. I already know.' Stepping out of the shadows, Nancy saw everyone turn and stare at her. When she had emerged from the kitchen two minutes ago to find her friends and her mother missing from the pub, nobody appeared to know where they might have gone. When she pushed open the front door and heard Rose outside the pub berating someone, astonishment had rooted her to the spot. Lurking where no one would see her, she had listened in disbelief. But rather than Jonathan's affair, it was her mother's reaction that was truly confounding her.

She'd never heard her mother like this before, hadn't known she was capable of such a rant. It was like Gaby Roslin peeling off her face to reveal Anne Robinson underneath. Even more astounding was the discovery that Rose didn't adore Jonathan and worship the ground he walked on. At this moment she seemed more likely to spit on it.

Everyone was still gazing at her, Nancy realised, waiting for her to say something else. It was like stepping out onto a stage without learning your lines.

'I know,' she said again, trembling half with the cold and half with emotion. 'But Mum, how on earth did *you* find out?'

'I was in the right place at the right time.' As shocked as Nancy, Rose said, 'But I can't believe *you* know. Oh darling, why didn't you *tell* me?'

'Because I didn't want to spoil your Christmas. I knew you'd be upset.'

Rose shook her head in disgust. 'Upset? I'm not upset, I'm livid!'

At that moment the door swung open and Jonathan appeared in the doorway. Taking in the situation at a glance he said, 'What's going on? Why is everyone out here?'

'You may be stupid, Jonathan,' Rose retorted, 'but you aren't brain-dead. Even you must be able to work it out.'

Overwhelmed by the transformation in her mother, Nancy glanced across at Paula McKechnie, shivering in her sequin-strewn dress and looking utterly miserable. As she reached up to brush snowflakes from her face, a diamond glinted on her right hand. Watching her watch Paula, Rennie said by way of explanation, 'That's the Christmas present.'

How had he found this out? Nancy couldn't begin to imagine. While she'd been busy helping Nora in the kitchen, slicing onions and grating a mountain of cheese, all this had been going on without her.

'Cheating on your wife.' Rose eyed Jonathan with disdain. 'That is so low. How could you? She's not even as pretty as Nancy! You should be ashamed of yourself. My daughter adores you—'

'Mum, it's OK. I'm going to leave him.' A lump sprang into Nancy's throat, because she couldn't believe she was telling Rose this, wrecking her Christmas and breaking her heart. Except her tiny, frail mother wasn't actually looking that heartbroken. In the glow from the street lamp, she swung back round to face Nancy, a look of hope on her pale face.

'Really? Truly? Oh darling, thank God!' Clasping her thin fingers together, Rose said anxiously, 'Are you sure?'

'Absolutely sure.' Nancy's smile had gone wobbly with relief. 'I thought you were mad about Jonathan. I thought you'd be devastated.'

'Sweetheart, are *you* mad? I've known for years that he wasn't good enough for you! I wouldn't trust that little worm further than I could toss a caber.'

'Look, this is ridiculous,' Jonathan blustered. 'You can't talk about me as if I'm not even here! So what are you trying to make out, that some-thing's been going on between me and Paula?'

'Lies, lies. See what I mean about him being pathetic?' Rose shook her permed head with contempt.

'Jesus, after all we've done for you,' Jonathan shot back. 'D'you seri-ously think I *wanted* you here with us over Christmas? I only put up with it to keep Nancy happy.'

Outraged by this attack on her mother, Nancy opened her mouth to protest but felt Rennie's hand on her arm. 'Let her get on with it,' he murmured, nodding at Rose. 'She's doing fine.'

'And didn't you do a great job of that,' Rose riposted with spirit. 'Never mind, you've certainly cheered me up. This is turning out to be my happiest Christmas in years.' Turning back to face the rest of them she said brightly, 'Brrr, I'm getting a bit chilly. Shall we go now?'

Grinning at Nancy and Carmen, Rennie said, 'Whatever you say, Rose. You're the boss.'

'Wait,' Jonathan called out as they were about to leave. Paula had already scuttled back inside, but he had never been able to handle not knowing the answer to something that was bothering him. 'How did you find out?'

It was snowing heavily now. Surveying him, Nancy thought how pretty the lit-up pub looked, how festive and inviting, and how having his hair plastered wetly to his forehead really didn't suit Jonathan at all.

Comforted by the feel of Rennie's warm hand against the back of her neck, she said, 'If I told you that, it would spoil the fun. When it's time to start cheating on Paula, you'd make sure it didn't happen again.' She paused and added more cheerfully than she'd imagined possible, 'This way, it just might.'

Chapter 8

'How are you doing?' murmured Rennie at dinner that night.

'D'you know, I haven't the faintest idea.' Nancy was touched by his concern; he was a virtual stranger, after all. Even if the fact that her marriage had broken up this afternoon was pretty much entirely down to him.

'You're in shock,' Rennie told her. 'Hey, but you did the right thing.'

They were in the restaurant of the Kincaid in Edinburgh; Rennie had insisted on booking them into the hotel and treating them to dinner, as arranged. Following their departure from the Talbot Arms, the four of them had returned to Nancy and Jonathan's house and helped Nancy to pack.

'You don't need to leave,' Carmen had reminded her. 'Why should you have to be the one to go?'

'I'd rather.' Nancy hadn't needed to think about it, her mind was already made up. The house had always felt more like Jonathan's than hers. He paid the mortgage, the property was in his name, he'd invariably had the final say when it came to decorating or buying furniture. Well, he was welcome to it. Right now she didn't care if she never saw Kilnachranan again.

Nodding at the waiter who was wondering if they'd like their glasses refilled, Rennie speared a scallop and said, 'What if he wants you back?'

From across the table, Rose put down her own fork and said, 'She'll tell him to take a running jump. Don't worry, I'll make sure of that.'

Nancy smiled, she couldn't help it. 'Honestly, it's like having a whole new mum. You've never been like this before.'

'I know. I'm making up for lost time. Could you be an angel and bring me some more butter?' Touching the young waiter's arm, Rose confided, 'I've had two bread rolls already, but they're so gorgeous I'm going to have a third. Don't worry, pet, I'll pay the extra.'

Rose was loving every minute of her evening. Watching her sitting there at the table, a tiny grey-haired figure in a pale blue shirt and her favourite dusty pink knitted twinset, Nancy marvelled at the change in her.

'You don't have to pay extra. Mum, why didn't you ever tell me how you felt about Jonathan?'

'Och, Nancy. Surely you know the answer to that. Remember Darren,' Rose chided gently.

Nancy suppressed a shudder. Oh yes, she remembered Darren. Her first love. Darren had been two years older than her – eighteen, gosh, *so* grown-up – and every mother's nightmare. He drove like a lunatic, drank like a . . . well, lunatic, had regularly stood her up in order to go clubbing with his mates instead and had generally made her life a misery.

When Rose had pointed this out to her, at the same time making clear her own views on Darren, their relationship had been stretched to the limit. The last thing Nancy had needed was her mother making her miserable too. She had a clear memory of herself, over-hormonal and consumed by the unfairness of it all, yelling, 'You don't understand, I LOVE HIM! And he loves me!' before stomping up to her room and slamming the bedroom door so hard that her Spandau Ballet poster had fallen off the wall.

After that she'd felt morally obliged, as only a sixteen-year-old can, to carry on seeing Darren for another eight and a half humiliating months.

What a dickhead he'd been. How masochistic she'd been. When it came to spiting her face, it was a wonder she'd had any nose left.

'Well,' Rose said now, across the table, 'I wasn't going to run the risk of *that* happening again. And to be fair, Jonathan did seem all right to begin with. It was a while before I decided I really didn't like him. But you were about to be married and you wouldn't have thanked me for telling you, so what else could I do? You might have cut me out of your life.'

'Oh God, I wouldn't—'

'Well, I wasn't going to take that risk.' Rose shrugged and calmly buttered her roll. 'Far simpler to pretend to adore him. Anyway, it's over now, and that's the best Christmas present I could have asked for. You have the whole of your life ahead of you. You're young and beautiful and you can do anything you want.'

Nancy prayed she wasn't about to start crying. The suddenness of it all had knocked her for six. 'I don't know what I want to do. I don't know what I *can* do.' A mental image of herself in a hideously jaunty baseball cap serving behind the counter of Burger King sprang to mind. Hastily she pushed it away.

'Hey, you don't have to worry about that. Give yourself time to think about it,' said Rennie.

Feeling panicky and helpless, Nancy said, 'But I don't have anywhere to live.'

Opening her mouth, Rose began to say, 'Darling, you—'

'Now you're being daft,' Rennie said forcefully. 'You can come and stay with us.'

'Of course you can,' Carmen joined in. 'Get away from here for a while, take a little holiday. It'd be great to have you in London.' Turning her attention to Rennie, she raised her eyebrows and added pointedly, '*Us?*'

He looked mystified. 'What?'

'You just said *us*.'

Rennie shrugged. 'The rest of the tour's been cancelled. I'm free for the next couple of months.'

'So that's settled, is it?' Carmen sounded rattled. 'Last night you asked if you could stay for a few *days*.'

Nancy, watching her reaction, wondered what this was all about.

'And since then I've decided you could use the company.' Unperturbed, evidently treating Carmen's reaction as a challenge rather than an insult, Rennie said, 'I did promise Spike that if anything happened to him, I'd keep an eye on you.'

'You liar! That is bullsh— rubbish,' Carmen blurted out with an apologetic glance at Rose. 'He didn't ask you anything of the sort.'

'OK, maybe he didn't. But it was one of those unspoken things.'

'That you'd keep an eye on me? I haven't seen you for months!'

'And now I'm making up for lost time.' Tapping his fork against his plate, Rennie said, 'This prosciutto is fantastic.'

'What, twenty-four-hour surveillance? I don't need keeping an eye on.' Carmen was defensive. 'I'm fine.'

Turning his attention to Rose, Rennie said easily, 'Any Christmas decorations in your home?'

'In my flat, you mean?' Startled, Rose said, 'Well, of course there are. I didn't go overboard, what with it just being me on my own and not even there over Christmas itself, but I put a tree up, and lights in the window – and a lovely wreath with fir cones sprayed gold.' She looked anxiously at Rennie. 'Is that the kind of thing you mean?'

Carmen was watching him too, as mutinous as any teenager.

'When I turned up at Carmen's place yesterday, there was nothing,' said Rennie, his tone conversational. 'Not a fairy, not a strip of tinsel in sight.'

Rose looked at Carmen, as shocked as if Rennie had just announced that she was the star attraction in a lap-dancing club.

'Oh, pet. Not even a tree?'

'This is ridiculous,' Carmen blurted out. 'There's more to Christmas than decorations, you know! Just because I was too busy to put any up doesn't make me some kind of basket case—'

'Actually, don't worry about me,' Nancy said hurriedly. 'I think I'll just stay here in Edinburgh.'

'You will not,' declared Carmen, her eyes flashing. 'You're staying with me. And that way I won't need a . . . a childminder to keep an eye on me, because I won't *be* on my own, will I?'

'Oh, sweetheart,' Rose flapped her hands consolingly, 'he didn't mean it like that.'

'Yes I did, that's exactly what I meant,' said Rennie. 'And how's Nancy supposed to cheer you up when she's just getting over her own marriage break-up? The two of you would make a fine pair, living like a couple of hermits, each as gloomy as the other. What you both need is some fun. Hey, don't look at me like that,' he told Carmen more gently. 'I'm trying to help here. You need cheering up and I can do that, it's what I'm good at.'

'Should have been a Bluecoat,' muttered Carmen.

'He has a point,' Rose said hesitantly.

'Thank you, Rose.' Rennie nodded with satisfaction, beckoning the waiter over. 'We'd like a bottle of Veuve Cliquot please.'

'And it's only for a couple of months,' Rose added. 'It's not as if he'd be there forever.'

Gravely, Rennie said, 'Thank you, Rose. I'm sure you meant that in a flattering way.'

'I hate being cheered up,' Carmen grumbled. 'Insane people, whooping and clapping like orang-utans, bellowing at you to join in and have fun.'

'OK. No whooping and clapping, I promise.'

Wearily, Carmen said, 'You aren't going to let this drop, are you?'

'No,' said Rennie. 'Nancy? Would you mind an extra house guest? Just for a few weeks,' he reminded her. 'It's not as if I'd be there forever.'

'Oh, you.' Playfully Rose smacked his wrist. 'You know I didn't mean like that.'

'Of course I wouldn't mind.' Nancy didn't feel it was her place to object; it was Carmen's house, after all. 'But—'

'No buts. You know it makes sense. Carmen, if I promise not to behave like an orang-utan, will you let me stay?' He had hold of her hand now and was looking soulful.

Carmen, struggling not to laugh, said, 'You are *such* a worm. Just don't expect to be waited on hand and foot, OK? Because I know what you're like.'

Dark green eyes glittering, Rennie blew her a kiss across the table. 'No problem, we'll have Nancy there to do all that.'

'Sir, your champagne.' The waiter arrived, holding a bottle that was cloudy with condensation and wrapped in a white napkin.

'Perfect timing.' Rennie grinned up at him. 'We've got something to celebrate.'

'And no singing in the middle of the night,' Carmen warned. 'I hate it when you do that.' To Nancy she added, 'He's not remotely house-trained, you know.'

Nancy began to wonder what she might have let herself in for.

'She's making me sound as if I don't know how to use a litter tray,' Rennie complained to Rose.

'I'm sure you're not that bad.' Rose's tone was consoling.

'He's spent so long living in hotels,' Carmen complained, 'that he's completely institutionalised. He'll be putting his shoes outside the bedroom door and demanding round-the-clock room service.'

'I can't help it. I need the love of a good woman,' said Rennie.

'Tuh,' Carmen snorted. 'From what I hear, you've had the love of a thousand good women. What you need is a slave.'

Chapter 9

Connor O'Shea may have moved over from Dublin eleven years ago, making his home in London, but his Irish accent was as strong as ever. He fully intended to keep it with him for life. It suited him, went with his personality and had the desired effect when it came to the opposite sex. In all fairness, what more could you ask of an accent than that?

Sadly, the person currently on the other end of the phone was male and far more interested in moaning on about staffing problems and holiday rotas. Stretching and yawning, Connor let him have his say.

'. . . and Savannah's complaining that the staff T-shirts are too tight. She wants me to order some in size eighteen. I told her it was her fault for being such a whale.'

OK, now he really did have to interrupt. 'Neville, order the T-shirts and stop giving Savannah grief.' From the living-room window, Connor idly watched a taxi pull up outside.

'But she's so fat! It's just . . . ugh.' You didn't need to be able to see Neville to know that he was shuddering with revulsion. Neville was as fastidious as he was fit, and as fit as he was gay. Luckily, Connor knew that Savannah was more than capable of standing up for herself and, if need be, squashing Neville flat.

'Now, you know as well as I do that people go to fitness clubs for different reasons. Some of them are like you. They have bodies like yours and they enjoy keeping themselves in peak physical condition.' Connor wondered why he was even bothering to say this when Neville was already perfectly well aware of it. 'And then there are the other clients, the kind who just want to be a bit fitter than they are. If you couldn't swim, Neville, and you were going along to the pool for the first time, would you rather be put in with the beginners' class or the British Olympic squad?'

'OK, OK,' grumbled Neville.

'You wouldn't want to be intimidated,' Connor persisted. 'Made to feel stupid. Women carrying a bit of extra weight know perfectly well that they're never going to look like most of our instructors, but it boosts their confidence no end when they see someone like Savannah taking a class, because she might be a big girl but she's fit as well. And bloody attractive. They enjoy her classes because they can aspire to be like her. Half of them wouldn't attend a class run by a seven-stone stick insect. So just go ahead and order the T-shirts, will you?'

'Fine.' Neville was offended. 'Shall I tell you about the holiday rotas now, or wouldn't you be interested?'

'I'd love to hear all about them,' Connor lied, 'but I'm pushed for time. In fact, here's my taxi now. Better fax them through to me instead.'

God, for a super-fit male, Neville was such an old woman. Pressing the off button on the phone, Connor wondered why on earth he'd ever asked him to manage the Islington branch of the Lazy B. Because he'd been drunk, probably. The ethos of the entire chain of Lazy Bs was that everyone wasn't perfect and that there was more to life than physical perfection.

Anyway, who was that, climbing out of the taxi? Ha, the Invisible Woman. Smiling to himself, Connor watched her pay the driver – thanks to her brother-in-law he now knew that her name was Carmen – and waited to see if she would glance up at his window as she made her way into the house next door. Well, there was a first time for everything. If she did, he would wave and mouth hello, and – probably – scare the living daylights out of her.

She didn't glance up. Deliberately not glancing anywhere, Carmen scuttled into the house as if terrified she might be about to be mugged. Which, let's face it, in Fitzallen Square was unlikely. What he was doing here, God only knew. Absently scratching his chest and wondering if it was time for his next cigarette – he was currently attempting to ration himself to one every two hours, a project miserably doomed to failure – Connor moved away from the window and headed for the fridge instead. A wedge of Cambazola would hit the spot.

OK, he was a disgrace. He freely admitted it. Ten years ago he had opened the original Lazy B in Oxford. Traditionally, founders of gyms or fitness centres didn't eat too much, drink too much, smoke too much or regard an hour-long workout as an hour of sheer, undiluted misery. But this had turned out to be a good thing because it gave Connor O'Shea the impetus to open the kind of gym he wouldn't find completely unbearable. His dream had been to create a gym crossed with a really great pub, with the emphasis on enjoyment and socialising. In his time he'd visited plenty of fitness clubs that reminded him of laboratories – cool, clinical places full of sleek modern fittings, featuring obsessive fitness freaks pounding away on the machines like . . . well, lab rats. If there was anything to drink, it was a healthy drink. If there was anything to eat, it was bound to include salad. Which was fine for the fitness freaks, but not so fine for the vast majority of people who might – in a burst of enthusiasm – join one of these clubs but would, after the first few weeks, find increasingly feeble reasons not to attend. The drop-outs, which was what Connor had termed them, needed more of an incentive to turn up and to keep turning up, month after month. And, OK, maybe they'd be socialising more than they'd be exercising, but even a bit of exercise was better than no exercise at all.

This had been the original idea behind the Lazy B, and it had taken off in a big way. Ten years on, the business was going from strength to strength.

The doorbell rang as Connor was wrestling with the wrapper on a packet of Scotch eggs. Heading for the front door, he wondered if it was his neighbour, popping round to introduce herself and borrow a cup of sugar. Where had that expression come from anyway? Had people years ago really needed to borrow cups of sugar? Wouldn't they be more likely to run out of washing-up liquid or batteries or loo roll? He'd never run out of sugar in his life.

It wasn't his neighbour.

'Dad! Yay, you're here!' Blond hair flying, Mia threw her arms round Connor, knocking her baseball cap off in the process.

Astounded, he hugged her back. 'I don't believe it. Am I on *This Is Your Life*? Is Michael Aspel hiding behind a postbox?'

'Sorry, it's just me. Come on then,' Mia said bossily, 'invite me in. It's freezing out here.'

Connor's heart swelled with love for his daughter. 'What a fantastic surprise. Why didn't you let me know you were coming?'

'Duh, because then it wouldn't have been a fantastic surprise, would it?' Reaching down for her blue Nike cap and kicking the front door shut behind her, Mia beamed at him and wriggled her backpack off her shoulders. 'But I have to say, I'm glad you weren't out. I'll have a cup of tea and a fried egg sandwich . . . ooh, and I'd love a bath afterwards, my feet are killing me.'

'We're out of eggs,' said Connor.

'No you aren't, I've brought some.' In the kitchen, Mia unzipped her backpack and pulled out a canary-yellow fleece with Against Factory Farming printed across the front. Unwrapping the fleece, she triumphantly produced an egg box. 'Present from Mum.'

Wryly, Connor accepted the gift. This meant they were the most organic, free-range eggs imaginable, both inside and out. He just knew they'd be smeared with chicken poo, feathers and bits of straw. As far as Laura was concerned, running them under a tap would have meant washing the goodness off.

'Great. You fry the eggs, I'll make the tea.'

Mia, not fooled for a second, said cheerfully, 'Coward. Actually, *chicken*.'

Connor filled the kettle. He leaned against the worktop and watched his daughter briskly scrub the eggs she'd carried with her all the way from Donegal. It was almost impossible to believe that Mia was sixteen; not so long ago she'd been a strong-willed, tantrum-prone four-year-old in dusty orange dungarees. And look at her now, taller than ever, wearing distressed black jeans, pointy black boots and a black and yellow striped mohair sweater that made her look like a bee on stilts. Her shoulder-length streaky blonde hair was tied back with a pink band and the only make-up she wore was mascara.

Mia, his beautiful daughter. She was the most important person in his life, yet discovering her existence had caused him untold pain. Anger too. Was it any wonder that Mia was strong-willed, when she had Laura as her mother?

Laura had been running one of those hippy shops in Dublin when Connor first met her. He was seventeen, still at school and working part-time in the bakery next door to Laura's shop. With her waist-length blond hair, embroidered cheesecloth dresses and bewitching smile he had naturally been attracted to her. Well, let's face it, as a hormone-fuelled seventeen-year-old, he'd have been pushed to find a woman he didn't find attractive.

But Laura had bewitched him. Fascinated by her beliefs in crystals, her air of mystery and, OK, her glorious figure, Connor had taken to dropping into her joss-stick-scented shop on a regular basis. He bought his mother a china unicorn with luminous sapphire eyes for her birthday, which had alarmed her no end as she was more accustomed to Yardley gift packs of soap and talc.

When Laura had started inviting him upstairs to her tiny flat above the shop, he had felt as if he'd won the lottery. Sex was a revelation, better than he'd ever imagined, possibly because Laura, at twenty-seven, was an experienced woman of the world. In her bedroom, which smelled of patchouli and jasmine, she introduced him to the joys of love-making and taught him how to give pleasure as well as to receive it.

Their clandestine relationship had lasted three months. Connor was dumbstruck when Laura calmly announced one day, out of the blue, that she was leaving Dublin, giving up the lease on the shop and moving to a smallholding in Donegal.

He felt as if his air supply had been cut off.

'What? But . . . why?'

'I want to be self-sufficient.' Laura affectionately stroked his chest; they were in bed together at the time.

'But I don't want you to go!'

'Connor, you're seventeen, you're a fine handsome lad. Trust me, you'll find someone else in no time at all.'

'I love you,' he blurted out, and Laura smiled.

'You don't. You love having sex with me. I'm ten years older than you are. I know what I want to do with my life, and now I'm moving on to the next stage. I'll be growing my own vegetables, tending sheep and goats, spinning my own wool – it's going to be fantastic.'

Already bereft, Connor said, 'Can I come and visit you, at least?'

'I don't think so. There wouldn't be a lot of point. Hey, we've had fun.' Reaching over, Laura planted a warm kiss on his mouth. 'Life's a journey, right? And now it's time we went our separate ways. I don't have any regrets, Connor. I'll always be glad we had this time together. You're a wonderful person.'

Resignedly, Connor said, 'But not quite wonderful enough.'

Of course, Laura had been right. He'd missed her to begin with, but life went on and he turned out to be less heartbroken than he'd imagined. After a while he started seeing someone else, a pretty eighteen-year-old called Niamh, who was studying law at Trinity. Memories of Laura had gradually faded from his mind, just as she had promised.

He was still only seventeen, after all.

And that would have been that, had it not been for a chance meeting almost five years later.

Connor's girlfriend at the time, a beautician by the name of Clodagh, had been invited to the wedding of an old school friend. Unwillingly, Connor had found himself forced to go along with her. It wasn't what he wanted to do – truth be told, he was on the verge of finishing with Clodagh – but she had insisted, booking them into a nearby country hotel for a long weekend as an incentive.

The wedding was taking place in Donegal, and the hotel contained a health and beauty spa. Arriving there on Friday morning, Clodagh announced that as an extra treat she had booked both of them into the spa for the entire afternoon, for a mud wrap, massage, pedicure, manicure, Reiki healing and a sunbed. It was at that moment that Connor knew for sure that their relationship was over.

'I don't want any of that stuff,' he told Clodagh.

Bewildered she said, 'Why not? You'd love it.'

'I promise you, I wouldn't. *You'd* love it.' Connor reached for his jacket. 'I can't think of anything more horrible. You go ahead, have your pampering session. I'll see you back here at six.'

It was a hot sunny day in July. Wandering through the town, he had come across a small Friday market with stallholders selling a variety of cheeses, sausages, Irish linen, vegetables, pottery, souvenirs for visiting tourists and hand-woven baskets. Hungry, Connor stopped off at a small pub selling food and sat at one of the tables outside to drink his pint of Guinness, enjoy a plate of ham and eggs with fried potatoes and watch the world go by. He was in no hurry, he didn't have to be back at the hotel until six o'clock. Maybe after lunch he'd drive on down to the beach and watch the surfers. Or walk the cliff path and admire the spectacular scenery. Or find a betting shop and decide if he was feeling lucky enough for a flutter.

Idly he watched a small girl in dirty orange dungarees fighting a losing battle to persuade her dolls to sit upright. The girl's blond hair hung loose down her back. Her T-shirt was purple, her feet bare and she was kneeling on the pavement arranging the four shabby stuffed dolls along the top of an upended packing crate. Like spinning plates, every time she reached the fourth doll one of the others would topple over. Amused, Connor realised that the girl was talking to the dolls, threatening to get very cross indeed if they didn't all sit up *straight*.

'Now behave, or I'll give you a big smack,' she declared bossily. The first doll promptly keeled forward and landed face down on the pavement. Picking it up, the girl said, 'Did that hurt? Well, serves you right. Don't do it again. You're all *very* naughty.'

'I think she hit her teeth,' said Connor and the girl looked over at him as if he were mad.

'She hasn't any teeth. She's a doll.'

Tempted to get competitive, Connor almost asked why she was bothering to speak to the dolls then, seeing as they didn't have any ears either. But since arguing with a small child in the street wasn't entirely dignified, he said, 'You're right, I'm sorry,' and took a gulp of Guinness instead. Reaching for a cigarette, he was about to light it when a stallholder to his left suddenly rose from her seat in order to serve a customer.

Moving forward, her long purple skirt swirled around her legs and in that split second Connor recognised her. He stared at Laura as she piled courgettes into a brown paper bag, handed them to her customer and slipped the money into a shabby leather purse slung round her waist.

It had been almost five years. He was looking at his first love. How incredible to see her again now. Realising that the cigarette was still dangling unlit from his lips, he wrenched it out – ouch – and rose to his feet.

'Laura!'

Chapter 10

Laura turned as the customer wandered along to the next stall. Their eyes met and the first thought that flashed through Connor's mind was that she didn't seem nearly as delighted to see him as he was to see her.

Did she think he was going to declare his undying love for her, sink to his knees, perhaps, and cause an embarrassing scene right here in the street?

Because he wasn't. There was no surge of love and overwhelming regret. He hadn't spent the last five years pining for her. It was nice to bump into her again, that was all.

'Laura. Great to see you. You're looking . . . um, fantastic.' This wasn't exactly true, but you could hardly tell an ex-girlfriend she was looking old. With her long hair in a plait, her thin, weather-beaten face and droopy clothes, she looked like a woman who lived off the land. She was thirty-one, but looked forty. Still, never mind, he must be looking older himself.

'Hello, Connor. Nice to see you too.' Laura devoted herself to reor-ganising the sacks of vegetables around her stall. Normally so cool and composed, he could tell that she was on edge.

'How's the self-sufficiency thing going?' said Connor, because there weren't any other customers around and it would be downright rude to turn round and walk off.

'Oh, pretty good. Hard work of course, but it's what I—'

'Mum, can I have a drink?'

Looking down, Connor saw the small girl in the orange dungarees poking her head round the side of the stall.

'In a minute, darling. I'm busy.'

'This is your daughter?' Amazed, Connor said, 'Hey, that's grand news. Congratulations.'

'Thanks. Mia, go and play with your dolls.'

'They're stupid. I hate my dolls.' Puffing out her cheeks, the girl said, 'I'm thirsty.'

'Why don't I fetch her something from the pub?' Connor suggested, because Laura was looking agitated. 'A Coke or something?'

He was only trying to be helpful. Mia gazed up at him, her eyes like saucers. From Laura's expression you'd think he'd suggested buying her daughter a triple bourbon on the rocks.

'She doesn't drink that rubbish. I'll get her some water in a minute. Well, it's been nice to see you again—'

'Mia. That's a pretty name,' said Connor. 'How old are you, then?'

'Three,' Laura said hurriedly.

'I'm *not*.' Mia was indignant. 'I'm four.'

Four. The answer was one thing, but the expression on Laura's face was what really made Connor take notice. Why would she lie?

Why indeed?

Feeling light-headed with disbelief, Connor said carefully, 'When's your birthday, Mia?'

Mia paused. Gave it some thought. Finally she said, 'When I get my presents.'

Connor was shaking. He looked carefully down at the small girl in front of him, with her huge grey eyes, her button nose and determined chin. Switching his gaze to Laura, who had gone pale, he said in a low voice, 'Is this . . .? Is she . . .?'

Except he already knew that she was.

One of the neighbouring stallholders was persuaded to look after Mia and keep an eye on Laura's stall.

Laura took Connor down a series of narrow side streets, away from the market. As he followed her, a million thoughts raced through his brain, tangling like elastic and shooting off in all directions. A baby, my God, not even a baby, a walking talking four-year-old girl. I'm a father, I've been a father for the last four years . . .

This was mind-blowing, almost too much to take in. Yet even as Connor was digesting the information, he was aware that he wasn't reacting with the sense of horror that overcame some men faced with the prospect of unexpected fatherhood. He had always faintly despised those of his acquaintance who, upon discovering their girlfriends were pregnant, claimed they simply weren't up to the challenge and promptly bailed out of the relationship. Or married men who decided family life was no longer for them and walked away from their wives and children, not caring about the devastation they caused. Connor was no goody-two-shoes but he'd never understood how these men could live with themselves. In his view, such selfishness was beyond belief. Then again, he had never found himself in such a situation. Maybe when it happened to him he wouldn't feel quite so principled and heroic.

But now it *had* happened and Connor instinctively knew that he was incapable of turning his back on Mia. He didn't even want to. She existed, she was his own flesh and blood. Against all the odds – and he was aware that he was still in a considerable state of shock – he already couldn't wait to see her again, get to know her, discover what she was *like*.

They finally reached a small park. Laura sat down on the grass and said, 'I'll get a crick in my neck if I have to look up at you.'

Connor lowered himself to the ground and sat cross-legged, facing her.

'She's my daughter,' he said evenly.

Laura nodded. 'Yes.'

'You should have told me.' Connor shook his head; what kind of a heartless bastard did she think he was?

'No,' said Laura.

'Yes! I would have stuck by you,' Connor exclaimed. 'OK, I know I was young, but I'd never have left you in the lurch! You didn't need to move away, we'd have coped somehow, between us we could have—'

'Connor, I know you would have stuck by me,' Laura said gently. 'You were a dear, sweet boy – you still *are* a dear, sweet boy – who wouldn't dream of leaving anyone in the lurch. But I didn't get pregnant by accident, you know.'

Bombshell number two.

'What?' Connor wondered if this was how it felt to be struck by lightning. 'But . . . but you were taking the pill.'

'Wrong. I told you I was taking the pill. Because if I hadn't, you'd have insisted on using condoms, which didn't fit in with my plans at all.' A ghost of a smile flickered across Laura's face. 'You see, I'd already made up my mind. I wanted a baby.'

She had always been the most fiercely independent and determined person he'd ever known.

'A baby,' echoed Connor, 'but not a partner? No husband or boyfriend to help you raise a child?'

'The baby was the most important thing.' Laura was calmer now, regaining control. 'Of course, if I'd met the perfect man I wouldn't have turned him down. But I didn't. I met you instead, and you were just a boy. I'd never have dreamed of landing you with the responsibility of a child. On the other hand, I couldn't have asked for a better father for my baby. You were tall, you had a great physique, you were healthy and bright and kind . . . let's face it, genetically you were perfect.'

Stunned, Connor said, 'Is that what I was? A sperm donor?'

'Oh Connor, don't make it sound horrible. I wanted a baby with your qualities. Can't you think of that as a compliment?'

'And what about Mia? Growing up without a father?'

'Lots of children grow up without a father.' Laura's jaw tightened. 'It never did me any harm.'

Since now wasn't the time to start an argument, Connor let this pass. 'So what happens now?'

'Nothing happens,' said Laura. 'Nothing's changed. You're free to walk away, forget you ever saw us.'

'Jesus, I don't believe I'm hearing this!' Anger welled up inside him. 'I didn't give you an old sweater, Laura! If I had, and you'd unpicked it and knitted it into a scarf, I can understand that I wouldn't have any right to march up to you and demand my wool back! But we've created a human being here. You can't seriously expect me to just walk away from my daughter as if she doesn't exist!'

'Why not? Plenty of people do that too.' A tear dripped from Laura's chin onto the front of her shirt and Connor remembered that her father had walked out on her mother shortly after Laura's birth.

'Well, I can't,' he declared.

'Connor, you're twenty-one years old. You had a teenage crush on me and we had fun, but we don't love each other. Mia and I are fine as we are, just the two of us. It's sweet of you to offer, but we don't need the hassle of a man in our lives. And you shouldn't smoke,' she added firmly as he fumbled in his shirt pocket for his cigarettes and lighter.

'Why not? Will it stunt my growth?' He was six foot two and he lit up with a don't-tell-me-what-to-do air of defiance.

'Maybe not, but it could certainly stunt your breathing. It could kill you,' said Laura. 'Plus, it's a very immature thing to do.'

Immature. Sensing the ammunition for further argument, Connor stubbed his Rothmans out on the grass, opened the packet and flung the remaining cigarettes into the air.

'Litter lout,' said Laura. But she was perilously close to smiling.

Having picked up the scattered cigarettes and ostentatiously thrown them into a nearby bin – apart from one, which he slipped into his shirt pocket for later – Connor came and sat back down next to Laura on the grass. Interestingly, he had no urge to kiss her.

'Look, you don't want me and I don't want you, but wouldn't it be handy for Mia to have a father? I wouldn't crowd you, I promise. I could just stay in the background, see her occasionally.' Connor presented his case with care. 'But I'd be there if I was needed. Think of me as emergency back-up. If you ever fancied a weekend away, I could look after Mia. If anything happened to you, she'd have someone she knew to take care of her – until you were well again,' he added hastily, because Laura was looking alarmed. With a shrug he said, 'Being a single parent must be exhausting. I'm just saying I could be useful.'

A lifetime of mistrusting men had left its mark on Laura. She held up her hands to stop him.

'OK, you're saying this now, but what about when the novelty wears off? If I tell Mia you're her father, how is she going to feel in a few years' time when you decide you can't be bothered to see her any more? She'd be devastated.'

'She wouldn't be,' Connor said patiently, 'because I'd never do that to her. But you don't believe me, so how about a compromise? We won't tell Mia I'm her father. I'll just be a friend of yours. That way, she'll have a chance to get used to me.' He paused, keeping a straight face. 'And then it won't come as too much of a shock on her fiftieth birthday when we do tell her the truth.'

'Mia? Come here, darling, and say hello to a friend of mine. His name's Connor.'

'Hi.' Connor crouched down on the pavement, so that he was level with Mia. 'It's very nice to meet you.'

Close up, he saw that the tips of her long eyelashes were golden, like his. Her eyes were silver-grey and watchful. There was a smudge of mud on one plump brown cheek. His daughter. God, he was actually looking at his *daughter*. It was an emotional moment to be—

'Like a box,' said Mia.

'Um . . . sorry?'

She abruptly turned away, disappeared behind the stall and reappeared moments later carrying an empty cardboard box. 'Like a box,' Mia explained, plonking it down on the pavement and pointing. 'There's a corner. There's another corner.'

'Very good. Nearly the same.' He hid a smile. 'But I'm Connor.'

Mia gazed at him, unimpressed. 'I know.'

'Connor's coming to see us on Sunday,' Laura said brightly. 'He'll be coming over to our house. That'll be nice, won't it?'

'Yes.' Obediently Mia nodded. 'You know dandelions?'

'I do.' Connor waited to hear what profound remark might follow.

'They're yellow.'

'You know cows?' said Connor.

'Yes.'

'They go moooo.'

He so longed to make his daughter laugh and decide she liked him. Instead Mia shot him a look of disdain.

'But cows aren't yellow.'

Hmm.

'Don't they have yellow cows where you live?' Connor looked dismayed.

'No. Cows aren't yellow, *ever.* Do you like biscuits?'

'Er . . . yes.'

Mia nodded. 'And me.'

'Here.' Taking pity on him, Laura passed over a slip of paper. 'That's our address, and a map of how to get there.'

Connor looked at it. Had she just made this up, plucking a false address out of the air and inventing a map to go with it?

'Don't worry.' Guessing what was running through his mind, Laura smiled. 'That's definitely where we live.'

It was Mia's tenth birthday. Connor said, 'Mia, sit down, I've got something to tell you.'

Mia was wearing purple shorts today, teamed with a lime-green T-shirt and grubby trainers. Obediently coming to sit next to Connor on the sofa, she hugged her tanned bony knees, spectacularly grazed from a recent fall from the apple tree, and said, 'What is it?'

Connor took a deep breath. He'd been practising this all morning. The thing was, no matter how you dressed it up, there really wasn't any way of lessening the impact. Since Mia was a past master at coming straight to the point, he'd decided to take a leaf out of her book.

'The thing is, you know your father.'

'What?'

Oh God, he was messing it up already. The whole point was that she *didn't* know her father. Great start, Connor told himself, well *done*.

'Well, it's . . . um, you know . . . me.'

'Connor, what you trying to say?'

'Me.' He pointed to his chest. 'I'm your father.'

Mia regarded him gravely for several seconds. Finally a slow smile spread across her face.

'Really?'

'Really.'

'Thought so.'

'Excuse me?'

'I thought you probably were,' said Mia.

Connor wondered if she'd understood.

'You thought I was probably your father?' When Mia nodded calmly, he said, 'How? Why?'

'Well, why else would you keep coming to see us? I'm ten now, and you've been visiting us for years. But you aren't Mum's boyfriend,' Mia patiently explained. 'So that seemed a bit weird for a start. And you play Monopoly and tennis with me. When Mum's boyfriends are here, they never want to do stuff like that. They always tell me to go out and play.'

Shaking his head, Connor marvelled at the logic. 'But you never said anything.'

'I did once. I asked Mum, but she said no, you were just a friend. So I left it after that. You know what Mum's like. But I still thought I was right.'

'And now?' Carefully, Connor said, 'Is it OK? Are you happy about it?'

Mia gave him an are-you-kidding look. 'Of course I'm happy! I love being right!'

'Dad, Dad, look what I've had done!'

Connor's mouth dropped open at the sight of his beloved daughter raising her top to reveal a daisy tattoo round her navel. Horrified, he croaked, 'You're only thirteen! I can't believe your mother let you have something like that! My God, what kind of tattoo parlour would risk—'

'It's not a real tattoo.' Grinning, Mia said, 'I do love you, Daddy. It's so easy to wind you up.'

'Happy birthday, sweetheart!' As Mia flew into his arms, Connor picked her up and swung her round.

'*Aaaarggh,*' cried Laura, because Mia's turquoise shirt had billowed up to reveal a tattoo of a dolphin peeping above the low-slung waistband of her faded jeans.

Plonking his daughter down in order to see what Laura was pointing at, Connor said, 'It's only one of those transfer things, it'll wash off in a day or two.'

'Actually it isn't.' Mia beamed with pride. 'It's a proper one.'

Appalled, Connor said, 'But you're only *sixteen.*'

'Exactly. I'm practically a grown-up.' Patting her stomach with pride, Mia said, 'But it's so sweet, Daddy, that you don't know the difference between a transfer and a real tattoo.'

'Sixteen,' Connor groaned. In his head, she was still a dungareed four-year-old with worms in her pockets and gaps in her teeth.

'Calm down, Dad. Honestly, you're such a dinosaur. You know, I'm officially old enough to get married.' Mischievously Mia said, 'Thank your lucky stars I haven't done that.'

Connor winced at the memory. At least there hadn't been any more tattoos in the last eight months. None that he knew about, anyway. Then he winced again, because his mouth had just caught fire.

'Oh, sorry,' said Mia. 'Bit hot for you?'

Through watering eyes, Connor saw that his daughter was calmly eating her way through a plate of fried eggs on toast, swimming in a pool of flame-red chilli sauce.

Pointing to the relatively modest dash of sauce on his own plate, he said, 'A bit hot for *me*? It's possibly the hottest chilli sauce on the planet. Where did you get this stuff?'

'There's this brilliant deli in Dublin. It's called Scotch Bonnet sauce. Here, have some water.' Mia was already on her way back from the sink with a brimming glass. 'Poor Daddy, I've only been here ten minutes and already you think I'm trying to poison you.'

Having downed the water in one, Connor gingerly checked his teeth hadn't fallen out. 'So how long are you staying, then?'

Mia put down her fork. 'Well, the thing is, I've been considering my future. Mum and I were having a chat about it the other day and basically I've spent the last sixteen years living in a self-sufficient smallholding in the wilds of Donegal. Which has been great, in its own way, but I feel I need a change of environment if I'm to become a fully rounded person.'

This was a more convoluted answer than Connor had been expecting. The chilli sauce was performing a kind of terrifying afterburn in his throat, ensuring he wouldn't forget it in a hurry. He nodded to show that he was still listening, in a distracted kind of way.

'I mean, there's so much more to life than cleaning out chicken coops and weeding the vegetable patch.' Raising her eyebrows, Mia said, 'At my age I should be expanding my horizons, discovering new people and places, experiencing new stuff—'

'If you ever, *ever* take drugs, I'll—'

'Oh shut up, give me a break Dad, drugs are for losers. Anyway, so like I said, Mum and I have had a really good talk about it and the thing is, how about if I came here and lived with you?'

The chilli was probably still burning but Connor was no longer aware of it.

'When?'

Mia spread her yellow and black striped arms and said encouragingly, 'Well, here I am, so how about now?'

'And where would you go to school?'

'I'm not going back to school. A-levels are meaningless these days. I'd rather get a job, start building a career. It's OK, Mum and I talked it all through.'

'What kind of work did you have in mind?' Connor didn't doubt for a moment that she had something in mind.

'Well, I thought I'd train to become the next national chilli-eating champion.' Mia grinned, trawled an index finger through the pool of chilli sauce on her plate and popped it into her mouth. 'Actually, I'd like to come and work for you.'

'And your mother's happy about that?' Connor had to ask, although it certainly sounded as though Laura and Mia had covered all the angles.

'Mum's great. She understands how I feel. I've spent long enough living in the middle of nowhere. It's time to move on, find out how it feels to live in the middle of *somewhere*.' Mia gazed anxiously at him. 'As long as you're happy about it too.'

Happy? He'd spent the last few years dreaming about this day. In his imagination he hadn't expected it to happen until Mia had finished university, but by then she'd be twenty-one and the chances of her even wanting to live with her old fogey of a father would be remote. What self-respecting 21-year-old would even consider it, after all, when she could be sharing a grotty flat in Hoxton with a crowd of equally grotty twenty-somethings and wall-to-wall squalor?

'I'm happy.' His heart expanding with love for his beautiful strong-minded daughter, Connor smiled and said, 'I can't imagine anything nicer.'

'Yay!' Jumping up from the table, Mia hugged him. 'Thanks, Dad. OK if I have my bath now?'

The phone rang fifteen minutes later. Sounding strained, Laura said without preamble, 'It's me. Listen, Mia's disappeared. I don't know where she is. Has she spoken to you at all? Oh God, the school rang and told me she hasn't been in—'

'Whoa,' Connor broke through the stream of jerky sentences. 'Mia's here. She turned up an hour ago.'

'*What?*' Relief was replaced within a split second by irritation. 'Connor,

58

did it not even occur to you that I'd be out of my mind with worry? You should have phoned me!'

'I thought you knew. Mia kept saying you were happy for her to leave school and come and live with me.'

'Oh, for crying out loud, are you serious? *Leave school?* She's supposed to be at school this minute! Put her on,' Laura ordered.

'She's in the bath.' Connor realised that he'd been well and truly set up.

'Send her back, then,' said Laura firmly. 'She can't do this, she's only sixteen. Just tell her she can't mess around like this, and send her back.'

'God, I love this house.' Wet-haired and wearing an oversized T-shirt emblazoned with the words Treat Animals With Compassion, Mia reappeared forty minutes later. 'You have no idea what a luxury it is to run the bath taps and know that hot water is going to come out. And dry yourself in real fluffy towels instead of horrible ancient ones that feel like sandpaper—'

'Why don't you give your mum a ring, just to let her know you've arrived safely,' Connor suggested.

Mia's eyes flickered guiltily away from him. Then she straightened her shoulders. 'OK, Dad, here's the thing. I lied.'

'Here's another thing,' said Connor. 'I know.'

'Oh.'

'Laura just rang. She was worried sick.'

'I'm sorry. I'm really sorry,' Mia blurted out. 'I did try and talk it through with her, but she just wouldn't listen, and I'd *so* much rather be here.'

'She wants you to go home.' Connor saw her wince. 'And I want you to promise never to lie to me again.'

'I won't.' Miserably, Mia shook her head. 'Lie, I mean. Oh God.' She buried her face in her hands. 'Do I have to go back?'

'No.'

Mia's head shot up. 'What?'

'I persuaded Laura to let you stay.'

'Really?'

'She's not happy about the school thing,' Connor warned.

'Well, I already knew that, we've been over it enough times. But I'd rather build a career,' argued Mia before he could start making going back to school a condition of staying in London. 'I mean, in the old days getting a degree meant something to employers, but these days everyone goes to college, *everyone* has a degree and it just seems . . . well, what's the big deal? Can they do a job?'

59

Luckily for her, Connor was in agreement. He'd interviewed more than his fair share of clueless graduates in his time. Instinct told him that Mia would achieve whatever she set out to do, workwise. She had more energy and determination than anyone he'd ever met.

'I said pretty much the same. That's why we're going to give it a go.'

'Daddy, you're a genius.'

'I know.'

'Shall I phone Mum now and apologise?'

'Might be an idea,' said Connor.

'Then I'll get dressed and we'll set off.'

Bemused, Connor said, 'Set off where?'

Mia shook her head in despair. 'Come on, Dad, keep up. To the Lazy B of course. I want to make a start on my job.'

Chapter 11

Nancy felt it was all wrong. The ease with which she'd got over Jonathan was actually embarrassing. She'd read the problem pages, watched the daytime TV shows, seen it often enough in the papers: when your marriage unexpectedly broke up, you were meant to be distraught for at least a year. It was a life-changing occurrence, after all. One minute she'd been married in Scotland. Now she was down here in London and single all over again. The least she could have had the decency to do was lose her appetite.

But instead of moping around feeling depressed, she was loving every minute. Staying married because you felt obliged to stick to your vows had – she was able to admit it now – been a burden. Being released from that obligation felt great.

Rrrrrinnnnggg went the doorbell, and Nancy jumped. Bugger, if that was Rennie she was in trouble.

Hastily wiping her hands on a yard of kitchen roll, she bundled every-thing into a bowl and hid it in the tumble dryer in the utility room. The object she'd spent the last two hours working on she shoved out of sight in the oven, which thankfully wasn't switched on.

Rennie's ability to lose his keys – or walk out of the house without them – was going to get him into the *Guinness Book of Records* at this rate. As she headed for the front door, Nancy wondered if tying one on a string round his neck might do the trick.

But it wasn't Rennie.

'Hi! I'm Mia Corrigan. I just moved in next door.' The bright-eyed girl in khaki vest and combats looked about seventeen, which Nancy couldn't help thinking was too young for their neighbour. 'Well, not just moved in. I arrived yesterday afternoon. The thing is, I thought I'd pop over and say hello anyway, but I'm trying to make a Yorkshire pudding. I've done all the egg-beating business and now I find out there isn't any flour in the house, so I was wondering if you had any to spare?'

Khaki combats. Long silver earrings. Small dolphin tattoo just visible beneath the vest. It was such an unlikely question that Nancy almost burst out laughing.

'Um . . . yes.'

'Great! Can you lend me a bit? Only these houses might be the bee's knees, but they aren't what you'd call handy for the shops. Well, not the sort of shops that sell plain flour,' Mia Corrigan amended. 'Of course if it's shoes you're after, costing thousands of pounds, we're spoiled for choice. And antique shops selling Ming vases for about a million. Sorry, am I talking too much? My mum says I talk for Ireland. Don't you think it's just mad though? How can some daft bit of pottery be worth that much just because it's old and hasn't got broken yet?'

The girl might be sparky and vivacious, but she was *way* too young for Connor O'Shea. Nancy hadn't met him yet – he'd only arrived back from holiday in Barbados, or wherever it was, a couple of days ago – but she'd glimpsed him leaving for work yesterday morning and knew from Carmen and Rennie that he was in his thirties. How could Mia's mother even allow her to move in with a man at her age?

'Now that's what I call a proper food cupboard.' Mia nodded approvingly as Nancy opened the cupboard and located the plain flour. 'You should see ours. Hopeless. I'm going to have my work cut out over there, I can tell you. There's milk and beer in the fridge, pizzas and ready meals in the freezer, and that's it. It didn't occur to me for a second that there wouldn't be flour in the food cupboard. Then when I opened it, I found a CD player and a rugby shirt.' Shaking her head in despair she said, 'Let me tell you, things are going to change. Give me a week and that kitchen won't know what's hit it.'

Realising that Mia had hoisted herself onto a kitchen stool and was making herself thoroughly at home, Nancy said, 'Would you like a cup of tea?'

'Love one, thanks.' The girl beamed at her. 'I don't know your name.'

'Nancy.'

'Nancy. That's a great name! Well, it's a pleasure to meet you.' Mia watched as Nancy made the tea, then she reached across the table and peeled something blue off the surface. 'What's this? Playdough? Hey, I didn't know you had kids! If you ever need a babysitter—'

'I don't have children. And this is my friend Carmen's house,' Nancy explained. 'I'm just staying here for a while.' Then, because it was almost five o'clock and she really wanted to get the job finished before Rennie came back, she headed over to the tumble dryer and took out the mixing bowl she'd bundled inside earlier. Mia, to her credit, didn't bat an eyelid.

Next, opening the oven door and retrieving the cake on its silver board, Nancy carried it over to the table.

'Wow,' said Mia. Realising that the playdough wasn't playdough after all, she popped the little wodge of rolled icing into her mouth. 'And I mean, seriously, *wow*. Did you actually make that yourself?'

The birthday cake was an edible plate of chicken Madras with three-colour pilau rice, complete with edible fork, side orders of mango chutney and cucumber raita, and with extra pickled chillies on top.

'It's for Rennie, Carmen's brother-in-law. He's staying here too,' Nancy explained, 'and it's his birthday tomorrow. Chicken Madras is his favourite meal.'

'That is so cool! How much of it can you eat?'

'The whole lot. It's sponge underneath. The glycerine makes the sauce shiny.'

'How'd you make the rice?'

'Squeezed the icing through a potato ricer, then chopped the strands up.'

'I can't believe it won't taste of curry! It's just the cleverest thing I've ever seen. Is this how you make your living?'

Nancy smiled. 'It's just a hobby. Look, I'm about to make the hot towel. Pass me that knife and I'll show you how it's done.'

Twenty minutes later, the front door opened and shut as they were putting the finishing touches to the folded hot towel. Rennie yelled out, 'Anyone at home?' and with commendable presence of mind Mia swung into action. By the time he reached the kitchen, everything was hidden once more.

Nancy, hastily wiping icing sugar from the table, said, 'Hi. This is Mia, she's just moved in next door.'

'Hi there!' Clutching her stone-cold mug of tea, Mia eyed him with undisguised curiosity. 'You're the music guy, yeah? Nancy's just been telling me. Sorry, I should probably recognise you.' She pulled an apologetic face. 'No offence, but it's not really my kind of music. I'm more of a Dolly Parton girl. My friends all take the mickey out of me, they think I'm completely weird.'

Rennie grinned. 'I wouldn't say no to Dolly Parton myself. Nice to meet you, anyway. Just moved to London?'

Nancy wondered where Connor O'Shea had met Mia. Not on holiday, surely. Her creamy skin clearly hadn't seen the sun for months.

'Just,' Mia agreed chattily. 'I'm brand new! But isn't this great, having friendly neighbours? It makes all the difference. I don't know a soul in London, apart from my dad.'

'And Connor,' Nancy reminded her.

'Sorry?'

'Connor. You know him as well. That makes two people.'

The corners of Mia's mouth began to twitch.

'I can't wait to tell him this. Did you really think he was my boyfriend? I'm sixteen,' said Mia, grinning broadly. 'Connor's my dad.'

Nancy blushed at her mistake. Rennie, roaring with laughter, flung an arm round her shoulders and said, 'The name's Pas. Faux Pas.'

Watching with interest, Mia said, 'How about you two, then? Is Nancy your girlfriend?'

Honestly, was it possible to turn any redder? Spluttering with fresh embarrassment, Nancy said, 'No I am not!'

Mia was unperturbed. 'You get on well, though. Look at you.'

'I'm a hopeless case,' said Rennie. 'She wouldn't be interested in someone like me.'

'Why not? You're about the same age, aren't you? You're good looking,' said Mia with alarming directness, 'and you seem pretty normal.'

Gravely Rennie said, 'I'm mad, bad and dangerous to know.'

'And I only split up from my husband two weeks ago,' Nancy blurted out. As if Rennie would be remotely interested in her anyway.

Mia said saucily, 'Nothing like a new man to get you over the old one,' then shook her head and said, 'Sorry, sorry, shouldn't be making light of it. But you're looking grand! You don't seem like a woman whose marriage just hit the rocks. Two weeks ago, blimey. Are you in bits?'

She's sixteen, thought Nancy. I'm being interrogated about my private life by a sixteen-year-old. For heaven's sake, any minute now she might start counselling me, doling out helpful sixteen-year-old advice.

She was saved from this indignity by the phone. Rennie, answering it, chatted briefly before passing the phone over. 'It's Rose, for you.'

Excusing herself from the kitchen, Nancy spoke to her mother for fifteen minutes. By the time she was finished, Mia had left with her bag of flour and Rennie was leaning against the worktop frowning at the instructions on a packet of Marks and Spencer boeuf bourgignon.

'It says Do Not Microwave. That's outrageous. Why would anyone buy a ready meal they can't microwave?' Perplexed, he gave the packet a shake. 'What would happen if I did?'

'You can't. It's in a foil container. You'd blow the microwave up.'

'Bloody hell. Forty minutes.' Tut-tutting with irritation, Rennie crossed the kitchen and switched on the oven. 'Mia had to get back to make her Yorkshire pudding. What's up?' Glancing over at Nancy, he saw that she was looking distracted. 'Something to do with Jonathan?'

'Hmm? Oh, no, not him.' Nancy frowned. 'It's Mum. She's lost her job. The old people's home has been sold to a property developer.'

'And she's out of a job, just like that?' Rennie's eyebrows shot up. 'What happened to the old people? Did they get chucked into a builder's skip?'

'It hasn't happened just like that. Mum knew about it weeks ago, she just didn't want to worry me. I think she was hoping to find another job, but it hasn't happened. She's sixty-eight. People aren't interested in taking on a sixty-eight year old. I can't imagine my mum not working,' Nancy went on. 'She's just not the type. And she needs that bit of extra money, it makes a diff—'

'What?' said Rennie as she skidded to a halt mid-syllable.

'Out of the kitchen.' Snatching the foil container from him, Nancy shooed him towards the door. 'I'll do that. Go and have a shower or something.'

'I must smell terrible,' said Rennie with a grin.

The moment he'd sauntered out of the kitchen, Nancy hared over to the oven and rescued the cake. Thankfully the oven hadn't had time to get hot enough to do any damage. Exhaling with relief, she waited until the boiler fired up – bless him, Rennie really was having a shower – and carried the cake carefully up to her room.

Rose wasn't the only one who needed a job. Gazing out of the bedroom window, Nancy knew that she had to sort out her own life. Staying here in London, just coasting along, wasn't something she could do indefinitely. Maybe she should think about heading back to Edinburgh and finding work herself. If she moved in with her mother, they could manage the rent on the tiny flat more easily. Perhaps she could get a job in a department store or something.

Nancy saw Carmen, bundled up against the cold, heading up the road towards the house. Tapping on the window, she caught Carmen's attention and waved. Rosy-cheeked and swamped by her navy coat and pink scarf, Carmen looked up and waved back, and Nancy thought how much more cheerful she'd seemed since Rennie had been staying here. He was good for her, teasing her and making her laugh. Nancy suspected that Carmen would miss Rennie dreadfully – and far more than she realised – when it was time for him to go.

Chapter 12

Carmen was still in the hall pulling off her gloves and unwinding the scarf from round her neck when the doorbell rang. She opened the door and gazed inquiringly at the stranger on the doorstep.

'Yes?'

'Oh. Hi.' The stranger on the doorstep, perhaps taken aback by her tone, said, 'Joe James.'

'And?' There was a bag slung over his left shoulder. Was he trying to sell her something?

Hurriedly he fumbled in the pocket of his leather jacket and produced a letter. As he offered it, Carmen wondered if maybe she'd been a bit brisk.

'I'm here to see Rennie Todd. I do have an appointment. For six o'clock. Um,' he consulted his watch, 'I'm a bit early. Sorry about that. I can wait out here if you prefer.'

'No, that's fine. Come on in.' Feeling guilty, Carmen ushered Joe James past her into the house. The letter-heading bore the name of some charity she hadn't heard of, called Top of the World. 'Come through to the living room and I'll find Rennie for you.'

'He's in the shower.' Overhearing her on the landing, Nancy banged on the bathroom door and shouted, 'Rennie, someone here to see you.'

'Joe James,' Joe called up politely, 'from Top of the World.'

'Joe James,' Nancy relayed through the bathroom door. She listened to Rennie's muffled response, then came downstairs. 'He'll be with you in ten minutes. Can I get you a drink?'

'Coffee would be great. Thanks so much. I don't want to put you out,' said Joe.

'Not a problem.' Nancy disappeared into the kitchen. Through the open door, Carmen was mystified to see her reaching into the tumble dryer and lifting out a glass mixing bowl piled high with assorted knives and packets of goodness knows what. Oh well.

In the living room, Joe sat down on one of the sofas and said, 'Sorry to be a nuisance.'

'You're not a nuisance,' Carmen lied, because she was obliged to keep him company now until Rennie appeared. He had a holdall next to his feet, into which he could stuff all manner of household objects if he was left on his own.

'It's really kind of Rennie to see me. We sent out loads of letters to celebrities. Hardly anyone else bothered to reply.'

Carmen looked again at the letter she was still holding. She was the one, just last week, who had caught Rennie going through a pile of mail forwarded by his record company. Appalled by the cavalier way he zipped through the various letters – keep this, chuck that, answer this one, definitely don't answer that one – she had given Rennie a big talking-to.

'What kind of charity is Top of the World?'

'A really small one. No one knows who we are. Yet.' Becoming more animated, Joe said, 'But we're doing our best. We help sick children do what they want to do, arrange trips and treats for them. We can't run to big foreign holidays like some of the other charities, but you can still make a child's day without spending thousands of pounds. And when you see the looks on their faces . . . well, it's just fantastic.'

Having overcome his initial nervousness, his whole manner had changed. Charmed by his uncomplicated enthusiasm, Carmen relaxed too. 'And how did you get involved?'

'My friend's sister died two years ago, of a brain tumour. She was nine. Her parents set up a charity in her memory. That's her photo at the bottom of the page,' said Joe. 'Her name was Lucy. She was just the most fantastic little girl.'

Carmen studied the photograph of Lucy, a blond-haired imp with a beaming gap-toothed smile. Heartbreaking.

'And you work full-time for the charity?'

'Crikey, no, I just do as much as I can in my spare time. I'm a plumber in real life.' Joe pulled a face. 'Not very glamorous, I'm afraid.'

'But useful.' Carmen found herself warming to him even more. 'My dad was a plumber. He loved his work, helping people when they had a crisis.'

'That's the good bit. You're their saviour when you turn up to mend a broken boiler or fix a burst pipe.' Joe's eyes danced. 'They're delighted to see you. They treat you like their new best friend. Then, when you send them the bill, they ring you up from their lovely warm house with its nice dry walls and bellow, "*How much?*"'

'And cross you off their Christmas card list.' Laughing, Carmen thought what nice eyes he had, how open and honest his face was. His hair was short and trendily tousled, he was wearing a blue polo shirt and cream chinos and his shoes were gleaming so much she thought he'd probably polished them specially in honour of this visit.

'They never invite me to their parties.' Joe shook his head mournfully. 'They walk straight past me in the street. People are cruel.'

Rennie, hair still wet from the shower, burst into the living room holding two mugs of coffee.

'Honestly, you can't get the staff these days. Nancy's just made me carry these through myself. I mean, doesn't she know who I am?'

'You're a spoiled rock star who has to learn that not everyone else is your servant,' said Carmen.

'She's so bossy,' Rennie complained to Joe. 'Has she been bossing you around too?'

'No, she's been fine.' Overwhelmed, Joe jumped to his feet, took the coffee mugs from Rennie, put them down on the table and shook his hand. 'Joe James. It's great to meet you. Thank you so much for agreeing to do this.'

'OK if I stay?' said Carmen.

'See? Bossy *and* nosy.' Sitting down, Rennie winked at her. 'Of course you can stay.'

Rennie drank his coffee and listened to Joe explaining the aims of Top of the World. In his holdall, he'd brought along T-shirts for Rennie to sign, which would then be auctioned. Rennie had also agreed to create an original design that would be printed onto more T-shirts and baseball caps.

'I've got a couple of tour jackets and a pair of leather trousers as raffle prizes,' said Rennie, 'but they're not back yet from the dry cleaners. When I finish the designs I'll courier everything over to you. By Wednesday, is that OK?'

'Brilliant. We're holding a fundraising ball,' Joe explained to Carmen. 'On Saturday night. It's going to be fantastic. But don't worry about getting a courier,' he turned his attention back to Rennie, 'you don't have to do that. I can pop round and pick the stuff up on Wednesday morning – or whenever it's convenient. Any time you like. It's no trouble.'

'You've got a meeting with your accountant on Wednesday morning,' Carmen told Rennie. 'I'll be here.'

'Great. Wednesday morning.' Nodding eagerly, Joe gazed at Carmen and she thought again how nice he was.

'Well, if that's all.' Rennie rose to his feet and glanced at his watch. 'There's somewhere I have to be by seven thirty.'

*   *   *

'Somewhere you have to be by seven thirty,' Carmen jeered, when Rennie had shown Joe James out of the house.

'In front of the TV watching *Coronation Street*,' Rennie protested. 'What's wrong with that?'

'You do have a reputation to keep up, you know. Rock star sex gods don't generally watch a lot of *Coronation Street*.'

'Their loss. Anyway, what about you and charity boy? He couldn't keep his eyes off you. What was going on down here while I was in the shower?'

Carmen felt her heart begin to beat a little faster. 'Nothing. We were just chatting.'

'Hmm. Got yourself an admirer, if you ask me. Better shave your legs before Wednesday morning,' said Rennie with a grin.

B-bump, b-bump, b-bump went Carmen's heart against her ribs.

'Luckily,' she told him as the *Coronation Street* theme tune began to play, 'not everyone is as obsessed with sex as you. Some people, people with morals and principles, actually understand that there's more to life than—'

'Sshh.' Rennie's attention was on the TV screen. 'What's Norris been up to now?'

'You big durr-brain,' Carmen exclaimed, when Nancy told her what she was planning to do. 'I love having you here. You don't have to go back to Edinburgh just because you're scared about outstaying your welcome. If you want to stay here for the next five years, that's fine by me. It's so much nicer having you in the house.'

'Really?' Nancy was incredibly touched.

'Really.'

'And me,' said Rennie, drawn to the kitchen by the end of *Coronation Street* and the smell of frying onions and garlic. 'It's much nicer having me in the house too.'

Carmen rolled her eyes, then batted his hand away with a wooden spoon as he tried to pinch a mushroom.

'It's much noisier, I'll give you that. And don't even look at that grated cheese. I'm making a Spanish omelette.'

'And there was me, thinking that getting flirted with by charity boy might cheer you up.'

'He wasn't flirting with me. Stop going on about it or I'll send you back to the Savoy.'

'The thing is, I'd love to stay,' said Nancy, 'but I'm worried about

Mum. Maybe I should go up and see her. She never moans or complains but she must be feeling horrible. I hate the thought of her worrying, all on her own.'

'Why don't we invite her down here?' said Carmen. 'Would she do that, do you think? Come and stay for a week or two, give her a bit of a break?'

'Great idea.' Stealing a mushroom while she wasn't looking, Rennie said, 'Someone to be on my side for a change. Me and Rose against you and Nancy. We can gang up on each other.'

'Really? Are you sure you wouldn't mind?' Nancy was searching Carmen's face for clues.

'It was my idea, wasn't it?'

'I'll give her a ring now.' Hugging Carmen, Nancy said, 'She's never been to London before. Not once in her life.'

'It'll be like Crocodile Dundee visiting New York.' Rennie grinned. 'When she steps off that plane she won't know what's hit her.'

'She's never flown in a plane.' Nancy knew what her mother would say. 'She'll want to travel down by coach.'

'Only because she thinks it'll be cheaper,' said Rennie. 'I'll book her onto a flight with EasyJet. Just tell her she'll hurt my feelings if she doesn't use it.'

'She doesn't like taking things from other people,' Nancy warned him. 'She's very proud.'

'Fine. Tell her to make me a chicken casserole and bring it down with her.' Rennie shrugged. 'Then we'll call it quits.'

It seemed churlish, after that, to mind that Rennie never did get to see his chicken Madras birthday cake. A call from his manager in New York had him throwing a few things into a case at midnight and catching a cab to Heathrow.

'It's Jessie, she isn't coping well,' Carmen explained the next morning when Nancy came downstairs to find Rennie gone. Dave, Red Lizard's drummer, was evidently having a rough time in rehab. Jessie, his highly strung wife, was finding it hard to manage without him and had taken to her bed with a bottle of vodka.

'Shouldn't she be in rehab too?' said Nancy.

'God, yes, but that's the thing, you have to want to go. If anyone can persuade her, it's Rennie. He's great with her,' said Carmen. 'She trusts him. Anyway, he's going to do his best to sort her out and hopefully be back by the weekend. Right, I'm off to work. Shall I pick up a takeaway on the way home?'

'Lovely.' By the weekend, Rennie's cake would be stale. Realising that she may as well just throw it away, Nancy tried hard not to feel miffed.

'Indian?' said Carmen.

Nancy, feeling she'd had enough of chicken Madras and three-coloured rice, said, 'I'd rather have a Chinese.'

Chapter 13

Carmen was glad to have Rennie out of the way for a few days. His teasing remarks about Joe James weren't what she needed right now. It was bad enough feeling the first flickerings of attraction for another man and discovering that you'd completely forgotten how to behave, without having to put up with Rennie's nudge-nudge attitude. For someone with so much experience with the opposite sex, he could be incredibly school-boyish when it came to taking the mickey out of his long-suffering sister-in-law.

Anyway, it was Wednesday morning and the good news was that he was currently thousands of miles away.

The bad news was that he'd just sent her a fax, an extraordinarily unflattering portrait of herself in a bra and big knickers, with scarily hairy legs. Underneath it he'd scrawled: Don't forget . . .

Even more annoyingly, she hadn't forgotten. Telling herself it had nothing whatsoever to do with Joe James calling round this morning, it was something she'd have done anyway, Carmen had shaved her legs last night.

Not that Rennie was going to know that. She'd chop off her own legs before she'd let him see them in their naked state and put up with yet more teasing. It was bad enough that she was here now, in her bedroom, wondering what to wear.

God, it was like being fifteen again. How long had it been since she'd last tried on a pair of trousers then taken them off again because they didn't look right?

For heaven's sake, all Joe James was doing was popping round to collect a parcel. He probably wouldn't even set foot inside the house.

How about the striped jeans and Nancy's lacy turquoise top?

By the time the doorbell rang at ten o'clock, Carmen had a plan. She told herself it wasn't a plan, but deep down she knew it was.

Luckily it was also common sense.

'Hi! Crikey, I didn't even realise it was raining! Come on inside, all the stuff's in the kitchen. What a filthy day. How are you anyway?' Gabbling, she led the way, praying her flushed cheeks would get themselves under control by the time she had to face him.

'I'm great. Sorry, my jacket's wet. Nice to see you again.' Joe followed her into the kitchen. When she finally turned, Carmen saw that there were raindrops caught in his hair and on his eyelashes. He was wearing a weatherproof navy jacket and faded denims. And he was smiling at her as if he really was glad to see her again.

B-bump, b-bump, b-bump.

'Now, Rennie had to fly to the States on Monday night, but I've got everything here. Leather trousers and tour jackets,' Carmen patted the bulky parcel, 'and all the T-shirts, signed before he left.' She touched the holdall Joe had brought along with him on Monday evening, then the envelope lying next to it. 'And he faxed his designs over last night. They're in that one.'

'Brilliant. We're really grateful. Actually, I was wondering if . . .'

'What?'

'No, nothing, it's OK.' Joe shook his head and exhaled. 'It's just . . . no, forget it.'

Breathless, Carmen said, 'Actually, I was going to ask you something too. We've had a bit of a problem recently with one of our showers. Sometimes the water goes cold for no reason. I was wondering if your company could take a look at it for us?'

There, she'd been subtle, hadn't she? And it was true, she wasn't making it up.

'Could be it just needs a service.' Joe shook his head slowly. 'But then we get that awkward thing, don't we? My boss sends you a bill, you think it's too high, you feel resentful and start to think you've been ripped off.'

'I wouldn't,' protested Carmen.

'Well, I'm sorry, but I can't take that risk. No, very bad idea.' Smiling slightly, Joe said, 'On the other hand, you could let me take a look at the shower now, then the company wouldn't have to send you a bill.'

'I can't do that.'

'Yes you can. It might just be a valve sticking. I could fix that in a flash. My boss would be none the wiser. And you'd be so grateful I might even end up asking the question I didn't have the courage to ask just now.'

Oh wow, this was thrilling, just so thrilling. Even if she had absolutely no intention of showing him her ultra-smooth legs.

'OK,' Carmen said shyly.

'Give me two minutes,' Joe told her, heading back to the front door. 'I'll just get my toolbox out of the van.'

Carmen perched on the edge of the corner bath and watched Joe expertly dismantle the shower. It was so lovely to watch a man who knew what he was doing. Now, minus his jacket, she was able to admire the way the muscles rippled in his forearms as he deftly unscrewed and checked each component in turn.

'So what's it like, having Rennie Todd as a boss?'

'Sorry?'

'What's he like to work for?' said Joe, reaching for a screwdriver. 'You seem to get on pretty well together.'

'We do.' Thinking of this morning's cheeky fax, Carmen said, 'Well, most of the time. But he isn't my boss.'

Joe looked surprised. 'He's not?'

'Rennie's my brother-in-law.' She was able to say it now, without worrying that her voice might go wobbly. 'I was married to Spike.'

'Oh my God, I didn't realise. I'm so sorry.' Mortified, Joe put down the screwdriver. 'I had no idea.'

'That's OK. Why would you?' Some rock star wives loved the lime-light, others didn't. Carmen had always preferred to remain in the back-ground.

'I thought you were his personal assistant or something. I'm really embarrassed now.'

'Don't be. It's fine. To be honest, I quite like people not knowing who I am.'

Reassured, Joe said, 'Still, it must be nice, staying here in his house.'

'Actually, it's my house,' said Carmen. Oh well, in for a penny, in for a pound. 'Rennie's staying here with me.'

'Bloody hell.' This time Joe looked truly appalled. His gaze took in the Italian marble bronze and cream bathroom. 'You mean all this is yours?'

Embarrassed, Carmen saw it through his eyes. 'Spike bought it.'

'I can't imagine what it must be like, to own a place like this.'

'The same as any other house, just bigger. When Spike and I first started going out together, we didn't have any money,' said Carmen. 'We lived in a really grotty flat in Edinburgh. But we were just as happy. Maybe happier,' she added, because those were the days before Spike had begun to experiment with drugs.

'It must have been awful for you when he died. I'm sorry.' Joe picked up a pair of pliers. 'You must miss him terribly.'

'I do. But it's been three years. I'm getting better.' Hearing the phone begin to ring downstairs, Carmen rose to her feet. 'I'd better answer that.'

Rennie had forgotten to cancel his appointment with the accountant. By the time Carmen had finished explaining to him that Rennie was out of the country and apologising on his behalf, Joe had come back downstairs.

'All done,' he said easily, rolling down his sleeves as Carmen hung up the phone. 'Good as new. The valve just needed a good clean.'

'You must let me pay you. Now that you know I can afford it.'

'Not a chance.' Joe smiled. 'On the house.'

'Well, thanks.' Feeling brave, Carmen said, 'But now you have to tell me what it was you were about to say earlier.'

'Oh, that. I can't.'

'Fair's fair. You promised.'

'Did I? OK.' Joe paused, running the fingers of his left hand thoughtfully through his dark hair. 'The truth? When I came over here on Monday evening I thought you were fantastic. I really felt we, you know, clicked? And all day yesterday I couldn't stop thinking about you. So I decided I'd ask you out. Then I wondered if you'd like to come along to the charity ball with me on Friday night, and I thought wouldn't it be great if you did, we'd have such a brilliant time together . . .' He stopped and waited, then looked regretfully away. 'But it's no good. There's no way in the world I can do that now.'

Feeling weirdly light-headed, Carmen said, 'Yes you can.'

'No I can't.'

'Why not?'

'Come on. You know why. I thought you were Rennie Todd's PA. But you aren't, are you? You're Spike Todd's widow. This is your house. How can I ask you out now? You're way out of my league.'

The trouble was, Carmen knew what he meant. It didn't matter that what Joe was saying wasn't true; he would feel uncomfortable because the fact that she had money did make a difference. This was why she'd never told anyone at the shelter who she had once been married to, and why she avoided the socialising that went on amongst the rest of the staff and volunteers. If they knew she lived in a house like this, they would treat her differently.

It was unfair, but it was a fact of life.

The way Joe was looking at her made Carmen want to start tearing up twenty-pound notes on the spot. It was the first time in three years that she'd actually experienced the crackle and spark of physical attraction.

Realising she was on the brink of not seeing Joe James again, she blurted out, 'Please ask me to go to the ball with you!'

Blimey, where had *that* come from?

'Believe me, I'd love to.' Joe looked longingly at her. 'But I'd just feel so . . .'

'I want to go to the ball.' Carmen couldn't quite believe she was doing this, but desperate situations called for desperate measures. 'Please take me with you. Nobody else has to know who I am, if that helps. I'd just really like to go,' she concluded helplessly. 'With you.'

There, now she'd made a complete and utter fool of herself. If Joe turned her down, there was nothing more she could do. Except maybe stick her head in the oven, if only it had had the common decency to run on gas.

'OK.' Putting his hands up, Joe broke into a smile. 'I'd like to go with you too. You've made my day.'

You've made my year, Carmen thought happily. He really had. Yikes, she had a date for Friday night!

Thank goodness Rennie wasn't here to tease her about it.

Chapter 14

You can lead a horse to water but you can't make it drink. Similarly, you can introduce your daughter to your girlfriend but you can't make them like each other.

From the safety of his office, Connor watched Sadie head over to reception and ask Mia a question. Both of them were smiling – well, baring their teeth at each other – but the body language said it all.

Damn it, why couldn't his life be uncomplicated?

Connor lit a cigarette, which wasn't actually allowed, but this was his club so what the hell. Sadie Sylvester was twenty-six and he liked her a lot, although sometimes he wasn't entirely sure why. Her hair was a riotous mass of ringlets dyed a vivid shade of magenta. She was curvy, voluptuous and terrifyingly fit. When she'd started working at the Lazy B four months earlier, teaching aerobics and dance classes, he'd found himself drawn to her brash, devil-may-care manner and sexy, slanting eyes. Before long, they were seeing each other regularly. Sadie could be bossy at times. She knew her own mind. When she'd first set her sights on Connor, it hadn't occurred to her for one moment that she might not get him. She was hot-blooded, emotional and could be blunt to the point of rudeness, but she was never boring.

All in all, Sadie and Mia had quite a lot in common. It would have been nice if they could have hit it off. But this hadn't happened; they had decided to hate each other from the word go.

Connor shuddered at the memory of their first meeting on the very evening Mia had moved in. Mia had given him a blow-by-blow account of it. Sadie, having decided to drop round on a whim – he suspected she liked to check up on him – had rung the doorbell at ten o'clock. Her hackles had risen instantly at the sight of Mia, whose version of pyjamas was a skimpy white vest top and low-slung cotton shorts.

'Who are you? What are you doing here? Where's Connor?'

Instantly offended by Sadie's unfriendly manner – and her hair was pretty offensive too – Mia bristled.

'You must be my father's girlfriend. Nice to meet you too. Dad's having a bath.'

'Oh, right. I'll come in. He didn't tell me you were visiting.' Sadie followed Mia into the living room, took off her coat and handed it to the younger girl with a forced smile. Fastidiously brushing away digestive biscuit crumbs, she then made herself comfortable on the sofa where Mia had been sitting.

Sweetly, Mia said, 'I'm not visiting. I've come to live with my dad.'

She watched with satisfaction as Sadie's lipglossed mouth dropped open.

When Connor arrived downstairs shortly afterwards, Sadie sprang up from the sofa and marched him into the kitchen.

'What's going on? Is this really going to happen?' Incensed, Sadie had bombarded him with questions. Having a sixteen year old hanging around the place didn't fit in with her plans at all.

'Hey, don't get worked up,' Connor told her. 'It'll be fine, you'll see.'

'How can you say that?' Sadie rolled her eyes in disbelief. 'This is going to change everything. For a start, how are we supposed to have fun together? We won't have any privacy!'

Wearily Connor rubbed his forehead. At this rate the house was going to end up like Beirut, with sniper fire zinging in all directions.

'It's all happened very suddenly. Once we've had time to get used to the situation, I'm sure things will settle down.'

'Ha,' snorted Sadie, who knew perfectly well they wouldn't. 'And what does she plan to do with herself all day? Go to school? Get a job? Laze around the place doing nothing at all, like most teenagers?'

'She already has a job. At the club,' said Connor.

Sadie's nostrils flared. 'At *our* club?'

'My club.' It occurred to Connor that this could signal the end of the line for Sadie and himself. Mia was here to stay, whether Sadie liked it or not. 'I've started her on reception. I think she'll do well.'

Sadie's glossy upper lip curled with derision, but she didn't say what she was clearly dying to say. Instead, sensing a change of direction was called for, she ran her fingers lightly down the gap at the front of Connor's white towelling dressing gown. His chest, so brown from their holiday, was warm and still damp from the bath.

'I came over here to see you. I thought we'd make love on the sofa in the living room.'

'Well, we can't. Mia's watching a documentary about battery farming and it doesn't finish until midnight.' Since Mia was passionate about the welfare of farm animals, the programme was required viewing. Connor made a mental note to himself to go out tomorrow and buy another TV set for Mia's bedroom.

'Fine. I'm adaptable.' Smiling for the first time, sliding both hands inside the dressing gown and raking her fingers gently down his sides, Sadie said playfully, 'We'll go up to your room. Do it the old-fashioned way, use the bed.'

Connor shook his head. 'We can't leave Mia down here on her own. It would look so obvious.'

'For God's sake! What does it *matter*? You're single, you're allowed to have a girlfriend,' Sadie protested. 'She can't stop you having a sex life!'

'I know, but it would be embarrassing.' Gently removing her arms from inside his dressing gown, Connor said, 'It's her first night here. Come into the living room and we'll all watch TV. Once you get to know each other, things will—'

'Oh please, they *won't* get better. Sitting down together to watch a documentary about battery farming isn't my idea of a wild time. Sex is my idea of a wild time, but I'm not allowed to have sex with my boyfriend because even though our uninvited guest wouldn't be able to see or hear us, she might know what's going on and be embarrassed. No, don't worry about me. I'll go home, leave you and your daughter in peace. Enjoy your battery hens.'

When Sadie had left, even more furious to discover that Mia had dumped her coat over the back of a chair instead of hanging it up properly on the coat stand, Connor rejoined his daughter on the sofa.

'Dad, I've got to say this.'

Thought you might, thought Connor. Aloud he said, 'What, sweetheart?'

Mia tucked her arm companionably through his. 'I'm an easy-going person. I like most people I meet. But that girlfriend of yours is something else, I'm telling you. You could do so much better.'

Connor was reminded of why he drank. In theory, he knew that alcohol was bad for you; it was a poison, it was capable of giving you diabolical hangovers, it did insidious things to your liver and, since he invariably smoked more cigarettes when he was drinking, would probably end up giving him lung cancer to boot.

The trouble was, he enjoyed drinking enormously. When he had a beer in his hand, he was happy. And when he had Sadie in his bed he was happy too. She was wildly sexy, so much so that, if he was honest, when they were in bed together, the less adorable aspects of her personality didn't trouble him at all. He was prepared to overlook these minor defects. What man wouldn't, when she had so much else to offer?

'We'll see,' he told Mia. 'She's not as bad as you think.'

Mia made a *tuh* sound under her breath. 'Dad, I think you'll find she is.'

'Anyway,' Connor decided he had to remind his daughter who was the parent around here, 'that's just your opinion. It's my life, not yours, and I'm not going to be running it to suit you. I'm not planning to dump every girlfriend you decide you don't like, either. So give Sadie a break, OK? She wasn't expecting you to be here tonight, but she'll get used to the idea.' *I hope.* 'You never know, you may end up the best of friends.'

Now, watching them square up to each other across the reception desk, Connor acknowledged that this was unlikely to happen. Perversely – and much as he loved his headstrong daughter – it only made him fancy Sadie all the more. She was wearing a midriff-baring violet Lycra sports top and violet and pink striped cycle shorts. Every inch of her tanned, super-toned body was beyond criticism. Sadie's thighs would never entertain the concept of cellulite. She worked like an Olympic athlete to keep her figure flawless, and equal attention was paid to her make-up. He had witnessed her spending forty minutes doing her face. Connor, who thought she didn't need it, wondered if this was another cause of Mia's distrust of Sadie. Mia thought there was something obscene about the idea of spending twenty pounds on a designer lipstick. Sadie, on the other hand, belonged to the Nancy Dell'Olio school of thought when it came to cosmetics: more wasn't nearly enough.

Her dark eyes were flashing now, her magenta corkscrew ringlets starting to bounce ominously. As their voices began to rise, Connor left his office and headed over to the desk.

'Ah, good.' Spotting him, Sadie said frostily, 'Back me up here, would you? Just tell your daughter to do as she's told and stop making a fuss about nothing.'

'Excuse *me*.' Mia had no intention of being intimidated. 'What's more important, the members who pay good money to come to this club, or your fake nails?'

'Girls, shhh.' Luckily the reception area was empty, but Connor was keen to avoid a squawking match. 'Tell me what this is about and let's sort it out, shall we?'

'She's sixteen,' Sadie exploded. 'She isn't going to boss me around like—'

'I'm not bossing you around, I'm protecting our members' interests!'

Turning to Connor, Mia said, 'Sadie wants to change the time of tomorrow's six o'clock advanced aerobics class. She's got an appointment with her nail technician,' her lip curled with derision as she enunciated the words, 'so she asked me to ring everyone in her class and tell them we'd be starting at five-thirty instead. So I phoned the first three people on the list but they all say they can't get here that early because they don't finish work until five-thirty. And now she's getting stroppy with me because I won't ring the rest of the numbers. It's just ridiculous, why should I? They're not going to be able to get here either, are they? Because bunking off early from the job you're being paid to do isn't professional!'

'Says the sixteen-year-old who has held down a job for all of three days,' Sadie sneered. 'And how did you get this job? Oh yes, that's it, your daddy gave it to you.'

'Right, stop this.' The time had come for Connor to put his foot down; the trouble was, he didn't know where to put it. 'Why don't you change your nail appointment?'

Sadie rolled her eyes at his stupidity. 'It's the only one I can get. Marco's flying over to LA on Saturday morning. He's an A-list nail technician, booked up for months ahead. God, I was so lucky to get this appointment at short notice, you have no idea.'

Clearly, as far as Sadie was concerned, missing out on her stint with Marco would be on a par with cancelling a private audience with the Pope.

'How about swapping classes with Leila then?' said Connor. Leila was the other aerobics instructor.

'I already asked her.' Sadie shook her head. 'She won't do it. Her parents are throwing a surprise party for her brother and she has to be there by eight thirty.'

Connor nodded, remembering Leila telling him about it. The party was being held at a hotel in Hertfordshire and she'd been fretting about catching a train because track repairs were causing delays.

'OK. You answer that,' he told Mia as the phone began to ring. Turning to Sadie he added, 'And you get back to the gym. I'll see if I can sort something out.'

The way Mia and Sadie narrowed their eyes at each other said it all. In the office, Connor rang Leila and did his persuasive thing on her.

'I would swap,' Leila protested, 'but I have to—'

'I know, I know.' Connor was sympathetic. 'It's that business with the trains. How about if I organise a car to pick you up and drive you to the party?'

Leila, who was a sweet-natured girl, accepted his offer. Connor hung up with relief. He was a fool, he knew. The car would cost a fortune. On the one hand, it was worth it to have the problem solved. On the other, Mia was going to give him grief when she found out what he'd done, while Sadie would feel she'd won their battle of wills.

God, nightmare. Why couldn't he have been attracted to gentle, thoughtful, eager-to-please Leila instead of fiery, sexy, eager-to-cause-havoc Sadie Sylvester?

Life was never that simple though, was it? Leila might be angelic but she did nothing for him.

Whereas Sadie did . . . well, quite a lot.

Connor leaned back in his chair and lit another much-needed cigarette. Having Mia and Sadie both working here was, he already knew, a big mistake. But Sadie was a damn good instructor with a devoted following. And Mia was attacking her job with relish, impressing everyone – apart from Sadie – with her enthusiasm, cheery manner and eagerness to learn. At this rate she was shaping up to be a dream employee. Her plan was to work her way up to club manager. She was probably fantasising already about giving Sadie the sack.

The phone rang on Connor's desk.

'It's me,' said Laura. 'How's she getting on?'

'Terrific.' Through the glass door, he watched Mia simultaneously booking a client into a class, handing a fresh towel to another client and buzzing a third who had mislaid his membership card through the turn-stile. 'Couldn't be better. Want me to transfer you so you can have a word with her yourself?'

'I've already tried having a word,' complained Laura. 'I rang her first. She told me it wouldn't give a good impression, people seeing the reception-ist yakking away on the phone to her mother, and besides, she was far too busy to take personal calls.'

Connor smiled to himself; between them, they had undoubtedly created something unique. Their daughter was the oldest sixteen-year-old he knew.

Chapter 15

Nancy, back from the shops, thought she was hallucinating when she glanced through the railings bordering the garden in the centre of Fitzallen Square. It was a dark grey afternoon and the air was thick with fog, but the small, bundled-up figure sitting on one of the wooden benches beneath a dripping ash tree looked uncannily like her mother.

Nancy made her way through the gate and peered more closely at the solitary figure.

'Mum! Is that *you*?'

Rose, her transparent Pacamac crackling as she pushed the hood down, waved and called back, 'Yoo hoo, darling. Hello!'

Nancy hugged her tightly; it was so good to see her mother again, even if it was like hugging a cellophane-wrapped sweet. Rose even smelled comfortingly familiar. Nancy shook her head in disbelief.

'You're not supposed to be here yet! Rennie booked you onto the four o'clock flight. I was going to meet you at the airport.'

'I know you were, darling. That's why I thought I'd save you the trouble.' Beaming, pink-cheeked with the cold, Rose said, 'I'm here now, so you don't have to trudge all that way.'

'But . . . how did you *get* here?' The reason Nancy had planned to meet her at Stansted was because she knew Rose would be traumatised by the prospect of finding her way to Chelsea. Suspiciously, she said, 'Don't tell me you caught the coach.'

'The coach? Not a chance.' Rose looked shocked. 'Why would I do that, when the plane's so much quicker? No, no, I just looked up the Easy-Jet website on the internet and found out the flight times. Then I rang them and a lovely lad there was able to swap me onto the earlier flight.'

'Website? *Internet?*'

'Sweetheart, I'm not senile. It's a marvellous system,' Rose confided. 'They have computers at the local library, and the librarians are wonderful at showing you how to use them. You'll never believe what I found on there the other day. Something completely outrageous!'

'What?' Nancy dreaded to think.

'A recipe for cloutie dumpling,' Rose exclaimed, 'from a lady in Wellington, in New Zealand! And when I emailed her to ask where she was originally from, she told me she'd never visited Scotland in her life. Yet her recipe was excellent. Imagine that!'

Nancy, her brain in a whirl, said, 'So how *did* you get here from Stansted?'

'Och, it was simple! I just asked a really nice man how I should go about it, and he showed me where to catch the train to Liverpool Street. Then I met *such* a nice family on the train and they explained the whole underground system to me. So when we reached Liverpool Street I bought one of those A to Z books at WH Smith and worked out which tube station was nearest to here.'

Had she ever seen her mother looking more relaxed? Incredulously, Nancy said, 'Just like that?'

'Just like that. Easy as pie. Well, you can't go far wrong with the Circle Line, can you? Sooner or later you'll end up where you want to be.'

Honestly, Nancy marvelled, whatever next. Would Rose be announcing that she'd applied to run the London marathon? Joined the international space program? Become a weather girl?

Speaking of weather . . .

'What are we still doing out here? Come on, let's get inside. We'll put the kettle on and get you warmed up. How long have you been waiting?'

'Not long at all, pet. I've been sitting here enjoying the gardens.' Having bent to gather together her motley collection of bags, Rose straightened and broke into a broad smile. Thinking she was smiling at her, Nancy was startled to hear her mother call out, 'Bye, sweetheart. Bye, Doreen. See you again. Hope that leg's better soon.'

Spinning round, Nancy saw a man in his thirties with long blond hair heading towards them through the fog with a mongrel on a lead. From the depths of his parka, the man called back, 'Bye, Rose, lovely to meet you,' in a light, unmistakably camp voice that sent a shiver of alarm down Nancy's spine.

'Mum,' she hissed when the couple had trotted damply off down the path, 'that wasn't a woman. It was a *man*.'

'What? I'm not with you, pet.'

'You called him *Doreen*.' His name was probably Darren, and Rose had, embarrassingly, misheard him.

'Dear me, you really don't think I'm safe to be let out on my own, do you?' Looking amused, Rose said, 'His name's Zac and of course he's a man. Doreen's the name of his dear little dog. She managed to get her leg caught in a drain cover yesterday, that's why she's limping. Now, are we going to have that cup of tea or not?'

Rennie, phoning from New York, insisted on speaking to Rose when he heard she'd arrived safely.

'Oh yes, I'm having the time of my life,' Rose assured him. 'Everyone in London is so friendly and welcoming, it's like being at a lovely big party. And this *house*, well, it's like something out of one of those magazines with celebrities in.'

'Did you bring me that casserole?' teased Rennie.

'No, pet, I didn't. I was worried about turbulence on the plane. But I'll make you one as soon as you come back,' Rose promised. 'And Carmen's hankering for flapjack, so I'll be doing some of that this evening.'

'Is Carmen there? I'll have a quick word with her.'

'She's upstairs, pet, getting herself all ready for her big date.'

In New York, Rennie's eyebrows went up. 'Big date? Who with?'

'Oh my, she did tell me. Let me think, what's the name of Carmen's gentleman friend?' Brightening, Rose exclaimed, 'Ah yes, got it now. Joe.'

'Joe,' echoed Rennie. 'My God, she's actually going out on a date with him?'

'She's very excited,' Rose confided. 'Nervous too. All over the place, bless her heart. Well, it's her first try since Spike. Some people take longer than others to get over these things, don't they? Poor lamb, she's taken more time than most.'

'Tell her I'm glad the shaving did the trick,' said Rennie.

'Oh really?' Interested, Rose said, 'Did Joe have a beard until recently? I didn't know that.'

'Rennie asked me to remind you to give your legs another shave,' Rose dutifully reported to Carmen when she finally reappeared downstairs. 'He said nobody likes a girl with stubble. I did explain to him that you'd be wearing a long skirt so it's not as if anyone would know, but he still wanted me to tell you.'

I'll bet he did, thought Carmen. Luckily she was too busy dealing with the butterflies in her stomach to react to Rennie's less than subtle teasing.

'You look beautiful, sweetheart,' Rose said reassuringly.

Carmen did her best to relax her shoulders and not look as if she was about to go out on her first date in . . . well, practically her whole life. She and Spike had been so young when they'd started seeing each other

85

that their meetings had been more hanging-around-in-the-park-together than anything resembling a proper date.

Now, anxiously checking her reflection in the mirror above the book-case, she thought she looked more like Bambi about to be shot. The shoulder-relaxing wasn't working at all. Her dark blue dress, held up with thin straps and cut not too low at the front, was plain and simply cut. The full-length organza jacket, also dark blue, was randomly dotted with Swarovski crystals. She hadn't worn anything this smart since her brand new school uniform on her first day at Jessop Lane Primary.

Hopefully this time she wouldn't be coming home with red poster paint down her front and a couple of buttons hanging off.

'I'm having the best time of my life,' Joe whispered in Carmen's ear and she felt herself flush with happiness as his arms tightened round her. They were slowly circling the dance floor as the band played an old Mariah Carey number. The female lead singer wasn't up to Mariah Carey's standard but that didn't matter, they were performing free of charge and the ball had been a raging success.

'Me too,' said Carmen. She'd enjoyed herself, and she'd enjoyed being here with Joe. He had looked after her, proudly introducing her to people he knew. Everyone had been friendly and welcoming. Conversation at their table had flowed effortlessly; she hadn't felt awkward once. Joe had held her hand under the table. He looked so handsome in his borrowed dinner jacket. He told jokes and made her laugh. In his company she felt relaxed, normal, desirable again. It was like coming out of hibernation.

'Sheila took me to one side earlier,' Joe confided, 'and told me we made a lovely couple.'

Sheila, big and matronly, had organised the raffle. Innocently Carmen said, 'What, you and her? Isn't she a bit old for you?'

Joe grinned. 'Me and you. She said we look perfect together.' He paused then added, 'I can't believe that this time last week, I hadn't met you. And now, since meeting you, I can't think of anything else. You're probably going to get me the sack.'

'Why?'

'Couldn't concentrate at work today. I was useless.' He gave her a squeeze. 'It's all your fault. I'm not safe. If you hear on the news about a major gas explosion in Clerkenwell, you'll know who did it. I'll have to go on the run, I'll be a wanted—'

'Stop! I can't handle this. If I'm that much of a health hazard, maybe we'd better not see each other again.'

Joe stopped dancing. 'Never.' He shook his head, smiling at her. 'Don't say that. I couldn't bear it.'

'OK.' They still weren't moving. Carmen murmured, 'People are starting to look at us.'

'Let them. I don't care. Listen, I'm doing this all wrong and I know it's uncool, but we are going to see each other again, aren't we?'

A lump sprang into Carmen's throat. To think that she'd been worried about tonight being a let-down, that Joe might realise he'd made a mistake. Slowly she nodded. 'I'd love to see you again.'

'And again,' Joe prompted.

'And again and again,' Carmen agreed with a surge of happiness.

'OK, I know it's way too soon to be saying this, so I won't.' His breath warm against her cheek, he murmured, 'But right now I'm *thinking* it wouldn't take much for me to fall in love with you.'

Heavens. This was like a Hollywood film.

'Is that scary?' whispered Joe, beginning to dance again as the music changed to George Michael's 'Careless Whisper'.

'A bit.' Carmen nodded.

'Sorry. Nice scary or get-this-creep-away-from-me scary?'

He was so lovely. She was so lucky. And his fingertips, drawing light circles on her back as they moved together in time with the music, were making her skin tingle in the most delicious way.

'Very nice scary,' said Carmen.

Joe's dark eyes softened. 'That's good enough for now.'

Chapter 16

Rennie arrived back from New York on Sunday morning and reached Fitzallen Square at midday. Any fantasies of opening the front door and being greeted by the welcoming smell of a home-cooked roast dinner were cruelly dashed when he bumped into Nancy and Rose in the hallway. Rose was bundled up in a grey woollen coat, thick knitted scarf and hat.

'You naughty boy, you'll catch your death of cold,' she scolded, eyeing Rennie's crumpled T-shirt and jeans. 'You're not even wearing a vest. Now, are you hungry? Shall I make you something to eat before we leave?'

'That would be great. Roast lamb, roast potatoes, carrots, leeks, parsnips, Yorkshire pudding and gravy please,' said Rennie. Then, catching the worried look on her face he said, 'Rose, I'm joking. You're here on holiday, not to wait on us hand and foot. What have you been doing anyway?'

'Seeing all the sights. Oh, it's been marvellous.' Rose's eyes lit up. 'We went to see Downing Street yesterday, and Madame Tussaud's – what a place that was, all those marvellous people looking so *like* themselves. And Buckingham Palace. And the London Eye. We're just off out again now, to visit the zoo at Regent's Park. Why don't you come with us?' Rose gave his arm an encouraging pat. 'Oh come on, it's going to be such fun!'

Fond though he was of Rose, Rennie couldn't imagine anything more awful. Standing in the freezing cold watching penguins swimming around in even icier water wasn't his idea of a good time.

Catching his eye, Nancy said, straight-faced, 'I think Rennie's probably tired after his flight.'

Rennie nodded. 'Thanks, but I'll just stay here. Maybe take Carmen out to lunch.'

'Carmen? She's not around,' said Rose. 'She went out earlier, with Joe.'

'Joe again? You're kidding. What have I missed?'

'Loads.' Nancy's tone was playful. 'Carmen's in love. We've hardly seen her since Friday night.'

Rennie wondered how he felt about this. Carmen? Were they serious?

'Your leather trousers raised four hundred pounds, by the way. And the four jackets went for five hundred and fifty each.'

'Has he been . . . staying here?' In deference to Rose, Rennie phrased it as delicately as he knew how.

Rose looked shocked. 'Of course not! He's been the perfect gentleman. Drives her home, kisses her goodnight on the doorstep.'

Well, that was something.

'She's come over all dippy,' said Nancy. 'Like a teenager. If she isn't out with Joe, she's talking about him. I swear she counts the minutes before she'll see him again.'

Rennie knew he should be pleased that Carmen was returning to the land of the living at long last. He wished he could *feel* more pleased.

'Well, that's . . . great.' As he said it, Rennie wondered if this was half his fault. OK, maybe he'd teased Carmen about Joe, but he hadn't seriously expected her to take him up on it.

'I don't like the thought of leaving you here on your own.' Rose was looking concerned.

'Mum, he's not ten years old.' Waggling her eyebrows apologetically, Nancy attempted to edge Rose towards the door.

'Are you sure you wouldn't like to come to the zoo?'

Rennie said gravely, 'I'll be fine. I promise not to play with matches or climb out onto my window ledge. Now, you two go off and enjoy yourselves.'

When Rose and Nancy had left, Rennie hauled his case upstairs and lay down on his bed. His mobile beeped, signalling the arrival of yet another text.

Where r u? Fancy meeting up? Call me! Miss u loads. Luv Caz. xxx

Rennie knew he should be used to textspeak by now, but it still amused him. Wasn't this the kind of message a thirteen-year-old girl might compose? Luv, for heaven's sake. And kisses. Caz was a 28-year-old medical physicist, hugely intelligent and perfectly capable of spelling long complicated words if she so desired. Yet her text made her sound like the kind of person who'd leap at the chance of appearing on *Trisha*.

Still, she had the best figure in Finsbury Park. And he had the rest of the day free. Still lying on his back, Rennie replied to her text with a brief: 'See you at your place in an hour.'

He couldn't bring himself to abbreviate.

Nor could he bring himself to raise much enthusiasm for the prospect of spending the afternoon with Caz, lovely girl though she undoubtedly was. As he stood beneath the shower, vigorously shampooing his hair, Rennie recalled Nancy's comments about Carmen, how she had been counting down the minutes before she would see Joe again.

Thinking about it again gave Rennie quite a jolt. Counting down the minutes was what he did when he was starving and had a frozen lasagne in the microwave. (That bit on the packet instructing you to leave it to stand for one minute was the part that *really* irritated him.) But he honestly couldn't remember *ever* counting down the minutes before meeting up with a girlfriend, experiencing that sense of breathless anticipation, knowing that if something were to happen to prevent their reunion he would be distraught.

Which probably explained why he was so often late turning up for a date.

Maybe love just wasn't his thing, Rennie thought as he reached for the shower gel. He'd never been in love, not properly. He suspected it had something to do with the thrill of the chase. Or, in his case, the abject lack of it. If you had to work hard to attract a girl's attention, do your best to make her like you and endlessly worry that she might not be interested in return, actually overcoming all those obstacles might mean so much that you then automatically fell in love with her, because winning her heart, like reaching the summit of Everest, was such a fantastic achievement.

But that had never happened to him. What with girls being generally more forward nowadays, it had been years since he'd even had the chance to spot one he liked and make the first move. They always spotted him and made their move first. Whenever he visited a bar or a nightclub, pretty girls approached him, instigating conversation – if you could call it that – and offering him their phone numbers, their undisguised interest and their bodies before you could say floozy.

And that was the problem, Rennie decided, sluicing the last of the foaming gel from his body and stepping out of the shower. He'd never had to try. He didn't need to be wildly entertaining and witty, because these girls would shriek with laughter at the feeblest joke. If he treated them in an offhand fashion, they tolerated it. They were crazy about him even when he *knew* he didn't deserve it.

For crying out loud, where was the sense of hard-earned achievement in that?

Beeeep went his phone. For a moment, as he reached across to pick it up, Rennie fantasised that it would be Caz, texting him to say frightfully sorry but she'd changed her mind and couldn't see him this afternoon after all.

Or, in textspeak, frtfly sry, chngd mnd, cnt c u 2dy.

Didn't she realise how dramatically she'd shoot up in his estimation if she did that?

Well, he'd been half right. The message was from Caz.

It said: Ready 4 U! Luv C xxx

Rennie towelled himself dry. Maybe he should ring and be the one to cancel. Was it fair to take advantage of her like this? Wouldn't he be happier stretched across the sofa downstairs, watching *Casablanca* or *Citizen Kane*?

But Caz would think *that* was unfair. More than anything else, she wanted to see him – and sleep with him – this afternoon. She would be upset if he let her down now.

Wearily, Rennie dragged a clean pair of jeans and a fresh shirt out of his wardrobe. He'd spend the afternoon with Caz and be home early. Tonight he'd have a serious talk with Carmen and find out exactly what was going on between her and Joe James.

Buttoning his denim shirt, Rennie wondered what time Carmen would be back.

The answer to this question was a bit bloody late for his liking.

'Yay, you're still awake,' Carmen said cheerfully, letting herself into the house at two thirty in the morning and discovering Rennie making his tenth cup of coffee in the kitchen.

Of course I'm still awake, Rennie thought crossly. I've been waiting for *you*.

Aloud he said, 'And what on earth time do you call this? Where have you been? What have you been doing? Don't you have to be up early for work? And why's your shirt on inside out?'

Carmen grinned and gave him a hug. 'Yes, Mum, no, Mum, sorry I'm late, Mum. We were having such fun I didn't notice the time. But I promise to get up at seven o'clock for work. And my shirt isn't on inside out.'

'I should hope not.' Rennie wondered if she could tell that he was sounding jokey but deep down he actually meant it. Although Carmen was clearly in such a daze of euphoria he doubted she'd notice if he was wearing a dress.

'How was New York? How's Jessie?' Having poured herself a glass of water, Carmen perched on the nearest stool. Her eyes were sparkling; he had never seen her looking so happy.

'Jessie's OK. She was just going through a bad patch. Her sister's with her now. So what's happening with you and this chap?'

This time Carmen's whole face lit up. 'We just clicked. He's so . . . great. We never stop talking. That's what we've been doing today. We went for a walk, we had lunch at Pizza Hut, we went to his flat and watched TV, then we played Scrabble, then we went for another walk, then back to the flat, Joe cooked us scrambled eggs on toast and we listened to music and it was just so . . . so exciting, not scary at all! It's like we've known each other our whole lives. And no, I haven't slept with him yet,' Carmen went on, because it was so transparently what Rennie wanted to ask her. 'We're taking things slowly. We both know how we feel about each other, so there's no hurry. People jump into bed together all the time and it means nothing. We want it to be extra special.'

Rennie, who had spent the afternoon in bed with an ecstatic Caz having completely meaningless sex, helped himself to a Jaffa cake.

'So you might be seeing him again then.'

Carmen pulled a face at him. 'Of course I'm seeing him again. Tomorrow night, in fact.'

'Bet you can't wait.'

'I can't.' She beamed, immune to his teasing.

'You'll be counting the minutes,' said Rennie.

'Right, I'm shattered, I'm off to bed.' Yawning widely, Carmen headed for the kitchen door. Then she paused and gazed seriously at Rennie. 'And yes, I *will* be counting the minutes. I feel as if I'm allowed to be happy again. That's a good thing, isn't it?'

Rennie softened, unable to begrudge her a bit of much-deserved happiness. 'Definitely a good thing.'

'I like Joe. He likes me.' Carmen hesitated then said, 'I think if Spike met him, he'd like him too.'

Not very logical, but Rennie knew what she meant.

'I'm sure he would.' Rennie nodded, because what else could he say?

'And it's all thanks to you,' Carmen went on happily. 'If you hadn't agreed to help the charity, I'd never have met Joe.' Blowing him a kiss she added, 'It's like you're my fairy godmother.'

Rennie waited until she'd gone before exhaling slowly and saying, '*Bugger*.'

Chapter 17

Rose was a firm believer in the benefits of the great outdoors. Why be stuck inside a stuffy old house when you could be outside breathing in great lungfuls of real, un-centrally heated fresh air? Besides, as well as being good for you, venturing out into the square enabled you to interact with the outside world, to nod and smile and exchange a few cheerful words with pleasant-looking passers-by.

Not that all of them fell into this category. Yesterday a rigid-looking couple – husband and wife, presumably, and not necessarily happily married if body language was anything to go by – had taken the path that led past Rose's bench. The man, in his sixties or thereabouts and with a military air to him, had narrowed his eyes suspiciously at the sight of her. Rose had set down her knitting and smiled at them perfectly politely, but the pair had remained hatchet-faced.

'Morning,' Rose called out as they drew level. 'Beautiful day, isn't it?'

'Hrrmmph,' the man snorted in reply. His wife, averting her thin face, behaved as though she hadn't noticed Rose's presence.

And they had marched on by, not looking very cheerful at all. Feeling sorry for them, Rose had picked up her knitting and smiled to herself. *Separate Tables*, the film that had earned lovely David Niven an Oscar, that was what the couple reminded her of. They'd have fitted right into that hotel dining room, sitting stiffly and in silence in the background.

Rose took a packet of homemade fudge out of her bag and popped a square into her mouth. She gazed around with satisfaction, listening to the birds twittering in the branches of the ash trees overhead. It might only be Tuesday, but already she regarded this bench as *her* bench. The weather had improved dramatically since the weekend and the sun was out. What, Rose thought contentedly, could be nicer than sitting here in the garden square with her knitting and her fudge, admiring the trees and the beautiful houses beyond them?

Reaching the end of a row, Rose heard a rustling noise from the bushes to her left. Next moment there was a yelp of pain and the sound of frantic whimpering. Jumping to her feet, she headed over to the bush and saw a pair of terrified brown eyes peering out at her.

'Doreen, Doreen!' shouted a voice, and the young man called Zac rounded the bend in the path. When he saw Rose on her knees, he broke into a trot.

'She's in here,' Rose told him, attempting to part the spiky branches and wincing as a thorn scraped her wrist.

'Oh Doreen, you are hopeless,' Zac chided, reaching Rose's side and tut-tutting at the little dog's predicament. 'Come on, baby, sshh, keep still, let me just untangle you . . .' Bravely he plunged in, ignoring the vicious thorns, separating the branches until there was enough of a gap to ease Doreen through. 'There, you silly thing, you're safe now.' Leaning back on his heels, he pulled Doreen onto his lap and soothingly stroked her ears. 'Honestly, what are we going to do with you? Thanks,' he turned to Rose, 'she's a hopeless case, a bit too intrepid for her own good. She thinks she's Indiana Jones. I spend my life having to rescue her from ridiculous places.'

'She has an enquiring mind,' said Rose, 'and the spirit of adventure. That's not such a bad thing. Och, look at her wee nose, that's what made her yelp.'

There was a small scratch just above Doreen's nose. Zac gently wiped away the beads of blood and kissed the top of her trembling head. 'Poor baby, never pick a fight with a hawthorn bush. They'll always win.'

'She's not the only one in the wars. Look at you.' Rose tut-tutted, pointing to the injuries Zac had sustained while plunging fearlessly to the rescue. There were several scratches on the backs of his hands and a deeper one on his wrist that was actually bleeding quite a lot.

'I'll live,' said Zac.

'But you might drip blood on your clothes.' Rose pushed back the sleeve of his completely impractical lime-green suede jacket. Rising to her feet, she said, 'I've got an Elastoplast in my bag. Come on, let's sort you out.'

As they reached the bench, Doreen began to snuffle excitedly. Opening her capacious bag, Rose said, 'She can smell the fudge. OK if she has a piece?'

'Homemade,' marvelled Zac. 'My word, it's like meeting Mary Poppins.' Clipping Doreen back on her lead, he accepted two pieces of fudge, one for himself and one for Doreen, then allowed Rose to mop at his wrist with a tissue before carefully placing the Elastoplast over the scratch. Shaking his head, he said, 'This fudge is phenomenal. And you knit as well.' His gaze fell upon the hastily abandoned heap of knitting on the bench. 'What's it going to be? Can I see?'

Rose had never before had interest expressed in her knitting by a member of the opposite sex. Maybe men really were different in London. Reaching for the needles and holding up the work in progress, she said, 'It's a bit of an experiment, I'm just seeing how it works out. My daughter wanted a kind of light lacy jackety thing to wear over a long yellow dress she has. Between you and me,' Rose lowered her voice, though they were the only two people in the square, 'she'll probably tell me it's perfect and never wear it. Still, it's always fun to try something different.'

At their feet, Doreen was bouncing around, recovered from her incarceration in the hawthorn bush and agitating for another piece of fudge.

'No, darling, bad for your teeth. Where's the pattern?' said Zac, studying the front of the knitted jacket and picking the already completed back and sleeves out of the carrier bag on the bench.

'I'm not using one.' Intrigued by the attention he was paying to the frilled, pointy-edged sleeves, Rose said, 'I'm just making it up as I go along.'

'Clever.' Zac ran his fingers along the edge of the sleeve, assessing the neatness of the stitches. She had chosen a thin silky two-ply thread in pale silvery-yellow; the effect she was aiming for was glamorous and cobwebby, more like lace than knitwear. He had nice hands, Rose noted; long-fingered and sensitive like a piano player's. He smelled nice too, kind of peppery and lemony. What he was doing growing his hair so long she couldn't imagine; surely a nice short back and sides would be more flattering.

'Is your wife a knitter?' Rose said eagerly, because it worried her that young women these days seemed to have lost interest in such a rewarding hobby. Nancy was a fine cook but she'd rather stick pins in herself than knit.

'I'm not married.' Zac gave her a quizzical look, as if she'd said something funny without realising it. 'Nor likely to be.'

'Oh now, don't be such a pessimist! You never know who might be just around the corner,' Rose encouraged him. 'There are so many lovely young girls, you're bound to meet someone one day.'

Zac grinned. 'Can't see it happening, somehow. Maybe a lovely – no, sorry.' He shook his head. 'Actually, I'm the one interested in knitting.'

'Really?' Rose was delighted. 'Well, that's just wonderful! I've never understood why more men don't—'

'I can't knit,' Zac cut in apologetically. 'But I do design knitwear. I have my own shop, just around the corner in Levine Street.' Proudly he added, 'I'm a clothes designer.'

'Really?' Rose cast a dubious glance at his lime-green jacket, mustard-yellow sweatshirt and frankly bizarre trousers – black, with white squiggles randomly hand-painted over them. It looked to her like the kind of get-up more commonly worn by those frenetic presenters on children's TV.

Sensing her doubt, Zac said good-naturedly, 'I'm actually quite successful. Well, in a minor way.'

Rose hurried to reassure him. 'Oh, I'm sure you are, pet! I didn't mean—'

'It's OK. Listen, I employ out-workers to knit for me. I don't know if that's something you'd consider.' Zac was still fingering the intricate sleeve of Nancy's jacket. 'But if you think you might be interested . . .'

Rennie, glancing out of the window, called out, 'Come and take a look at this.'

Nancy was emptying the dishwasher in the kitchen. Hurrying through to the living room, she followed Rennie's pointing finger and said, 'Oh God, what's she up to now?'

Below them, Rose had emerged from the gardens across the street, chattering animatedly to a long-haired man with a small dog. As Nancy and Rennie watched, the three of them happily set off along the pavement.

'Does she have a thing for toy boys?' Rennie suggested helpfully.

'How many times have I told her not to speak to strangers.' Nancy heaved a sigh. 'And does she take a blind bit of notice?'

'Want me to go down and bring her back?'

There were con artists around, Nancy knew, who specialised in tricking old ladies into emptying their bank accounts and handing over all their money. Heading over to the chair where Rose had left her handbag, she reassured herself that her mother's purse, credit cards and chequebook were all still here.

'Don't worry. We saw him there the other day, walking his dog.' Why that should make a difference, Nancy didn't know, but somehow it did. 'Mum was chatting to him before. The dog's called Doreen,' she remembered. 'I think she'll be safe. He looks too clean to be a mugger.'

'I'm sure the police will be impressed,' Rennie said with a grin, 'when you tell them that.'

Chapter 18

'Here we are, home sweet home.' Zac pushed open the door with a flourish. 'Well, shop sweet shop. Small but perfectly formed. Jacintha, could you be an angel and take Doreen upstairs? She's gasping for a drink.'

Jacintha, with her glossy chestnut hair and painstakingly applied make-up, looked like one of those It-girls, thought Rose. Pushing her copy of *Tatler* to one side, she clicked her French-manicured fingers at Doreen and disappeared through the door at the back of the shop, having already ascertained at a glance that the woman Zac had brought back with him was in no shape or form a potential customer.

Rose gazed around with interest. From the outside the shop was small, painted sugar-almond pink and bore a sign above the window with Zac Parris Designs inscribed on it in grey and silver lettering.

Inside, the shop space itself was perhaps ten feet wide and twenty feet long with silver-grey walls, fuchsia-pink carpet and lots of gauzy irides-cent netting forming a draped and tented ceiling, from the centre of which hung an ornate pale pink and white chandelier. Rose, who had never seen a shop resembling it in her life, exclaimed, 'My word, it's like one of those TV programmes, isn't it? You know, where the people decorate each other's living rooms and end up getting such a fright they burst into tears. Oh! I didn't mean that this isn't gorgeous,' she went on hurriedly. 'It's just beautiful, like a fairy palace! Anyone would be delighted if they got something like this! It's the kind of thing that lanky long-haired one would produce, have you see him? With all the freckles. Lovely man. My friend Morag thinks he's . . .' Rose lowered her voice and half mouthed the words, 'one of those *homosexuals*, but I still like him. He's always so friendly and cheerful.'

Hearing a sound like a cross between a laugh and a cough, Rose realised that Jacintha had rejoined them.

'Sorry, listen to me wittering on.' Rose turned her attention to Zac's designs, sparsely displayed on narrow racks against the walls. There was only one of each item, which seemed strange; it was nothing like your run-of-the-mill shop. 'Is this the kind of thing you'd be after?'

The sweater she was examining was of nubbly oatmeal-shaded lambs-wool with ivory satin facings round an asymmetric neckline. The back of the sweater was U-shaped and split like a pair of coat tails, one tail distinctly longer than the other. Extraordinary, thought Rose, blanching as she glimpsed the ornately inscribed price tag. Good grief, she'd expect the sweater to be embroidered with diamonds and come with a free house for that.

'It's an exclusive business. My clientele expect individual designs. They don't want to turn up at a special event to find someone else wearing an identical outfit,' Zac explained.

Trust me, thought Rose, the chances of *one* woman wearing something like this to a special event would be virtually nil. As for two, forget it. They'd have to be out of their minds.

Politely she said, 'It's lovely.'

'Knitted by a woman in Devon,' said Zac. 'I send her my drawings, tell her what I'm after. She makes up the garment. Do you think you could do that?'

Rose, who had been knitting incessantly for the last forty years, said, 'That's like asking me if I know how to breathe. So I'd be able to post the garments off to you, would I? Only I don't live in London, you know, I'm just down here on holiday for a couple of weeks.'

'That's fine,' said Zac as the phone on the desk began to ring. 'We'd have to have a trial run, of course. If I give you a sample of work, could you do it in the next day or two? Jacintha, can you answer that, please?'

Jacintha, who had just finished painting her nails, flapped her hands and said tetchily, 'I'll kill you if these get smudged. Hello, Zac Parris Designs, how may I help you? Oh, right. Hang on.' Dropping the exaggeratedly polite telephone voice, she held the phone out to Zac. 'For you.'

Whoever it was on the other end caused Zac to flush red. Excusing himself, he slipped through to the workroom and closed the door. Jacintha, rolling her eyes in despair, declared, 'Zac's latest no-hoper.'

'Oh.' Another prospective home-knitter, Rose guessed, who had failed the test. Well, she wouldn't do that. Watching Jacintha carefully turn the glossy pages of the magazine, she said brightly, 'He's nice, isn't he?'

'Who, Zac?' Jacintha tore her attention away from an article on 'The New Celibacy!' which, Rose privately wondered, surely couldn't be all that different from the old kind. 'He's OK.'

Heavens, such enthusiasm. Rose said, 'But you must enjoy working here.'

This made Jacintha smile. Gesturing towards the spare chair, uphol-stered in baby-pink satin, she said, 'Have a seat. Zac could be gone for some time. Shall I tell you why I handed in my notice here last week?'

Startled, Rose felt as if she'd opened a can expecting to get beans and had found worms instead.

'Um, only if you want to, pet.'

Maybe Zac had made some kind of unwanted pass at her. Surely not – he seemed such a nice boy.

'Men,' said Jacintha.

Oh dear.

'I mean, why do I have a job? What's the main reason for coming to work in the first place? To meet *men*,' Jacintha exclaimed, because Rose was looking blank. 'To *flirt* with men and have men flirt with me! All my friends have the *wildest* time at work, they have great social lives, they're always having fantastic nights out and they get boyfriends out of it. My friend Shona married her boss, for crying out loud. Now she doesn't *have* to work any more and they live in this fantastic five-bed detached on Primrose Hill. And what do *I* do?' Jacintha demanded, her eyebrows arching up into her hairline. 'I work here, that's how dumb I am. I actually chose to come and work in a shop where you meet no men at all!'

Rose was bemused. 'None? What, never?'

'Well, there's the postman, I suppose. And the fat bloke who waddles in to fix the computer when I've spilt coffee in it. But it's a clothes shop for women, so the only time a man comes in is when his wife or girl-friend drags him along to flash the old credit card. Anyway, I've learned my lesson and I'm out of here.' Jacintha nodded with satisfaction. 'I've got a job with a PR agency in Soho. Loads of men, non-stop partying – ha, I can't wait.'

Nancy blew on her icy hands and hung back as Rose tapped on the door of Zac Parris Designs. It was nine twenty-five in the morning and the door was locked, but there were lights on inside. She couldn't believe she'd allowed her mother to drag her here – she was twenty-eight years old, it was *embarrassing* – but Rose's mind had been made up.

'Ah, there he is,' Rose exclaimed happily as Zac appeared in the shop and unlocked the door. 'Morning, pet, how are you? I've brought you the sample you wanted. And this is my daughter, Nancy, the one I was telling you about.'

'Of course, come along in.' Zac was smiling but his eyes were shadowed as if he hadn't had much sleep. 'Coffee's on if you'd like some. My word, you were quick. I wasn't expecting to see you today.'

'Och, it was no trouble.' Rose coloured with pride as he lifted up the sample she'd done for him. 'I'm a fast worker. Well, what d'you think?'

Nancy watched him expertly scrutinise the stitching of the strappy, swingy top he'd sketched for her mother to copy.

'You're a pro,' said Zac. 'It's perfect. Now, I'd pay you on average sixty pounds per item. Forty for something smaller, like this. Up to eighty for anything more intricate. Are you happy with that?'

'Are you sure?' Rose, her eyes widening, nodded vigorously. 'That sounds wonderful. I can't believe you'd pay that much!'

Nancy hid a smile. When it came to striking a bargain, Richard Branson had nothing to fear from her mother.

Zac looked amused too. 'Good. In that case we have a deal. Now, how about that coffee?'

'Where's Jacintha?'

'Oh, she'll roll in at some stage. Mornings aren't her forte. Takes her a good couple of hours to put her make-up on.'

Zac was obviously gay. Nancy, observing his camp manner and flamboyant hand gestures, realised that this detail had escaped Rose entirely.

'Well, she's going now. Off to a new job in Soho.' Rose fixed her gaze on Zac. 'She tells me you haven't found anyone to replace her yet.'

'I haven't.' Zac was busy fiddling with the coffee machine and setting out little silver cups. 'Now, do you take sugar?'

'The thing is, my daughter needs work. She'd be perfect.'

Zac paused, spoon in hand, and spun round to look at Nancy. Under the impression until now that her mother had already suggested her for the job, Nancy realised that he'd had no idea; it was a complete bolt from the blue.

'Um . . .' said Zac.

'You wouldn't regret it,' Rose went on proudly. 'She's punctual, efficient, good at dealing with people. She wouldn't sit around painting her nails and reading magazines, either.'

'Mum—'

'But you *wouldn't*,' Rose told her. 'You'd be great at this job.'

Nancy squirmed; this was truly mortifying. It was like being a sixteen-year-old wallflower at a party and having your mother march up with some boy she'd found to dance with you. In fact, having already declared several times what a lovely boy Zac was, this was probably Rose's attempt at matchmaking. *Oh God.*

'Well . . .' floundered Zac, who clearly didn't want to dance.

'And she could start as soon as you like,' Rose went on encouragingly. Right, that was enough.

'Mum, stop it,' Nancy blurted out. 'I can sort this out myself, OK? Let me speak to Zac. Why don't I see you back at the house?' And strangle you then, she added silently. Honestly, what was her mother *on*, these days? Had she secretly been attending assertiveness classes?

'Good idea.' Rose nodded and looked pleased with herself, evidently satisfied that her matchmaking skills had paid off. 'I've a spot of shopping to do, anyway. You two have a nice chat, get to know each other. I'll hear all about it when you get back.'

Chapter 19

'I'm so sorry,' Nancy groaned as soon as the shop door had clanged shut. 'It's OK, you don't have to give me the job. I had no idea she was going to spring it on you like that. I've never been so embarrassed. Here, let me do that,' she added, because Zac was making a complete pig's ear of trying to spoon sugar into his coffee. Most of it had spilled onto the tray. His hands were shaking, Nancy saw as she re-sugared, stirred and handed him the silver cup. 'Are you OK? You look a bit . . .'

'Overwrought? Knackered? Suicidal? It's OK, you can say it. No need to be polite.' Gesturing for her to follow him, Zac led the way through to his work studio, behind the shop. He was wearing ultra-baggy orange combats, a white long-sleeved T-shirt and a customised navy gilet awash with zips and odd-shaped pockets. He was in his late thirties, Nancy guessed, and his thin face was taut with the effort of containing whatever was currently on his mind.

'Here, take a seat.' Zac hastily gathered up a mass of fabric swatches and gestured for her to occupy the red velvet upholstered two-seater sofa. 'Rose is a nice lady. If she thinks you'd be good at the job, you probably would be.' He paused and took a gulp of scalding hot coffee. 'She tells me your marriage just broke up.'

'My husband was cheating on me.' Nancy decided that if he could be blunt, so could she. Although he probably knew all the details already, from her mother.

'Yeah. Well, I know how that feels.' Zac managed a wry smile. 'If you're wondering why I look like something that crawled out of the gutter.'

It was easier for women, Nancy realised. At least they could hide the ravages of misery with make-up.

Sympathetically she said, 'Did it just happen?'

'*Just* happen? It's *always* happening.' Zac heaved a heartfelt sigh and perched on the velvet arm of the sofa. 'It happened again last night. Story of my life. If there was a category in the *Guinness Book of Records* for

Most Hopeless Lovelife, I'd be in there. Talk about a walking disaster.' He shook his head dejectedly, combing his fingers through his long hair. 'I don't know how I do it, I just get it wrong every time.'

'I only got it wrong once,' said Nancy, 'but it was a pretty big once. And now I'm here in London,' she added, 'five hundred miles away from home. I was only supposed to be staying down here for a couple of weeks with my friend Carmen. Now she's trying to persuade me to move in for good.'

'Aren't you the lucky one,' said Zac. 'It's the other way round for me. I meet someone, they move in with me and – I'm sorry, I *know* I'm deluded – I honestly imagine we'll be together for ever. Then next weekend they pack their bags and move out. After that, I never see them again. I mean, how pathetic is that?'

He was putting on a brave face but there were tears glistening in his blue eyes.

'Not pathetic at all,' Nancy fibbed, to be kind. 'You just haven't met the right one yet.'

'Just an awful lot of Mr Wrongs.' As Doreen pattered down the stairs and into the workroom, Zac held out his arms to the little dog. 'Just as well I've got you, sweetie pie, isn't it? At least you'd never leave me, run off with my entire CD collection and my favourite pair of Jean Paul Gaultier trousers accidentally packed in your bag.' Giving Doreen a cuddle, he said hopefully, 'Were you devastated when you and your husband broke up?'

'I thought I would be. And I know you probably want me to say yes, but I wasn't.' Nancy struggled to explain. 'It was a huge shock at first, but then I kind of felt . . . well, relieved. Like when you've been invited to a party you know you *have* to attend but you don't actually want to go to. You're quietly dreading it but putting on a brave face, then all of a sudden something happens out of the blue and you realise you don't have to go any more.'

'So if he turned up on your doorstep this afternoon and begged you to take him back?'

'I wouldn't. It's over.'

'Would you not even be tempted?'

'No.' Nancy shook her head and meant it. 'Not for a second.'

'You're so strong.' Zac sighed and stroked Doreen's silky ears. 'I wish I could be like you.' Brightening, he said, 'You can be my role model. Stop me being such a hopeless pushover. Give me pep talks every morning, hit me over the head whenever I—'

'Hang on,' said Nancy, 'does that mean you're offering me the job?'

'Of course.' Zac sounded surprised.

'But . . . don't you have other people to interview?'

'No.' Zac looked faintly embarrassed. 'To be honest, I hadn't got round to organising anything. I'm a clothes designer,' he protested. 'Admin isn't my thing. I kind of hoped Jacintha might come up with someone.' Brightly he added, 'But I'd much rather have you!'

'Because it would save you the bother of having to advertise,' Nancy said drily.

'No! Well, yes. But Jacintha's friends are . . . how can I put this? . . . just like Jacintha. And Rose did say you'd be perfect for the job.'

Nancy rolled her eyes. 'She's my mother. She thinks I'd be perfect for the Olympic relay team, for the position of Chancellor of the Exchequer *and* to represent the country in the Eurovision song contest.'

'Blimey. If you can do all that,' said Zac cheerfully, 'you can definitely handle working here. How soon can you start?'

Nancy smiled. 'As soon as I've taken off my gold medal and finished preparing my Budget speech.'

'Next Monday then?'

This was unlike any interview she'd ever attended before. Working for Zac Parris was going to be an education.

'Next Monday,' Nancy said happily.

'You won't meet any men,' Zac warned. 'That's why Jacintha's leaving, because there's never anyone to chat up.'

'Not meeting any men,' said Nancy, 'is what's going to make this job perfect.'

Rennie was still asleep when the doorbell rang. Groaning, he rolled over in bed and covered his head with a pillow.

Rrrrinnggg.

God, he hated doorbells. They could seriously damage your health.

But since he was now awake, and appeared to be the only one in the house, he may as well answer it.

Naked, carrying his jeans in one hand, he made his way downstairs and pressed the intercom. 'Yes?'

'Um . . . is that Rennie Todd?' It was a girl's voice, one he didn't recognise.

Rennie paused. Could he get away with pretending to be the butler or something?

Finally he said, 'Who is this?'

'Look, I'm sorry,' the girl sounded nervous, 'but I need to speak to you about, um, Carmen.'

'Why?'

'Please. It's important.'

Rennie heaved a sigh and climbed into his jeans, almost sticking his foot through the frayed hole in the left knee. Opening the front door, he saw a girl with ash-blond hair pulled back from her face in a tight pony-tail to reveal dark roots. She was pretty, in her mid-twenties, and huddled up against the cold in a red leather jacket, smart black trousers and high-heeled boots.

'Carmen isn't here.' Rennie shivered too as the icy wind blasted his bare chest.

'I know. I wouldn't be here if she was.'

He watched her inwardly registering the fact that she was talking to Rennie Todd, someone who up until now she had only seen on televi-sion. It was something he was used to. Briskly – God, it *was* cold – he said, 'Is this going to be quick?'

'Um . . .' The girl shook her head apologetically. 'Not that quick, no.'

Typical. No chance of getting back to sleep then. In which case, caffeine was called for.

'You'd better come in. Coffee?'

'Thanks.' The girl followed him through to the kitchen. 'Sorry if I woke you up.'

'Let's just hope it's worth it.' Filling the kettle and managing to splash icy water from the tap all over his chest – *ugh* – Rennie said, 'What's this all about then?'

As if sensing that he wasn't yet awake enough to listen and simulta-neously perform simple domestic tasks, the girl took the kettle from him and said, 'Why don't I do that?'

Rennie sank gratefully onto a kitchen stool. There was a KitKat in the fruit bowl, which would do nicely in lieu of breakfast.

He held up the KitKat. 'Want half of this?'

'No thanks. You have it.'

Good. Correct answer. 'So what's your name?' said Rennie.

'Tina.'

'And you know Carmen from where?' It occurred to Rennie that she might be something to do with the homeless shelter.

'I don't know Carmen, I just know *of* her. Here.' Tina plonked a far-too-strong coffee down in front of him and said, 'OK, here we go. I'm Joe James's ex-girlfriend.'

'Oh.' Bloody hell, this was all he needed. A jealous ex, come round to stir up trouble.

'No.' Tina was evidently able to read his mind. 'It's not what you think. I just need to warn you about Joe.'

'Shouldn't you be talking to Carmen?' Bleeurrgh, no sugar either. The woman was trying to poison him.

'I don't want her to know this is coming from me. She'd tell Joe and he'd go mental. Anyway, from what I hear, she's mad about him. Sorry, you should have said.' Tina handed him the sugar bowl and a teaspoon. 'I don't want you to tell her I've been here.'

Frowning, Rennie said, 'But Joe gave you this address?'

'No, he didn't. I knew it was Fitzallen Square, because he mentioned it before he came round the first time to see you. When I turned up this morning, I thought I might be able to guess which house it was.' Looking slightly embarrassed, Tina smiled and said, 'You being who you are, know what I mean? I sort of expected yours to be the house with all the Lamborghinis and stretch limos parked outside, the rock music blasting from every window, the groupies queuing up at the front door.'

Gravely, Rennie said, 'Sorry. The groupies don't get here until midday. So how did you find us?'

'Asked the postman.'

Oh well. Rennie nodded and began peeling the silver foil off his KitKat. 'Carry on.'

'Joe is only with Carmen because she's rich,' Tina said bluntly. 'He's after her money.'

'Did he tell you that?'

'We went out together for almost a year. Last week he dumped me. And yes, I was upset.' Tina shrugged. 'I'm being honest here, OK? I thought we'd stay together, get engaged, the whole thing, so of course I was upset. Anyway, yesterday I rang Joe and told him I'd found his car insurance and MOT certificates in my bag, from when we'd been to the post office to tax the car. He dropped round at lunchtime to pick them up.'

'And you ended up in bed,' Rennie guessed. Well, it's what he would have done.

'No! But Joe was so pleased with himself, he couldn't help bragging about him and Carmen, and how crazy she is about him.' Tina paused, then went on, 'He said his life was about to change, big time, which got on my nerves a bit. I told him he wasn't that great a catch, and *he* said he wasn't about to let a chance like this slip through his fingers. You see, his dream is to start up his own plumbing business, but you need money to do that, which Joe doesn't have. Anyway, he boasted that he was going to persuade Carmen to help him set up on his own. He said twenty grand would be nothing to her, she wouldn't even miss it. Which I think is a pretty crappy thing to say, even if it *is* true. And I think Carmen deserves to know what he's up to. There, now I've said it. You don't have to believe me if you don't want to, but it's the truth.'

'You want me to tell Carmen,' Rennie said slowly, 'so that she'll finish with your ex-boyfriend. And then what? You can have him back?'

Tina shrugged. 'Maybe. I can't give Joe twenty grand because I don't have any money. But I still love him.'

'Carmen isn't going to believe me.'

'Fair enough. I'm not asking you to tell her so that she'll dump Joe.' Reaching across the table and snapping the last stick of KitKat in half – God, he *hated* it when girls did that – Tina said levelly, 'I'm just suggesting you warn her, so that when he does start dropping hints about twenty grand solving all his problems, she'll stop and think it through before whipping out her solid gold, diamond-studded chequebook.'

Chapter 20

The weather had taken a dramatic turn for the worse. Pewter-grey clouds loomed overhead, the temperature plummeted and icy rain began to pelt down as Nancy prepared to leave the house. By the time she reached the pavement, the icy rain had turned to hail, hammering onto her umbrella with the force of gunfire. Pellets of hail bounced and ricocheted in all directions like a mini Wimbledon gone mad. Shuddering as a car swished past, sending a wave of water over her feet, Nancy wondered just how desperate you had to be for a haircut to venture out in a hailstorm. Well, *this* desperate, clearly. Otherwise she'd be in the bathroom now with a comb and a pair of scissors, rather than out here getting soaked to the skin.

Except she'd done the comb-and-scissors thing before, and getting soaked to the skin was a small price to pay in order to avoid that awful sinking feeling when you gazed at yourself and your economy DIY haircut in the mirror and knew without a doubt that this was your Biggest Ever Mistake.

Anyway, she needed highlights as well as a cut. A new job definitely merited new highlights. And if she waited until the storm had passed, there wouldn't be enough time for a hairdresser to do both before—

'Oh my God,' shrieked Nancy as she turned and saw the bicycle careering straight towards her. The cyclist, having completely lost control, hit the kerb with a metallic crunch and Nancy leapt back to avoid the bike. Sadly she was unable to avoid the cyclist, who shot over the handlebars and landed against her chest with a lung-crushing thud.

Whoomph, Nancy promptly lost her footing and went over backwards. The cyclist, a teenager wearing an anorak and spectacles streaming with sleet, crashed down on top of her. Clearly horrified at finding himself in such close physical contact with an older woman, he yelped, 'Sorry, sorry', and scrambled to his feet. Nancy, still on the ground, gazed openmouthed in disbelief as he ran to retrieve his bike from the gutter, leapt onto it and pedalled furiously away.

Feeling like a wino, she hauled herself into a sitting position and gingerly examined her grazed hand. Hail was still hurtling down, her umbrella was bowling merrily across the road and her handbag – oh, *perfect* – had burst open in a puddle.

'It's OK, don't move,' called a voice behind her. As if she might be about to jump up and break into a Riverdance routine.

Still winded by the impact, Nancy concentrated on getting her breathing back to normal. Carmen's neighbour, Mia's father, crouched beside her and said, 'Want me to call an ambulance?'

Nancy shook her head. 'I'll be all right. Nothing broken.'

'That bloody idiot,' Connor said in disbelief. 'I saw it happen from the window.'

'Like Batman.' Nancy managed a shaky smile. 'He appears out of nowhere, then shoots off again before you know what's hit you.'

'Except he doesn't usually crash into you on his bicycle,' said Connor. Gravely, he held out his hand. 'By the way, I'm Connor.'

'I know. Mia's dad. Nice to meet you.'

Solemnly they shook hands. He was getting drenched, Nancy realised as the hail continued to clatter down like painful confetti.

'Well, this is stupid. Like trying to pretend it isn't raining at some posh garden party. Think you can stand up?' said Connor.

Nancy nodded and allowed him to help her to her feet. The pavement was slippery with slush and she began to tremble as shock belatedly set in.

'OK,' Connor murmured, leading her to the railings. 'Just wait here a second while I fetch your stuff.'

He was wearing a blue and white rugby shirt and dark blue corduroys. Nancy leaned feebly against the railings and watched him gather together everything that had exploded out of her bag, including a box of tampons and a lipstick that had rolled into the gutter. He then raced up the road to collect her umbrella.

'Come on,' said Connor when he returned, 'let's get you inside.'

His front door was wide open. He helped her up the steps into his house.

'Really, you don't have to—'

'Hey, don't spoil my big moment. I've never come to the aid of a damsel in distress before. When I was a kid I always wanted to be a superhero,' Connor confided. 'I used to dream about rescuing people from burning buildings, saving their lives.'

'That's so noble.' Nancy smiled at him, picturing him as a boy.

'Actually it wasn't. I wanted to rescue them so they'd be eternally grateful and give me some fantastic reward. Remember Charlie and the

Chocolate Factory? I especially wanted to save Willie Wonka's life, so he'd give me his factory and I'd have a lifetime's supply of sweets. Now, shall I help you off with your coat?'

Nancy discovered that her hands were still shaking too badly to unfasten her belt. Feeling stupid, she stood there like a child while Connor did it for her.

'I can't manage a factory full of sweets, I'm afraid. But you're welcome to the packet of orange TicTacs in my bag.'

Connor grinned and something inside Nancy went *twaannggg* as she looked at him properly for the first time and realised how attractive he was. OK, maybe not take-your-breath-away good looking like Rennie, whose chiselled cheekbones and wicked dark eyes had girls going feeble at the sight of him, but attractive in a down-to-earth way. Connor O'Shea looked rumpled and lived-in and . . . well, just downright *nice*.

Oops, she was still gazing at him. Right, stop it. *Ouch.*

'Sorry.' Having peeled off her wet coat, Connor had gently pushed back the sleeve of her favourite olive-green sweater. Flinching, Nancy saw the nasty graze that ran the length of her forearm, with blue-grey bruising and blood seeping out through the broken skin.

'Hang on, let me get the first-aid kit,' said Connor. 'I think we're going to have to amputate.'

He had such a fantastic voice, lazy and humorous and with that impossible-to-resist Dublin accent.

'Can I keep the arm as a souvenir?' Nancy watched as Connor, having fetched the kit, began to clean her forearm with antiseptic lotion.

'Now that's what I call thrifty. You could mount it on a plaque,' he said approvingly. 'Hang it on your wall. Great conversation piece, and so much cheaper than an oil painting.'

'And when the novelty's worn off, I could sell it on to Charles Saatchi.' As she turned her arm outward, enabling him to lay sterile gauze over the wound, Nancy caught his eye and felt that jolt of attraction again. He smelled gorgeous, he had a sense of humour and she just loved the way his eyebrows moved when he smiled, as if they had a life of their own.

'There, all done. Anything else need looking at?'

'I'm fine.' Since she could hardly strip off and show him every painful bruise – what could he do, kiss them better? – Nancy carefully rolled the sleeve of her sweater down over the bandage. 'Nice job. Thanks. How can I ever repay you for saving my life?' Reaching for her bag, she said, 'Here, take my TicTacs. I want you to have them.'

Was she being suitably playful and light-hearted, or making a complete twit of herself? It was so long since she'd flirted with anyone that she couldn't remember for the life of her how it was done.

Mildly shocked, Nancy ordered herself to get a grip. For heaven's sake, Carmen had mourned the loss of her husband for three whole years, and yet here *she* was behaving like a twittering teenager just three weeks after the end of her own marriage. Surely that couldn't be right?

'Listen,' Connor interrupted her thoughts, 'what are you doing tomorrow night?'

Nancy's heart began to palpitate.

'Sorry? Um . . . nothing planned.' Feeling herself going red, unable to believe this was all happening so fast, she said, 'Why?'

Serve her right if he asked her to babysit.

'How about coming round for a drink,' Connor suggested, 'and we can get to know each other properly. Without the smell of antiseptic.'

'Love to. Sounds great!' As she said it, Nancy wondered if that was too eager. But he'd asked her, hadn't he? What was wrong with saying yes? If she pretended to hesitate, he might change his mind. OK, act normal, just act norm—

'Around seven, then? You, Rennie and Carmen?'

Oh.

'Fine!' Nancy smiled extra brightly to hide her disappointment. Oh well, that was understandable; Connor probably thought it would be rude not to invite Rennie and Carmen along too. He wouldn't want them to feel left out.

He was being subtle, that was it.

'Always good to get to know your neighbours,' Connor said easily. 'I haven't met Carmen yet, not even to say hello to. Here, give me your hand.' Reaching for her left wrist, he dabbed carefully at her upturned palm with a tissue. 'It's still bleeding. Maybe I should put a dressing on this one as well.'

'What's going on?'

Startled, Nancy twisted round on her chair to find herself being stared at by a girl with wild magenta curls and a beautiful but none too friendly face. She was wearing a great deal of intricately applied make-up, a white shirt that presumably belonged to Connor, and nothing else.

'This is Nancy, one of our neighbours. She had a bit of a run-in with a cyclist,' Connor explained. 'Nancy, this is my girlfriend Sadie.'

Sadie nodded briefly, in acknowledgement. Nancy, attempting a friendly smile, felt as if she'd just stepped into a lift shaft without noticing the lift wasn't there.

111

'Which neighbour?' demanded Sadie.

'That side.' Connor pointed to the left. 'With Rennie and Carmen. I've invited them over for a drink tomorrow night, so you'll be able to meet everyone properly then.'

'And will Mia be here?'

'Of course Mia'll be here.'

'In that case, let's hope she behaves herself,' said Sadie shortly. 'Connor, it's gone four o'clock. We have to be at the club by five.' The implication was clear as her narrowed gaze fixed on Connor's fingers round Nancy's wrist: *put her down.*

'I need to leave too.' Glad that she was no longer shaking, Nancy pulled her hand free and rose to her feet. 'Thanks for the first aid.'

'Thank *you* for making a lifelong fantasy come true.' Connor grinned, oblivious to the effect his words were having on trap-mouthed Sadie. 'Now, don't forget, seven o'clock tomorrow.'

'Absolutely.' Nancy wondered if she could manage to break both legs before tomorrow afternoon. 'See you then.'

Chapter 21

Carmen didn't cry, or shout at him, or call him hideous names, but Rennie knew she was thinking them.

'Sweetheart, I'm sorry. I just thought it was only fair to warn you,' said Rennie. 'Don't shoot the messenger.'

Carmen looked at him as if he were her worst enemy.

'But who *is* the other messenger? You can't not tell me! I have a right to know who's saying this stuff about Joe.'

'I can't. They made me promise, cross my heart and hope to die. But they're on your side, that's the thing. They don't want to see you get hurt.'

Except he was hurting her now, Rennie knew that. He'd just told her that the man she was besotted with was stringing her along and not in love with her at all.

'Right, well, thanks.'

'Just bear it in mind,' said Rennie. 'They may be wrong, he might be completely on the level, but—'

'Yes, yes, I get the message, you think Joe is a con artist. I'll make sure I hide my credit cards and never take my eye off my purse.'

'That's not what I meant,' Rennie shot back. 'OK, fine, just forget I said it.'

'How can I forget it?' howled Carmen. 'You *have* said it! Tell me who told you!'

'No.' He was emphatic.

'No? Oh, and why not? Maybe because they don't exist?'

'What?' said Rennie.

Carmen jabbed an accusing finger at him. 'It's what *you* think, but you know I won't take any notice if it's just you, so you've come up with this mystery visitor instead. Do you have any idea how insulting you are? You can't believe that Joe likes me for my personality. You're saying that if I didn't have money he wouldn't look at me twice.'

'But—'

'No, shut up, I don't want to hear another word,' Carmen hissed and grabbed her coat. 'You said you wanted me to be happy, but you didn't actually mean it, because the moment I finally meet someone and start to *feel* happy, you have to come along and spoil it all. And, let me tell you, all the girls you sleep with wouldn't look twice at you if you just had a normal job. They're only interested because you have money.'

Luckily Rennie's feelings weren't hurt because he knew this wasn't true. Carmen knew it too, but he didn't remind her of this. He just stood there and let her get the insults out of her system. Right now, he felt it was the least he could do.

'. . . and that's why you've never even had a proper girlfriend!' Carmen flung at him five minutes later. 'You're just pathetic, immature and . . . and *shallow*.'

'You're right.' Nodding in agreement, Rennie reassured himself that he was also a damn fine lay.

'I feel sorry for you,' Carmen said disdainfully. 'Deep down, you wish you could be as happy with someone as I am with Joe. You're just jealous.'

'Hey, what's up? You're quiet tonight.'

Carmen shook her head and said automatically, 'Nothing, I'm fine.' They were walking hand in hand across Leicester Square after leaving the cinema. She'd been looking forward to seeing the new Steven Spielberg film, but if Joe were to start quizzing her on the plot, she'd fail miserably. The trouble with being told something unpleasant was that whether it was true or not, you couldn't put it out of your head. When she'd yelled at Rennie she'd meant every word, but now the doubts were starting to trickle through her mind. It wasn't true, she was ninety-nine per cent sure. But what if it was? What if Rennie had a point?

'I'm hungry,' said Carmen.

'OK. How about if we grab a takeaway and head over to your place?'

Carmen shivered, less than keen to go back to Fitzallen Square. Rennie might be there. Oh God, what if Rennie *was* right?

She blurted out, 'I don't want a takeaway. Can't we eat in a restaurant?'

'Fine. Somewhere around here?' Letting go of her hand and sliding his arm round her waist, Joe said, 'You choose. Anywhere you like.'

It was Friday night, the streets cold and busy. As they headed up a narrow road, Carmen spotted a restaurant that she'd visited before.

'This one,' she announced when they reached it.

Joe paused, looking doubtful. The restaurant was French and frighteningly expensive.

'Sure? Only, we're wearing jeans.'

Carmen's stomach tightened at this sign of reluctance.

'That's fine, they won't mind.'

'OK.' Joe gave her a reassuring squeeze. 'If it's where you want to go.'

Hating herself for doing this – and hating Rennie for making her do it – Carmen said, 'Listen, this place costs a bomb. Let me pay.'

Joe gave her a stern look. Then he shook his head. 'No way. My treat.'

'But it costs—'

'Sshh, it's all right.' He placed a finger over her mouth. 'I can afford it.'

'But—'

'No, don't argue. This is where you want to eat, so this is where we'll eat. And I'm paying the bill.'

'We could split it,' said Carmen.

'No,' Joe smiled and kissed her on the mouth, 'we couldn't. I've never let a lady pay for dinner before and I'm not about to start tonight. I may not be able to afford to bring you here every night of the week, mind you, but every once in a – hey, what have I said now? Are those *tears*?' Turning her round, peering at her under the amber glow of the streetlamp, he said worriedly, 'Why are you crying? Have I done something wrong?'

Blindly Carmen shook her head. As she wiped her eyes, she felt the ton weight of doubt lift away. 'Nothing's wrong.' This time she truly meant it. Flinging her arms round Joe, she whispered happily, 'Everything's right. Let's go back to your place.'

Joe looked concerned. 'What about food? I thought you wanted to eat here.'

Carmen smiled, because he *still* wanted to treat her to an expensive meal. How could she ever have doubted him?

'I've changed my mind. I want to go home.' Between kisses, she said, 'I'd rather just be with you.'

'Dad never knows when to stop,' Mia told Nancy with cheerful resignation as she sloshed wine into glasses. 'Once he'd invited you lot over for drinks, he got carried away and started asking along a whole load of people from the club. His motto is, why have a small party when you can have a thundering great huge one. Which is fine,' she went on, 'until he goes, "Oh Mia, you're so great at cooking, quickly rustle up enough food for eighty people, would you?" I mean, for a supposedly intelligent man, he can be awfully thick sometimes. If I hadn't bumped into your mum this morning, we'd all have been eating bowls of porridge.'

'Och, it was nothing.' Rose, pink-cheeked with pleasure, was busy ladling chilli and rice into bowls.

'It was a *lot*,' Mia corrected her. 'You were like a fairy godmother flying to my rescue. She overheard me as we were leaving our houses,' she explained to Nancy. 'I was on my mobile to Jason, the chef at the Lazy B, having a quick panic attack and asking if he could help out. Which of course he *couldn't*, the lazy bum. Next thing I knew, Rose was offering to give me a hand.'

Rennie, helping himself to a bowl of chilli, said, 'If Rose overheard a bunch of crooks planning to rob a bank she'd offer to give them a hand. She can't help herself.'

'Behave.' Rose flicked him with a tea towel.

'You would, Rose. You know you would. If you heard a drugs baron complaining that he couldn't get anyone to smuggle a load of coke through customs, you'd say, "Oh hen, that's no problem, I can do that for you."'

'He's a wicked boy.' Rose's eyes were twinkling. 'Such a tease. Here, make yourself useful and drain this pasta.'

'Hey, hey, what's going on here?' Connor exclaimed, appearing in the kitchen. 'You're supposed to be enjoying the party, not draining pasta.'

'It's Rose,' said Rennie. 'You wouldn't believe how bossy this woman is. She's working me like a dog.'

'Ignore him,' Rose told Connor, 'he's nothing but a moaning Minnie. We're almost done here, pet,' she promised. 'As soon as everything's in serving dishes, everyone can help themselves.'

Nancy, busy collecting forks and spoons from the cutlery drawer, was appalled to discover that Connor's arrival had caused her heart to start galloping, even though she now knew he had a girlfriend. Sadie was in the living room, less than twenty feet away, looking even more formidable tonight than she had yesterday. She was poured into a slinky silver dress and wearing more make-up than ever. Yet her terrifying presence wasn't having the desired effect. Nancy, try as she might, was unable to stop herself reacting physically to the sight of Connor, or to the sound of his voice. It was like being fourteen again, and having a violent crush on the boy next door. Except it was that much more humiliating when you were twenty-eight.

'Right, that's it,' Mia declared, wiping her hands on a towel and grabbing a can of Tropical Lilt from the fridge. 'We're done. Time to start enjoying ourselves. Come on,' she urged Nancy, sensing reluctance. 'Don't you like parties?'

'The last party I went to, I came face to face with my husband's mistress.'

'Then this one will be *much* better.' Unfazed, Mia chivvied them through to the living room. 'I'll introduce you to everyone from the club. They're all really nice. Well, with one hideous exception, obviously.'

Rennie grinned. 'Who's the hideous exception?'

'The one in the Bacofoil. Sadie Sylvester. She's my dad's girlfriend and she hates me. But that's OK,' Mia went on chirpily, 'because I hate her too.'

'Not very Waltons,' said Rennie.

'I'll say it isn't. You don't get people in the Waltons dancing like *that*.' Mia pulled a face as Sadie gyrated like a lap dancer. 'Yuk, she thinks she's *sooo* irresistible. Actually,' she brightened and gave Rennie a nudge, 'you could chat her up, she'd probably go for someone like you. Then, when she starts flirting back, Dad can get really annoyed and dump her. That'd be perfect.'

'Or deck me,' Rennie drily observed. 'Anyway, I wouldn't do that to Connor.'

'But you'd be doing him a *favour*. Crikey, you'd be doing *all* of us a favour. Isn't that what neighbours are for?'

'Sorry, not a chance.' Pointing to a willowy blonde across the room, Rennie said, 'Who's that?'

'Zoe? She's one of the lifeguards at the club.'

'Single?'

Mia rolled her eyes. 'Single.'

'Hooray,' said Rennie. 'Maybe she'd like to save my life.'

They watched him go.

'Men, honestly.' Mia tut-tutted. 'No help at all. How am I supposed to get rid of Sadie?'

'Arsenic?' Nancy suggested.

Mia squeezed her arm. 'Wouldn't that be great? Honestly, it's so unfair. Why can't Dad go out with someone lovely like you?'

Hear, hear, thought Nancy, draining her glass of wine and feeling the warmth spread through her stomach. Why couldn't he? She'd spent the morning in the hairdresser's getting three shades of blond highlights, and the afternoon deciding what to wear tonight, finally settling on an electric-blue jersey top and white trousers. Except now that she was here surrounded by outrageously dressed, seasoned party-goers, she felt like a Blue Peter presenter.

117

'You could give it a whirl,' Mia persisted.

'Oh yes, that'd work.' Nancy watched Connor, now laughing with Rennie and Zoe-the-lifesaver. He had a cigarette in one hand and a bottle of lager in the other, and just the thought of talking to him was glueing her tongue to the roof of her mouth. But how were you supposed to control the way you felt about other people? Maybe Connor could stand to lose a couple of stone, maybe he wasn't the world's sharpest dresser and maybe he could do with a visit to the hairdresser himself, but there was just something about him that made her go weak at the knees with longing.

Presumably Sadie Sylvester felt this way too.

'You could join the Lazy B,' said Mia, ever hopeful. 'Act like you're interested in Dad.'

'Look, I'd love to help, but I couldn't pretend to be interested in your father.' At least this much was true. 'And Sadie would definitely deck me.' And Connor wouldn't be remotely interested in me either, but never mind that.

'Oh well, I'll think of something. Maybe what we need's another drink.' This time Mia didn't bother with Tropical Lilt. Grabbing a fresh bottle of wine, she refilled Nancy's glass, then deftly emptied the rest of the bottle into her empty Lilt can.

'Should you be doing that?' Nancy glanced across to see if Connor had spotted the manoeuvre.

'It's a party. I've been working my socks off all day.' Clanking the can against Nancy's glass, Mia added gaily, 'Anyway, I'm sixteen, not six. Cheers!'

Chapter 22

By ten o'clock the dancing was in full swing. Connor pulled Nancy energetically onto the dance floor, not realising what he'd done until he saw her flinch and bite her lip.

'Oh God, oh Jesus, I'm *sorry*.' Hitting his own forehead in despair, he reached for her wrists and examined the angry grazes on her palms. 'What an idiot I am. I completely forgot. Feel free to kick me as hard as you like – go on, right there on my shin.'

Nancy smiled, the twin explosions of pain slowly receding as Connor made his over-the-top apologies. It wasn't easy to behave in a natural friendly manner when you were being invited to kick someone you had a violent crush on. It was harder still when you were aware that his girlfriend, standing less than six feet away, was watching you like a kestrel watches a baby shrew.

But Connor, determined to make amends and oblivious to Sadie's glares, pulled Nancy into an ungainly bear hug and said in her ear, 'I'm glad you came tonight.'

It wasn't a romantic gesture, Nancy knew only too well. He was just being friendly. But it still felt wonderful.

Behind Connor, she could see Mia giving her the thumbs up, nodding and winking encouragingly.

'I'm glad we came along too,' Nancy told Connor.

'But it's . . .' he frowned at his watch, 'gone ten, and still no Carmen. Are you sure she's coming?'

Nancy wasn't sure at all. Carmen was barely on speaking terms with Rennie. Upon hearing about the party, she had announced that she was working at the shelter until nine and *might* come along later. And no, she most certainly would not be bringing Joe. What, with Rennie there? Was Nancy serious?

'Maybe not,' Nancy admitted. 'She . . . um, might have to work late.'

'Sounds like a dodgy excuse to me. I'm starting to wonder if we're ever going to meet her.'

'Of course you'll—'

'Whoops, sorry,' trilled Sadie, 'didn't mean to step on your foot! Now, have you two finished chatting, because I'd quite like to dance with my boyfriend. This is our favourite song, isn't it, darling?'

Shania Twain was belting out of the speakers. Connor, looking bewildered, said, 'Are you sure?'

But Sadie had already inveigled herself in front of him, tossing her magenta ringlets and gyrating her hips as only an aerobics teacher could. Making her escape before the ringlets could whip her painfully across the face, Nancy headed over to Mia and a couple of girls from the Lazy B.

'Got your marching orders, then,' observed the taller of the girls, whose name was Therese.

'Take it as a compliment,' Jess, the shorter girl, consoled Nancy. 'She doesn't get nearly as het up when Connor's talking to someone ugly.'

'But that's the thing,' said Therese. 'Connor chats to everyone as if he fancies them. It's just his way. He's such a charmer, all he has to do is ask you if your verrucas have cleared up and you get that gorgeous squidgy feeling in your stomach. I mean, he doesn't *mean* to do it, he just can't help it, can he?'

Well, that tells me, thought Nancy. So much for thinking that the way Connor had been talking to her might have been in any way special.

Jess said, 'Sadie's going to have her work cut out keeping that jealousy of hers under control. She's mad about Connor. God, look at the way her boobs are jiggling.'

'Whose boobs are jiggling?' Rennie joined them, swigging from a bottle of Pils. 'Oh, right. Implants.'

Mia's eyes widened with delight. 'Are you serious? Is that a boob job? Really?'

Rennie said, 'Trust me, I'm an expert.'

'Ha!' Mia took another gulp from her Lilt can. 'Fabulous. Did she have a sex change as well?'

'Sshh.' Jess gave her a nudge, because she was getting loud and Sadie had just shot them a suspicious glance. 'If Connor marries her, she'll be your stepmum.'

Mia spluttered and began to choke. 'I'd rather cut off my own feet. No, no, he can't do that. I won't let him.'

'My cousin said that when her dad started seeing this hotshot magazine editor,' said Therese. 'They couldn't stand each other. My cousin couldn't *believe* her dad had such terrible taste. When she found out they were thinking of getting married, she threatened to run away from home.'

120

'What happened?' Mia was eager for tips.

'They got married. The hotshot magazine editor gave up her job and had four kids in five years. They've all got names like Archie and Alfred. It's like walking into an old people's home.'

Mia looked horrorstruck. 'What did your cousin do?'

'Ran away from home. No other choice. Well, they explained to her that at nineteen, you couldn't technically *call* it running away from home, but that's what she ended up doing. Moved into a disgusting bedsitter in Clapham. And she and her stepmother still hate each other.' Therese gave Mia's arm a comforting pat. 'So you see? It could be a lot worse. Count your lucky stars Sadie isn't pregnant.'

Jess, gazing over at Sadie, said, 'Imagine a baby with hair like that.'

This was serious. This was *seriously* serious. Now that the thought had been implanted in her mind, Mia found she couldn't let it go. She couldn't believe it hadn't occurred to her before. How many women, desperate not to lose the man of their dreams, 'accidentally' became pregnant? God, zillions. And Sadie was how old? Thirty-three? Her biological clock was probably clanging away inside her surgically enhanced chest. She'd do anything to hang on to Connor. She knew he wouldn't leave her high and dry, because Connor was an honourable man, a devoted father who would never renege on his responsibilities.

It all made sense. Mia slipped out to the kitchen and found Rose loading the dishwasher.

'Oh pet, are you all right? Headache?'

Feeling hot, and unaccustomed to drinking, Mia pressed her head against the cold metal of the upright freezer. She nodded. 'Big headache.'

'Hang on, I've painkillers in my bag.' Rose scuttled off and Mia took the opportunity to refill her Lilt can with chilled Frascati. There was a terrifying image in her brain of Sadie, hugely pregnant, firing out babies – pop, pop, pop, pop – like bullets from a machine gun. Gulping down half the Frascati and feeling her head start to buzz, Mia made her way slightly unsteadily across the kitchen in search of inspiration. This couldn't happen, it really *mustn't* happen. Was this how James Bond felt when he knew that if he didn't act now, the world would be destroyed?

'Here we are!' Rose was back, clutching her brown patchwork leather handbag. Rummaging efficiently through the contents, she found a packet of Nurofen and popped a couple out of their plastic casings. 'That's it, sweetheart, wash them down with some of that Lilt. They'll perk you up in no time.'

'Perk me up. You make me sound like a pair of bosoms. Like Sadie with her permanently perky bosoms – in fact, permanently perky *protu-berances* . . .' Mia was dimly aware that she was wittering on, but a thought was currently unfurling in her brain, courtesy of Rose and her patchwork leather bag.

As she knocked back the Nurofens and sluiced them down with Frascati, wine dripped down the front of her purple top. Rose promptly whisked a tissue from a mini-pack in her bag and handed it to Mia.

Because that was the thing about handbags, you kept your whole life in them. A woman's handbag was capable of telling you an awful lot about its owner. And Sadie 'Perky Bosoms' Sylvester's handbag was currently hanging on a hook in the cupboard under the stairs. Just dangling there, all on its own in the dark, potentially bulging with secrets . . .

'Still feeling a bit poorly, pet? Whoops-a-daisy.' Rose caught Mia's arm as she swayed and almost toppled over. 'Why don't you go upstairs and lie down for a few minutes?'

Mia nodded vigorously. 'Have a little rest. Oh yes. Good idea.'

The hall was empty. Everyone was in the living room singing and dancing along to Abba's 'Waterloo'. Honestly, old people could be so sad some-times; Mia hoped she wouldn't end up like that.

She opened the under-stairs cupboard and saw Sadie's bag hanging from one of the coat hooks. Most people kept theirs with them but Sadie had been paranoid about drink being spilled on her precious pale blue suede Prada. Mia's fingers itched to open it but, pressing though her need was, she was aware that it wasn't the height of good manners to go rooting through your dad's girlfriend's personal private things.

If, on the other hand, she accidentally nudged the straps and the bag *happened* to fall open on the floor, well, that would be OK, wouldn't it? It was pretty much what had happened to her dad yesterday when Nancy had been knocked down by that boy on the bike and he'd had to gather up everything that had spilled out of her bag. He'd told her all about having to scoop tampons out of the gutter.

Fantastic. Thanks, Dad.

Double-checking that the coast was still clear, Mia gave the handbag straps a casual nudge. Then, when that didn't dislodge the straps, a bigger nudge. Oh, for heaven's sake, were they superglued on? Impatiently she lifted them over the coat hook, let the bag drop to the floor and . . . bingo!

The sound of footsteps made Mia jump. She froze as someone in stilettos tip-tapped across the parquet floor between the living room and the kitchen.

Hastily, Mia slid into the under-stairs cupboard and pulled the door almost shut behind her. Moments later the doorbell rang, giving her another shock.

Her dad called out, 'I'll get it,' and Mia heard him emerge from the living room.

As he passed the under-stairs cupboard she glimpsed him through the one-inch gap in the door.

Then . . . *click* went the door as Connor closed it. Mia, inside the cupboard, was abruptly plunged into darkness. How she was going to get out again she had no idea; there was no handle on her side of the door.

Oh well, look on the bright side, at least she had privacy now. Her dad was opening the front door; she could just about hear him greeting some late arrival or other. Feeling about in the dark, Mia located the light switch. As light flooded the interior of the cupboard, she smiled down at the handbag on the floor and made herself comfortable on a crate of books. It was actually quite cosy in here, like playing house as a child.

Just as well she didn't need the loo.

Chapter 23

'Hey,' Connor exclaimed with delight, 'my mystery neighbour. We meet at last.'

Carmen, finding herself being hugged then enthusiastically kissed on both cheeks, felt ashamed of herself. Rennie and Nancy had both told her that Connor O'Shea was a thoroughly nice man.

'There. Now we know each other.' Connor eventually released her. 'I was beginning to think you were avoiding me.'

'I was.' Dimpling, Carmen said, 'Sorry, don't take it personally. I was avoiding pretty much everyone.'

'No need to apologise. Rennie told me about your husband. You've been through a rotten time.' Connor helped her out of her coat. 'And neighbours can be tricky. It's like meeting new people on the first night of your holiday, realising after twenty minutes that you can't stand the sight of them and having to spend the next fortnight hiding round corners.'

He *was* nice. Grateful to him for understanding, Carmen said, 'It's been a rough three years, but I'm over all that now. Back to normal. Well, normal-ish.' Let's face it, since marrying Spike, had her life ever really been normal?

'It must help, having Rennie and Nancy around.'

'Kind of.' This was true, but Carmen still wasn't ready to forgive Rennie for last night.

'And I've been hearing about your new chap,' Connor went on. 'That's great. You should have brought him along tonight, the more the merrier.'

Presumably he'd heard about Joe from Nancy. Carmen said, 'It might not be so merry if he was here. Rennie doesn't have a high opinion of my boyfriend.'

'Ah well, he's your brother-in-law,' Connor replied easily. 'Bound to be protective. I'd be just the same with my daughter.'

'But Rennie isn't my dad. What's that noise?' said Carmen.

Connor, busy adding her coat to the pile heaped on the chaise longue, said, 'What noise?'

'Your bell was working just now.' Carmen was puzzled. 'Is that someone knocking on the door?'

When Mia had embarked on her search, she'd had her hopes pinned on finding a diary in Sadie's bag, with any luck containing incriminatingly chirpy entries along the lines of: Still two-timing Connor – let's hope he never finds out! or: Help, I'm pregnant and George has dumped me. Never mind, I'll tell Connor he's the father. Or: Up to 2 grams of crack cocaine a day now. *Really* expensive habit!

Or, best of all: Connor has *no* idea I was born a man, hooray for sex-change ops!

Oh God, wouldn't that be great?

The problem was, there was no diary in the bag. Mia, perched on her packing crate of books, rifled through the various compartments examining old receipts, a perfume atomiser, keys, pens, yet more receipts for annoyingly boring items, three packets of Wrigley's Extra and a hairbrush.

No hidden bottle of vodka, not a rock of crack cocaine in sight.

She opened Sadie's pink and blue striped make-up bag. Shiseido mascara, No. 7 foundation and eyeshadows, Elizabeth Arden Eight Hour cream, Estée Lauder blusher, three different lipsticks and . . . oh now, what was this?

What indeed?

Bingo, Mia thought triumphantly, zipping the make-up bag back up. Perfect. Jumping to her feet, she cracked her head against the cupboard's sloping roof. Ooch, never mind, let me out now. She knocked on the door and heard voices – was it still Dad? – outside in the hall.

Having tried the front door and found no one on the doorstep, Connor frowned, puzzled, at Carmen. The next moment they both heard more knocking behind them.

'Did you ever see that film *Poltergeist*?' said Connor.

'I think it's coming from in there.' Carmen pointed to the under-stairs cupboard.

'Can't be. It's a cupboard. And we don't have ghosts,' said Connor.

'In that case, brace yourself. You could have a really massive spider.' Carmen, who was closer, pulled open the door.

'Hi,' said Mia, swaying slightly and clutching her Lilt can. She beamed. 'Thanks. You must be Carmen.'

Taking the can from her, Connor sniffed it then took a swig of luke-warm Frascati.

'Mia. My daughter,' he told Carmen. 'Drunk.'

'Tiddly,' Mia corrected him, wagging a finger. 'Not legless, just . . . pleasantly relaxed.'

'Relaxed enough to shut yourself in a cupboard,' Connor observed.

'Ah, but you're going to be jolly glad I did.' Looking determined, Mia said, 'Dad, I need to have a serious talk with you. About condoms.'

Carmen did her best to keep a straight face. The look of horror on Connor O'Shea's face was fabulous.

'OK. Maybe some other time.' Clearly appalled at the prospect of his daughter wanting to discuss her sex life, Connor began to steer Mia back towards the living room. 'Why don't we all—'

'No, you don't understand.' Mia dug her heels in like a dog. 'Some other time may be too late.'

'Look,' said Connor, 'you don't even have a boyfriend. Can't we just—'

'I know I don't have a boyfriend, *duh*. But *she* does.'

They'd reached the door to the living room. As Mia pointed an accusing finger at Sadie, the CD playing on the sound system chose that moment to come to an end, plunging the room into silence.

'What?' said Connor.

'Condoms, Dad. You have to use them, every time. I'm *serious*,' Mia insisted as he started to smile. 'She's trying to catch you out. She thinks if she gets pregnant, you'll marry her. Women do it all the time, it's the oldest trick in the book!'

Carmen saw that Sadie Sylvester was shaking her head in amused disbelief, exchanging glances with her co-workers that signalled, see what I have to put up with?

'It's *true*,' Mia insisted.

Everyone was staring. Sadie said, 'Connor, isn't it time your daughter went to bed? Then we could all enjoy the party in peace.'

Connor put his hand on Mia's shoulder. 'I think that might be a good—'

'Dad, get off, she's taking you for a fool!' With the air of a conjuror magicking a rabbit out of a hat, Mia stuck her hand down the front of her khaki vest and drew out a folded piece of paper. 'Maybe when you see what I found, you'll realise I'm right.' Triumphantly she unfolded the page torn from a magazine. 'This article is titled, "How I bagged my man!" and it's written by a girl who was desperate not to lose her boyfriend. He kept saying it was way too soon to think about settling down with one woman, but she knew how much he loved kids so she came off the

126

pill without telling him. When she got pregnant he realised he loved her after all, and asked her to marry him. That was eight years ago and they're still happy together. She says, "I know it was a high risk strategy, but it worked like a charm. My husband's always telling me how glad he is that our darling daughter came along when she did. Of course, he still doesn't know I did it on purpose, but that's my little secret. Sometimes the end result justifies the means!"'

Everyone was agog as Sadie stalked across the room and snatched the magazine page from Mia's grasp.

'Where did you get this?'

'Cupboard under the stairs. Your handbag accidentally slipped off its hook and everything fell out onto the floor.'

'And my make-up bag accidentally unzipped itself, I suppose.' Acidly Sadie said, 'My God, you are an evil piece of work.'

'OK, so maybe I was looking through it.' Mia shrugged defiantly. 'And maybe that was a naughty thing to do.' Pleased with herself she added, 'But then again, sometimes the end justifies the means.'

White with fury, Sadie turned to Connor. 'This is too much. I've had it up to here with your precious daughter.'

'I'm just trying to protect my dad,' Mia retaliated.

'You're a poisonous little witch! You rummaged through my handbag.' Sadie's eyes were sparking like fireworks. 'Through my private and personal belongings. And then you have the nerve to accuse me of planning to trap your father into marrying me. Well, let me tell you, the last thing I want is a baby. Especially when there's an outside chance I might end up with one like you.'

'So what were you doing with that article hidden away in your bag?' Mia demanded heatedly.

'Therese?' Sadie glanced across the room, to where her co-workers were clustered. 'Why don't you tell Mia what's wrong with your father?'

Startled, Therese said, 'My dad? He's got Parkinson's Disease.'

'Thank you.' Returning her attention to Mia, Sadie said evenly, 'He's really not very well at all. Therese is worried sick about him. So when I was flicking through a magazine yesterday and happened to come across an article about a revolutionary new treatment for sufferers of Parkinson's, I thought Therese might like to see it.' Turning over the ripped-out page, she showed the relevant section to Connor then slowly crossed the room and handed it to Therese. 'Here you are. You never know, it might help your dad.'

'Th-thanks,' stammered Therese.

'Don't mention it.' Marching back to where Mia was standing, Sadie said, 'So there you go. I hadn't actually noticed the article on the other side of the page.' Coolly she added, 'Feel free to apologise any time you like.'

Mia stood her ground. 'Just because you wriggled out of it this time? I'd rather stick pins in my eyes than apologise to you.'

Carmen wondered if everyone else in the room was secretly enjoying this, loving every excruciating moment as much as she was. There was something horribly fascinating about witnessing a no-holds-barred argument that didn't personally involve you. This was better than an extra riveting episode of *EastEnders*. And now Mia was beginning to realise that she had made a mistake after all, while Sadie was looking as if she was on the verge of giving Mia a resounding slap.

Gripping stuff, and you didn't have to worry about the showdown coming to an abrupt end, leaving you on tenterhooks for the next episode in two days' time.

'Could someone put some music on please?' said Connor, keeping himself between the two warring girls like a boxing referee.

'No, *don't*.' Sadie turned to glare at a thin, nervy looking male guest who'd had the temerity to make a move towards the CD player. 'Let's sort this out once and for all, shall we? I'm your girlfriend,' she told Connor, 'and she's your daughter. Clearly, you have a choice to make here. Do you want to carry on seeing me? Or are you going to allow this interfering brat to stay and make the rest of your life a misery? Because it's either me or her, Connor. One of us has to go.'

Carmen held her breath, enthralled. Sadie was looking confident. Mia was looking . . . actually, she was looking a bit green around the gills. And Connor had to make his decision right here, right now . . .

Connor turned to Mia and said evenly, 'What you did was very, very wrong. I can't believe you rifled through somebody's handbag and accused Sadie of planning to do something like that. I'm ashamed of you.'

Mia said nothing. Sadie preened and looked smug, like the beauty queen who, having slept with all the judges, knew she was about to be pronounced the winner.

'Sweetheart.' Taking her hand, Connor said, 'I'm sorry.'

Sadie gave his fingers a triumphant squeeze. 'You don't have to apologise. She's the one who should be doing that. Oh, darling—'

'No, what I mean is, *I'm sorry*.' Connor shook his head. 'You gave me an ultimatum. I know Mia's behaved appallingly, but she's still my daughter.'

Sadie, her magenta hair quivering with disbelief, said tightly, 'You mean she's *won*? Are you completely *mad*?'

'Look,' Connor attempted to explain, 'it's not as if—'

Crack went Sadie's hand across his face. What with her being so fit, it must have hurt, but Connor didn't even flinch.

'You bastard.'

'I know,' said Connor.

'She's going to ruin your life,' Sadie spat, 'and you're just going to stand back and let her do it.'

'I'm not—'

'Well, I feel sorry for you. From now on, your life is going to be miserable. I'm out of here.' Addressing Mia, Sadie said icily, 'Is there still enough money in my purse to pay for my taxi home, or did you help yourself to that too?'

Pale and swaying, Mia looked as if she'd just witnessed her first autopsy. Without a word, she turned abruptly and shot out of the room.

Sadie's upper lip curled with derision. As she headed for the door she hissed at Connor, 'I hope you realise you're making the biggest mistake of your life.'

Mia hadn't had time to close the bathroom door. Nancy found her crouched on the floor next to the lavatory, wiping her mouth with a crumpled-up length of loo paper.

'Sorry, do you need the bathroom?' Mia glanced up apologetically. 'I'll be out in a sec.'

'I came to find you, see how you are.' Relieved to have missed the pyrotechnics, Nancy ran a white flannel under the cold tap, then wrung it out and handed it to her. 'Feeling better now?'

'Much. I'm not that great at drinking. Haven't had the practice. I keep forgetting you aren't supposed to glug it down like water. Thanks,' said Mia as Nancy helped her to her feet. She pressed the cool flannel to her forehead and exhaled with relief. 'That feels nice. Has she gone?'

'Oh yes. Didn't you hear the front door flying off its hinges?'

'Dad's going to hate me. I suppose I should be sorry, but I'm not.' Perched on the side of the bath, Mia watched as Nancy squeezed tooth-paste onto her pink glittery toothbrush.

'You went a bit over the top.'

'I know. I don't make a habit of snooping through people's hand-bags, honestly. And I'm not out to ruin Dad's life either, but she was just such a nightmare, wasn't she? Once he gets over being cross with me, he'll realise I was right. He'll end up thanking me for it.'

'Hmm.' Much as she agreed with Mia's verdict on Sadie Sylvester, Nancy couldn't help feeling she was being overly optimistic.

'I mean, I do *want* him to be happy,' Mia went on, between vigorous bouts of tooth-brushing. She slooshed Colgate foam around her mouth then spat into the sink. 'I'd just love it if he met somebody nice. Like you.' She caught Nancy's startled eye in the mirror above the sink. 'It'd be great if he got together with someone like you. I wouldn't be a night-mare daughter if that happened, I promise.' Brush, brush, more slooshing and spitting. 'What d'you reckon then? Think you could fancy my dad if you set your mind to it?'

Good grief, did this girl never give up? Feeling the familiar rush of heat to her cheeks, Nancy was just glad that Mia currently had her head bent over the sink and was unable to see it.

'You're not saying anything.' Mia finished rinsing her mouth from the tap and righted herself once more. As tenacious as any terrier, she prompted, 'Well? Yes or no?'

'Look, it doesn't work like that,' Nancy said helplessly.

'Of course it does! How else is it going to work? Trust me, I've got a real feeling about this.' Reaching for a towel, Mia wiped her mouth. 'The two of you could be great together. I'm serious, all my friends say how brilliant I am at fixing people up. I just know these things. I have the eye for it. In fact, I think I could be romantically psychic.'

'Really.' Just because Mia wasn't slurring her words and staggering around, Nancy was discovering, didn't mean she wasn't still three sheets to the wind.

'OK, marks out of ten,' Mia went on, holding up her fingers like a bossy teacher. 'Don't be shy, let's get this out in the open, we'll score him for looks, personality and—'

'Right, that's enough.' A voice behind them caused both Nancy and Mia to wheel round. Nancy winced at the sight of Connor in the doorway. Just how much had he heard? Oh God, did he think she and Mia had cooked up this entire scheme between them?

Thank heavens she hadn't started giving him marks out of ten.

'Excuse my daughter. Thanks for keeping an eye on her.' Connor nodded briefly at Nancy, his expression grim. 'I'll take over now.'

'Time for my talking-to,' said Mia, pulling a face. 'Time for my big telling-off. If you don't see me for the next six months it'll be because Dad's locked me in the cellar.'

'What you did tonight wasn't funny,' Connor countered.

'Just as well we aren't giving you marks out of ten after all,' Mia grumbled. 'You wouldn't get a very high score while you're being this mean.'

'I'll leave you to it.' Relieved to be escaping, Nancy edged her way out of the bathroom. 'See you . . . um, later.'

'Probably in July or August,' Mia flashed her an unrepentant smile, 'when I get out of the cellar. That's if the rats haven't eaten me by then.'

'Personally,' said Connor, 'I'd feel sorry for the rats.'

As she made her way downstairs, two unwelcome thoughts struck Nancy.

Connor looked knee-tremblingly magnificent when he was angry. Which was bad news, because it meant she only fancied him all the more.

Worse still, would the fact that Mia had effectively forced her father to end his relationship in such an abrupt fashion result in him only fancying Sadie Sylvester all the more himself?

Chapter 24

Carmen was clearing the tables after lunch at the shelter, carrying piles of plates through to the kitchen where Nick and Annie were ploughing through a mountain of washing-up.

'Carmen, stick up for me,' Nick pleaded as Carmen began scraping left-over shepherd's pie into the bin. 'Annie's making fun of my wardrobe again.'

Annie shook her head at him. 'I'm not making fun of your wardrobe, I'm making fun of the clothes you keep in it. Carmen, he just doesn't understand how embarrassing it is, being seen out with him in public. You're on my side, aren't you? Explain to Nick that real men don't wear Mr Blobby T-shirts.'

Carmen smiled; she really liked Nick and Annie, and enjoyed their bickering arguments. Annie was short, bouncy and in her early twenties. Nick, tall and endlessly cheerful, sported lots of dark hair that seldom saw a hairbrush and had that cut-it-myself-without-looking-in-the-mirror air about it. He thought it was funny when strangers visiting the shelter mistook him for one of the homeless rather than a volunteer helper. He and Annie lived together in a flat just round the corner and had, over the course of the last year, invited Carmen along to several parties, each of which she had invented some spurious excuse or other not to attend.

'Some of your T-shirts aren't too bad,' Carmen said diplomatically – actually this was a lie, they *all* were – 'but maybe it's time to let Mr Blobby go.'

'Have him put to sleep, more like,' said Annie.

'But it's a perfectly good T-shirt.' Nick plucked at the front. 'There's months of wear in it yet. And it makes people smile.'

'It's got *holes* in it.' Annie, who wasn't troubled by the need for diplomacy, poked her finger through one of the offending holes. 'And people aren't smiling, they're sniggering at you because you look such a dork.'

'Ah well, everyone's entitled to their opinions. It's a free country. If anyone doesn't want to speak to me because they don't approve of the

T-shirt I'm wearing, that's their loss.' Stacking up washed plates on the drainer, Nick added, 'If Annie here decided not to speak to me, well, frankly that'd be a bonus.'

Carmen said, 'My boyfriend's got a pair of purple socks with goldfish on. He knows I hate them so he'll deliberately wear them to embarrass me.' Well, it had only happened once, but it was nice to be able to join in on the anecdote front. Just talking about Joe was enough to give her a warm glow.

'Shows he's got a sense of humour,' said Nick. 'Doesn't take clothes too seriously. Good for him.'

'Cut them up into tiny pieces,' Annie stage-whispered to Carmen. 'Chuck them in the bin. Nip it in the bud before things get completely out of control and he ends up like Nick.'

'You know who she drools over when we're at home watching TV?' Nick raised his eyebrows. 'The chap from *Will and Grace*. Mr Immaculate, I ask you. This girl's a lost cause.'

'It's his eyes. Anyway, he's not really gay.' Annie looked dreamy for a moment, then turned to Carmen. 'So, how long have you been seeing your chap?'

She'd said it ultra casually, but Carmen guessed they were curious. She had kept herself so much to herself over the course of the last year, it was practically the first personal detail she'd volunteered since coming to work at the shelter.

'Not long. Early days. But, you know, it's going well.'

'That's great.' Annie was genuinely pleased. 'What's his name?'

'Joe. He's a plumber.' Gosh, it felt brilliant to say his name.

'You two must definitely come along to our next party then,' said Annie. 'We'd love to meet him.'

Nick, dumping a just-washed baking tin into her hands, said, 'But only if he's wearing his purple goldfish socks.'

'Oh, and could you write Tasmin Ferreira in the appointment book for four o'clock tomorrow afternoon? She's coming in for a second fitting,' Zac called through from the workroom. 'Doreen, sweetie, if you sit there you'll get your tail chopped off. Go and see Nancy. Tell her I'd love a cup of tea, white, two sugars.'

Nancy smiled as Doreen came trotting into the shop. It was only Wednesday, but already she knew she was going to enjoy working here. Zac was fun, gossipy and indiscreet, filling her in on all the background details of his clients. The website also brought in a fair amount of business and she was kept busy replying to emails, answering the phone and chasing up orders for new and original materials. Zac was extra chirpy this morning because a shop in Tokyo had placed an order for twenty of his studded suede skirts, evidently oblivious to the fact that while they looked great, the sharp-edged backs of the studs meant you couldn't actually sit down in them.

'You have to suffer to look fashionable,' Zac had airily declared when Nancy had pointed this out to him. 'Sitting is for wimps.'

The phone rang as Nancy was dropping tea bags into two cups.

'Zac?' She covered the receiver with one hand. 'It's your father.'

A mixture of emotions crossed Zac's face as he put down the taffeta bodice he was currently working on and came through to take the phone. Perching on the edge of the desk in his lemon-yellow trousers and pink V-neck merino wool sweater, he said, 'Hi, Dad, how are you?'

Not in a camp way at all.

Nancy, making the tea, was unable to avoid listening to Zac's half of the conversation, which swung from carburettors to football, then to central heating systems and finally gardening.

'OK, Dad, you look after yourself now,' Zac said eventually, with genuine affection in his voice. 'I'll be down to see you next weekend. Take care. Bye.'

The tea was no longer as hot as it might have been, but Nancy gave it to him anyway. For the past ten minutes Zac had sounded so completely heterosexual that it almost came as a shock when he took a slurp and said, 'Ooh, yum, just what I needed!' in his normal voice.

Catching the look on her face, Zac waggled his free hand in embarrassment. 'OK, you don't have to say it, I know how pathetic I am. The thirty-five-year-old male who can't tell his father he's gay. I'm sorry, but if you start lecturing me, I shall have to sack you.'

'I wasn't going to. I'm the one who couldn't tell her mother her husband was having an affair, remember?' Pushing the biscuit tin towards him, Nancy said comfortingly, 'Have a Hobnob.'

'He's retired now.' Zac heaved a sigh. 'But he worked on the docks for forty years. Mum died when I was twenty. I love my father, but he's a man's man. He wouldn't understand. And I don't want to upset him.'

'Really, you don't have to explain. I think it's nice that you care so much about him. Where does he live?' said Nancy.

'Weston-super-Mare. I'm all the family he has. Every two or three weeks I go down there for the weekend. Put on my proper manly clothes,' Zac said with a wry smile, 'and my butch manly voice, and we spend our time together doing manly things like stripping car engines, fishing, gardening and watching hours of football on the TV.'

'He never remarried after your mum died?'

'No. There've been a couple of lady friends. One lasted almost two years, but it fizzled out last summer. I asked him where Deirdre was and he just said, "Son, she couldn't hold a candle to your mother." I didn't try and find out what had gone wrong. Well, we don't really talk about those kind of things.' With an elaborate shudder Zac said, 'Which I'm quite happy about. Imagine if he'd started telling me about their sex life.'

'Does he ever ask when you're going to settle down and make him a grandfather?' Nancy was curious; surely Zac's father must suspect by now that something was amiss.

'I invented a girlfriend.' Zac bit into a biscuit. 'Samantha, her name was. We had an on-off relationship for eight years. Long-distance too,' he mumbled through a mouthful of Hobnob. 'I told Dad she was working in Australia. Anyway, it did the trick. When Sam and I broke up a couple of years ago I was devastated. She was the love of my life. Going to take me a good long time to get over her – ooh, I'd say a decade at least.'

The things we do to protect our parents, thought Nancy as he crunched happily on his biscuit. She swung round on her chair as the bell above the door went ting, and saw Rennie enter the shop. Zac, spotting him too, promptly began to choke and spray crumbs all over the desk.

'Oh *my*,' Zac murmured, clearly impressed.

'What are you doing here?' said Nancy.

'I used to be a big star. How the mighty are fallen.' Rennie shrugged tragically. 'These days I'm nothing but a lowly errand boy. Rose has finished her latest creation and she sent me down here with it.' He handed the plastic carrier bag over to Zac and said, 'Hi, I'm Rennie.'

Zac looked as if he'd forgotten how to breathe, let alone open a carrier bag and peer inside. 'I know who you are. Good to meet you. Zac Parris.'

'Why couldn't Rose deliver it?' said Nancy.

'She's out in the back garden cleaning the outsides of all the windows. I'm telling you, that house has never been so clean. She's supposed to be down here on holiday,' Rennie marvelled, 'and she never stops. Is that a cup of tea?'

'Actually, it's a wild alligator,' said Nancy.

Looking excited, Zac hopped down from the desk. 'I'll make you a cup of tea!'

'Also, your ex rang,' said Rennie.

Nancy's heart jumped. 'Jonathan?'

'Of course Jonathan. How many ex-husbands d'you have? If he asked you to go back with him, would you go?'

'No.' For heaven's sake, why did people keep *asking* her that?

'Good. So you won't be cross when I tell you that he asked to speak to you and I said you were too exhausted to come to the phone because we'd been up all night shagging.'

Zac exploded with delight. Nancy gasped and said, 'You didn't!'

'I did. And in my best rock star voice, too.'

'What did Jonathan say?'

'Jonathan the jerk? Didn't know whether or not to believe me. Sounded a bit taken aback.' Rennie's eyes glittered. 'Asked me to tell you to give him a ring. I said presumably not a diamond one.'

'No!' Nancy exclaimed.

'Bloody did. Why not?' demanded Rennie. 'He deserves it.'

Zac was gazing at him, lost in admiration. His eyes travelled speculatively over Rennie's lean, hard body from the turned-up collar of his old leather jacket to the frayed hems of his jeans.

'I'm working on something at the moment that would be perfect on you.' Zac blurted the words out in a rush. 'Double-breasted jacket, black and white stripes, leather-trimmed velvet lapels. If I make one up for you, would you wear it?'

Rennie hesitated. He looked at the supermarket carrier bag containing the green and gold cobwebby cardigan Rose had completed this morning.

'Would it be knitted?'

Zac frantically flapped his hands. 'No, *no.*'

'Stripes.' Rennie looked thoughtful. 'Will it make me look like Richard Whitely?'

'It would not,' Zac said very firmly indeed. 'Look, let me whizz it up, then it's yours to do what you want with.' Nancy held her breath, praying Rennie wouldn't suggest giving it to Rose to finish cleaning the windows. 'If you hate it, fair enough. If you love it, just tell people where it came from. Can't say fairer than that, can you?'

'Absolutely not. Start measuring,' said Rennie with a grin, because Zac's fingers were already twitching towards his tape measure. 'One more thing.'

'What?' From the look on Zac's face, if Rennie suggested he licked the floor clean with his tongue, he'd be only too happy to oblige.

Gravely, Rennie said, 'Please don't make me look like Elton John.'

Chapter 25

'Oh my God, he is *divine*,' Zac breathed twenty minutes later when Rennie had sauntered out of the shop. 'Couldn't you just—'

'I don't think you could,' said Nancy, before his imagination rocketed into overdrive. 'Rennie probably wouldn't let you.'

'Spoilsport. I know he's straight. But he just has that . . . *thing* about him, doesn't he? It's in his eyes. When he looks at you, he makes you feel so special, you start thinking anything could happen. David Beckham's the same,' Zac drooled. 'He has those eyes too.'

'I didn't know you knew David Beckham.' Nancy was impressed.

'Well, I don't. I mean, I've never actually *met* him,' said Zac, 'but you only have to see the photos.' Mischievously he added, 'You can't help wondering if you might be the one to change them.'

'Well, don't get your hopes up.'

'Must be fab sharing a house with Rennie though.' Zac was going all dreamy-eyed again. 'Like living inside a copy of *OK* magazine. I mean, he's just so . . . glamorous.'

Nancy, picturing Rennie stretched out across the sofa dipping crisps in Heinz salad cream while engrossed in *Emmerdale* or *EastEnders*, said, 'It's more like living inside a copy of *TV Soaps*. And he's useless around the kitchen. Any excuse not to do the washing-up.'

Zac looked scandalised. 'He has *charisma*. You can't expect people with charisma to do the washing-up.'

'It's Carmen's house,' said Nancy, 'and she's known Rennie since she was sixteen. As far as Carmen's concerned, Rennie's a lazy sod and there's no reason why he can't do his share of the work.'

Pained, Zac said, 'That's like inviting the Queen to a party, then handing her a black binbag afterwards and asking her to clear up the empties.'

'Yes, well. Carmen still isn't happy with Rennie. She hasn't forgiven him yet for the Joe thing. Rennie might have charisma,' Nancy added drily as the phone began to ring, 'but Carmen's immune to it.'

*   *   *

Carmen may not have forgiven Rennie for the below-the-belt comments he'd made about Joe, but they'd turned out to be unfounded and it was probably about time they put the awkwardness behind them.

Besides, Nancy had taken Rose off to the West End to see *Miss Saigon* – Rose was a sucker for a musical – so she didn't have much choice.

'Rennie!' Carmen yelled down the stairs.

Nothing.

'Rennie!' She remained rooted to the spot.

'What?' Rennie called up from the living room.

'Can you come up here?'

'What?'

'UP HERE!' Carmen bellowed, wanting to stamp her feet but not daring to. 'NOW!'

Probably deliberately, he took his time. *Coronation Street* was on; she wouldn't have put it past him to wait until the episode titles were scrolling up the screen. Finally she heard Rennie reach the doorway behind her.

'Up here. *Now,*' he mimicked lightly. 'It's my body you're after, I take it. Overcome with lust all of a sudden, couldn't bear to wait a minute longer—'

'*Moth,*' Carmen interrupted, still with her back to him. She knew it was ridiculous to be terrified of something so harmless but moths, especially big ones, had been a phobia of hers since childhood. If she took her eyes off this one for a split second it might flutter out of sight. And that would be enough to give her nightmares for a fortnight.

'Sorry?'

Rennie was such a bugger. If she could only bring herself to move, she would have clocked him one. He knew perfectly well what she'd just said.

Still, the words beggars and choosers sprang to mind.

'Moth. Over there. On the curtain pole.' Clutching her raspberry-pink bath towel round her, Carmen pointed a trembling outstretched finger.

'Yuk, moth. Let's hope it's not a big one.' Cautiously reaching her side, Rennie shuddered exaggeratedly and cried, 'Oh God, it's massive! Get it away from me! Call the *police.*'

'Shut up.' Carmen spoke through gritted teeth, because Rennie wasn't remotely scared of moths. 'Just get rid of it.'

'Please,' prompted Rennie. *Dammit.*

'Please.'

'So are we friends again now?'

Bloody Rennie. 'OK.'

'Don't sound very sure.'

Exasperated – and still frozen to the spot in terror – Carmen hissed, 'I'm sure, I'm sure. We're friends again, *OK*?'

Rennie was in front of her now, clearly enjoying himself. 'Best friends?'

'Just stop buggering about and get rid of the sodding thing, will you? *Yes*, best friends,' squeaked Carmen as he headed for the door.

Grinning broadly, Rennie turned back and made his way over to the curtain pole. Scooping the moth into his hand, he opened the bedroom window and flung it out. It wasn't until he'd closed and locked the window that Carmen was able to breathe again. Weak with relief, she sat down on the edge of the bed and said grumpily, 'Thanks.'

'You'd make a rubbish spy. Imagine how easy it'd be to interrogate you.'

'All right, don't rub it in.'

'You know where you went wrong, don't you? You didn't keep insects as pets when you were a kid. Me and Spike had a whole collection,' said Rennie. 'We used to keep them in matchboxes and give them names. What with our family being so poor,' he explained, 'we couldn't afford a dog.'

'Get the violins out,' said Carmen.

'It's true! We could barely afford matchboxes. Anyway, that's why I'm not afraid of moths. Because they're my friends.'

'I hope you don't go around throwing all your friends out of high windows.'

Rennie bent down and planted a kiss on her cheek. 'I promise not to throw you out of a high window. Hey, why don't you come downstairs and I'll make us a cup of tea?'

Carmen thawed. This was Rennie's way of saying he was sorry too.

'OK.' She smiled at him. 'Give me ten minutes. I'll be down as soon as I'm dressed.'

'Looking good, Mrs Todd,' said Rennie, handing her a mug as she appeared in the kitchen.

There was a tea bag still floating in it, Carmen discovered, but it was the thought that counted. Glad that Rennie had realised he'd been wrong, she did a quick twirl to show off the new dress she'd bought specially for tonight. Bronze silk, fitted and Audrey Hepburnish, it was a million miles from her usual jeans and sweatshirts.

'You scrub up pretty well,' Rennie told her. 'Where are you off to?'

'Joe's taking me out to dinner. At Passione.' Carmen's chest tightened for a moment, in case Rennie made some snide comment like asking who'd be paying for the meal. Much to her relief, he didn't.

'Great place. You'll love it. You aren't drinking your tea.'

Obediently Carmen took a sip of tea. The tea bag slooshed against her upper lip and her teeth shrivelled in dismay at the strength of the brew. At that moment, thank goodness, the doorbell rang.

'That'll be my minicab.' Grateful for an excuse not to have to drink the brick-coloured contents of the mug, Carmen grabbed her bag and coat. 'Aren't you off out tonight?'

'Not until later. Now you have a brilliant time.' Helping her into her long black coat, Rennie said, 'You'll dazzle everyone in the restaurant.'

'Thanks.' Touched by the compliment, Carmen gave him a quick kiss.

'Just, don't get too carried away, OK? Remember what I said the other night.'

Carmen froze. 'About what?'

'I'm not going to say it, because I don't want us to have another falling out. But you know what I mean.' As he spoke, Rennie carried on fastening the buttons on her coat.

Carmen slapped his hand away, hard.

'I don't believe this is *happening*. You *had* to say it, didn't you? You just had to stick the knife in and spoil everything!'

'I *didn't* say it.'

'You bastard, you bloody selfish bastard!' Seething with the unfairness of it all, furious with herself for having been taken in and thinking that Rennie actually might have been admitting he'd made a mistake, Carmen whacked him again on the shoulder.

'I'm not being selfish,' Rennie protested as the doorbell rang again. 'I'm trying to protect you.'

Storming out to the hall, Carmen yanked open the front door and yelled, '*Two seconds*,' at the waiting driver, who was so startled he almost fell off the step.

'Right, I've had enough of you,' she bellowed at Rennie. 'I mean it, more than enough. I'm sick of the sight of you, and I'm *extra* sick of you meddling in my life. You can pack your things and get out, d'you hear? *Now.*'

'OK.' Placatingly, Rennie held up his hands.

'I *mean* it,' Carmen repeated, her heart thudding against her ribcage like ominous footsteps. 'You've gone too far this time. When I come home tonight I want to find you *gone.*'

*   *   *

Passione, on Charlotte Street, was divine. Having determinedly put Rennie out of her mind – he was just impossible to live with, it would be a relief to get him out of the house – Carmen concentrated instead on enjoying the evening.

And how could you not enjoy it, with food like this? Better still, she was here with Joe, who was being funny, sweet and wonderfully attentive.

'That's it,' Carmen sighed, patting her stomach and sitting back in contentment. 'I'm full. I couldn't eat another thing.'

'Just coffee.' Joe signalled to the waiter for two espressos and reached for the half-empty bottle of wine. 'And we'll finish this.'

'I don't think I've even got room for any more wine.'

'You have to,' he protested as she half-heartedly attempted to cover her glass. 'It's a special night. I've got something to celebrate.'

'You have?' Carmen was interested; now that he mentioned it, he *had* seemed as if he had some secret he was longing to impart.

'I made a big decision yesterday. Well, it's something I've been planning for a long time,' said Joe, 'but making plans is one thing. Acting on them, actually carrying them out, is another matter.'

Intrigued by the sparkle in his eyes, Carmen said, 'And? What have you done?'

'Handed in my notice.'

Carmen's eyes widened. 'Why?'

'Because nobody ever got rich working for someone else's company. Well,' Joe amended with a grin, 'I don't suppose that's true, because some people must do. What I'm trying to say is, I know *I'm* never going to get rich working for my boss. But I'm a bloody good plumber. It's always been my dream to have my own business. So that's what I'm going to do, set up on my own. It just makes sense, don't you think? This way, the harder I work and the more hours I put in, the more money I'll make.'

'I think that's fantastic,' Carmen exclaimed. 'It makes *perfect* sense. Why work for someone else when you can be your own boss?'

'And so many people dream of doing this, but they're too afraid to take the leap,' Joe went on eagerly. 'But that's the beauty of plumbing, there *is* no risk. You can't lose. It's a win-win situation. Everyone needs plumbing and heating engineers. And I'm going to work my socks off to make it a success. Give me a few years and I'll be the plumbing king of London.'

'Well, good for you.' Carmen gave his hand an encouraging squeeze. 'When do you start?'

'As soon as I've got everything sorted out. You see, I need a decent van, plus a computer of course, and then I had this *other* brilliant idea this afternoon.' Gazing into her eyes, Joe said, 'How about if you and I were partners. You know, went into this together.'

'What?' Carmen laughed. 'I'm not a plumber.'

'You don't need to be. I mean a business partner. Well, more of a sleeping partner really,' explained Joe. 'You wouldn't have to *do* anything, just put up some of the money we'd need to get this thing up and running. I mean, it's not as if there'd be any risk of losing it, because like I said, it's a win-win situation. And it would save all that faffing around, getting bank loans and stuff. So what d'you think?' He gazed at her intently. 'How does that sound? Great idea or what?'

Carmen's face was frozen; she couldn't tell if she was still smiling or not. There was a buzzing sound in her ears and beneath the table her legs were wound tightly round each other like corkscrews.

She felt sick.

How did it sound? Like Rennie, whispering in her ear: *See? Ha, told you.*

'I . . . don't know, Joe.'

'Oh, come on, it's not as if we'd need loads of money. I'm not talking about half a million here.'

Was she as white as she felt? With difficulty Carmen cleared her throat. 'Well . . . um, how much?'

'I've worked it all out. Twenty thousand, that's all. Crikey, that's *nothing*.' He smiled and stroked her wrist. 'Cheer up, you look terrified. It's not scary, it's an adventure!'

It wasn't an adventure. It was her worst nightmare come true. The waiter brought their bill at that moment and Joe took out his credit card at once.

'Can we go halves?' Carmen began searching for her bag, but he shook his head.

'No way. Let me do this.' He waited until the waiter had departed. 'Now, what do you say?'

The quicker she said no, the quicker they could change the subject and move on. Taking her courage in both hands, Carmen said as cheerfully as she could, 'Joe, to be honest, I think it'd be easier if you just got a bank loan. Thanks for offering me the . . . opportunity, but—'

'You're saying *no*?'

In that split second, Carmen saw something alter behind his eyes, a shift of emotion that sent a chill down her spine.

'But like you said, you can get a loan from the bank.' She watched Joe's hand leave hers, retreating like the tide. 'That's what banks are for!'

'Oh yes.' Joe's mouth narrowed. 'With their endless interrogations and forms to be filled in and petty bloody rules and regulations. Jesus, that's what I thought we'd try and avoid.'

Carmen realised that he was waiting for her to say, 'Oh, all right then, I'll put up the money.' Instead she shrugged, reached for her glass of wine and said nothing.

'You don't trust me,' Joe blurted out suddenly. 'Is that it?'

'No.' She shook her head, feeling sicker than ever. 'It's not that. I just think it's better if you go to the bank.'

'But you've got all that money sitting there doing nothing.' Joe was bewildered. 'Piling up, earning interest, making *more* money. And it's not as if you even earned it yourself. You were just lucky enough to marry the right bloke. Twenty grand would be a drop in the ocean as far as you're concerned, but it would buy me a van, a computer, everything I need . . . My God, I really can't believe you're *being* like this.'

I can't believe you're being like this, thought Carmen. She was feeling hot and dizzy now, as well as sick. Was it physically possible to faint when you were sitting down? If she did faint, would Joe even bother to help her?

'I feel so stupid.' Joe shook his head, his expression a mixture of resentment and hurt. 'I thought what we had was special. Jesus, I thought you liked me.'

Ditto, Carmen thought miserably, aware that people at neighbouring tables were beginning to nudge each other.

'I do like you.'

'Enough to let me pay for dinner,' Joe said bitterly. 'Oh yes, that's absolutely fine, isn't it, even though you know I can't afford it. But when it comes to you having to dip into *your* precious bank account, that's diff— Where are you going?'

'Home.' Jerkily, Carmen pushed back her chair. Rummaging in her bag, she took out all the money in her purse and threw it onto the table. 'There, that should cover dinner. Bye, Joe. It's been an education knowing you.'

'But—'

'No, that's it,' Carmen said evenly. 'I'm going now. And don't worry, I'm sure you'll meet another rich girl soon.'

'No, wait, I'm sorry.' Appalled, Joe jumped up too. 'Don't go, I didn't mean it! Carmen, please, I *love* you!' he yelled desperately as she stumbled past startled waiters and neighbouring tables.

Too late.

Carmen had already gone.

Chapter 26

Rennie was making a hopelessly cack-handed attempt at ironing his favourite shirt when he heard the front door open. He was due to meet up with a group of friends at a new bar in Soho and had rather hoped that Nancy and Rose would be back from their trip to the theatre before he left – Rose was a spectacular ironer who could always be relied upon to exclaim, 'Will you look at what you're doing to that poor shirt? Here, give it to me, pet, *this* is how it should be done.'

Now, congratulating himself on his excellent timing, he assumed a helpless expression and waited for Rose to come bustling into the kitchen and whisk the iron from his incompetent male grasp.

Except it wasn't Rose.

'You're still here,' said Carmen accusingly.

'I wasn't expecting you back so soon. I've booked a room at the Savoy,' Rennie lied. Pointing to the furiously steaming iron, he said, 'As soon as I've finished this, I'll pack my things.'

Carmen's gaze alighted on the cornflakes packet standing open on the table.

'What's that doing out?'

She was still furious with him.

'Sorry, I had some cornflakes. I was hungry,' said Rennie. 'I'll put it away in a—'

Zzinnggg went the packet as it whistled past his head. Ducking, Rennie heard it hit the wall behind him. Cornflakes showered in all directions. Carmen gazed around wildly, seized the biscuit tin and hurled it after the cornflakes packet. The lid pinged off, sending biscuits bouncing to the floor.

Cornflakes were one thing, but chocolate digestives was taking it too far. The floor might be sparkling clean, thanks to Rose, but broken biscuits somehow never tasted as nice as whole ones.

'OK, stop,' Rennie ordered as Carmen grabbed the tea caddy and flung it wildly at the door. '*Stop.*' His voice rose as she reached for the sugar bowl, because sugar was definitely no laughing matter.

'*No,*' bellowed Carmen, hurling the sugar bowl across the kitchen and watching with grim satisfaction as it smashed against the fridge.

Racing across the kitchen, Rennie grabbed her arms and cornered her between the oven and the dishwasher.

'Let go of me.' Carmen was wriggling like an eel; a straitjacket would have come in handy. Her eyes blazed as she hissed, 'I hate you. How *dare* you? Let me go!'

'Look, the kitchen didn't do anything wrong.' Refusing to release his grip, Rennie nodded at the cereal-and-sugar-strewn floor. 'I'm the one who upset you and I'm going, I promise. You're right, I should have kept my opinions to myself. You can do whatever you like with Joe. Run off and marry him, if that's what you—'

'It's over, OK?' Carmen's tone was venomous.

'Fine, I know. I'll call a cab and pack my things. Just promise me you won't throw any more food while I'm upstairs.' As he took a cautious step back, cornflakes and biscuits crunched under his feet.

'It's over between me and Joe, you idiot.' Carmen swallowed hard before defiantly meeting his gaze. 'You were right and I was wrong. And if you say I told you so, it'll be bits of your body strewn around this floor.'

Over. *Thank God for that.* Inwardly digesting this news – while he still had a digestive system intact – Rennie said, 'What happened?'

'You're thinking it,' warned Carmen.

'I'm not, I promise.' Rennie decided to think it only in the privacy of his own room. That would be safe enough, surely.

'He wanted the money.' Carmen's eyes were blazing. 'Twenty thousand pounds, just like you told me. *Bastard.*'

'Who's the bastard? Him or me?'

'Him. Oh God.' Her face abruptly crumpled as the realisation sank in. 'I can't believe he did it. *Shit.*'

'Absolutely.' Rennie nodded. 'He *is* a shit.'

'Not him. Your shirt.' She was pointing behind him.

'How can it still be steaming? I switched the steam off,' said Rennie.

It was Carmen's turn to march across the kitchen. As she lifted the iron from the shirt, she said, 'That's not steam, you berk. It's smoke.'

The phone on the worktop began to ring. Carmen froze.

'I'll get it.' Answering the phone, Rennie said briskly, 'Yes?' then listened.

'Is that him?' whispered Carmen.

'Yes, she's here.' Rennie's green eyes narrowed. 'And no, she still doesn't want to give you twenty grand.'

Carmen felt her stomach disappear. As she held out her hand, she saw that it was trembling. 'Let me speak to him.'

Joe sounded distraught. 'I'm sorry, I'm so sorry. I don't want to lose you. Please . . . forget about the money, it doesn't matter. Sweetheart, I love—'

'It's over, Joe. Don't ring this number again.' Carmen heard her voice begin to wobble, but knew she had to say it. 'Leave me alone, OK? I don't want—'

'But you mean everything in the world to me,' Joe cried out in desperation.

'I think you mean I meant all the money in the world to you.' Trembling all over, Carmen hung up.

Thirty minutes later the first doubts began to creep in. Carmen gazed blindly at the TV and wondered if she was in fact making a terrible mistake. Changed out of her smart bronze dress into her old white dressing gown and with her make-up brutally scrubbed off, she took a sip of the brandy Rennie had insisted on pouring for her.

From the kitchen she could hear the sound of him wielding the Dyson with as much expertise as he had earlier tackled the ironing. Sucking up granulated sugar, broken biscuits and the best part of a family-sized box of cornflakes was a noisy business.

Which meant that if the phone rang again in the kitchen, she wouldn't be able to hear it.

Oh God, why had this had to happen to her? Burying her face in her hands, Carmen went over the conversation in the restaurant again, word for agonisingly painful word. What if she *had* misunderstood Joe's proposal?

The Dyson went quiet in the kitchen, undoubtedly because it was full to bursting with cornflakes and Rennie couldn't be bothered to empty the cylinder again.

'All done.' He came into the living room.

Carmen managed a faint smile. 'Really?'

'Well, kind of.' Rennie sat down next to her on the sofa and pulled her bare feet companionably onto his lap. 'Feeling better now?'

Carmen marvelled at the question; was thirty minutes as long as Rennie took to get over the end of a relationship with someone he liked a lot?

Actually, dumb question. Knowing him, thirty minutes was generous.

'I've been thinking. It's not as if he asked me to *give* him twenty thousand pounds,' Carmen blurted out. 'What if I'm being unfair? It was a

147

straight business proposition, after all, just a loan – *ow*.' She jerked her left foot away as Rennie pinched her toe. 'But I'm just saying, what if it was completely innocent and I overreacted because of what you'd said? Ow, will you *stop* that?'

'No, *you* stop it,' said Rennie. 'Stop making excuses for him. OK, tell me the truth,' he went on. 'I know I'm right and logically you know I'm right, but you aren't one hundred per cent convinced. So how convinced are you?'

God, he was bossy. Carmen tucked her feet securely under her so he couldn't pinch her toes again.

'Ninety-five per cent.' She exhaled slowly. 'But there's still that—'

'Five per cent that isn't sure.' Rennie gave her a nudge. 'See? I knew that GCSE would come in handy one day.'

'It's just, he does so much for charity!' This was what had been bothering Carmen; to her mind, someone who gave hours of their spare time fundraising for a charity, especially one that helped sick children, surely *had* to be a good person.

'So does Jeffrey Archer,' said Rennie.

'Who was it who told you about Joe?' Carmen didn't expect him to reply; every time she'd asked this question before, Rennie had refused to tell her. She had decided he'd invented the supposed mystery visitor. Except now she knew he hadn't.

Unexpectedly Rennie said, 'She made me promise not to tell you while you were seeing Joe. He mustn't know.'

Carmen nodded; she just wanted this to be settled once and for all.

'Joe's ex-girlfriend. He dumped her when he met you. Her name's Tina,' said Rennie.

'Hmm. Ex-girlfriend. So she came here to stir up trouble.'

'She wants him back.' Rennie nodded in agreement. 'But the reason she came here was to let you know the truth. Joe boasted about you, about what he was planning to do. She thought you deserved to know.'

'And now she's won. He'll probably go back to her.' Taking another sip of brandy, Carmen said, 'Are you telling me the truth?'

'You can ring her if you like.' Rennie took out his mobile. 'I persuaded her to give me her number.'

Oh God. Did she want to speak to this girl? Would it dispel those last nagging, niggling doubts?

Swallowing the remains of the brandy in her glass, Carmen took a deep breath and said, 'Go on then.'

* * *

'He's such a shit,' said Tina, when Rennie had explained the situation to her and passed the phone over to Carmen.

'But you still want him back.' This was definitely a surreal experience, discussing Joe with his ex-girlfriend.

'I love him. You were a temptation he couldn't resist. Well, your money was.' Tina's tone was pragmatic. 'But I haven't got any money, have I? So when we're together I know it's because he wants to be with *me*.'

'Joe didn't know who I was when he first met me. He thought I worked for Rennie.' The brandy was bringing out Carmen's defensive side; somehow, it was important to let this girl know that.

Tina laughed. 'Is that the way he played it? Of course he knew who you were. Joe's been Red Lizard's greatest fan for years.'

'B-but . . . he didn't know *me*,' Carmen stammered.

'He's got scrapbooks at his mum's house. Anything to do with that band went into those books. Look, I'm sorry,' Tina sounded embarrassed, 'but he knew where you lived. When your husband died, Joe came along to the vigil outside your house.'

Carmen felt the last flicker of doubt die inside her chest. That was it, all over. Then the sound of a bell ringing on the other end of the phone cut through the silence and she heard Tina gasp, 'Oh my God, he's here!'

'Joe?' This surely had to be the ultimate farce.

'I just looked out of the window. He's standing on my doorstep.' Tina was unable to disguise her joy and relief. 'I have to go. Promise you'll never tell him it was me, OK?'

'That's easy enough. I'm never going to be speaking to Joe again,' said Carmen.

'And you mustn't ring this number again either. He'd go mental if he knew what I'd done. Right, well, it's been nice talking to you but I have to answer the door now . . .'

'You aren't crying,' said Rennie. 'I thought you would.'

So convinced had he been that he'd even thoughtfully placed a box of Kleenex on the coffee table.

'I'm hurt. I feel stupid and ugly and made a fool of, and I really hate it that you warned me and I refused to believe you. But it isn't the end of the world.' Resting her head against the back of the sofa, Carmen said, 'I cried when Spike died. Compared with that, this is . . . nothing. I'll feel empty again, but I'm used to that. I can handle it.' She picked up Rennie's phone once more and punched out the number for directory enquiries. 'Plenty of practice. Oh hi, I'd like the number of the Savoy Hotel in London, please. Yes, can you put me through?'

Rennie said, 'Why don't we have another drink?'

'Hello, could you tell me if Rennie Todd has a room booked for tonight? No? OK, thanks very much. Bye.'

'I booked under a false name,' Rennie protested when Carmen looked at him. 'I'm a celebrity, we have to consider security, I have *stalkers* . . .'

'You sad, deluded old man.' Carmen gave his arm a sympathetic pat. 'Whoever in their right mind would want to stalk you?'

'Don't worry. I'll go.'

'Oh, shut up. You know you won't.'

'I just feel I could be more useful here,' said Rennie. 'You need looking after. It's my mission in life to get you through this traumatic episode.'

'Plus you get bored in hotel rooms,' Carmen reminded him. 'You're hopeless at being on your own. You buy houses and sell them again without even moving into them.'

'I moved into the last one.' Rennie was indignant.

'For a whole week. Then you got lonely and sold it to that racing driver.'

'It was too bloody big.' He groaned at the memory of the eight-bedroomed mansion in Berkshire, bought on a whim because he'd been so taken by the stained-glass window on the landing. If only he'd just bought the window; that house had been such a mistake.

Oh well, at least he'd sold the place for a quarter of a million more than he'd paid for it.

'You're a hopeless case,' chided Carmen.

'I've got a few of those upstairs. Still want me to go and pack them?'

'Oh, give it a rest.'

Rennie knew he'd won. Life was great here with Carmen, Nancy and Rose, and now that Joe James – thankfully – was out of the picture, they could all get back to normal. He planted a kiss on Carmen's cheek. 'You love me really. And you aren't ugly or stupid either.' Forcing her to look at him, he said, 'You do know that, don't you?'

Carmen sighed. 'Who was that American billionaire? He was two hundred years old and in a wheelchair when he married a Playboy model. That's kind of how I feel.'

'Boobs aren't big enough,' said Rennie. 'I mean, sorry and all that, but they just aren't.'

'You know what I mean. I liked Joe for who he was. I thought he liked me for who *I* was. But he didn't. God, how could I have been such an idiot?'

'Forget him,' Rennie said bluntly. 'The guy's a twat and a dickhead. The *good* thing is that you've spent the last three years thinking you'll never find another bloke and be happy again, but now you know you can.'

Carmen wrapped the ends of her dressing gown belt around her fingers. 'I don't know if you've noticed, but I'm not actually feeling that happy right now.'

'But you will. You'll meet someone else and fall in love.' Something tightened in Rennie's chest. 'At least you know it's possible now. It can happen and it will. And with any luck, next time he won't turn out to be a dickhead.'

'Listen to you.' Carmen broke into a smile. 'Talking about falling in love, all this girly stuff. Very New Man.'

'Hey, I'll be wearing Birkenstocks next. Eating tofu salad and reading the *Guardian* before you know it. Anyway, I'm just saying don't be too hard on yourself. You've turned a corner,' said Rennie. 'You're on your way back to the real world. Give it a couple of weeks and you'll be out clubbing every night, getting chatted up and pulling left, right and centre.'

'Turning a corner's one thing,' Carmen pulled a face. 'But that would be turning into you. Oh, here they are.'

Rose and Nancy were back.

'Good show?' said Rennie.

'Heaven! The most wonderful thing I ever saw.' Rose, her face blotchy and her eyes pink-rimmed, exclaimed, 'I've never cried so much in all my life. I couldn't stop!'

'Women.' Rennie shook his head. 'I'll never understand them.'

'And what's been going on in the kitchen? Did World War Three break out while we were away?'

'Sorry.' Sensing Carmen's embarrassment, Rennie said, 'I did that. Bit of an accident with the cornflakes.'

'You're a butterfingers,' Rose scolded good-naturedly. 'Never mind, I'll have it cleared up in no time. *And* you've ruined your favourite shirt; honestly, you are hopeless.'

Deciding he'd been quite noble enough, Rennie said, 'That wasn't me. It was Carmen.'

Chapter 27

'About time too.' Jonathan's tone was terse when Nancy returned his call the following morning. 'I was expecting you to ring me yesterday.'

'I've been busy.' Reaching across the kitchen table for her gloves, Nancy was interested and relieved to discover that the sound of his voice did absolutely nothing for her. It left her cold. In the space of just a few weeks she was over Jonathan. It was even possible to find him faintly pathetic.

'How have you been?'

'Fine.' It was true, she had. In fact, better than fine.

'We need to talk,' said Jonathan.

'Isn't that what we're doing now?'

'I mean properly.' He paused and cleared his throat. 'Face to face. I could . . . come down to London, if you want.'

'What for?' Nancy checked her watch; she really had to leave for work in five minutes.

'To sort this out. Decide what we're going to do.'

'Get a divorce. It's simple enough, isn't it? There's no need for you to fly down,' said Nancy. 'I'll find a solicitor, tell him to—'

'Look, I don't want a divorce.' Hurriedly Jonathan went on, 'I'm not with Paula any more. It's over.'

Well, well. Who'd have thought it? 'Over? That was quick. Did you get the ring back?'

'It was never serious. Paula was just a bit of—'

'A floozy?' guessed Nancy.

'A bit of fun, I was going to say. But I suppose that's not right. She was just *there*,' Jonathan said weakly, 'and she was available. She was the one who made all the running. To be honest, she threw herself at me. And I suppose I was . . .'

'Stupid? Unfaithful?' Nancy suggested helpfully. 'A complete shit?'

'*Flattered*.' Jonathan sounded irritated. 'But it was never meant to be anything important. The last thing I wanted was to jeopardise our marriage.'

'Should have thought of that before you got her knickers off.'

'I know, I *know*,' he exploded with frustration, 'but you were never supposed to find out!'

'Ah, but I did find out,' Nancy said easily. 'And what's more, I'm *glad* I found out.'

'Nancy, listen to me, I don't want a divorce! I still love you! I made one tiny mistake,' Jonathan groaned, 'and I'm *sorry*.'

'Well, that's incredibly generous of you, but the answer's still no. Because I don't love you and I definitely want a divorce.' God, it felt so great to be saying this and to actually mean it. Re-checking her watch, Nancy said, 'Look, I'm sorry, but I do have to go now.'

'It's him, isn't it! Jesus, you *are* sleeping with him.' She heard disbelief mingled with fury in Jonathan's voice, reverberating down the phone.

'What?' Nancy smothered laughter.

'Rennie Todd,' Jonathan shouted. 'You're letting him screw you! Is he spinning you a line, is that it? Do you think he's serious about you? Because I'm telling you now, you're kidding yourself if you do. He's sleeping with you because you're there, willing and available.'

'Bit like you and Paula then.' Nancy couldn't resist it.

'He can have anyone he wants, for fuck's sake! He's just *using* you.'

'Or,' Nancy said cheerfully, 'I could be using him.'

Jonathan made a noise like an old-fashioned kettle coming to the boil. Rennie, choosing that moment to wander into the kitchen wearing nothing but the blue and white striped shorts he'd slept in, yawned and said, 'I don't know about you, but I could use a cup of tea.'

'Is that him?' roared Jonathan. 'Jesus, don't tell me you're in bed with him now! He'll dump you, you do realise that, don't you? Men like him have a different groupie for every night of the week.'

'Thanks, Jonathan, but you don't need to worry about me. I can look after myself.' As she said it, Rennie raised his eyebrows enquiringly and Nancy nodded, grinning.

'Sweetheart,' said Rennie, 'aren't you cold with no clothes on? Here, let me warm you up.'

'I have to go,' Nancy said hastily, cutting an outraged Jonathan off in mid-splutter.

'Sounds a bit agitated,' observed Rennie.

'He thinks we're having an affair.'

'Serves him right. Before you know it, he'll be deciding he wants you back.'

'He already has.' Taking a last hasty gulp of lukewarm coffee Nancy said, 'Just now. I turned down his generous offer.'

153

'Hey, that's great.' Rennie sounded genuinely pleased. 'Good for you. Fancy a quickie to celebrate?'

'Sorry, late for work already.' Smiling, Nancy grabbed her handbag and inwardly marvelled at how fantastic she felt. Turning down Jonathan had done wonders for her self-esteem. Maybe one day an attractive man would make her an offer along the lines of the one Rennie had just suggested and actually mean it.

Wrenching open the front door, she unexpectedly came face to face with the attractive man she had secretly hoped might be the one to make that offer. Almost cannoning right into his chest, Nancy jumped and let out an undignified yelp of surprise.

'Sorry, sorry.' Connor held out his hands and steadied her, which did nothing to calm her frantically racing heart. 'Didn't mean to give you a fright. I was just about to ring the bell.'

'Caught me by surprise.' Clutching her chest, Nancy took deep breaths and tried not to notice how gorgeous he was looking. OK, maybe not gorgeous – Connor was too scruffy for that – but irresistible all the same. 'Um, did you want to see Rennie?'

'You, actually.' Apologetically Connor said, 'But I can see it's not a good time, you're rushing off to work.'

'What about?'

'No, it's fine, I don't want to make you late.'

Which was like plonking a huge, thrillingly gift-wrapped present into a six-year-old's arms, then snatching it back and saying, 'Actually, don't open it yet.'

'You're here now. I'm not going to be late.' The big lie tripped effortlessly off Nancy's tongue. Poor Zac, less than a week and already she was turning into Jacintha. Reversing back into the hall, she said, 'Now, what was it you wanted?' and briefly – shamelessly – allowed her imagination to run riot.

'OK, this won't take two minutes. It's actually Mia's idea,' Connor admitted, which Nancy felt was promising. Had Mia persuaded him that if he wanted a new and *far* nicer girlfriend than Sadie Sylvester, he need look no further than next door?

'Mia's full of ideas,' said Nancy, aware that this was a less than dazzling response but powerless to come up with anything witty at short notice.

'Tell me about it. Let's hope this one's better than the last.' Connor pulled a wry face, which was less encouraging. 'Anyway the thing is, my secretary's eight months pregnant and she's starting her maternity leave on Friday. We're holding a party at the club. I was going to buy a cake, then Mia told me about the one you'd made for Rennie.'

'Hi.' Emerging from the kitchen clutching a slice of toast and Marmite, Rennie said interestedly, 'What cake?'

'Hey there.' Connor greeted him with a cheerful nod. 'The one Nancy made for your birthday. The curry cake.'

'Curry cake?'

Connor turned back to Nancy. 'Did I get this wrong? Chicken Madras and pilau rice, Mia said. She described it to me down to the last detail.'

'I know I eat weird stuff,' Rennie complained, 'but not that weird.'

'It's OK.' Nancy waved her hands, embarrassed. 'I made a cake for your birthday but you flew over to New York so you didn't get it. I threw it away.'

'Bloody good job,' declared Rennie, who could sometimes be *too* blunt. 'I'm glad I went to New York now.' Gazing in horror at Nancy he said, 'Whatever were you thinking of?'

'Will you shut up and listen?' Nancy wished she'd never made the bloody thing now. 'It didn't taste of curry, OK? It was a normal sponge cake inside, decorated to look like a plate of chicken Madras and rice.'

'Mia said it was fantastic,' Connor added supportively.

Feeling cross and a bit stupid, Nancy said, 'It *was* fantastic. But don't worry, I won't be making you another one, that's for sure.'

She was glaring at Rennie. Raising his eyebrows in apology, Connor said, 'Hey, I'm sorry, I didn't come here to cause trouble.'

'No, *I'm* sorry.' Rennie shook his head with genuine regret. 'Misunderstanding. It sounds great. Going to all that trouble, just for me. I'm really touched. You shouldn't have thrown it away.'

Nancy felt her cheeks burning, because they were both looking at her now and Connor was probably thinking she must have a bit of a crush on Rennie. Dammit, Rennie was undoubtedly thinking the same thing.

'It would have been stale by the time you got back. Look, forget it, no big deal.' She turned abruptly to Connor and said, 'So you want me to make one for your secretary, is that it?'

'Well, that was the idea . . . I mean, I'd pay you of course,' Connor added hastily. 'But if you're too busy, that's fine, I'll just buy one from—'

'I have to go to work now.' Feeling hot, frazzled and ashamed of herself for behaving like a teenager in a strop, Nancy said, 'Of course I'll do you a cake. Look, I'll be home by six. Why don't you come over this evening and we'll talk about the kind of thing you want.'

* * *

'Afternoon, Jacintha,' said Zac, when Nancy arrived out of breath at the shop.

'I know, I know, I'm so sorry.' In her hurry to unwind her scarf, Nancy wound it the wrong way and almost garrotted herself. 'It won't happen again. I've just had a bit of a frantic morning, my husband wants me to go back to him and he thinks I'm having an affair with Rennie and our neighbour called round just as I was leaving the house and then—'

'Hey, relax, we're only teasing you.' Zac, with Doreen on his lap, was beaming all over his face. 'It's eight minutes past nine, silly, not eight minutes past three. Anyway, never mind about that.' He bounced on his chair so excitedly that Doreen's ears jiggled like wings. 'Enough about you, let's talk about me! *Guess* who I met last night?'

So this was why he'd been waiting impatiently for her to come in.

'Boy George.' Reaching across him to switch on the computer, Nancy hoped Zac wasn't going to be wittering on for the next twenty minutes; she had a heap of emails to get through.

'More like Boy George's gorgeous blond Scandinavian son,' Zac said happily. 'If he had one.'

'I don't think he has. Go on then, tell me everything. Well,' Nancy hastily amended, 'not *everything* . . .'

'His name's Sven.' Zac gazed dreamily at the wall, where a hologram of the glorious Sven was evidently hovering. 'He's twenty-five, blue eyes, white-blond hair, teeth to die for. You should see him, he looks like a model. I told him he should approach an agency.'

'What kind of work's he doing now?' Nancy's attempts at opening her emails were hampered by Doreen's determination to capture the mouse with her paw.

'Well, nothing right now.' Did Zac sound defensive? 'I mean, back in Malmo he's in PR, but he took a few months off to come over here and last night we just clicked. I walked into the bar and there he was, all on his own. He took one look at me. I couldn't *stop* looking at him. So I offered to buy him a drink and that was that, from then on we were just chatting non-stop. I'm telling you, if you could *see* this boy's cheek-bones . . .'

'OK, put Doreen down and listen to me. Concentrate,' Nancy ordered, because Zac was lit up like a fairground ride. 'Don't rush into anything. Don't get carried away. Take your time and *don't* do anything stupid like ask him to move in with you.'

Zac's shoulders slumped. Resentfully, he said, 'I can't believe you're being so mean.'

'I'm not being mean. You told me to say all those things,' Nancy reminded him. 'Two days ago, remember, when you announced you were turning over a new leaf?'

'Oh God, I know, I *know* I did.' Impatiently Zac waved the reminder away, like a dieter fed up with saying no to cream cakes. 'But Sven is different, I promise. This time it's for real. We get on so well, he's just a genuinely nice guy, if you could meet him you'd see I'm right.'

It was Carmen and Joe all over again. You couldn't order people to control their emotions, Nancy was discovering. Zac wasn't going to take a blind bit of notice of anything she had to say.

'Fine. I'm happy you're happy. Now, can I make a start on these emails?'

'Hang on, what was it you said when you came in?' Belatedly Zac slipped out of me-mode and did a double-take. 'Your husband wants you to go back to him? Back to *Scotland*?'

Nodding, Nancy said, 'Could be handy, couldn't it? Perfect timing. You can persuade Sven to come and take over my job.'

Zac was visibly shocked. 'Are you leaving?'

'No, I'm not. And don't look so disappointed.' Nancy blew him a kiss. 'I'm staying here to make your life a misery, whether you like it or not.'

Chapter 28

Nick, ambling into the kitchen at the shelter, said, 'The trouble with playing chess against Albert is how do I *know* he's a Grand Master?'

'OK, clue,' said Annie. 'If you beat him, he probably isn't one.'

'But that's what's so annoying.' Frustratedly, Nick pointed through the door to where Albert, a recent arrival at the shelter, was dozing peacefully in a tartan armchair. 'We start playing, I *start* doing well, I start to think that this time I might actually win. Then the next thing I know, I hear the sound of snoring and when I look up, Albert's fallen asleep again. So I never *do* get to beat him. When he wakes up and I suggest we carry on, he says he can't because he's lost the thread of the game.'

'That's Nick for you,' Annie told Carmen cheerfully. 'They said he was gullible and he believed them. Face it, Albert is no Grand Master, Old Eamonn isn't really the son of God and Peg Leg Jack's real parents probably weren't Winston Churchill and Bette Davis.'

The older visitors to the shelter tended to make colourful claims regarding their family histories. Nick, picking up a potato peeler and joining Carmen at the sink, said conversationally, 'I used to be married to Shirley Bassey, you know.'

'That's nothing,' Annie airily retaliated as she chopped carrots. 'My first husband was Sylvester Stallone.'

'She's always had this thing for Sylvester Stallone.' Nick gave Carmen a complicit nudge. 'Does that make any sense to you? I mean, what *is* the attraction there?'

Carmen smiled absently, struggling to pay attention to their banter. Last night she'd dreamt that Joe and Tina had invited her to their wedding and at the reception Joe had publicly announced that she was paying for the whole thing because she could afford it.

'Miles away,' Nick tut-tutted, waving a hand in front of her face. 'Please don't tell me you're fantasising over Sylvester Stallone's oiled biceps. Heyyy, payyy atten-shunn.' He mimicked the low-pitched Stallone drawl. 'Whattaya doin' . . . starin' at my biceps?'

Distracted, Carmen said, 'Hmm?'

'Heyyy, she ain't even listenin' to meee,' Nick protested. 'Like she don't even know who I aaaam.'

'Oh, shut up, Nick, give it a rest, will you?' Annie rolled her eyes despairingly. 'You're such a hopeless case.'

Mystified, Nick said in his normal voice, 'Why am I hopeless?'

'Because Carmen's not in the mood, OK? Honestly, why is it that men never notice *anything*?'

Gazing around the kitchen in search of clues, Nick said, 'Notice *what*?'

Carmen turned and caught Annie silently mouthing something at him. Since Nick's talents didn't include lip-reading, he continued to look baffled.

'It's OK,' said Carmen, because someone had to put him out of his misery. 'I'm having a bit of an off day, that's all. Joe and I broke up.'

'Oh. Hey, I'm sorry.' Nick looked accusingly at Annie. 'How did you know?'

'I'm a girl.' Annie was scornful. 'We have this thing called intuition, otherwise known as common sense. I'm sorry too,' she told Carmen. 'What a rotten thing to happen. Poor you.'

Touched by their concern, Carmen said, 'Thanks. I'll live.'

'His loss.' Nick's tone was bracing. 'So what happened? Caught him with another woman, did you? *Hey*,' he dodged out of the way as Annie threw a carrot at his head. 'What was that for? I'm not the one who cheated on Carmen.'

'You don't ask questions like that, you big hopeless wazzock. It's not what people *do*.'

'But if we don't ask, how are we supposed to find out?'

'Really, it doesn't matter,' Carmen said hastily before another relationship could crumble before her very eyes. 'I didn't catch him with another woman. I just found out he wasn't . . . well, as honest as I'd thought.'

'Honesty. Honesty's important.' Annie was sympathetic. 'You don't want to be involved with someone you can't trust.'

'Nick, dear boy.' Albert, in his fifty-year-old dinner jacket and grubby brown corduroys, stood in the kitchen doorway. 'Just finished the game without you.' His plummy tones emerged through his long untrimmed beard and his eyes sparkled with triumph.

'Really, Albert? Did I win?'

'Frightfully sorry, old thing. Checkmate in four. Still, better luck next time, eh?' Shuffling back out of the kitchen, Albert executed a regal wave. 'Can't expect to beat a Grand Master.'

'Like I was saying,' Annie whispered when the door had closed behind him. 'Honesty's important.'

Nick winked at Carmen and said, 'In that case, your bum looks enormous in those jeans.'

Carmen loved the way they bickered together, like a couple who'd been married for fifty years.

'One other hint,' Annie told Nick. 'Never say that to a girl with a sharp chopping knife in her hand. Or you could really live to regret it.'

The heavens opened as Carmen left the shelter at five thirty. Skulking in the doorway with hunched-shouldered commuters bustling past, she realised that her black wool coat would soak up the rain like a sponge, and that of course today was the day she'd forgotten her umbrella.

Well, what else could you expect?

Bugger it, thought Carmen, today was the day for a cab.

But even the cab drivers, it turned out, were against her. Evidently they were less inclined to stop for someone huddled in an oversized coat on the steps of a shelter for the homeless.

'Ugh,' shivered Nick, joining her five minutes later and shuddering as the icy rain hit him in the face. 'What are you still doing here?'

'Waiting for it to ease off before I head for the tube,' Carmen lied.

Nick shook his head. 'It's not going to stop for ages. God, sometimes I hate this country.' Giving Carmen a nudge he said, 'Come on, let's run off together.'

'The Caribbean,' said Carmen through chattering teeth. 'Or Sydney. Sydney would be nice. Or – ooh, I know, Capri.'

'Damn, if only I'd thought to bring my passport today.' Pointing through the rainswept darkness down the street, Nick said, 'How about a coffee at Giacomo's instead?'

Inside the warmth of the friendly Italian cafe, Carmen's coat began to steam gently. By the time Nick arrived at their table with two cappuccinos, her feet had begun to thaw out.

'Proper coffee.' Nick inhaled appreciatively. 'Nothing like it.'

Carmen said, 'And the coffee at the shelter is definitely nothing like it.'

He grinned, because back at the shelter they got through catering-sized tins of horrible powdered instant stuff.

'Hey, I'm sorry if I put my foot in it earlier. Annie told me off after lunch for being such a klutz. I didn't mean to be insensitive.'

'You weren't,' Carmen assured him. 'I'm fine, really. I thought Joe was special. Turns out he wasn't. That's all, no big deal. Happens to everyone.'

'But it still hurts. When I was nineteen I was absolutely crazy about my girlfriend,' said Nick. 'She was everything I'd ever wanted. I thought we were officially the happiest couple on the planet. Until I came home early one day and caught her in *our* bed with *my* sociology lecturer.'

Carmen knew she mustn't laugh. She mustn't, she really mustn't. But the look on Nick's face wasn't helping; his eyebrows were wounded but his eyes were bright with laughter.

'That's . . . tragic,' Carmen managed finally. 'Is it true?'

'True?' Nick bristled with indignation. 'I've got the anguished diaries to prove it. Go on, you can laugh, but I was destroyed at the time. And my friends, needless to say, were no help at all. They said it served me right for doing sociology in the first place. You've got cappuccino foam on your lip, by the way. No, don't wipe it off. A moustache suits you.'

Carmen wiped away her frothy moustache; she was feeling better already. This was why Nick was so popular at the shelter, he had the ability to make fun of himself, chat effortlessly to anyone and invariably cheer them up.

'So how did you get over her?'

'Hey, I was a student! I got legless in the union bar and persuaded my ex-girlfriend's less attractive best friend to come back to the flat for wild sex.'

'Of course you did.' Carmen nodded solemnly. 'And did that work?'

'After nine pints of cheap cider and six shots of tequila? Are you kidding? *Nothing* worked,' said Nick. 'I couldn't do a thing. Which was hugely embarrassing of course, because all I needed now was for this girl to spread the word that I was impotent and my life would be over, I'd have to leave the country. So I did the only thing I could do under the circumstances.'

'Which was?'

'Told her the reason I couldn't sleep with her was because she was too ugly.'

Carmen spluttered and grabbed a paper napkin. 'You *didn't.*'

'I did. Had to.' Nick shrugged soulfully. 'My manhood, my university career, *everything* was at stake.'

'And what did she do?'

'Cried. Got dressed. Ran off down the street with her cardigan on inside out.'

'I can't believe you did something so horrible,' Carmen protested.

161

'It was important. Plus,' Nick went on, 'I was drunker than I'd ever been before in my whole life.'

'That poor girl. Whatever happened to her?'

'Funnily enough, I saw her on TV not long ago. She's a Tory MP now.' Nick stirred his coffee. 'So it clearly scarred her for life.'

'She'll probably push through a bill to bring back hanging for drunken students who humiliate girls.'

'And I'd deserve it. I know, but you did ask. At least I was honest with you.'

'A bit *too* honest. But you managed to get over the break-up with your ex-girlfriend,' said Carmen. 'How long ago did you meet Annie?'

'Two years ago? Maybe a bit more than that.'

Annie had left work early that afternoon to visit her dentist and have a loose filling replaced. Glancing at her watch and realising that it was already gone six, Carmen said, 'Should you give her a ring and let her know where you are? She'll be wondering why you're late.'

Nick shrugged, unconcerned. 'She won't be. I'm old enough to be out on my own.'

Honestly, were all men as selfish as each other?

'I know you're *old* enough.' Carmen rolled her eyes in despair. 'But what if Annie's cooked dinner and is expecting you home by six? If you're going to be late, it's only polite to call and—'

'Whoa, whoa, you're starting to sound like my mother. For a start,' Nick began counting on his fingers, 'Annie's just been to the dentist, so all she'll be doing is slurping Cup-a-Soup through a straw. Second, she's the world's worst cook, so any opportunity to miss one of her terrible meals is a bonus. And third,' he said, dodging out of the way as Carmen took an indignant swipe at him on Annie's behalf, 'she won't even be at home. She's gone out with her boyfriend.'

Carmen froze in mid-swipe. *Boyfriend?*

'Sorry?'

'They've gone to the cinema to see the new Richard Curtis comedy. You know the one.' Nick waggled his hands in a Hugh Grantish kind of way. 'Drives me insane, all those cute quirky characters with posh voices, pratting around doing cute quirky things. But Annie loves all that.'

Boyfriend?

Bemused, Carmen said, 'Don't you . . . um, mind?'

'You're joking. I'm more of a *Great Escape* man myself.'

'I meant the thing about the boyfriend. Isn't that a bit . . . you know . . . unusual?'

Nick shrugged. 'I suppose. Blokes don't go for that kind of film as a rule, do they? I should think he's hating every second but putting up with it for Annie's sake. Gets him some Brownie points,' he added wryly. 'Probably hoping she'll sleep with him.'

'And will she?' Carmen was astounded; it had never occurred to her that Nick and Annie might have an open relationship. Weren't they normally the preserve of permatanned women who wore plunging leopard-print dresses and men with too much aftershave and medallions round their necks?

'Maybe. I don't know.' Nick drank his cappuccino. 'He seems all right.'

Carmen was perplexed. 'And you're OK with that?'

Half smiling, Nick ran his fingers through his messy hair. 'Annie's a grown-up. She can do what she wants.'

'Right. Of course she can. Gosh, I just . . . well, it's just a surprise. Sorry,' said Carmen. 'I must sound like somebody's maiden aunt.'

Nick slowly finished his coffee, gazing at her over the rim of the cup as he did so. He looked as if he might be trying not to smile.

Finally he put down the empty cup and Carmen saw that his mouth was twitching at the corners.

'Annie isn't my girlfriend.'

'She isn't?' Carmen was confused. When had they broken up? Why hadn't they told her? How could they carry on laughing and joking together at work, as if nothing had happ—

Oh.

A great crimson blush swept up her neck as she realised her mistake.

'I'm not Annie's boyfriend,' Nick carried on. 'We aren't a couple. We never have been.'

'Oh my God, I don't *believe* it.' Covering her face, Carmen let out a squeal of shame. 'I'm such an *idiot*.'

'You aren't an idiot. You just got hold of the wrong end of the stick and—'

'Never managed to find the right end,' Carmen finished for him, sliding her hands down her cheeks and watching Nick struggle heroically to maintain a straight face. 'It's just, when I came to work at the shelter, someone told me you lived together.'

'We share a flat. Separate bedrooms,' said Nick.

'So anyway, I thought you were a couple,' Carmen went on, 'and the two of you got on so well together, I suppose I just carried on thinking it. Nothing ever . . . nobody ever said anything to make me think otherwise.'

Even as the words were spilling out, she knew that she might have cottoned on earlier if she had paid a bit more attention to other people and not kept herself quite so much to herself.

Which was shaming, but at least she was over that now. And Nick, generously, wasn't pointing it out.

'Me and Annie,' he said with a chuckle. 'Ha, wait till she hears about this.'

'You *act* like a couple,' Carmen protested. 'You talk about the TV shows you watched last night, you invite people round for dinner, you throw parties—'

'That you never come to,' said Nick.

'I'm sorry. Next time I will.' Carmen nodded vigorously to show she meant it.

'Promise?'

'Definitely promise.' Crikey, it was the least she could do, to make up for paying so little attention to them over the past year.

'Come along then.' Nick pushed back his chair and stood up.

'What?'

'Dinner party. Our place. Before you have time to change your mind.'

Startled, Carmen said, 'Dinner party? You mean, *now*?'

'Absolutely. Do you think we don't know how to do them in Paddington?' Reaching for her hand, Nick indicated his scruffy, moth-eaten green sweater and said, 'I know I may not look it, but I'm actually rather posh.'

Chapter 29

Nancy had to physically restrain herself from putting on more make-up before Connor's arrival. It was hard, because he was clearly keen on the kind of girl who got through a couple of tubes of orange foundation and one and a half lipsticks a week. Which she wasn't, although with enough incentive she could always learn.

But there was such a thing as playing it cool and not looking like a woman in the desperate grip of a crush. Plus she couldn't trust Rennie not to say, 'Hey, what's with all the slap? You never make this kind of effort for me.'

You could never accuse Rennie of being discreet.

Anyway, *she* was. Having resolutely gone without lipgloss, eye shadow and mascara, she had changed into plain black trousers and a grey sweater that was casual, deliberately unflashy and couldn't possibly be construed as dressing to impress.

Which would have been perfect if Connor hadn't turned up at seven o'clock wearing . . .

'Come in.' Rennie greeted Connor with a broad grin. 'She's waiting for you in the kitchen.'

Then, unable to resist it, he'd led the way through in order to announce wickedly, 'Hey, Nance, your other half's here.'

Connor started to laugh when he saw Nancy.

'Tell me you don't have concealed cameras in my bedroom.'

'Actually no,' said Nancy. 'I used a periscope to peep through your window. When I saw you putting on your grey sweater and black trousers I rushed to my wardrobe and changed into mine.'

The sweaters were both lambswool, both pale grey, both V-necked.

'Your cleavage is better than mine,' Connor said cheerfully.

'Well, maybe you should try a Wonderbra. It really helps.'

'Beer?' said Rennie, over by the fridge.

'A Wonderbra's better.' Patting her stomach, Nancy explained, 'Beer tends to settle further down.'

'Right, I'll leave the pair of you to it.' Rennie handed Connor a bottle of Beck's. 'Got a hot date waiting for me in the living room.'

'Rose,' Nancy explained when Rennie had left the kitchen. 'They're watching *Gone with the Wind*. Now, about this cake you're after.'

They sat down side by side at the kitchen table with a notepad between them. Nancy did her level best to ignore the fact that Connor's right forearm – with the sleeve of his sweater pushed up – was touching her left arm. She prayed the little hairs on her own forearm wouldn't get all excited and start sticking up.

'OK, what I *did* have in mind was a baby in a cot waving a set of dumb-bells,' Connor began. 'Then I thought maybe that wasn't such a great idea after all, and anyhow the baby isn't here yet. So Mia said why didn't we make a cake out of all the food cravings Pam's been having, like orange juice and piccalilli, mashed banana and macaroni cheese with chillies.'

'That wouldn't make a cake,' said Nancy. 'That'd make a really horrible soup.'

Connor gave her a playful nudge and *pinggg* went all the little hairs on the back of her arm. 'Now you're making fun of an innocent country lad.'

He was neither of these things, Nancy knew perfectly well, but the sound of his voice was irresistible, like being stroked with brown velvet mittens . . . OK, don't think about it, put brown velvet mittens *out* of your mind . . .

'Are those all the things she likes?' Oh Lord, had her voice gone squeaky?

'You're joking, Pam's been a seething mass of cravings since the day she found out she was pregnant. Garlic mushrooms,' said Connor, counting on his fingers. 'Jammy Dodgers. Raw carrots dipped in barbeque sauce. Matches.'

Nancy had been scribbling them down. 'D'you mean Matchmakers?'

'I wish. Matches. She lights them, blows them out, breathes in the smell then chews the wood at the other end. Chewing matches, I ask you.' Despairingly Connor rolled his eyes. 'I've told her she looks like Clint Eastwood. *And* she's a fire hazard. But she won't stop.'

'OK.' Nancy was sketching a lace-trimmed Moses basket packed with the different foods he'd listed. 'Something like this?'

Impressed, Connor surveyed the drawing. 'You're a star. That'd be fantastic. With spent matches and indigestion tablets scattered around the basket,' he added. 'She's getting through six packets of Rennies a day.'

'I'm not surprised.'

'Oh, Pam doesn't have indigestion. She just loves that chalky crunchy grittiness against her teeth when she bites into them. So can you really do this?' Connor nodded in admiration as Nancy continued to sketch. 'By Friday?'

'I can make a start now.' Swivelling round on her chair, Nancy reached for the Union Jack cake tin on the worktop behind her. 'Rose made a couple of sponges this afternoon. Plain OK? With raspberry jam and buttercream?'

'Not got any with Branston pickle and Coal Tar soap?'

'Hang on, let me just ask Rose—'

Connor dragged her back by the belt loop on her trousers, which sent the nerve endings around Nancy's hips into a complete frenzy.

'Come back, come back. I want to see how you do this. And you have to let me pay you, by the way.'

Oh God. 'I don't want any money.' Nancy pulled a face, because she'd guessed he'd do this. 'Really. It's just a hobby, something I do for fun.'

Connor nodded. 'Mia said you'd say that.'

To change the subject Nancy said hastily, 'How is she?'

'Working a double shift. Busy making up for being so bad the other night.'

'Have you forgiven her yet?' As she spoke, Nancy took a knife from the cutlery drawer and lifted the sponge cake from the tin.

'Hey, nobody ever said having daughters was easy.' Connor's smile was wry. 'Maybe some are easier than others. Mia went about it the wrong way, but she meant well. To be honest, it's not as if Sadie was the great love of my life.'

'No?' Foolishly, Nancy's spirits lifted.

'You know these things deep down, right? I mean, Sadie has her good points.'

Those would be the ones up her jumper, Nancy thought childishly.

'But you have to try and imagine yourself with someone in fifty years' time,' Connor went on. 'Can you picture me and Sadie together then? Jesus, she'd be nagging me to do sit-ups.'

What a witch, thought Nancy. I'd *never* nag you to do sit-ups.

'I wouldn't be allowed proper milk.' Connor looked mournful. 'Only that awful skimmed stuff like when you're a kid and you swirl your paintbrush in a jam jar of water.'

Nancy longed to tell him she always bought proper milk, but that would sound competitive.

'She'd try and make me wear Lycra. Imagine,' Connor said in horror, 'being forced to jog down to the post office for my pension, dressed up like Jimmy Savile.'

Smiling, Nancy finished shaping the sponge base and went to fetch the airtight container of ready-rolled icing.

'How are Sadie and Mia getting on at work?'

'Like a couple of grenades, each trying to pull each other's pins out.' Connor shook his head and took another swallow of beer. 'I'm keeping out of the way, I tell you. Leaving them to it. As long as the members aren't affected, those two can glare at each other as much as they like.'

'And the members aren't bothered by the glaring?' Nancy began expertly shaping the icing around the sponge to form the Moses basket.

'Bothered? They're loving every minute. What they really have their hearts set on is a huge fight in the swimming pool,' said Connor. 'Like that scene with Alexis and Krystle in *Dynasty*.'

'Just as well Sadie wasn't the great love of your life.' Feeling daring, Nancy glanced up at him.

'You're telling me. Ah well, it'll happen one day.' Pinching an off-cut of icing, Connor said easily, 'Love at first sight, that's what I believe in. One of these days I'll be at work or in a bar or just driving down the street and *bam*, there she'll be. Our eyes will meet and that'll be it. In a split second I'll know she's the one for me.'

Which was all very admirable and romantic and lovely, of *course* it was, but hardly the kind of thing you wanted to hear under the circumstances.

'Does that make me sound like a big old girl's blouse?' As he said it, Connor's hand was edging across to steal another bit of icing. Nancy briefly contemplated nipping at the tips of his fingers with her knife.

Then again, maybe not. It was unlikely to make Connor fall in love with her on the spot.

'If I grew a moustache,' Rennie was back in search of more beers, 'do you think I'd look like Clark Gable?'

'You'd have to learn to drive a horse-drawn carriage,' said Nancy.

'Rhett Butler fell in love with Scarlett the first time he saw her.' Connor sounded encouraged. 'And you couldn't call him a big girl's blouse.'

'They didn't live happily ever after,' Nancy reminded him. 'What if you set your heart on someone who wasn't interested in you?'

'Easy.' Accepting another bottle of Beck's from Rennie, Connor said, 'I'd march her down to the Lazy B and strap her to one of the treadmills.

Then I'd turn it up to maximum speed.' He winked at Nancy. 'And wouldn't let her off until she said yes.'

'What time do you call this?' Rennie demanded when Carmen arrived home. 'Where have you been? It's two o'clock in the *morning*.'

'What are you, my parole officer?'

'I was worried about you.' His eyes narrowing, Rennie said suspiciously, 'You haven't seen *him*, have you? The pilfering plumber?'

'Of course I haven't.' Carmen peeled off her coat. 'And you know where I was, I left a message on the answering machine.'

'*I* leave messages on answering machines.' Rennie was scornful. 'It doesn't mean I'm telling the truth.'

'Well, I'm not you,' said Carmen, 'and I always tell the truth. Nick from work invited me back to his place for dinner. We had bacon and eggs with tinned tomatoes and fried bread. And doughnuts with custard for pudding.'

'I like doughnuts. Did you bring one back for me?'

'No. Anyway, we talked for ages, and it was great. Then his flatmate Annie came home with her boyfriend and we ended up playing Monopoly. It was fun. We had a brilliant time.'

'Hang on.' Rennie was frowning. 'I thought Nick and Annie were a couple.'

'Nooo,' Carmen said scornfully. 'Just flatmates.'

'So this Nick bloke, what's he like?'

'Nice. They're both nice. Oh, don't look at me like that.' Carmen flapped her hands in protest. 'I don't fancy Nick. He's just someone I work with.'

'But does he fancy you?'

'No way! He just bought me a coffee to cheer me up after I told him it was all over between me and Joe. You,' she rolled her eyes, 'have been watching too many soaps.'

'Did you tell him why you and Joe broke up?' Rennie persisted.

'No.'

'Does he know who you are?'

'No.' Carmen looked defensive.

'That you live in this house?'

'*No.*'

'So he hasn't asked to borrow any money yet?'

Carmen's eyes flashed. 'Don't *start* that again.'

'OK.' Rennie shrugged. 'Why don't they know?'

'Because Nick and Annie are just people I work with. I've never told

169

anyone at the shelter who I was married to because it isn't relevant.'

'D'you think they might resent the fact that you're loaded and they aren't?'

'Nick and Annie? No, of course they wouldn't. They're not like that,' Carmen said defensively. 'It's just . . . easier this way. Like this morning, Annie was having a moan about their electricity bill, trying to figure out ways to reduce it. At lunchtime we discussed the best cheap shampoo you can buy. And this afternoon we were talking about what we'd do if we won the lottery. You see?' She spread her hands. 'We wouldn't be able to do *any* of that stuff if they knew I lived in a house like this.'

Rennie nodded. 'I think you're right.'

'Blimey, don't say you're actually agreeing with me.'

'Just this once. Don't worry, I won't make a habit of it.' Reaching into the fridge, Rennie took out a foil-covered bowl of leftover apple crumble.

'I'll share that with you,' said Carmen.

Rennie looked like an eight-year-old being asked to give away half his sweets. 'It's fattening.'

'Good, that's why I like it. If it was a salad,' Carmen told him generously, 'you could eat the whole lot yourself.'

'Actually, we've got a bit of an emergency situation on our hands. Our supplier's threatening to leave the country.'

'What?'

Rennie was busy searching through the cutlery drawer. 'Rose and I were watching *Gone with the Wind* tonight. When Scarlett said, "I must go home again, to Tara," Rose said she must go home too. I just thought she was joking. Then when it was finished I said that one of Vivien Leigh's other old films was coming out on DVD next week and we'd have to watch it together.' Turning, he handed Carmen a teaspoon and a small bowl, keeping a dessertspoon for himself. 'That was when she told me she wouldn't be here, it was time she headed back to Scotland.'

Carmen was shocked. 'Why?'

'That's what I asked. She said she couldn't impose on your hospitality indefinitely. I told Rose she wasn't imposing and not to be ridiculous, but I think she's made up her mind.'

Carmen looked down at the tiny bowl in her hands, into which Rennie was doling thimble-sized amounts of apple crumble. She gazed around the gleaming kitchen, ran an index finger along the spotlessly clean cooker top, then watched as Rennie greedily dug into his own, much larger, helping of crumble.

'OK.'

'OK what?' Rennie spoke with his mouth full.

Carmen knew he was imagining a world devoid of casserole, crumble and crisply ironed shirts. 'I'll have a word with Nancy. See what I can do.'

Chapter 30

Yesterday's torrential rain had given the square a jolly good clean. As Rose made her way through the iron gate leading into the communal gardens, she breathed in the cool fresh smell of damp earth and greenery. All the dust and grime of the city had been washed away overnight; leaves were glossy, the gravel path looked as if it had been varnished with Cuprinol. A pair of squirrels, darting up the trunk of an ash tree, skittered along its silvery branches before leaping intrepidly across to a neighbouring conifer.

Rounding a bend in the path, Rose saw that her bench was already occupied. Oh well, never mind, it was plenty big enough for two.

As she drew closer, Rose recognised the woman sitting rigidly on the bench. A couple of weeks ago she had seen her walking through the garden with her husband, had called out a cheery greeting to them and been pointedly ignored. The pair of them had exuded an air of chilly, haughty disdain, not helped by their rigid posture and long noses.

As she reached the bench, it struck Rose that the woman wasn't looking so haughty today. Her face was drawn with misery, her eyes red-rimmed. Upon realising that her space was about to be invaded, she gathered her Burberry mackintosh more tightly around her chest and prepared to move off.

'Oh, don't do that,' Rose protested. 'I don't have leprosy, I promise!'

'I was just going.'

'No you weren't. I'm so sorry, I didn't mean to drive you away. It's such a beautiful morning I couldn't resist coming out for a breath of fresh air. Isn't it lovely to see the sun again? Please don't go,' said Rose. 'You'll make me feel terrible.'

The woman, who looked as if she was feeling pretty terrible herself, wearily sank back against the bench. Her thin lips were pressed together and she was twisting a mangled tissue between bony fingers. Having made herself comfortable, Rose took her knitting out of her bag then delved in again for a mini-pack of Kleenex.

172

'Here.' She offered them to the woman beside her.

'Oh. No thank you. Well, OK.' Realising that her long nose was about to drip and that her own tissue was no longer up to the job, the woman took the proffered pack. 'Thanks.'

'Don't mention it. You've had some sad news, by the looks of things. What happened, pet, did somebody die?' Rose's years of working in the care home enabled her to ask the question without a hint of awkwardness; she had learned from experience that her elderly residents appreciated the straightforward approach.

The woman next to her shook her head. Tears slid down her drawn cheeks. Recalling the grim expression on the face of the woman's husband as they'd marched through the garden the other day, Rose said, 'Problems at home, then,' and saw the woman's thin fingers clench the tissue more tightly. This was the reason she'd left her house on a bright but cold winter's morning and come out into the square.

'You know, I remember how I used to envy other women,' Rose went on easily, her knitting needles click-clacking as she worked on a lilac sleeve. 'I thought they all must have such happy home lives compared with mine. Although you never really know if they do, do you? Maybe other people envied me.' She paused and shook her head. 'My husband was a complete waste of time, but of course I didn't go around shouting it to the rest of the world. I only stayed with him for the sake of our daughter. She never knew how unhappy I was, oh no. I made sure I kept that to myself. She still doesn't know, for that matter. What would be the point of spoiling her childhood memories, all these years later? Young people nowadays seem to get divorced at the drop of a hat, don't they? But it wasn't the done thing when we were their age. You made your bed and that was it, you lay in it. For better or for worse.'

A sob escaped the woman next to her on the bench, and Rose knew that she'd been right. For a couple of minutes they sat together in silence – apart from the stifled sobs – and Rose thought how much better the woman would feel with all those pent-up tears out of her system.

Finally the woman said stiffly, 'I don't speak to strangers on park benches.'

'You don't have to, pet.' Rose carried on placidly knitting. 'But sometimes it's easier to talk to a stranger than someone you know.'

More silence, apart from the birds rustling in the trees overhead and the occasional swoosh of a car bowling down the wet street. A tiny *splat* caused the woman to sit up and exclaim despairingly, 'Oh, *perfect*.'

Rose, whose attention had been on her knitting, said, 'What was that?'

'*Bloody* bird. Thank you *so* much.'

Leaning forward, Rose saw the generous white splosh of bird poo decorating the tip of the woman's expensive-looking brown suede shoe.

'Don't worry. Here, use one of these.' Having delved into her bag once more, Rose produced wet-wipes. 'Honestly, these birds pick their moments, don't they? There, that'll get the worst of it off. Leave the rest to dry, then go at it gently with a toothbrush.'

When the woman had finished she handed the mini-pack of wet-wipes back to Rose. She hesitated, as if wanting to speak but unable to say what was on her mind.

'Go ahead.' Rose gave her an encouraging nod. 'Ask me anything you like.'

'I've seen you before. Here on this bench.' The woman's tone was tentative. 'You live here on the square?'

Rose smiled. 'In my wildest dreams. No, pet, I've just been staying down here for a couple of weeks, with friends. I'll be heading back home in the next day or two.'

Evidently having picked up on the accent, the woman said, 'Scotland?'

'Edinburgh. Back to my own little flat.' Rose experienced a pang as she said it; she *was* looking forward to seeing her flat again, but she knew she would miss Rennie, Carmen and Nancy dreadfully. Still, no need for them to know that.

'And you live alone? Is that a . . . hard thing to do?'

Tilting her head to one side, Rose proceeded with care.

'Honestly? It has its ups and downs. I've already told you my marriage wasn't a happy one. When my husband died, a part of me half expected to be relieved. And I think probably a part of me was, but at the same time I still missed him, far more than I'd imagined. We'd been married for so many years, you see. I was used to being unhappy.' Drily she added, 'Being unhappy and doing a terrific job of hiding it. I thought that was my role in life. But I still grieved when he died.'

'And now?'

'Oh, I'm much happier,' Rose nodded. 'No question about it. I have my dear little flat; it's only rented, not really mine, but everything's as I'd like it to be and there's no one to please but myself. There's a lot to be said for that. I'm happier now than I was then, and I've learned to enjoy my own company.' She paused, picturing the neat-as-a-pin kitchenette in her flat, where only one coffee mug from the matching set was ever used and a two-pint carton of milk invariably went off before it could be finished. 'But it can still be lonely, at times.'

'I'm married,' the woman next to her blurted out in despair, 'and I've never been lonelier in my life.'

Rose reached across and gave the woman's cold hand a sympathetic squeeze. 'Then maybe you don't have anything to lose. D'you have children, pet?'

Fresh tears sprang into the woman's eyes. 'A daughter. She has her own life.'

'Well, so do *you*,' said Rose.

'I've never lived on my own. Never. Oh God, I can't believe I'm telling you this. If my husband knew, he'd—'

'Sshh, stop it. He isn't going to know, is he?'

'He'll be wondering where I am.' The woman wiped her eyes and checked her watch. 'I should be getting back. I don't suppose we'll meet again.' Shaking Rose's hand, she said awkwardly, 'Thank you.'

'I hope everything works out for you, pet.' Rose's smile was warm. 'Whatever you decide. It's been really nice to meet you.' Realising that they didn't even know each other's names, she added, 'I'm Rose, by the way.'

The woman said, 'Marjorie,' and managed a wan smile of her own. 'Well, have a good journey back to Edinburgh.'

Edinburgh. Feeling oddly bereft, Rose reached for her knitting and said cheerily, 'Oh, I shall, don't you worry. Bye!'

'Roast beef?' Wandering into the kitchen, Rennie sniffed the air. 'Roast potatoes? Yorkshire pudding and gravy?' Taking the lid off the saucepans bubbling away on the hob, he looked disappointed. 'And carrots and broccoli. I'm not really in the mood for a roast.'

'Aren't you, pet? That's a shame.' Rose dried her hands on a towel and began taking plates down from the dresser. 'I can do you sausages and fried potatoes if you'd prefer – *oof.*'

'Rose!' Breaking into an enormous grin, Rennie swung her round in the air. 'It was a *joke.* How can you think I wouldn't be in the mood for one of your roasts?'

'Put me down,' squeaked Rose, clutching two dinner plates. 'You fool, how am I supposed to know when you're joking?'

'That's what I most love about you.' Lowering her to ground level, Rennie planted a noisy kiss on her forehead. 'You never do.'

'Only because you spend your whole life changing your mind about everything,' Rose scolded. 'Especially girlfriends. One minute they're great, the next minute you're bored to tears with them. Why wouldn't you be the same with roast dinners?'

'Girls are for fun,' said Rennie. 'A roast is for life.'

'Well, this one doesn't seem to be having much fun at the moment.' Rose took a slip of paper from the pocket of her Argyle cardigan and waggled it accusingly under his nose. 'Poor girl rang five times today. You can't keep your own phone switched off,' she chided, forcing Rennie to take the list of increasingly desperate messages from Nicole. 'If you don't want to see her any more, you have to tell her. Put her out of her misery, pet.'

As if Nicole were a small furry animal, thought Rennie. It wasn't kind to keep her hanging on when the situation was hopeless. The good thing was, he didn't have to squeeze her into a cat basket and take her down to the vet.

If he wanted, he could do it by text.

UR dmpd.

'Go on then,' said Carmen twenty minutes later. 'You ask her.'

'Me?' Rennie was helping himself to the world's best roast potatoes. He raised his eyebrows, double-checking with Nancy and Carmen. 'Now?'

Startled, Rose realised that they were all looking at her. 'Ask me what?'

'We don't want you to go back to Scotland,' Rennie told her. 'But if you *want* to go, we can't stop you.'

Rose put down her knife and fork. Her expression softening, she said, 'That's sweet of you, pet. I've had a wonderful holiday down here.'

'You don't have to leave,' said Rennie. 'We'd love it if you'd stay. This house wouldn't be the same without you in it.'

'Oh, but—'

'Rose, we don't know how we'd manage without you,' Carmen chipped in. 'You've cleaned the house. You cook brilliant meals. You're taking care of us. If you think you might like to stay, we'd be so happy. And we'd pay you, of course, to carry on doing everything you've been doing. You could give up your flat in Edinburgh. If you want. It's up to you.'

Rose gazed at her, then at Nancy. Finally she turned to Rennie.

'Is this another of your jokes?'

'No.' Rennie smiled, because only Rose could think it might be. 'We love you. None of us want you to leave.' Teasingly he added, 'Plus, we think we may starve to death without you.'

'Mum?' said Nancy. 'So what d'you think?'

Rose was unable to speak. She was unbelievably touched. The three of them had plotted this between them, but why? Had they any idea how

176

much she loved being here, *being useful*, and how much she'd been inwardly dreading going back to her old life?

'She doesn't want to,' Rennie declared.

'I'd love to stay.' Rose's voice quavered with emotion. 'If you're sure you want me.'

'Oh, we do.' Carmen grinned.

'I definitely want you to stay,' said Rennie. 'And there aren't many ladies I say that to.'

'Well, in that case, you're going to have to behave yourself.' Clearing her throat, Rose said briskly, 'Do as you're told.'

'Not the washing-up.' Rennie was appalled.

'Never mind the washing-up.' Rose gave him a severe, I-mean-it look. 'You're going to do the right thing and finish with that poor girl.'

Chapter 31

Rennie came downstairs an hour later. He found Rose alone in the kitchen scouring the washing-up bowl.

'Right, all done. I told Nicole I couldn't see her again.'

'Good boy.' Rose had her back to him.

'Not what she called me. Any leftover roast potatoes in the fridge?'

'Middle shelf, in the blue dish. Help yourself,' said Rose, still scouring away and sounding distracted.

'Hey, what's up?' Turning her round to face him, Rennie saw that her eyes were wet with tears. 'Oh God, Rose, don't cry. Did we force you to stay? Do you really hate us? Here, wipe your eyes.' He couldn't bear to see her upset.

'You fool, that's a tea towel,' Rose protested, half crying and half laughing at his well-meaning incompetence. 'And I'm crying because I've never been so happy. I love it here in Fitzallen Square. I love being here in this house with all of you. I love feeling *needed*. This is the very best thing that's ever happened to me.' Dragging a tissue out from the pushed-up sleeve of her blue cardigan, she wiped her eyes and said, 'Where are you off to, then? Somewhere nice?'

'I've been a good boy, you just said so yourself.' Rennie, freshly showered and changed into a dark suit and white shirt, flashed her a wicked grin. 'Now I'm going out to be bad. God, I'm glad I'm not a woman.' Shaking his head in disbelief, he said, 'Crying when you're sad is one thing. But doing it when you're *happy*, now that is just plain weird.'

Rose gazed down at the damp tissue in her hand, reminded of her brief conversation in the square with Marjorie. Had it only been this morning that she'd been putting on a brave face, pretending that she really didn't mind the prospect of leaving London?

'I'll have to go back and fetch the rest of my things. What'll I do with my furniture?'

'Keep what you want to keep, sell the rest.' Rennie shrugged and headed for the fridge. 'There's plenty of room here.'

178

This was true. The second-floor bedroom Carmen had given her was in fact larger than her entire flat in Edinburgh. 'Don't eat *all* the roast potatoes,' Rose chided. 'Save some for Carmen and Nancy.'

'I'm a growing boy. You wouldn't want me to waste away.'

'You're a greedy boy. And behave yourself tonight. Don't go breaking any more hearts,' Rose scolded.

'Save myself, you mean?' Rennie's green eyes glittered with amusement. 'Until the right girl comes along?'

'Why not? It's worth a try. Who knows, it may even do the trick.'

'Rose, I love you to bits and I'm sure you're absolutely right.' Having located his keys on the dresser, Rennie headed for the door. Over his shoulder he added with a wink, 'But *what if it doesn't?*'

As Rose was leaving the house the next morning, the glossy black front door of number sixty-two opened simultaneously. Turning to greet for the first time their left-hand side neighbours, Rose's mouth dropped open in surprise.

'Marjorie! Well I never, I had no *idea* you lived there!'

Marjorie stiffened, clearly taken aback and not thrilled to discover that the woman in whom she had in a moment of weakness confided yesterday was, literally, quite so close to home.

'Oh.' Her chin lifted in a gesture of defence. 'Hello.'

'Isn't that just typical?' Rose said happily. 'Neighbours all along and we didn't even know it.' Lowering her voice she said conspiratorially, 'How are things with your husband?'

Appalled, Marjorie glanced back at her closed front door, the tendons in her neck so tense they stood out like guy ropes. 'Very well, thank you. All sorted out.'

'Oh, I'm so pleased.' Rose doubted they were, but the woman was evidently reluctant to discuss the situation. 'Listen, I'm just off to the shops now, but if ever you fancy a cup of tea and a chat – well, you know where I am, pet.'

Marjorie looked at her as if she was mad.

'Edinburgh,' she said, startled. 'You'll be in Edinburgh.'

Rose beamed. 'Ah, but that's it, I won't be. Everything's changed now. I'm here to stay!'

If Marjorie had looked pale before, she was positively translucent now. Fear radiated from her pale eyes. Hastily collecting herself, she approached the black railings separating them and muttered through gritted teeth, 'Look, I only said those things yesterday because you told me you were going back to Scotland.'

'Oh.' Taken aback by her vehemence, Rose said, 'Well, I *was*.'

'But now you tell me you *aren't*. I confided in you because I didn't *know* you. And now,' Marjorie gestured angrily up at Carmen's house, 'I find out you're my next-door neighbour, that you're actually living with those . . . those dreadful *people*.'

'Oh no, no.' It was Rose's turn to be genuinely shocked. 'You can't say that. They aren't dreadful!'

'I most certainly can say it,' Marjorie retorted sharply. 'The girl's husband died of a drugs overdose. He was an alcoholic, took cocaine and heroin, and now his brother's moved in. Who needs people like that living next door to them? This is a respectable square—'

'Carmen's husband died three years ago,' Rose said firmly, 'and she loved him very much. You can't call Carmen a nightmare neighbour.'

Marjorie was defiant. 'What about the brother? He has long hair. He wears a *diamond earring*.' Her voice rose. 'He came home in a taxi at *four o'clock* this morning.'

'Really? I didn't know.' Meaningfully, Rose said, 'I was asleep.'

'And you can't tell me he doesn't take drugs too.'

'Well, I most certainly *can* tell you that,' Rose retorted, 'because Rennie's *never* taken drugs.' She was dimly aware that this was a ludicrous situation; only yesterday Marjorie had been confiding in her about her miserable marriage and she had been comforting her, squeezing her hand. Yet now here they were on the front steps of their respective multimillion-pound residences, practically having a stand-up fight. But having to listen to this woman criticise Carmen and Rennie – *when she didn't even know them* – was something Rose simply wasn't prepared to tolerate.

'He's one of those wild music types.' Marjorie's sniff registered her opinion of wild music types. 'They all do that kind of thing. If I were you, I'd think twice about staying in a house like that.'

If you were me you wouldn't be invited to stay, Rose thought furiously. Feeling her fists clenching deep in the pockets of her coat, she said tightly, 'Maybe you shouldn't criticise people you don't even kn—'

'What's this? What's going on here?' barked a male voice as the front door of number sixty-two burst open. The tall iron-grey man Rose recognised as Marjorie's husband was glaring at his wife.

The change in Marjorie was remarkable; she appeared to shrink before Rose's eyes, almost to cower away.

'Nothing, dear. Nothing.'

'I heard voices. You've been talking to someone.' His manner as clipped and bristly as his moustache, the man turned to Rose. 'And who are you?'

180

'Rose McAndrew. Carmen Todd's new housekeeper,' Rose replied pleasantly.

The man didn't attempt to shake her hand. He looked as if he'd never smiled in his life; wouldn't know how to go about producing something so irrelevant as a smile.

'What have you been talking about?' he demanded.

Simultaneously Rose said, 'Carmen,' and Marjorie blurted out, 'The weather.'

'Both,' Rose amended. 'Now if you'll excuse me, there's something I've forgotten.' Taking out her key, she pointedly turned her attention to getting back into the house. With a snort of disdain, Marjorie's husband retreated into his own hallway and slammed the front door shut.

'Listen,' Marjorie whispered, her face creased with anguish. 'I'm sorry. I shouldn't have said those things. Please . . . you won't say anything about, you know . . .'

The woman was clearly terrified of her bad-tempered husband. Rose, envisaging their home life, wondered if he beat her whenever she incurred his wrath.

'*Please*,' Marjorie begged. 'Promise me you won't.'

'Don't worry.' Rose shook her head, filled with pity for her. 'I won't breathe a word.'

Rennie was padding barefoot around the living room chatting on the phone to Ed, his manager, when Rose let herself back into the house. He ended his call and shook his head sorrowfully at her.

'Brawling in the street, Rose? I don't know, I really don't. Is that lady-like?'

'Now stop it. I wasn't brawling.' The living-room window, Rose noticed, was open an inch. 'I was just . . . introducing myself to the neighbours.'

'Ah, the Brough-Badhams. Brigadier Brough-Badham.' Rennie stiffened his spine and imitated the man's haughty, mouth-turned-down-at-the-corners grimace. 'And his lovely wife, the Honourable Marjorie.' His imitation of Marjorie was uncannily similar to that of her husband. 'She fancies the pants off me, you know.'

'I hate to be the one to break this to you,' said Rose, 'but I don't think she does.'

'Can't you just picture her peeling off that face like a rubber mask? For all we know, she could look like Claudia Schiffer underneath.'

Sometimes Rose despaired. She'd just told Marjorie – categorically – that Rennie didn't take drugs.

'OK, only joking,' said Rennie. 'We call them the Glums. And I did

181

happen to overhear the bit where you were defending us. That was very sweet.'

'Maybe if you tried being a bit more friendly,' said Rose. Heavens, what was she doing now, defending the other side?

'Can't.' Rennie shrugged. 'Hate them. Almost as much as they hate us. Do you know, when Spike and Carmen moved here, the Brough-Badhams started up a petition to get them out?'

'Why can't people just be nice to each other?' Perplexed, Rose said, 'Life would be so much easier if everyone just . . . got along.'

'Easier,' Rennie agreed with an unrepentant grin, 'but not nearly so much fun.'

Chapter 32

'All done.' Nancy held out the box containing the cake as Connor opened his front door. It was six o'clock on Friday evening and pregnant Pam's leaving party at the Lazy B was due to start at eight.

'Bring it on inside. Here, let me give you a hand.' As he took the pink and white striped box from her, Connor's hands brushed against her own and the by now familiar zapping sensation shot up Nancy's arms. Was this something she'd ever get used to?

'Yay! Let's see it.' Mia, clearing a space on the kitchen table, said bossily, 'Come on, Dad, take the lid off.'

Connor paused, looked at Nancy. 'What if I don't like it?'

'Don't worry. I'll just go away and quietly commit suicide.'

'Fine, but where would we get another cake at such short notice?'

'Oh, get on with it,' Mia exclaimed, briskly removing the lid. 'Bloody hell, Nancy, it's all broken.'

'*What?*' Nancy stopped gazing helplessly at Connor and spun round so fast she got a crick in her neck.

'Ha, got you.' Mia beamed at them both.

'Hey,' said Connor, studying the cake. 'That's amazing. You've done an incredible job.'

Praise from Connor was like warm honey trickling down her spine. Basking in the sensation, Nancy watched him examine the more intricate details of the cake. She wondered if putting on perfume to bring it over to his house had been a mistake.

Then she thought maybe not as Connor put an arm round her shoulders – yes, yes! – and said, 'You're a clever old stick, aren't you?'

The warm honey abruptly vanished. *Stick?* Clever old STICK? What kind of an endearment was *that* when it was at home?

'Ignore him.' Sensing her alarm, Mia said consolingly, 'It's just one of those stupid things Dad says. He called me that once. So I called him a fat old fart,' she remembered with satisfaction. 'That soon put a stop to it.'

'Please don't try that.' Connor turned to Nancy. 'I'm sorry, I just meant you were clever. You don't look a bit like a stick. Anyway, we'd better be getting ready.' He nodded at Mia. 'D'you have it?'

Mia patted her jeans jacket pockets, found what she was looking for.

Embarrassed, Nancy said hurriedly, 'I told you, I don't want any money.'

'It isn't money,' said Connor.

'Oh.'

'Here.' Mia handed Nancy a laminated card. 'Now you're a member of the Lazy B.'

Overwhelmed, Nancy took the card. 'You don't have to do this.'

'Hey, wasn't I saying just the other day that you should come along to the club?' Mia, whose idea it had been, was looking delighted with herself. 'Well, now you'll have to.'

Nancy turned the card over. Oh God. 'You really didn't have to do *this*.' Horrified, she gazed at the photograph of herself, purportedly there for identification purposes. This one, taken almost ten years ago, showed her with over-plucked eyebrows, truly hideous perm and the startled look of someone perched in a photo booth, unsure when the flash might be about to go off. Except that she hadn't been in a photo booth, she'd been at one of Spike and Carmen's parties.

'I asked Carmen yesterday for a picture of you,' Mia explained. 'See? All planned.'

Nancy said wryly, 'And to think she used to be my friend.' God, even her passport photo wasn't as awful as this.

'You can have another one taken at the club. We'll do you a replacement card,' Connor's tone was consoling. 'Hey, look on the bright side. At least you've improved with age.'

'Thanks.' Nancy forced herself to smile; he probably didn't mean to imply that these days she looked passable, whereas back then she'd been a *complete* dog.

'Anyway, I like curly perms, my aunties all used to have them.'

'Dad.' Mia gave him a pitying shake of the head. 'You aren't doing yourself any favours, you know.'

'Aren't I?' Connor turned to Nancy. '*Aren't* I? Am I getting it horribly wrong?'

'Now you happen to mention it,' said Nancy, 'yes.'

'Bugger, I've lost my blarney.' He clutched his forehead, looked tortured. 'I'm sorry. I don't know where it's got to.'

'Try looking down the back of your sofa,' Nancy suggested. 'When we lose anything, that's where it usually turns up.' Readying herself to leave she said, 'Anyway, thanks for the membership. Maybe I'll give the club a try over the weekend.'

'Come with us tonight,' Mia exclaimed. 'We'll be leaving here in half an hour. I can give you the guided tour, introduce you to people. And you'll see Pam getting her cake. Fancy that?'

Nancy hesitated, glanced at Connor to see his reaction.

'Of course you must come with us.' Connor clutched her arm. 'That's a great idea. Why didn't I think of it?'

'Probably because you're losing your marbles along with your blarney.' Mia flashed him a sunny smile. 'I'll be having to put you in a home soon.'

'How about it then, Nancy, are you free?' said Connor.

Nancy was having trouble concentrating; the electrical currents were still zip-zapping excitedly up and down her arm. Gathering herself, she said, 'I'm free.'

'Great.' Connor looked pleased.

Mia winked at her and Nancy blushed, suspecting that she and Connor had both just been expertly set up. Mia was clearly a girl with a plan.

It was ten o'clock and the bar at the Lazy B was bursting at the seams, Pam was still having her photograph taken with her much-admired cake and Nancy had met practically everyone who worked at the club. She had also been glared at from a distance by Sadie Sylvester, who evidently didn't trust her an inch and suspected her – heavens above, *surely* not! – of having her sights set minxily on Connor.

'Just ignore her,' Mia had breezily remarked. 'I do. Every so often I just ask people to pull the knives out of my back.'

Which wasn't as comforting as it might have been, given the killer looks Sadie was shooting them across the room.

Rejoining Nancy now, Mia said, 'Pam's shattered, I'm just going to call a cab for her. Have you seen Dad?'

'One of the members lost their locker key. He went to find the master,' said Nancy.

'I haven't even had time to show you around the rest of the club.' Mia knocked back her glass of orange juice and checked her watch. 'I had no idea there were going to be so many people here. So, you and Dad getting on OK?'

There was that knowing look again. Honestly, did Mia have any idea how embarrassing it was to be in this situation, set up by a meddling sixteen-year-old?

'I'm having a nice time. And you don't have to show me around,' said Nancy because Mia was clearly busy. 'I can do that any time.' Glancing down at her shoes she added, 'Maybe when I'm wearing something more appropriate.'

Mia disappeared to call the taxi firm and Nancy sipped her drink, shifting from one pencil-thin high heel to the other. Her feet were starting to hurt now. Four-inch stilettos wouldn't have been the ideal choice for exploring a fitness centre anyway. Sitting down and giving her aching feet a rest would be nice but a quick scan of the room revealed only one free seat and that was too close to Sadie Sylvester for comfort.

Determined not to look but sensing that Sadie's narrowed gaze was trained upon her like a sniper's rifle, Nancy headed in the direction of the bar instead. Within seconds, she smelled the overpoweringly heavy scent Sadie wore.

'I know exactly what you're up to,' Sadie announced. 'Getting all friendly with Mia. Offering to make cakes for Connor. Wheedling your way into his life, making yourself—'

'Actually,' Nancy turned to face her, 'I didn't offer to make the cake. Connor asked me to.'

'And now you're here, at Pam's leaving party. My God, talk about infiltration.' Sadie shook her head in mock admiration. '*And* I hear you're joining the club. Don't you worry that you might be making a bit of a fool of yourself?'

Cruel accusations were always painful to hear, Nancy discovered, particularly when there was more than a smidgen of truth in them.

Aloud she said, 'I don't know what you mean,' and saw Sadie's glossy red mouth curl with disdain.

'Oh, come on. Your husband had an affair, am I right? He's found someone else and you're desperate to do the same. My God, I bet you couldn't believe your luck when you found out you had Connor living next door to you. I mean, I'm not saying I *blame* you – let's face it, he's quite a catch – but there's such a thing as being too obvious.'

Oh hell, did it really show that much? Her heart thumping unpleasantly, Nancy said, 'Connor's just a friend.'

'Of course he is. As far as *he's* concerned,' Sadie drawled. 'The trouble is, your marriage hit the rocks and your confidence has taken a battering. So when a man comes along and starts being nice to you, you get all over-excited and think it's because he's romantically interested. Whereas in reality, that's just Connor's way. It means *nothing*,' she emphasised, her eyes glittering with a mixture of pity and triumph. 'So don't be fooled into thinking you're special, because you aren't.'

Chapter 33

The gym was more or less deserted; almost everyone had by this time given up exercising and gravitated towards the party downstairs. Nancy, clutching her impractical shoes, padded barefoot past the darkened aerobics studio – where she *wouldn't* be joining the classes run by Sulphuric Sadie – and began investigating the fitness equipment.

One of the rowing machines was occupied by a fit-looking student type with a Walkman clamped to his ears. Envious of his tanned legs, but not of those scarily bulging calf muscles, Nancy made her way over to the running machines and cross-trainers. A middle-aged woman with a huge bosom bouncing up and down inside a baggy pink T-shirt was puffing and panting her way up some kind of never-ending ladder.

'It's a Stairmaster,' she said breathlessly, greeting Nancy with a cheerful smile and sensing her bemusement. 'Ghastly, of course, but does wonders for your bum. It's like climbing mountains without the worry of slipping into a ravine and having to be hoisted out by Mountain Rescue. Thinking of joining the club, then?'

'Well, yes.' It was such a relief to talk to someone friendly again. 'I mean, I already have.'

'Oh, you'll love it. Jolly nice shoes, by the way.' Using a white towel to mop her perspiring face, the woman nodded at the stilettos Nancy was cradling like kittens. 'This is a great place. I was always joining gyms then giving up on them, but here's different. Have you met Connor yet?'

'Um . . . yes. Actually, he's my next-door neighbour.' Nancy prayed she wouldn't blush.

'Is he really? I say, lucky old you!' The woman beamed, her legs still pumping away. 'All I've got next door is a neurotic music teacher and her five yowling cats. Connor's a gem, isn't he? Half the women who come here are in love with him – whew, that's it, time's up!' Heaving a noisy sigh of satisfaction, she hit the Stop button and jumped down from the Stairmaster. 'Fifteen minutes, that's my lot. Now I can go and have a lovely glass of wine as a reward. Maybe see you in the bar,' she said

188

happily as she headed off for a shower. 'In case you don't recognise me with my clothes on, I'll be the one with the wonderfully toned bum.'

Nancy spent some time wandering around, investigating the mysteries of the various scary-looking machines. There was a row of exercise bikes that had computer games connected to them, requiring pedal power in order to function. There was a climbing wall with sticky-out hand and footholds that she could only too easily envisage herself falling off. The weight-lifting equipment was scary. A punchbag looked fun. There were hundreds of photographs pinned up around the walls depicting club members in a variety of poses. Smiling, Nancy spotted a jaunty photo of the woman she had just been talking to, labelled 'Magnificent Mags collects the Krispy Kreme Doughnut award for most enthusiastic exerciser of the week. Sadly, Mags won't be winning it again as she didn't offer prize-giver Connor O'Shea a single doughnut'.

There really weren't that many fitness clubs like the Lazy B. Nancy, thinking that she might like it here after all, wondered if Mags had a bit of a secret crush on Connor herself . . . Now, where did that corridor lead to, past the glass-fronted dance studio and off to the left?

The corridor led to the back stairs. A spiral staircase winding down to the ground floor would take her back to the party. Still clutching her shoes, Nancy began to descend the staircase, pausing only when she heard a voice she recognised.

Then a second voice.

She was almost directly above Connor's office, Nancy realised, glancing out of the window and getting her bearings. And the door to the office was open, enabling her to overhear every word of Connor's conversation with Mia.

'. . . you just can't go around ordering people to do things because *you* want them to happen.' Connor was sounding exasperated.

'I'm not ordering you, I'm just helpfully suggesting you invite her out to dinner,' Mia wheedled. 'Come on, Dad, I know she'd say yes. You'd have a great time.'

Three-quarters of the way up the spiral staircase, Nancy froze. A waft of smoke drifted up the stairwell, indicating that Connor had just lit a cigarette.

'Mia, give this a rest, will you? It isn't going to happen. Nancy's a nice person, I like her as a friend, but that's as far as it goes. For one thing, she's only just separated from her husband. And even if I *did* fancy her rotten, I wouldn't get involved because women in that situation are just too . . . vulnerable. It wouldn't be fair on Nancy, or on me.'

Nancy was barely able to hear him now; the buzzing in her ears was so loud she felt as if she'd been dragged underwater. What if she fainted and toppled down the staircase, landing in a heap outside Connor's office? Oh God, how was she going to get out of here without stumbling on the stairs?

'You don't fancy her at all?' Mia sounded accusing. 'I thought you *did*.'

'And you're only sixteen,' Connor retaliated, 'which just goes to show how much you know. Listen, Nancy's self-confidence has taken a knock. If I can make her feel that little bit better about herself, I will. But it doesn't *mean* anything. Basically, there are some girls you fancy and some you don't, and nothing anyone can do will change that. I'm not interested in Nancy, OK? She's not my type and she's never going to be my type, so can we please close this conversation and head on back to the party?'

'More fool you,' Mia said scornfully. 'You'd rather mess around with Sadie the human cyanide pill.'

'OK, now pay attention.' Clearly tiring of the argument, Connor's tone was brusque. 'You may have stopped me seeing someone I do like, but I'm damned if I'll let you bully me into seeing someone I don't.'

Nancy forced her legs to move. Clinging to the banister, she crept silently back up the spiral staircase. At least the stairs, made of steel rather than wood, didn't squeak and give her away.

Retreating back through the gym, she heard the student-type on the rowing machine singing along with his Walkman. Evidently thinking he was alone, he was warbling ambitiously along to REM. As she sneaked past him he closed his eyes and bellowed, 'Everybody hurrrrrts . . . sometiiiiime.'

Nancy quelled the urge to run up behind him and shove him off his rowing machine. That would hurt him. Jolly well serve him right for singing one of her favourite songs so hideously off-key.

'I'm getting really cross now,' Mia grumbled. 'I gave Marcus my Dolly Parton CD two hours ago and he *still* hasn't played it. Why do we have to listen to this boring old rubbish anyway?'

'It's not boring old rubbish, it's U2.' Connor found it hard to believe his own daughter had such tragic taste in music. 'And you're on your own with Dolly Parton.'

'But she's great! If Marcus would just *play* the CD, you'd—'

'We'd still hate it,' said Nancy, 'and there's nothing you can do to make us change our minds.'

Mia looked as if her favourite teddy bear had just punched her on the nose. Her expression wounded, she said, 'I thought you were my *friend*.'

'I am.' Nancy checked her watch. 'But you can't force me to like Dolly Parton.'

'Well said.' Delighted, Connor clapped her on the shoulder.

Just like Mia can't force you to like me, thought Nancy. Aloud she said, 'And now I have to go.'

'Oh, stay a bit longer,' Mia begged. 'If you hang on for another hour we can share a cab.'

'Thanks, but I'll head off now. It's been great. Bye.'

As Nancy headed for the exit, she held her head high. Inwardly she might be a cringing ball of disappointment and humiliation, but on the outside she was serene, ice-cool and in control. Nobody was going to know how she felt, and, on the bright side, at least she hadn't made a full-scale fool of herself.

OK, so eavesdroppers might never hear good of themselves, but sometimes it was worth it to hear the truth.

Sadie Sylvester, passing her in the doorway, said with a smirk, 'Home alone?'

Bitch. Silicone-breasted bitch. Flashing a sunny smile, Nancy said, 'Absolutely. You should try it some time. And you've got lipstick on your chin.'

'What are you doing?' Mystified, Nancy found Carmen stretched out across the navy sofa, sucking a pen and poring over a copy of *Time Out*.

Carmen pulled the end of the pen out of her mouth with a *plop* and said, 'Moving.'

'What?'

Sitting up, Carmen showed her the adverts she'd circled in Apartments to Let. 'I've made a few appointments. Will you come along with me after work tomorrow? Take a look at them?'

Nancy peeled off her coat and plonked herself down on the sofa next to Carmen. 'Why?'

Rennie, lying on his side on the floor watching *Citizen Kane*, said, 'She hates us all.'

'Not *all* of you.' Carmen stretched out one foot and prodded her toes against his jutting hipbone. 'Only the ones who won't let you watch what you want on TV because they just have to watch ancient films on video.'

Taking a closer look at the ads Carmen had ringed, Nancy said, 'Clerkenwell? Good grief, where's that?' Her head jerked up. 'Are you serious?'

'She's barking,' said Rennie, earning himself a kick. 'Ow. And cruel to flatmates.'

'Shut up,' Carmen told him, 'it's something I have to do.' She turned to Nancy. 'After the Joe thing. I never want to go through that again.'

'But you aren't really moving out?' Nancy was worriedly reading the ads for one-bedroomed flats in unglamorous locations.

'Of course not. Not properly moving out. But . . . OK, it's like with Nick and Annie from work.' Carmen waggled her hands and said falteringly, 'They're just so nice, and it's not that I fancy Nick or anything, *because I don't*, but I don't want them to know where I live, in case it, you know, spoils things between us. But I've been to their flat three times now,' she hurried on, 'and it's starting to get embarrassing because it's about time I invited them back to mine.'

'So you're going to rent one and pretend it's where you live?'

'Somewhere really grotty and horrible,' Rennie said with relish. 'With cockroaches the size of terriers.'

'I've lived in cheap flats before.' Carmen was defiant. 'So have you. They don't have to have cockroaches. You can still make them nice. Remember the first bedsitter Spike and I got together? Couldn't get cheaper than that.'

'The one with the rats in the cupboard under the kitchen sink? Oh yes, that was a palace. If that's the kind of place you're after, better buy yourself a pair of wellies,' said Rennie. 'Rats find it hard to chew through the rubber.'

'Do they find it easier to chew through videotapes of old Hollywood movies?' Carmen turned back to Nancy. 'So will you come along with me tomorrow?'

'Of course I will.' Nancy understood why Carmen needed to do this.

'Can I come too?' said Rennie.

'Oh yes, that'd be really helpful. Nobody would ever guess who Carmen Todd was if she turned up with Rennie Todd in tow. Now shut up and watch your stupid film, while I ask Nancy how she got on tonight at the club.'

'Great,' lied Nancy. 'Everyone was really nice. Well, apart from Silicone Sadie, obviously. I've got an appointment with one of the instructors on Sunday morning to have a fitness assessment and learn how to use the machines.'

There was no way in the world she could tell Carmen the humiliating truth about what had happened this evening, not with Rennie in the room.

'Sex,' Rennie announced from the floor. 'Trust me, that's all you need to keep fit.'

Tuh, thought Nancy, chance would be a fine thing.

Chapter 34

Sixteen B, Arnold Street, was the third flat they visited and Carmen knew at once that this was the one.

'Yes,' she said, gazing with satisfaction around the living room. 'This is it. It's perfect.'

Nancy was gazing worriedly up at the ceiling. 'Are you sure?'

OK, it wasn't perfect, but it suited Carmen's needs and wasn't completely grotesque. They were in a quiet backstreet of Battersea and the landlord had assured her that the neighbours kept themselves to themselves. The first-floor flat comprised a tiny kitchen, an even tinier bathroom, one bedroom and a living room that looked out over the street. The decor was tatty, with floral wallpaper peeling at the edges. The last person to have wielded a paintbrush appeared to have bought a job lot of tester pots and painted each floorboard a different colour. The window frames were rotting, the furniture was mismatched and shabby and bare bulbs dangled sadly from every light fitting. But there was a new white bathroom suite, which was a comfort, and the kitchen was reasonably clean. With a bit of luck there wouldn't be rats lurking in the cupboard under the sink.

Nancy was still peering in fascination at the multi-stained ceiling. 'It's like a map of Europe up there. Look, there's Spain. And there's a mushroom!'

It wasn't a mushroom, it was a frilly-edged patch of fungus.

'I'll give the whole place a proper clean,' Carmen said happily. 'Buy some lampshades and rugs, make it homely. It'll be great.' She went through to the kitchen, where the landlord was reading an old *Evening Standard* and smoking a cigarette. 'I'll take it.'

He yawned. 'Five hundred quid deposit and first month's rent in advance.'

Carmen nodded and signed the rental agreement he spread out in front of her. She handed over the money in cash and watched the man's bald head gleam in the reflected light from the bare bulb directly above him

as he wrote out a receipt. He lived downstairs and seemed entirely unin-
terested in his new tenant, which suited Carmen down to the ground.

Finally he passed her the front door keys and they shook hands.

'And keep the noise down,' he said tetchily. 'You don't look noisy, but
you never can tell. Any racket and you'll be out on your ear. Got that?'

'Got it. And in return I'd appreciate total privacy,' said Carmen pleasantly. 'I won't be living here full-time. In fact I may not be staying here
much at all. But when I *am* here, and friends come to visit, I don't want
them to know that. Basically, you don't even need to speak to them.'

The landlord eyed her with suspicion. 'You on the game?'

'No. And I'm not a drug dealer.' Carmen smiled. 'It's just . . . for
personal reasons.'

'I don't want any trouble. No police, no ambulances screaming up the
street.' He wagged a plump warning finger at her and repeated, 'I won't
have trouble in this house.'

'I'll be the quietest tenant you ever had. There won't be any trouble,'
said Carmen. 'I promise.'

'He thinks you're married and having an affair,' said Nancy. 'That's why
he went on about police and ambulances. He's worried that your jealous
husband might find out and come storming round with a shotgun.'

They had found a quiet table in the Queen's Head, on the corner of
Arnold Street. A traditional working-class pub, it made a nice change
from the trendy, done-up-to-the-nines wine bars of Chelsea. Carmen,
tearing open a packet of smoky bacon crisps with her teeth, said, 'If Spike
could see what I was doing, he'd laugh his head off. Renting a flat just
so I can pretend to be poor. Do you think I'm barking mad?'

'Not really.' Innocently Nancy said, 'Why don't you tell me a bit more
about Nick?'

Carmen's eyes darted guiltily to her glass of red wine. 'Nick?'

'Nick-from-work. Nick-and-Annie Nick. The Nick you're doing all of
this for,' Nancy reminded her, 'despite not finding him even remotely
attractive.'

'Oh, that Nick.' Taking a huge gulp of wine, Carmen spilled some
down the front of her orange T-shirt.

'The one you thought wasn't single, but now it turns out he is. And
you don't fancy him, he's just a really nice person you enjoy being with.'

'He is. I do. He's a *friend*,' Carmen protested, mopping at her front
with a tissue. 'And you have an evil mind.'

'Excuse me, can we just cast our minds – evil or otherwise – back a bit? Remember when we used to walk through the park on our way home from school and Spike Todd used to try to run us over on his pushbike? And he used to tease you about your haircut?'

'Witch,' said Carmen.

'And the next thing we knew, he's got you riding around on the back of his bike and you're laughing together and going to his house to listen to him play his guitar,' Nancy continued remorselessly. 'But when I asked you what was going on, you said, "Oh nothing, don't be daft, Spike's just a *friend*."'

'I've finished my drink.' Carmen held up her empty glass. 'Your round.'

'So would Nick be *that* kind of friend?'

'Shut up. I'm embarrassed.'

Nancy pulled a face. 'Let me tell you, you don't know the meaning of the word embarrassed. I had Sadie at the club last night telling me what a show I've been making of myself over Connor.'

'Oh well, don't take any notice of *her*.' Carmen gestured dismissively with her bag of crisps. 'She's just jealous.'

Which wasn't as reassuring as: Of *course* you haven't been making a show of yourself. Nancy said with trepidation, 'Have I? Oh God, has it been glaringly obvious?'

'Nooo, not *glaringly*.' Carmen was consoling. 'I mean, *I* can tell you like him, because I know you. But it's not as if you've been twirling your bra around your head and purring at him like Eartha Kitt. Anyway, men are so thick that if you aren't a tiny bit obvious, they'll never cotton on to the fact you like them.'

Oh hell. Nancy's skin prickled with shame.

'Anyway, forget Sadie,' Carmen went on. 'She's been dumped by Connor and isn't happy about it, that's the only reason she had a go. But he's a free agent now, and you get on brilliantly with Mia, so there's abso-lutely *no* reason why you and Connor—'

'OK, I haven't told you the other embarrassing thing that happened last night. I overheard him and Mia talking in his office. Mia was saying pretty much the same thing. It isn't going to happen.'

'But—'

'No, really, it's *never* going to happen. I heard what Connor said.' Nancy shuddered at the memory and glugged down her wine. 'He doesn't fancy me and that's that. Really, nothing there. I'm a nice person, of course. He likes me as a friend. But that's as far as it goes. I'm not the kind of girl he'd ever get involved with, because I'm not his type. Because basically, as far as Connor's concerned, I'm just a *clever old stick*.'

Oops, she hadn't meant to raise her voice that much. The pub had fallen silent. Even the group of teenagers clustered around the pool table had stopped playing. How to announce to the world that you really were a sad and lonely woman.

Obligingly, one of the teenagers called over, 'Don't worry, love, I'd give you one.'

Over at the bar, a middle-aged man said, 'I wouldn't say no to being beaten by a stick.'

Another of the teenagers began tapping his friend's rear with a snooker cue, while his friend pulled Britney-type faces and bellowed, 'Hit me, baby, one more time.'

So much for friendly local pubs. Carmen looked at Nancy.

'Shall we not bother with that other drink?'

Naturally, everyone went, 'Ooh,' and 'Ow,' and hilariously clutched their backsides as Carmen and Nancy squeezed their way past them out of the pub.

On the pavement, Nancy exhaled slowly and said, 'Thank goodness we went there. I feel so much better now.'

'They were just having a bit of fun.' Carmen gave her arm a squeeze. 'I'm sorry about Connor.'

'Life goes on.' Nancy had already mentally steeled herself. 'It would've been nice, but never mind. Connor can't help having no taste when it comes to girls. Anyway, ready now?'

'Ready for what?'

'To admit that there might secretly be a bit of a spark going on between you and Nick?'

Carmen smiled. She knew when she was beaten. 'OK. Maybe a bit of one.'

'A baby spark,' Nancy said encouragingly.

'A sparkette,' Carmen agreed, blushing under the streetlamp. 'God, but what am I turning into? No men for three years, not a single hint of a man, and now all of a sudden I'm turning into Zsa-Zsa Gabor. First Joe, now Nick . . . I mean, is it my hormones, d'you think? Are they rampaging out of control?'

'I think they're just waking up after a long, long sleep. I think it's great news.' Winding her purple scarf round her neck, Nancy said, 'I especially think it's a good job I got you away from the poor defenceless boys in that pub.'

Chapter 35

Janice Hazzard was intensely proud of her liposuctioned legs. She loved them almost as much as she loved Zac.

'Bit shorter, darling. Up a bit, up a bit . . . yes, there, that's it. Got to give the fans what they want to see, haven't we? Ooh, mind where you're putting that hand, you naughty boy!'

'Janice, I'm pinning the hem.' Zac rolled his eyes at the thought that he might be deliberately groping Janice's thighs. 'If you don't keep still, you're going to get hurt.'

'He's a genius,' Janice smugly informed Nancy. 'Nobody else designs dresses like Zac Parris.'

Well, that was certainly true. Janice was currently wearing an almost finished emerald-green creation with one long narrow sleeve and one voluminous batwing one, with a fuchsia-pink maribou trim around the plunging neckline and triangular mirrors appliquéd across the bodice. The skirt, short and tight, emphasised Janice's generous bottom. Her shoes were fuchsia pink with emerald-green heels. She looked like a drag queen with a sense of adventure.

Nancy, having brought in two cups of coffee, wondered how many make-up remover pads Janice got through each night, taking off that much slap.

'Is the coffee made with Evian?' Janice was peering suspiciously into her cup. 'I only drink coffee made with Evian.'

'Give it a rest, darling.' Zac spoke through a mouthful of pins, like a ventriloquist. 'You aren't being interviewed for *Hello!* now. It's tap water and you can like it or lump it.'

'He's so rude,' trilled Janice, ruffling Zac's hair as he crouched at her feet.

'Now I know how Doreen feels.' Ducking away, Zac shook his hair back into place.

'Oh, do stop whingeing. D'you want to come along to this premiere with me or not?' Winking at Nancy, Janice said, 'I could always invite that pretty boy of yours instead.'

Janice was in her sixties now. In *the* sixties, she had been a gloriously pretty young actress with a bawdy laugh and an insatiable appetite for men who treated her badly. As she had grown older, the men had become younger and more adept at relieving Janice of her earnings. She had continued to work like a trouper, basically by becoming one of the nation's more downmarket treasures.

An endearing mixture of vanity, vulnerability and self-deprecating humour had won Janice new fans over the years and she never minded being made fun of. Five years ago she had unexpectedly married the septuagenarian multimillionaire Malcolm Hazzard, a man as reclusive as his new wife was outgoing. Even more unexpectedly, the marriage appeared to be a success. Janice had famously announced to the press that after years of being the older woman, becoming the younger woman was the biggest ego boost of all time and she couldn't imagine for the life of her why she'd never done this before. There really was nothing nicer than being spoiled rotten by an adoring, appreciative, hugely wealthy man.

'There, all done.' Having finished pinning, Zac stood up and allowed Janice to survey herself in the full-length mirror. 'And leave Sven out of it; he's my pretty boy, not yours.'

'Scared he'd prefer me, is that it?' Janice wagged a teasing finger at him; these days she collected gay acquaintances like other people collected china figurines – they entertained her, flirted with her and posed no risk to her marriage. 'Oh yes, this'll knock 'em dead.' Admiring her reflection, she struck a few 'Hello boys' poses. 'Perfect, darling, you've done it again. Now, I'll send someone over to pick it up when it's finished. Malcolm and I are off to New York for a couple of days, but I'll speak to you before the end of the week . . . ooh, I say, those are new!'

Her darting gaze had alighted on a couple of bags protruding from a box in the corner of the workroom. Fetching them to show her, Zac said proudly, 'I've just finished working on them. They're for next season's collection.'

'They're the business.' Janice ran an admiring manicured hand over the pink satin and suede shoulder bag lined with lilac shot silk. 'How much?'

'For you, five fifty.'

'I'll have this one, and this one.' Janice lovingly smoothed the second bag, turquoise lined with sunset-orange silk. 'And can you do one the colour of a Cadbury's chocolate wrapper? Purple with hot pink inside?'

199

Without missing a beat Zac said, 'Darling, you're my favourite kind of shopper.'

'Just send the bill to Malcolm. God, I *love* saying that.' Janice beamed at Nancy. 'Before I met my husband you can't imagine how broke I was. Couldn't even afford Top Shop!'

At lunchtime, Zac took Doreen out for a walk. Upstairs in his flat, Nancy heated the cartons of wild mushroom risotto from his favourite delicatessen and put together a salad. She enjoyed their lunches in Zac's kitchen. When summer came, they would eat out on his roof terrace. For a single man with no family money behind him, Zac had a beautiful flat.

By one thirty he and Doreen were back. Nancy served up the risotto and said, 'Can I ask a really impertinent question?'

'No.'

'Oh.' Bum.

'*Joking.*' Zac grinned. 'Hey, I love impertinent questions. About me and Sven, right?'

'Yuk, *no.*' Zac was still besotted with Sven. 'Actually, it's about this place.'

Zac broke off a chunk of bread. 'And?'

'Well, I just wondered. Your dad worked on the docks. You've told me yourself how hard it can be to keep a business like yours afloat. But you have the shop downstairs, and this flat, and we're here in the middle of poshest Chelsea . . .'

'So you're wondering how the heck I manage to pay the bills,' Zac finished for her. 'Well, that's easy. I'm actually a high-class prostitute.'

'No you're not.' Nancy pulled a face at him. 'You're too ugly.'

'Flattery'll get you everywhere. OK,' Zac admitted, 'I was left money when my godmother died. She was my mother's best friend and didn't have any family of her own. Wanda, her name was. She was a stylish lady, liked fashion, encouraged me when I told her I wanted to become a designer. Of course that was when I was thirteen.' He broke off another piece of bread and fed it to Doreen. 'So there you go, that's how I managed to afford the down payment on this place. All thanks to my fairy godmother – ooh, let me phone Sven before I forget.'

As if *that* was likely. Nancy watched him key in Sven's number, listen expectantly for a few seconds then visibly deflate when the answering service kicked in.

'Hi, you, me here!' Zac adopted his buoyant, haven't-a-care-in-the-world manner in order to leave a message. 'All set for tonight? Pick you up at eight. And I'll bring that yellow shirt, OK? See you later, alligator! Bye-ee!'

Nancy helped herself to more risotto.

'Was that all right?' Zac raised anxious eyebrows at her.

'Fine.'

'Not too over the top? Just nice and casual?'

'Maybe leave out the alligator next time,' said Nancy.

'It was only meant to be a bit of fun. Oh God, does it make me sound ancient?'

'You aren't ancient. Eat your lunch and stop being such a worry-guts.'

'It's just that his phone's switched off. Why would his phone be switched off?' Sounding fretful, Zac checked his watch. 'It's quarter to two. Why would anyone switch off their phone at a quarter to two?'

'He probably went to the cinema. What was the name of your godmother?'

Zac looked blankly at her for a moment. 'What? Wanda, I told you. Why?'

'Just forgot, that's all. Now, are you going to finish that risotto or shall I?'

Nancy hadn't forgotten; she was checking if Zac had. If that was the official line, she wasn't going to argue with him. But there was definitely something about his story that didn't ring true.

'Is this a fashion statement?' Nick nodded at Carmen's hair as she arrived at the shelter on Wednesday morning.

Since her dark spiky hair was anything but styled, Carmen said, 'Sorry?' Had she forgotten to comb it after getting out of the shower?

'Those turquoise bits. Mainly at the back.' Helpfully Nick pointed them out. 'And some at the side here. I like them.'

'Oh.' Patting her head and feeling the stiffened spikes, Carmen said, 'I've just moved into a new flat. Been redecorating.'

'Really? Hey, you should have said. I'm a demon with a paintbrush.'

'Demon being the operative word,' Annie chimed in. 'He can't bear the thought of wasting paint, so anything left over has to go *somewhere*. Which, in case you'd been wondering but were too polite to ask, is why our bathroom ceiling is red.'

'Ignore her, she has no sense of adventure. Much left to do, or have you finished?'

'Well, I've done the bathroom and the kitchen.' Guessing what was coming, Carmen pretended she hadn't. 'Still got the living room and bedroom to go.'

Nick said easily, 'So you could do with a hand? I'm free tonight.'

A warm Ready Brek glow spread through her stomach. 'If you're sure, that'd be . . . great.' It *would* be great. She hadn't left the turquoise paint streaks in her hair on purpose, but if she'd thought of it she would have.

'Where's the new flat?'

'Arnold Street, Battersea,' said Carmen.

'Right, that's settled.' Nick rubbed his hands together in let's-get-painting fashion. 'We'll go straight there from here.'

'Don't say I didn't warn you,' said Annie.

Chapter 36

'Hey, you did the right thing. This is a pretty nice place.'

Was this perverse? As she showed Nick around, Carmen realised that she felt ridiculously proud of her scruffy little flat in a way that she never could about the house in Fitzallen Square.

'See? Here's the bathroom. There was some mould up on that wall, but I scrubbed it off and bleached it.' She pointed to the painted-over stain. 'And down there in that corner I filled the hole with scrunched up newspaper and covered it with Polyfilla.'

'Good work.' Nick ran his fingertips appreciatively over the repair, then straightened up. 'Right, let's get this show on the road, shall we? You can put the kettle on, then tell me where to start. And I promise not to paint any ceilings red.' Squeezing behind her to get out of the bathroom, he rested his hands on her shoulders and whispered, 'Unless you really want me to.'

The next three hours flashed by. Carmen didn't know where the time had gone; one minute they'd been pulling on oversized painting shirts and prising the lids off tins of emulsion; the next minute it was nine thirty, the living room was finished and her stomach was rumbling like a tank.

'I can't believe we've done four walls in less than three hours.' Perched on the stepladder, Carmen gazed down at Nick. 'Now you're the one with paint in your hair. Pistachio green.' Tapping his head with her brush she added playfully, 'And parma violet.'

'Big mistake. *Big* mistake.' Nick sighed as he gripped each side of the ladder. 'Never think you can get away with *anything* like that when you're the one stuck up there like a parrot on a wibbly wobbly perch.'

'*Waaah*,' squealed Carmen as he gave the stepladder an experimental shake. Instinctively her arms shot out and she slithered down, half stumbling against Nick's chest.

'See what I mean? Now you've got paint on your nose.' Nick's mouth twitched as he wiped the bridge of her nose. 'And you're all speckled, like an egg. Blimey, was that your stomach again?'

'You must be hungry too.' Carmen was conscious of how close to each other they were. 'I haven't got any food in yet. How about a takeaway?'

Nick was gazing down at her. Carmen felt her heart leaping like an antelope being chased by a wildebeest. They had spent the last three hours talking non-stop, yet all of a sudden she was unable to utter a single word.

The silence lengthened between them as she waited for Nick to slide his fingers through her hair and kiss her. He wanted to, she knew he did. And she definitely wanted him to, so why wasn't it happening? What was he waiting for? Why didn't he just *get on with it*?

Then she realised that Nick was deliberately leaving it up to her. She had to be the one to make the move. OK, well, she could do that. Reaching up, breathing in the mingled smells of peppermint and paint, she brushed her mouth against his. Then pressed more firmly, before relaxing into the kiss.

Oh *yes*.

Finally, Nick pulled away. Smiled. 'So. I've wanted to do that for quite a while.'

Recklessly Carmen said, 'Me too.'

'It might have been more romantic if you could have stopped your stomach rumbling.'

'I know. Sorry about that.'

'Stomachs are like small children. No sense of occasion. They don't like to be ignored.'

'We'll get a takeaway.' Nodding decisively, Carmen wiped her hands on her paint-spattered shirt. 'There's an Indian just around the corner in Donovan Street.'

When the doorbell went, Carmen jumped as if a spider had just crawled out of her cleavage. Who on earth was that?

'Nervous,' Nick observed with amusement. 'Don't tell me you forgot to mention your jealous husband.'

Downstairs Carmen found Nancy on the doorstep, pink-cheeked with the cold and clutching a plastic food container. 'Surprise! Thought you might be hungry.'

'Or you thought you might be nosy.' Carmen wasn't fooled for a minute. When she'd rung Nancy earlier to tell her she would be coming straight here from work, she had added that Nick would be giving her a hand tonight.

'Nosy? Me? How can you even think that? Is he here?'

'No. Left an hour ago.'

Nancy's face fell. 'Bugger.'

'Yes, he's here.' Breaking into a grin, Carmen ushered her into the cramped hallway. 'Just don't be too obvious, OK?'

'I won't. I'll be wonderfully discreet. You've got paint on your nose, by the way.'

Remembering the tender way Nick had attempted to wipe it off, Carmen said happily, 'I know.'

Upstairs she said, 'This is Nancy, my oldest friend. Nancy, this is Nick from work.'

'Hi,' Nancy beamed. 'I come bearing shepherd's pie, made by my mother. Carmen told me she was so busy painting last night she forgot to eat.'

Carmen knew at once they'd get along. Nick had that easy-going air about him that enabled him to strike up an instant rapport with the most difficult-to-get-along-with visitor to the shelter. Viewing him as if she were Nancy, she saw the messed-up hair, big nose, kind eyes and execrable dress sense. Tonight Nick was wearing a blue and grey striped sweater with holes in the elbows, a green and brown checked shirt and scruffy khaki combats. She knew he'd bought the sweater and shirt from Oxfam; cutting-edge fashion wasn't a priority as far as Nick was concerned, and why should it be?

All the same, she was glad he wasn't wearing the Mr Blobby T-shirt.

'Shepherd's pie, my favourite. And to think we were about to grab a takeaway.' Nick beamed. 'I'm even more pleased to meet you now.'

'You've done all this.' Nancy gazed around the finished room. 'It's looking great.'

'Wait until tomorrow, we'll be in the bedroom then.' Realising too late what he'd just said, Nick hastily backtracked. 'I mean, um, decorating it.'

Sensing the chemistry in the room, Nancy hid a smile. 'I'm just going to stick this in the oven. There's apple crumble too.'

'Can it get any better? Annie's going to be so jealous. I'd better wash all this stuff before it goes solid.'

Nancy watched him lope through to the bathroom with the rollers, trays and paintbrushes. Nudging Carmen, she whispered, 'He's *nice*.'

Carmen's eyes were bright with long-overdue happiness as she clutched Nancy's arm and whispered back, 'I *know*.'

When his brother had died three years ago, Rennie had taken care of Carmen. During the first few days, when she had been paralysed with grief, he had moved into the house in Fitzallen Square and dealt with everything. The funeral had needed to be arranged, a task that had been beyond Carmen. Journalists and mourning fans had congregated outside on the pavement and it had been necessary to organise security to keep them under control. When the initial shock and numbness had begun to wear off, Carmen had been tortured by the thought that she should have been able, somehow, to prevent Spike's death. Night after night Rennie had sat up with her, rocking her in his arms, comforting her and allowing her to weep the worst of the overwhelming feelings of guilt out of her system. He had loved his brother too. Their grief had been shared. But, back then, he'd known that Carmen was the one who most urgently needed support. And he had given it to her, to the best of his ability.

It was a habit that had stuck. Now, three years later, Carmen was back on her feet and capable of living her own life again. A normal life, with all that entailed. Rennie, lying on his bed smoking a cigarette, knew that he should be taking a mental step back now. He should allow her to make her own decisions, her own mistakes.

He'd already interfered once, with Joe – whom he'd never entirely trusted – and that had turned out to be the *right* thing to do. But Carmen hadn't appreciated it, to the extent that she'd now rented this damn flat in Battersea and was conducting her love life away from his critical gaze.

Rennie sighed. He didn't mean to be critical, it was just that old habits died hard. And now, hot on the heels of Joe, she was plunging into a new relationship from which he was entirely excluded.

The phone rang in his jeans pocket. Levering it out and exhaling a plume of smoke, Rennie said, 'Yes?'

'Hi! Sheryl!'

He frowned. His name wasn't Sheryl and he was fairly sure he didn't sound like a girl. 'Excuse me?'

'It's Sheryl, remember? Last night at the Met Bar?'

Taking another drag of his cigarette, Rennie recalled the bouncy terrier-like blonde who had approached him at the bar and spent a good twenty minutes telling him how much she idolised Red Lizard.

'Right. I remember. And?'

'I gave you my number.' Sheryl sounded as if she was pretending to pout. 'I've been waiting all day for you to ring, but you haven't.'

Clearly the shy and retiring type. After enthusing about his band, Rennie recalled, she had gone on to list all the Premiership footballers she had *been out* with. In the euphemistic sense of the word, no doubt. How had she put it? Oh yes: 'I mean, it's not as if I even like football that much, but they're just such great lads, aren't they? Really, like, fantastic company!'

Not to mention wonderful conversationalists, thought Rennie. What might they have discussed? Proust? Third World debt? The Man Booker shortlist?

'So?' Sheryl demanded when he didn't reply. 'Fancy meeting up? I'm free today.'

'You gave me your number. I didn't give you mine.' Rennie frowned. 'How did you get hold of it?'

Giggling, Sheryl said, 'When that ugly girl asked for your autograph, your phone was on the bar next to your drink. I just had a quick peep.'

Bloody hell. He'd turned away for, what, less than twenty seconds? And in that time this predatory female had investigated the contents of his own phone.

'Wouldn't you class that as an invasion of privacy?' As he asked the question, Rennie idly wondered if the girl would have turned out to be a nicer person had she not been born with striking good looks. If hanging out at the Met Bar blatantly propositioning celebrities hadn't been a viable option, might she have settled for less and ended up leading a happier, more contented life instead?

'Look, I really fancy you,' said Sheryl. 'I'd like to see you again, that's all. And I promise you, I'm a great lay.' Persuasively she added, 'Everyone says so.'

Rennie blew a series of smoke rings up at the ceiling. Then he sighed.

'Not interested, thanks. Don't call this number again.'

'*But*—'

'Goodbye.' He hung up.

Silence. Stubbing out his cigarette, Rennie stood up and went over to the window. It was a grey, cold day and he had just turned down the opportunity to spend the afternoon in bed with a pneumatic girl whose immodesty knew no bounds. Was this what it was like to grow old? Would he be buying himself sheepskin slippers next?

There was nobody out in the square this lunchtime. The house was empty too. Carmen and Nancy were both at work. Rose, no longer a visitor to Chelsea but a bona fide resident, had trotted off to get herself registered at the local health centre. From there, she was heading over to Battersea to inspect Carmen's new flat and, no doubt, clean it to within an inch of its life. When Rennie had offered to go along with her, Rose had looked at him pityingly.

'You great daftie, you'd ruin the whole thing,' she'd chided. 'Carmen's taken the place because she wants to be *normal*. Now, I won't be back until tea time but there's a nice fish pie in the fridge so you'll not starve, pet . . .'

Now, resting his hands on the window ledge and listening to the silence, Rennie wondered what on earth the point was of turning down an offer of wild sex from an undeniably attractive admirer when there wasn't anyone around to hear him do it.

Had he made a mistake? How else was he going to spend the rest of the day? Well, there was always other stuff he *could* do, like getting his brain into songwriting mode and coming up with ideas for the next album, whenever *that* was likely to happen.

Boring.

Twenty minutes later, Rennie checked his phone and rang a number. Slightly despising himself, he waited until it was answered then said, 'Hi, it's Rennie. Can we meet up?'

Chapter 37

The return of the bitingly cold weather had brought more visitors than usual to the shelter. In the recreation room every chair was occupied, the TV was blaring and at least a dozen regulars were crowded around the refectory table where a rowdy game of Trivial Pursuit was in progress. A cheer went up from one of the teams as their dice-thrower rolled a six.

'Piece of cake,' bellowed Charlie, who was eighty-two. 'We're up for a piece of cake! OK, Art and Literature. Concentrate now, lads, concentrate.' His hands as he rubbed them together made a rasping noise like sandpaper.

Baz, sitting opposite him, pulled out a card and cleared his throat importantly.

'Who wrote the novel *The Mill on the Floss*?'

Pandemonium broke out.

'Charles Dickens!'

'Nah! That posh old bird with the eyelashes. Barbara Cartland.'

'Jeffrey Archer, wasn't it?' said Charlie.

'Jackie Collins, she's got eyelashes. I dunno, would you call her posh?'

'She's not posh,' Charlie remonstrated. 'She wears leopardskin. Do you ever see Her Majesty the Queen wearing leopardskin? No you don't. And that's because she's posh.'

'Madonna writes books.' Alf, barely visible behind the cloud of smoke billowing from his pipe, said confidently, 'I reckon Madonna's the answer.'

'What's a Floss when it's at home, anyway? I've never heard of a Floss,' grumbled Charlie.

'There's all sorts. Candy floss. Dental floss. Don't you know what dental floss is?'

Charlie cackled with laughter. 'Ain't had teeth for forty years, have I? What would I be doing with dental floss? Hey, Nick, give us a hand here, lad. Who wrote *The Mill on the Floss*?'

'I'm Switzerland.' Nick was busy clearing the table of mugs. 'Strictly neutral. Doesn't Harry know?'

'Harry? Any ideas?' Charlie gave the middle-aged man next to him a nudge. Harry looked up from the battered Mills and Boon novel he'd been absorbed in and said quietly, 'What?'

'*The Mill on the Floss*, lad. Who wrote it?'

'George Eliot,' Harry muttered.

'Never heard of him. Sure about that?'

Harry rolled his eyes. '*Yes.*'

'Then why didn't you say so?' The thing about Harry was he seldom *bothered* to speak, but when he did he was always right. 'George Eliot!' Charlie declared with confidence and a great roar of triumph went up from his team as Baz threw down the card in disgust.

Carmen had finished mopping the floor. Harry, evidently finding the noise too much for him, left the table and settled himself on one of the chairs pushed against the wall at the far end of the room in order to read his paperback in peace. Another of the chairs was occupied by a new visitor to the shelter. Grubby and dishevelled, with rheumy grey eyes and a matted beard, he was probably in his forties, though it was never easy to tell. He had the nose of a hardened drinker and smelled strongly of beer. He'd barely spoken to Nick when he'd shuffled through the door an hour ago, refusing an offer to have his clothes washed and dried for him and accepting only a mug of coffee. Since arriving, he had smoked several cigarettes and silently observed the goings-on in the recreation room. Carmen was used to this kind of behaviour. New visitors were always welcomed, never interrogated. They preferred to stay in the background and make up their own minds about the shelter. If they decided it was too quiet, too chaotic or too smoky, or that the staff were too bossy or the food not to their taste, they would shuffle out and never be seen again.

'Carmen, Carmen, over here!' Charlie was energetically patting the empty chair beside him. 'Harry's buggered off, the bugger. You'll have to take his place.'

'Let me just put my mop and bucket away.' Carmen decided half an hour of Trivial Pursuit wouldn't hurt.

'Here, I'll take them.' Relieving her of the task, Nick added in a low voice, 'Don't eat the biscuits. Baz just sneezed all over them.'

Carmen inwardly squirmed with pleasure as Nick's hand brushed against hers. 'I'll try to remember that.'

'I think you've got an admirer, by the way. New chap over there. Can't take his eyes off you.'

'Really?' Carmen didn't look over.

Nick grinned and murmured, 'Who can blame him? He's got good taste.'

'Oh, bloody hell, pink. Entertainment.' Charlie snorted in disgust. 'Get yourself sat down, girl, and put your clever head on.'

Baz, reading aloud from the card, said, 'What was the name of the sixties recording artist, the Singing Nun?'

'Easy. Julie Andrews,' Charlie said promptly. 'Always fancied her.'

'Mother Teresa,' cried one of the older members of the team.

Alf, sucking noisily on his pipe and scratching his unwashed head, said ponderously, 'I reckon it's Madonna.'

Annie was tidying up in the kitchen with one of the other helpers. Having put away Carmen's mop and bucket, Nick headed back through to the recreation room and made his way over to where Harry and the new visitor were sitting. Taking the empty chair between them, he said easily, 'So how are you doing, Harry? Chest better now?'

Harry nodded and carried on reading his Mills and Boon.

'Good book?'

'Very good. Driving narrative. Plenty of emotional tension. Nice plot twist in Chapter Seven.'

'Excellent.' Nick watched Harry's hands begin to tremble as he closed the battered paperback. 'Ever thought of writing a book yourself, Harry?'

'Oh, I have. I mean I *did*,' Harry said quietly.

Crikey. Intrigued, Nick said, 'You actually wrote a book?'

'Several.'

'Harry, that's fantastic. I'm impressed.' As he spoke, it occurred to Nick that Harry might be doing an Albert, that he could be about to announce that he was, in fact, J. K. Rowling.

But Harry simply shook his head. 'Don't worry. No need to be impressed.'

'Hey, you're wrong,' Nick insisted. 'Just *writing* a book is an achievement in itself. It doesn't matter if you don't get published, you've still—'

'I did get published, though. That was the problem.' Harry turned his head to look properly at Nick. 'I wrote a novel and sold it to a publisher. The editor took me out to lunch and told me how fantastic the book was. He said it would be the making of me, that I had a glittering new career ahead of me, that my book would hurtle into the bestseller charts, because his company would do everything in their power to make sure it happened.'

Nick waited, didn't speak. He'd never heard Harry say so much before; today was evidently the day for unburdening himself.

'My wife was so excited,' Harry went on eventually. 'We felt as if we'd won the lottery. This was it, our lives were about to change. The publisher had offered me an advance. It wasn't huge, not one of those mega deals you read about in the papers, but decent enough. We both decided I should give up my job in the Civil Service and write full-time, because the sooner I produced the second novel, the sooner we could sell that one too. It made sense, so that's what I did.'

This time the silence was more prolonged. Nick, aware that the new visitor to his left was listening too, finally said, 'So the first book was published?'

Harry nodded, first examining the cracked spine of the Mills and Boon, then his blackened nails.

'It was. But it didn't hurtle into the bestseller lists. It barely sold at all. We were disappointed, but the publisher explained that this often happened with a first novel. People prefer to buy books written by authors they've heard of. Anyway, I had the second novel finished by then, so we pinned all our hopes on that.' Leaning forward on his chair, Harry wearily rubbed his face. 'Except the publisher didn't like it. Said it wasn't of publishable standard. He suggested changing it and I tried to do as he asked, but it was just so *hard*, and six months later he rejected the rewrite. By this time we'd remortgaged the house and my wife was running up credit card debts. That's when it all started to go really wrong. She kept yelling at me to write *better*, and the more she yelled, the more impossible it became to write anything at all. So for the next year I struggled with another book, but the publisher didn't want that one either. They dropped me. My wife left me three weeks later. Then the house was repossessed and the credit card companies started asking when I might be thinking of paying them back. Can't blame them really, I suppose. Anyway, that's when it all became too much for me. I'd failed at everything. Lost everything.' He paused. 'That was six years ago.'

Nick shook his head. Behind every homeless person there was a story.

'That's a rotten thing to happen, Harry. I'm sorry.'

'Look on the bright side.' Harry's smile was wry. 'At least I have my health.'

'You could have a go at writing again,' said Nick. 'No pressure on you this time. Just write because you want to, not because you have to.' Encouragingly he added, 'All it takes is a notepad and pen.'

Harry shrugged. 'I don't think so. Nothing to write about any more.' Wiping his nose with a handkerchief he said gruffly, 'Thanks anyway. I've never told anyone before.'

'I'm glad you did.' Nick gave his arm a brief, reassuring squeeze. 'And Harry, if there's ever anything I can do to help, just let me know. I mean it.'

'Thanks.' Harry nodded.

'Now, why don't I get us a nice cup of tea?' Turning to the newcomer who smelled so strongly of alcohol, Nick wondered what his story was. Heavy drinking presumably, leading to problems with his family . . . divorce . . . losing contact with the kids . . . 'How about you, cup of tea?'

There were tears in the man's eyes, Nick saw; hearing Harry's story had evidently brought back to him how much he himself had lost.

Then again, you could never guess.

'No thanks.' The man cleared his throat and gazed fixedly across the room, clearly unwilling to be drawn into any form of conversation.

'OK. Just tea for you and me then, Harry.' To lighten the mood, Nick said, 'Hey, I've never met a real author before! What's the name of the book you had published?'

'*Pay Day*.' With a grimace, Harry said, 'Appropriately enough.'

'Well, I'll look out for it.'

'I saw a copy in a charity shop before Christmas.' Harry absently scratched his neck. 'Thought I wouldn't mind reading it again myself.'

Eagerly Nick said, 'Great!'

'It was one pound fifty.' Harry shook his head. 'Couldn't afford it.'

As she rounded the corner into Fitzallen Square, Rose couldn't remember when she'd last been happier. She was really here now. Who would have thought that life could turn out like this?

It had been such a wonderful day. Working to brighten up Carmen's little flat had been a pleasure rather than a chore. Now she was heading home – *home!* – to cook dinner for everyone and this evening she would sit watching TV with Nancy and Rennie, and crack on with her knitting, an off-the-shoulder pink and green sweater designed by Zac for one of his overseas clients.

Alerted by the sound of footsteps, Rose saw Brigadier Brough-Badham making his way along the pavement towards her, hatchet-faced as usual and marching briskly along with his hands thrust into the pockets of his long beige trenchcoat.

As he reached Rose, without slowing down or sparing her even the briefest of glances, he said curtly, 'Get rid of him.'

Astounded, Rose whirled round to gaze at his departing back. Indignantly she shouted, 'Get rid of *who*?'

But Brigadier Brough-Badham carried on walking without deigning to reply.

Having assumed he was referring to Rennie – who, at a guess, had either said or done something disreputable again – Rose realised her mistake less than a minute later. The man sitting on the front step of the house, leaning against one of the white pillars, was what Brigadier Brough-Badham would no doubt term as *undesirable*. His hair was dirty and straggly, Rose saw as she approached. He was bearded, bleary-eyed and possibly the worse for drink judging by the way his legs were sprawled in front of him. Poor fellow, he must be freezing. Well, it clearly wouldn't be sensible to invite him into the house, but she could certainly bring him out a mug of hot soup and put together a parcel of food.

'Hello, pet.' To be polite, Rose said gently, 'Are you waiting for someone?'

The man gazed blearily up at her. Finally, in a hoarse voice, he said, 'Yeah. I'm looking for Carmen.'

Chapter 38

Carmen got the shock of her life when she arrived home an hour later and recognised the man sitting at her kitchen table. Almost jumping out of her skin, she saw the dinner plate in front of him, the half-full mug of coffee, the grubby grey woollen scarf hung over the back of the chair.

Her heart palpitating wildly, Carmen hung back in the doorway. Oh God, this was seriously creepy. What was he doing here? How had he known where she lived? And what on earth did Rose think she was doing, allowing him into the kitchen and feeding him beef stroganoff?

'Hi, sweetheart,' Rose said gaily. 'Hungry?'

Hungry? Was Rose out of her *mind*?

'What's going on?' Carmen addressed the visitor to the shelter – the one who, according to Nick, had spent the entire afternoon covertly watching her. Although whenever she had in turn glanced over at him he had appeared to be more interested in Nick. Heatedly she demanded, 'Have you been following me?'

'No.'

'Then how did you find out where I *live*?'

'God, I'm good,' drawled the man, sitting back in his chair and peeling off his beard. 'I should be an actor.'

'You bastard!' shrieked Carmen as Rennie pulled off his wig and broke into a broad grin. He still looked so hideous she could barely take it in. As she watched, he popped out the soft contact lenses with their ageing pale grey lines around each iris.

'Here, clean yourself up.' Delighted with her part in the subterfuge, Rose was at the ready with a pack of wet-wipes. 'That's not really dirt on his face, pet,' she consoled Carmen. 'It's all make-up. Isn't it clever?' she went on admiringly. 'He certainly fooled me.'

'Fooled Carmen too.' Baring grotesquely stained teeth at her, Rennie dragged off the holey brown sweater he'd been wearing, to reveal one of his own T-shirts underneath. 'Better now?'

'Bastard.' Carmen was tempted to hit him. 'And your teeth are revolting.'

215

'I wanted false ones but it was too short notice. Remember Lisa?'

Carmen nodded. Lisa, an ex-girlfriend of Rennie's, had worked as a make-up artist for the BBC.

'I rang her this morning.' Rennie sounded pleased with himself. 'Went round to her house and got her to grubby me up. Gave myself a fright when I looked in the mirror, I can tell you. Then again, it has its good points. Had a whole carriage to myself on the tube.'

'I'm not surprised. You smell like a brewery,' said Carmen.

'Splashed half a can of Tennant's Extra over me for that authentic, reeking-of-alcohol touch. Nice job, don't you think? Oh, come on, you know you can't resist the rough and ready look.' Advancing towards her, Rennie leered, 'Come over here and give me a kiss.'

Carmen had been marvelling at the lengths he would go to to play a trick on her. She was about to open her mouth and tell him he had far too much time on his hands when it struck her that she'd got it all wrong.

'Hang on, hang on.' Holding up her hands to ward him off, she said, 'What made you do this?'

Still smiling lasciviously, Rennie bared his hideous brown teeth. 'Wanted to see where you worked, find out what you do all day.'

'Really? Or is that a big lie?'

He looked mystified. 'Sorry?'

'Oh, don't give me that. You came to spy on Nick!'

Rennie instantly conceded defeat. 'OK, is that so terrible? You said I mustn't come to the flat because I'd be recognised. But it's OK for Nancy and Rose to go there. Why did Nancy turn up at the flat last night? Because she was dying to meet Nick. And I wanted to meet him too, but I wasn't allowed to,' he said simply. 'So I did it the only way I could, by making sure nobody would recognise me. Not even you.'

'You wanted to spy on him,' Carmen repeated evenly.

'I wanted to see what he was like.'

'Because you don't trust me! You think I'm incapable of choosing someone nice!' Carmen was torn between feeling outraged and touched by his concern.

'Look, calm down,' said Rennie. 'I was right about Joe, wasn't I? He seemed OK to begin with, but deep down I had this feeling he wasn't on the level. And now here you are, rushing into another relationship. I just wanted to check him out for myself, that's all. What's so terrible about that?'

Carmen sighed and sat down opposite him. Warily she said, 'Fine, so now you have. And?'

'The truth?'

'Fire away,' Carmen said flatly.

'OK.' Rennie nodded. 'He seems like a good guy. Dodgy clothes.'

'You can talk.'

'Don't be defensive. He's no fashion icon. But I liked him and I'm pretty sure he's on the level.'

'Of course he's on the level.'

'It was fun, actually, watching the two of you together. Pretending not to be flirting with each other.' Amused, Rennie said, 'He's mad about you. It's so obvious.'

'No need to sound so surprised.' Now Carmen really wanted to hit him. 'I'm not a complete troll.'

He rolled his eyes. 'Don't be so touchy. I'm on your side. And I think you've chosen the right one this time. Nick's a decent bloke.'

'Well, thank you.' Should she feel flattered or patronised on Nick's behalf?

'If you marry him,' Rennie's eyes glittered, 'will I be invited to the wedding?'

'Not a chance,' said Carmen as Rose brought her a plate of stroganoff and rice.

'Could I just lurk at the back of the church if I dress up as a tramp?'

'Still no.' Carmen smiled sweetly at him. 'And do you think you could go and brush your teeth now? They're starting to make me feel sick.'

Nancy's muscles didn't know what had hit them. Her calves were on fire, her lungs were close to bursting and there was barely enough strength in her neck to keep her head from flopping onto her chest.

But in the weirdest way she was actually enjoying herself.

Then again, it was always nice to stop.

One point nine seven miles on the treadmill. Nearly there. Willing herself on, Nancy watched the computerised counter move to one point nine eight . . . keep going, keep going . . . one point nine nine . . . oof, just a few more seconds . . . here we are, any second now . . .

Yes. Two miles. Triumphantly slamming the flat of her hand onto the Stop button, Nancy felt the blissful slowing of the machine as it began to wind down. She clung to the side bars, panting and perspiring. Savannah, coming up to see how far she'd run, clapped her hands and said encouragingly, 'Way to go, girl! You'll be entering the London marathon next. Don't overdo it though. Give your muscles time to recover. Now, off you hop and have a rest.'

Nancy, whose legs had now turned to not-quite-set jelly, gasped '*Hop?*'

After a shower, Nancy made her way back through to the bar. It was her third visit to the Lazy B since Sunday and already she was being recognised and greeted by other friendly regulars. Spotting Mia taking a break, she carried her coffee over to join her.

'Hey.' Mia put down the magazine she'd been engrossed in, something to do with animal rights, and gazed approvingly at Nancy's yellow track-suit. 'You're looking fit.'

'Looking fit, feeling knackered.' Stirring her cappuccino, Nancy said, 'Knackered, but smug.'

'Does it hurt?'

'Well, when I do this.' Nancy leaned forward to put her coffee cup back on the table in front of her and winced. 'I think this must be how it feels to be in labour.'

'But you're still glad you decided to come here? You don't have to work yourself so hard, you know.' Mia took a slurp of mocha milkshake. 'It isn't compulsory. You could always give the exercise malarkey a miss and just have fun.'

Nancy knew that, but it wouldn't have felt right. Mia and Connor had given her the membership and it seemed rude not to use it properly.

Well, that was the official line. The real reason was because she didn't want to appear to be angling for attention from Connor, only turning up in order to waft around the place eyeing him longingly from a distance. Which was how it *would* look, both to Connor and, even more excruciatingly, Sadie.

At least this way she could pretend she was here purely for the exercise. And it *was* fun in a masochistic kind of way.

'I'm enjoying it.' Nancy flinched as she reached forward again for her coffee. 'Ouch. Maybe it's easier to just hold the cup rather than keep picking it up and putting it down.'

'Speaking of picking up.' Mia's eyes danced. 'What d'you think of Cyanide Sadie's latest victim?'

Nancy knew all about this. The whole club had been buzzing with the news that Sadie had taken up with Antonio, the club's new personal trainer. Antonio – never, *ever* shortened to Tony – was as sleek as a seal. With his shaven head, liquid brown eyes and sinuous body he actually strongly resembled a seal. Instantly, upon his arrival at the Lazy B, he had attracted a great deal of fluttery attention from the female members of the club. Antonio was twenty-three, single and super-fit. He was also heterosexual. The fact that he waxed the hairs off his chest didn't seem to bother them in the least.

Sadie had wasted no time getting in there first. Nobody else had stood a chance. Antonio was beautiful and he was hers. Within a few days they had become an item. Mission accomplished.

If Sadie had done it to take her mind off Connor, it appeared to have done the trick.

'He certainly seems to have cheered her up,' said Nancy.

'Hmm.' Mia smirked.

'What? Isn't that a good thing?'

'She wouldn't be quite so cheerful if she'd seen the way he was flirting with me this morning.'

'*What*?'

Lowering her voice, Mia leaned closer and added gleefully, 'Or the way he pinched my bum.'

'My God! Seriously?'

'Oh, he was serious all right. Nothing accidental about it.' Mia mimed sliding her hand behind an invisible bum, first squeezing then giving it a lascivious pinch. 'He came behind the reception desk to pick up his booking sheet. Too much Italian testosterone, if you ask me. I slapped him away and told him he could be done for sexual harassment, but he just laughed. *That's* when he came over all flirtatious.'

'So then what did you do?' Nancy pictured the scene: Mia giving Antonio a no-holds-barred piece of her mind and possibly a slapped face for good measure.

'Ha, flirted back at him of course.'

'You flirted with Antonio?' Astounded, Nancy said, 'Do you like him?'

'*Duh*. He's way too old for me. Plus, if a man waxes his chest hair, what other hideous bits and pieces might he secretly have waxed? *And* all he likes to talk about is nutrition and ab-curls, which is enough to do any normal person's head in.'

'So why . . .?' Nancy broke off as she realised belatedly why Mia was flirting with Antonio.

'Because I can,' Mia said mischievously. 'And because it's going to have Cyanide Sadie foaming at the mouth with fury.'

Was this what was known as a death wish?

'It's over between Sadie and Connor,' Nancy protested. 'You don't have to hate her any more.'

Checking her watch, Mia knocked back the rest of her milkshake. 'Are you joking? She's still bad-mouthing me – it's her mission in life to get me the sack. Anyway.' Jumping to her feet she said chirpily, 'Compared with drawing up rotas, fighting with Cyanide Sadie's much more fun. It brightens my day.'

It was obvious that Mia had no intention of backing off. As Nancy left the club ten minutes later, Mia was behind the reception desk, swinging her blond hair and doing her flirty thing while Antonio leaned across, whispering provocatively into her ear. For a mad moment Nancy almost felt sorry for Sadie, whose advanced aerobics class was currently in progress upstairs. Then she gave herself a mental shake, because Sadie was poisonous. Plus, if she found out about Mia and Antonio, they were the ones who were going to be in need of sympathy. Not to mention hospital treatment.

Catching sight of Nancy, Mia waved and called out, 'You just missed Dad.'

Nancy smiled and waved back. Had she?

Good.

Chapter 39

Except she hadn't. As Nancy turned left out of the club and began to make her way towards the tube, Connor's conker-brown Bentley pulled alongside the pavement. The passenger window slid down.

'Hi, thought I recognised you.' Eyes sparkling, Connor leaned across from the driver's seat and beckoned her over. 'Hop in and I'll give you a lift.'

Oh God, difficult, *difficult*. Why did he have to be so nice? Why couldn't she make herself not like him? What were those tap dancers doing in her chest?

'No thanks, I'm fine.' Nancy shook her head, frantically searching for a feasible excuse. 'Um, I've got my return ticket for the tube.'

Connor's mouth twitched. 'I wasn't actually planning to charge you for the ride.'

'But I hate wasting tickets.' Nancy pulled a regretful face. 'And my mother always warned me not to accept lifts from strange men.'

'I have sweeties too.' Persuasively Connor patted the glove compartment. 'Fruit pastilles, Dime bars – you name it, I've got it.'

'Really, I don't—' As Nancy spoke, a lorry blasted its horn behind Connor, making her jump.

'Come on, you're holding everyone up.' Leaning across still further, Connor swung open the passenger door. 'They all think you're a hooker now, haggling over the price.'

More horn-tooting. Oh, for heaven's sake. Hastily clambering into the car, Nancy couldn't help thinking that with her trainers, old jeans and wet hair escaping from her baseball cap, she'd be a low-rent hooker.

'I lied about the sweets by the way,' said Connor as he pulled away from the kerb.

'What, no Dime bars?'

'Well, there were, but I ate them. Off out anywhere this evening?'

'No.' The cold night air had dried out Nancy's lips; she fumbled surreptitiously in her bag for her stick of lipsalve.

'Only I've been invited to the opening of a new restaurant on the King's Road. God knows what it'll be like.' Cruising along, Connor squeezed the Bentley between two cabs as effortlessly as if it were a wafer-thin mint. 'Full of braying Hoorays, probably, but you never know. Could be fun. Fancy coming along?'

Yes.

'No thanks,' said Nancy, as casually as she knew how. What would be the point? Why was Connor inviting her anyway? Well, clearly because he didn't have anyone else to ask at short notice.

'No?' Connor pretended to look hurt. 'I'm not that awful, am I? Come on, don't be mean, you can't let me go on my own. There might be girls there after my body. Pestering me, pawing me, not giving me a minute's peace.'

'And that would be a tragedy.'

Having pulled up at a red traffic light, Connor said, 'What's that smell?'

'Sorry?' Oh help, had she forgotten her deodorant?

'Kind of fruity.' He sniffed the air. 'Peachy?'

Phew. 'Apricot lipsalve,' said Nancy.

'Really? Hey, I like it. Say it again,' Connor prompted.

Now he'd turned to look at her. This was torture. Doing her best to breathe normally and not pant like a dog, Nancy repeated, 'Apricot . . . lip . . . salve.'

Connor inhaled slowly. 'That is so nice. Does it taste like apricots?'

Oh Lord, how was he proposing to find out? Nancy knew she couldn't handle being kissed purely in the spirit of investigative research. What if she humiliated herself, got carried away, welded her body to his and shoved her tongue down his throat then refused to let go when he frantically attempted to prise her off?

'What's this? What are you doing?' Startled, Connor jerked his head away.

'Sshh, keep still. You wanted to know how it tasted.' Willing her hand not to shake, Nancy carefully applied the stick of lipsalve to his mouth.

'Mm. Mmm. Hey, this is *fantastic*.' Noisily licking his lips, smacking them together with relish, Connor peered at his reflection in the rear-view mirror. 'Does it make me look like a girl?'

It was colourless lipsalve. 'More like a big old rugby-playing transvestite,' said Nancy. 'And the lights have gone green. Stop admiring yourself and drive.'

'Come with me to this opening night.'

'No.'

'Why not?'

Because I fancy you so much I can't stand it, and you don't feel the same way about me. Because I don't want to make a fool of myself by giving my feelings away. Because you might spot a girl there who makes *your* heart skip a beat.

Thank goodness it was dark in the car. Slowly breathing in the smell of apricot lipsalve and expensive leather upholstery, Nancy said, 'Because you look like a big old rugby-playing transvestite.' Then, after a pause, 'I just feel like an early night, that's all.'

For the next few minutes Connor drove in silence. As they approached Fitzallen Square he said, 'Have I done anything to upset you?'

Yes.

'No.' Her fingernails dug painfully into the palms of her hands.

'Sure?'

Nancy wondered how he'd react if she turned to him and said, 'Actually, yes, you *have* done something to upset me. You see, I have this monster crush on you and it would have been really nice if you could have returned the compliment, but I know that isn't going to happen because you don't find me remotely fanciable, because I'm *not your type.*'

Well, maybe some outbursts were better kept to yourself.

Aloud she said, 'Of course I'm sure.'

'Only you seem a bit . . . I don't know, distant.'

'How can I be distant? I live next door to you.' Feigning a yawn, Nancy said, 'I'm just tired.'

'So we're still friends.' Connor pulled up outside their adjoining houses and switched off the engine.

'Still friends.' And *only* friends, Nancy thought with a sigh of resignation. Just good friends and nothing more. Absolutely definitely nothing more.

'Well, I'm glad to hear that.' Connor relaxed visibly. 'I'd hate to think I'd done something awful.' Glancing up at the lit windows of Carmen's house, he said, 'Hey, is Rennie doing anything tonight? Maybe he'd like to be my date, seeing as you've turned me down.'

'Just because you're wearing apricot lipsalve,' said Nancy, 'doesn't mean Rennie's going to want to be your boyfriend.'

Following her into number sixty, Connor asked Rennie if he felt like going along with him for the opening night of the new bar.

Rennie and Rose had just finished watching *Ninotchka*. Brightening, Rennie said, 'Will there be girls there?'

Connor thought about it. 'There is that possibility.'

223

'In that case, sounds like my kind of bar.' Rennie hauled himself up from the sofa.

'You've got that meeting with your manager tomorrow morning,' Rose reminded him. 'You told me you had to be up at seven.'

Rennie winked, touched by her concern. 'Rose, I'll make you a promise. If I'm not in bed by midnight, I'll come straight home.'

*   *   *

'Mum, could you do me a massive favour?'

Never happier than when she was helping others, Rose said at once, 'Of course I can, pet. What is it?'

'I'm at the Chinese takeaway around the corner from Carmen's flat.' Nancy was sounding frazzled. 'The thing is, I've lost my credit card, but I think I know where it might be.'

Rose had been scrubbing the kitchen floor, tiled in black and white like a chess board on the slant. Wiping her wet hands on her apron she said, 'Up in your bedroom, on the dressing table?' because this was where Nancy usually left it. 'OK, sweetheart, no problem, I'll find your card and jump on the tube. Tell the Chinese people I can be there in twenty minutes, I'm sure they'll understand—'

'No, no, the takeaway isn't the problem. Carmen's paid for it.' Nancy sounded as if she was smiling. 'I'm just worried about where the card is. Now, I used it this morning to book theatre tickets over the internet and I *think* I might have left it on Zac's kitchen table, because I was borrowing his laptop. But if I didn't leave it there, it could be really lost and that means I'll have to ring the card people and get it cancelled.'

'Oh, you'd need to.' Rose, who didn't trust credit cards one bit, immediately began to worry; you heard such terrifying stories of thieves running up horrific bills on other people's accounts. 'Shall I ring Zac and ask him if your card's there?'

'I already tried. No answer. He must be out.' Lowering her voice Nancy said, 'Hang on, I'm just moving into the street so I'm not over-heard. OK, this is why I need a favour. Could you take my spare key and go over there? Let yourself in through the shop, switch off the burglar alarm and just shoot upstairs to the kitchen. Zac won't mind. Then you can ring me from there and let me know if you've found the card.'

'OK pet, I'll do that. Give me the number for the alarm and I'll go straightaway.'

It would be cold outside. Rose was still in the hallway pulling her woollen gloves on and tucking the ends of her scarf inside her coat when the front door opened. Rennie, back from a day of meetings with his manager and agent, was wearing a sea-green shirt, faded jeans and a thin gold chain round his neck in place of a scarf. How he'd never succumbed to pneumonia, she couldn't imagine.

'Rose. Are you sure they've offered you a job at Spearmint Rhino?'

Rose enjoyed being teased by Rennie. The infamous pole-dancing club had featured on last night's news.

'Cheeky boy. There's a baked ham in the fridge if you're hungry, and a Dauphinoise that just needs heating up.'

'Where are you going?'

Rose explained about the missing credit card, concluding, 'I'll be back in half an hour.'

'It's late,' said Rennie. 'Come on, I'll give you a lift.'

'Really, I'll be fine,' Rose protested.

'It's dark and it's freezing outside.' Rennie jangled his car keys at her. 'Anyway, you shouldn't be out on your own. You could get mugged.'

'And then who'd slice the ham and heat up the Dauphinoise?'

Rennie's green eyes sparkled. 'There is that too.'

Chapter 40

It was as warm as toast inside Rennie's black Mercedes. Rose, feeling as cosseted as the Queen, stroked the wonderfully comfortable leather upholstery and carefully fastened her seat belt. Glancing up, she saw Marjorie Brough-Badham standing stiffly at the window of number sixty-two, gazing down at them.

Rose couldn't resist giving her a regal little wave. Marjorie didn't wave back. Feeling snubbed, Rose watched her turn away from the window. Next moment the curtains were swished shut. It was like a door being slammed in her face. Well, that tells me, thought Rose as Rennie fired the ignition and ear-splitting music blasted through the speakers.

'My goodness, what a racket.' Rose shuddered and reached forward to turn it down. 'Who's singing *that*?'

'Me,' said Rennie. 'We're choosing tracks for the new album.'

'Oh pet, I'm sorry. I'm sure it's lovely.' Patting his arm, Rose said, 'Now put your seat belt on.'

In the car it took only a couple of minutes to reach Levine Street. Zac's shop was in darkness as Rennie pulled into a free space across the road.

'I won't be long,' said Rose.

'I'll come with you. Can't stand waiting in cars.' Rennie hopped out of the driver's seat. 'Besides, I want to see how Zac's getting on with my scary jacket.'

In the shop doorway Rose peeled off her gloves and took the key from her pocket. Peering at the numbers written on her hand, she carefully repeated them aloud and took a couple of deep breaths because other people's burglar alarms were always a bit nerve-wracking.

Once inside, she found the box easily enough and keyed in the code. Phew, done. Now she could relax.

'Hey, how about this?' Rennie was gleefully holding a shimmering silver shift dress decorated with huge purple lip-prints against himself. 'Does it suit me?'

'Put that down,' Rose scolded. 'Zac doesn't want your grubby finger-prints all over his clothes.'

Rennie raised a playful eyebrow. 'Actually, I think you could be wrong there.'

Rose did her best not to blush. When Nancy had told her that Zac was that way inclined, she'd been shocked. It was one thing seeing people on the TV who were gay, like Dale Winton and that little leprechauny Irish one, but somehow it had never occurred to Rose that she might know a homosexual in real life.

Frankly, if she weren't so fond of Zac she might have felt a bit funny about it.

Rennie was now investigating a pair of white trousers trimmed with black pom-poms. Rose, chivvying him towards the stairs, said, 'Come on, you. Nancy's waiting to hear if we've found her credit card.'

As they climbed the staircase Rose noted with approval that before leaving the flat Zac had left a couple of lights on in order to deter burglars. The kitchen was to the left, with the door closed. Hearing a faint scuffling noise, she realised that Zac had left Doreen at home.

'Honestly, what a hopeless guard dog,' Rose chided. 'Not a single bark.' Raising her voice before opening the door in order not to startle the little dog, she called out, 'It's all right, sweetheart, only me!'

The next moment her heart leapt into her throat as the door was abruptly yanked open. With her fingers already closed round the doorhandle, Rose found herself yanked along with it. Catapulting into the kitchen, she collided with Zac who had never looked more petrified in his life.

'Jesus, oh my *God*,' Zac gasped. '*Rose!* What's going on?'

There was a frying pan clutched in his right hand. Her own heart racing, Rose clasped her chest and stammered, 'I thought the flat was empty . . . Nancy told me you were out.'

'I could have killed you.' Zac was hyperventilating, his face chalk-white and his hands trembling violently. 'I thought you were a burglar. If you hadn't called out I'd have hit you over the head with this.'

The frying pan was Le Creuset, no laughing matter. Wobbly with relief that he hadn't swung it at her, Rose said, 'Oh pet, I'm so sorry. Could I sit down for a moment, get my breath back?'

'Um . . . well, I was just on my way out.' Zac shifted awkwardly, evidently not keen on the idea.

'Sit down, Rose.' Taking charge, Rennie steered her towards the kitchen table and pulled out one of the chairs. 'Nancy rang you, but there was no reply.' As he said it, Rennie's gaze flickered from Zac to the silver mobile phone lying on the table. 'She tried your mobile too, but it was switched off. Where's Doreen?'

'What? Oh, in the bedroom. Having a little sleep.' Wiping his perspiring hands together, Zac blurted out, 'I still don't know what you're *doing* here.'

'Oh sweetheart, what must you think of us?' Rose's forehead pleated apologetically. 'Nancy's lost her credit card. She thought she might have left it here in the kitchen. Have you seen it?'

'No.' Wildly Zac shook his head. 'Credit card? No, definitely haven't seen it. Sorry. Right, was that all? Only I really do have to go out!'

Rennie, sauntering over to the far side of the table where a slew of papers and magazines were scattered, began picking up each one in turn – *Vogue, Harpers, Car Weekly* – and flicked through them. Nothing. Then he moved Zac's laptop, which lay open and switched off next to a couple of discarded coffee mugs.

The credit card, which had slid beneath the laptop, was revealed. Clasping her hands, Rose exclaimed, 'Oh thank heavens, there it is!'

Zac looked relieved too. Relieved, thought Rennie as he passed the card over to Rose, but still downright twitchy.

'Good, good.' Zac began making chivvying gestures in an attempt to persuade Rose out of her chair. Hurriedly he said, 'Well, if that's all—'

'OK if I use the loo before we head off?' Sliding past him, Rennie made his way swiftly across the kitchen.

'No!' yelped Zac, lunging after him. '*No*, that's not the bathroom—'

Too late, he caught up with Rennie as he pulled open the door.

'*Oh God*,' Zac groaned, slumping against the fridge and covering his face.

'Sorry, my mistake.' Rennie beamed at him over his shoulder. 'I thought it was a bathroom. Turns out it's a broom cupboard. And you'll never guess what else you've got in here.'

A sound like a mouse being strangled issued from Zac's throat. Concerned, Rose said, 'Whatever's the matter, pet?'

'You know when customs officers open the back of a lorry and dozens of illegal immigrants come tumbling out?' Rennie's tone was conversational. 'That's just how I feel now.'

Rose was bemused. 'What?'

'Come on out,' said Rennie. 'It can't be comfortable in there.' He opened the door more widely and Rose's mouth dropped open as Brigadier Brough-Badham emerged from the broom cupboard.

'Good gracious. Oh my *goodness*,' Rose gasped. 'What's going on? Zac, do you know who this *is*?'

Zac looked at Rennie, whose mouth was twitching at the corners.

'Oh, I think he does,' Rennie assured Rose.

'But . . . but he lives next door to us,' Rose spluttered. 'With his wife, Marjorie. This is just . . . well, *extraordinary*. Whatever's he doing here in your flat?'

Bracing herself the next morning, Nancy let herself into the shop. Doreen came trotting over, her tail wagging eagerly, and she scooped the little dog up into her arms.

At least someone was pleased to see her.

'Hello, baby, how are you?' Nancy heard her voice go squeaky, as if she'd been sucking helium. 'Had a nice walk this morning? Been playing with your ball?'

Through the open door leading into the workroom, Nancy could see Zac with his back to her, pinning a swathe of midnight blue velvet round his tailor's dummy. Raising her Minnie Mouse voice, she called out casually, 'Hi, Zac. Everything OK?'

He stopped pinning and turned to face her. Said flatly, 'So they told you.'

Maybe not that casual then.

'Sorry.' Nancy moved towards him, feeling horribly responsible and clutching Doreen like a security blanket. 'Am I sacked?'

Zac heaved a sigh. 'Why?'

'Because it's all my fault. I sent Mum over here last night. She brought Rennie along with her. As far as I was concerned, the flat was empty.' Nancy pulled a face. 'I was sure you wouldn't mind.'

'Great timing.' Zac was wearing a pale grey shirt today, and plain dark blue trousers. It was as if he hadn't had the energy to choose his usual outrageous get-up. 'One thing. How did Rennie know Geoffrey was in the broom cupboard?'

Geoffrey. It was hard enough to believe that Brigadier Brough-Badham *had* a Christian name, let alone that it was Geoffrey.

'Well, he said you were as jumpy as a cat on a hot-plate. Then when he brushed his hand against the coffee mugs on the kitchen table,' Nancy explained, 'he realised they were both warm.'

And Rennie, being Rennie, had been overcome with curiosity.

'Have to start calling him Miss Marple.' Pushing his unwashed blond hair back from his face, Zac said wearily, 'Put the coffee on, will you? I suppose we'd better talk.'

'We don't have to.' Vigorously Nancy shook her head. 'Not if you don't want to.'

But Zac gave her a pitying look. 'Of course I don't *want* to, but we certainly *do* have to. Geoffrey's your neighbour. None of you has ever got on with him. How do you suppose he's feeling now? If his wife finds out, this'll kill him.'

'She doesn't know?' Nancy was incredulous. Then again, she had spent the whole of last night being incredulous. The thought of Zac and Brigadier Brough-Badham together was, frankly, mind-boggling.

'There are plenty of gay men who are married. Especially the older ones,' said Zac. 'Geoffrey had his army career to think of. His family. He did his best to fit in. You have no idea how difficult his life has been,' he added defensively. 'And now this. If Marjorie gets to hear about it, I don't know what he'll do.'

'We won't tell her.' Appalled, Nancy said, 'That's a promise. Truly, we won't breathe a word.'

'You might not,' Zac said soberly. 'But what about Rennie?'

'He won't either!'

'Really? He blurted everything out to you though, didn't he?'

Hot with embarrassment, Nancy recalled her and Carmen's arrival home last night. Rennie, greeting them at the front door, had practically dragged them over the threshold exclaiming, 'Quick, quick, get in, you are not going to *believe* this!'

'He did,' she admitted, 'but only because the Brigadier's always hated us so much. I mean, poor Carmen, he's been awful to her.' Hastily Nancy added, 'But Rennie would never tell Marjorie. That would just hurt *her*.'

'Try telling Geoffrey that.'

'Rennie isn't malicious.'

Zac said seriously, 'Geoffrey couldn't bear it. That's the truth. It would destroy both of them.'

'Don't worry.' Nancy vowed to speak to Rennie. 'And tell Brig – um, Geoffrey not to worry either. Really.'

'And the moral of this story is,' Zac grimaced, 'if your phone rings, answer it. We weren't in bed or anything, by the way, when you tried to contact me. We were in the kitchen, just talking and drinking coffee.'

'I didn't think that,' Nancy lied, flushing as the unthinkable mental image of Zac and Geoffrey in bed together flashed through her mind.

'OK, stop *picturing* it. Just sit down and I'll tell you the whole story.'

'I don't want to—'

'It's kind of relevant,' Zac said evenly, 'seeing that if it wasn't for Geoffrey, I wouldn't have this shop.'

Chapter 41

'I've always been hopeless with men. Well, you know that.' Zac gestured sadly with his hands. 'It's all over between me and Sven, by the way. He chucked me yesterday, texted me to say he's met someone else.'

'Oh God, I'm sorry.' Nancy winced in sympathy; he'd been crazy about Sven.

'Don't be. I'm used to it by now. Anyway, I met Geoffrcy eight years ago. I was coming out of a gay bar in Soho, pretty upset because some other boyfriend had just given me the boot in favour of someone prettier. Geoffrey was walking past when I literally bumped into him. He asked me if I was hurt and I said too right, I was *always* getting hurt. And he invited me to go for a drink. I wasn't some kind of gigolo,' Zac said defensively. 'I mean, I know he's twenty years older than me, but we really seemed to hit it off, you know? We talked for hours. He told me he was married. I told him about my disastrous love life. The thing with Geoffrey is, he's so buttoned up on the outside, keeping this stiff upper lip and going around like Disgusted of Tunbridge Wells. But inside, deep down, he's just another desperately unhappy man who hasn't been able to live the kind of life he was meant to live. He was ashamed of his feelings towards other men. He called it his weakness. I couldn't believe I'd found someone unhappier than I was.'

'So you started . . . um, seeing each other.' Nancy was eager to skim over the details.

'For about a year,' Zac agreed. 'And I did love him, but the age thing was always a problem. We were friends more than anything, two lonely people in need of company and someone to talk to. After a while the physical side fizzled out, but we stayed good friends.'

Nancy gestured around the shop. 'And this place?' Although she'd already half guessed.

'I was struggling to get my own business up and running. The banks wouldn't loan me enough to set up anywhere decent. I didn't ask Geoffrey to help me,' Zac said fiercely. 'I know what you're thinking, but it wasn't like that. He'd always encouraged me, been there for me during the hard times. Then one day he was driving down this street and he saw the For Sale sign up outside this place. It used to be an antiquarian book shop. Geoffrey rang and told me to come and take a look. So I did, but it was obviously way out of my price range. I mean, Levine Street in Chelsea, was he mad? But the next day Geoffrey came to visit me. He gave me an envelope with a cheque inside, for more money than I'd ever seen in my life.' Tears filled Zac's eyes and he blinked them back. 'I couldn't believe it. We weren't sleeping together. Geoffrey didn't want anything in return. He just told me he wanted me to take it, to make my dreams come true. Remember when you asked me about this place? And I told you my godmother left me the money when she died? That was a lie.'

'Well, the truth would have come as quite a shock.' Bemused, Nancy said, 'But what about his wife? Didn't Marjorie notice all this money missing from their bank account?'

'She's independently wealthy.' Zac shook his head. 'They have separate accounts. Separate beds, separate everything.'

No wonder they'd always looked so miserable. Glancing up, Nancy saw a baby-blue MG pulling up outside the shop – double-parking, because its owner didn't believe in searching for something as unbelievably tedious as a parking space.

'Lysette's here for her fitting.' She clasped Zac's hand. 'Don't worry about Rennie, I'll speak to him. He won't breathe a word.'

For a moment Zac looked as if he might be about to cry again. Then, visibly bracing himself, he stood up to deal with over-excitable Lysette and said, 'Well, let's hope so. Because apart from anything else, I'd really hate Geoffrey to ask for his money back.'

Carmen wondered if this was how Richard and Judy felt, working and living together and never tiring of each other's company. It was practically how she and Nick were nowadays. Apart from the evening before last, when Nancy had mislaid her credit card, they had been spending all their time together and it felt . . . well, fantastic. Unbelievably great. Last night they had gone ten pin bowling with Annie and her boyfriend before picking up takeaway pizzas and heading back to Battersea for a boisterous game of Monopoly. When Annie and Jonathan had finally left the flat just before midnight, Nick had slowly removed her clothes and made love to her, and she had given herself to him entirely, wondering if it was possible to feel happier than this.

And now, this morning, here they were on their way into work together, swaying in unison on the packed tube train, and Carmen couldn't help feeling sorry for her fellow commuters because none of them was as filled with such indescribable joy as she was. She felt like the sun, radiating happiness that must surely be visible. Were people covertly glancing her way, nudging each other and whispering, 'Look at her, see that girl over there, did you ever see anyone *glow* like that? Now that's a girl in love.'

'I hate to tell you this,' Nick whispered, 'but you're starting to scare people.'

Carmen squirmed with pleasure as his warm breath tickled her ear. 'Why?'

'That smirk on your face. You look like a spaniel who's just heard a really smutty joke.'

'I do not.' Reaching under his jacket at the back and pinching his bottom, Carmen murmured, 'Anyway, it's all your fault.'

'Excellent news. I'm delighted to hear that I'm capable of making you smirk like a spaniel. I shall be adding this talent to my CV.'

He bent his head and kissed her on the mouth, and Carmen had to hang on to the handrail for dear life as her knees turned to noodles. Behind her, someone sniffed loudly. Another person tut-tutted with disgust at such a wanton, early morning display of affection. Carmen pulled away and gave them a smug, pitying look as the train pulled in at Paddington. They weren't happy and she was. She'd never been so glad to be alive.

Clutching a laundry basket, Annie came through to the kitchen while Carmen was clearing up after breakfast.

'There's a wobbly one out there.' She pulled a face. 'Bit smelly, too. Been on a giant bender by the look of it. Nick says could you make him a coffee. White, two sugars.'

'No problem.' Carmen finished the last of the drying-up and reached for a clean mug. 'Have we seen him before?'

Annie shook her head. 'First-timer. Ask him if he'd like us to wash his clothes. I'll just get on with this lot.' She paused, her eyes sparkling. 'Still going well with Nick then?'

Since there was no point in even trying to deny it, Carmen grinned. 'Really well.'

'I'm so glad. You make a great couple.' Mischievously Annie said, 'Might not be long before I have to start looking for a new flatmate.'

'Too soon.' Carmen felt herself flush pink.

'Ah, but sometimes you just know when something's right.' Shifting the laundry basket to her other hip, Annie said, 'And when that happens, why wait? I mean, it's not as if you only just met each other, is it?'

'We'll see.' This was a bridge Carmen intended to cross in her own good time. Piling coffee and sugar into the blue and white striped mug, she said, 'What's this chap's name, anyway?'

'Russell.' Annie made calming-down movements with her free hand. 'Don't get your hopes up. He looks nothing like Russell Crowe.'

Russell. Russ. Carmen, standing frozen in the doorway, felt as if she'd been kicked in the stomach. The moment she'd seen him she'd recognised him and the implications were too hideous to contemplate.

Big Russ, that was how he'd been known when he'd worked as a roadie for Red Lizard. Numbly clutching the mug of hot coffee, Carmen worked out that it was five years since she'd last seen him. At the end of that year's world tour, Big Russ had been faced with an ultimatum from his wife: either he gave up travelling and took a job closer to home, or their marriage was over. Reluctantly, Big Russ had resigned from the job he loved, relinquishing it for the sake of the pretty blonde wife he adored.

What had happened since then? How had he been reduced to this? Finding it hard to breathe, Carmen watched Russ struggle to roll a cigarette, drop tobacco all over the floor and curse loudly. In such a state, how on earth was she going to make him understand that he mustn't mention her connection with Red Lizard?

Could she double back into the kitchen, escape through the fire exit and hide amongst the dustbins until he was gone? Would that work? Or maybe a paper bag over her head? Oh God, how could this be happening to her now?

'You're in my way,' grumbled Baz, attempting to shuffle past with a tray of empty plates.

Nick, from across the room, saw Carmen hesitating. Pointing over at Big Russ, he mouthed helpfully, 'Over there.'

Oh God.

Chapter 42

Big Russ looked up as Carmen gingerly approached him. His hair was greying and straggly, the lines more pronounced around his face. He must be in his mid-forties now. He looked sixty. And he had a bad attack of the shakes.

'Hi, here's your coffee.' Carmen risked meeting his gaze and saw his eyebrows knit together.

'Cheers, love. Feelin' a bit, you know, rough, like. Have we met before?'

He didn't recognise her! With a rush of relief, Carmen put the mug of coffee down on the table in front of him.

'No, I don't think so. Two sugars, is that right?'

Big Russ nodded, grunting as he leaned forward to pick up the mug. The next moment, coffee slopped all over the table.

'Sorry. Got the shakes. Couldn't give me a hand, love, could you?' His frown deepened as he blearily surveyed her. 'You sure I don't know you? Your face rings a bell. Ever worked down Cornwall way?'

'Never.' Shaking her head firmly, Carmen held the mug to his lips and said, 'There, not too hot?'

Not hot enough to burn his tongue and render him speechless, sadly. Having taken several noisy gulps of coffee, Russ sat back and said slurrily, 'Seen you before somewhere, know I have.'

'Maybe we just passed each other in the street.' Carmen forced brightness into her voice as Nick came over.

'Nah, only came down from Manchester yesterday.' Russ began another doomed-to-failure attempt to roll another cigarette. He looked up, puzzled. 'Ever been to Manchester?'

'Sorry.' Eager to change the subject Carmen said, 'Now, we can wash your clothes for you if you—'

'Seen her before,' Russ told Nick, nodding and pointing an unsteady finger at Carmen. 'Know her from somewhere. It'll come to me.'

Behind his back, Carmen rolled her eyes at Nick.

'Best way to remember something is to stop thinking about it,' Nick said easily. 'So what brings you down from Manchester then, Russell?'

'On my way to Cornwall. Back to Cornwall,' Russ slurred. 'To live with my brother in Penzance.' He coughed and dropped his cigarette papers into his lap. 'S'posed to change trains at Paddington yesterday.'

'Nick.' Annie had emerged from the kitchen waving the phone. 'Call for you.'

Carmen exhaled with relief as Nick apologised to Russ and went to take the call. She helped Russ to drink the rest of his coffee. 'Why didn't you catch the train to Cornwall?'

'Delayed, wasn't it? So I went into the pub. Ended up spending the ticket money on beer instead. Woke up in a doorway this morning. Someone told me about this place. Not bad here, is it?' Blinking, he peered at Carmen once more. 'Did you used to have long hair?'

Carmen's heart was racing. Any minute now, he was going to figure out who she was and broadcast it to everyone within earshot.

'Look.' Panicking inside, she forced her voice to remain calm. 'If your brother's expecting you, you really should get down to Penzance. We have an . . . um, emergency fund that can cover the cost of the train ticket. Would that be a help?'

Tears filled Russ's eyes. 'Bless you, love, it would. He'll be wondering where I am.'

'OK, I'll get you the money. But you have to promise that this time you'll buy a ticket.' Carmen jumped up. Hurrying through to the back office, she unlocked the drawer containing her bag and emptied her purse, thanking her lucky stars she'd stopped at the cashpoint on the way in to work.

'What are you doing?' Nick's voice behind her made Carmen jump. Guiltily she swung round.

'He's desperate to get down to Cornwall.'

Eyeing the giveaway bundle of tenners in her hand, Nick's expression softened. 'You can't afford to do that.'

'It's OK, really. I want to.'

'Yesterday lunchtime we were looking at lampshades for your bedroom,' said Nick, 'and you chose the paper ones because they were the cheapest. Now you're giving – what, a hundred pounds? – to a complete stranger.' Moving towards Carmen, he put his arms round her and slowly shook his head. 'God, you are amazing.'

Guilt welled up. Unable to look at him, Carmen said, 'I'm not.'

'You are. How many people would do that?' Stroking her face, Nick planted a tender kiss on her mouth. 'That's why I love you.'

'Yeeurch,' exclaimed Annie, shielding her eyes in the doorway. 'People *kissing*. Gross. Too early in the morning for all that lovey-dovey stuff.'

Releasing Carmen, Nick said, 'Never too early for me.'

Outside the shelter, Carmen pointed Big Russ firmly in the direction of the station. 'You have to buy a train ticket,' she repeated.

He nodded. 'I know. I will. My brother's waiting for me.'

Carmen hated herself for prying but she had to ask, needed to know. Gently she said, 'Do you have any other family? Were you ever married?'

Russ's eyes clouded over. For a few moments he was silent, his Adam's apple bobbing in his throat.

'I was. We were very happy. Josie, her name was. Then she died, four years ago. Brain haemorrhage. Bang, gone, just like that.'

'Oh Russ, I'm so sorry. That's terrible.' Carmen was appalled.

He nodded. 'Forty-one, she was. My Josie, the love of my life. I wanted to die too. Should've just blown my brains out. Instead I'm doing it the hard way, drinking myself to death.'

Carmen looked at him. 'And does it make you feel better?'

'No,' Russ said wearily. 'Worse.'

'Maybe it's time to stop. Josie wouldn't have wanted to see you like this.'

'I know. I know.' Shamefaced, he huddled deeper into his coat.

'I have to get back to work,' said Carmen. 'Listen, you take care of yourself. Moving down to Cornwall could be a whole new start.'

Russ didn't clap his hands together and cry, 'Yes, yes it *could*!' He mumbled pessimistically, 'Yeah, right,' and wiped his nose with the back of his hand. As he turned to leave, he said, 'Thanks for the money.'

'Good luck,' said Carmen.

Russ paused and glanced back. 'I *know* I've seen you somewhere before.' Pointing a stubby finger at her, he said again, 'It'll come to me.'

That's why I'm getting you out of here, Carmen thought guiltily, packing you off on a train before it happens and you mess up my life like you messed up yours.

'You're off at six, aren't you?' said Antonio. 'Come out for a drink with me after work.'

Mia was beginning to realise that maybe she hadn't done the wisest thing after all. Think Before You Flirt was a maxim to which she hadn't adhered and now she was living to regret it. Over the past couple of weeks Antonio had become keener and keener. It had been fun at first, but now she didn't quite know how to make it stop. And if Antonio and Sadie were to break up, that would leave Sadie on her own again. What if she decided to get back with Connor? Talk about divine retribution.

'Antonio, I can't. You're with Sadie.' She wished he wouldn't give her that soulful, baby-seal look.

'No problem.' Antonio raised his hands. 'She's got classes until ten.'

'I couldn't go behind her back,' Mia said firmly.

'OK, fine. You want me to finish with her, is that it?'

'No! I think you should stay together.'

'But I like you better.' Antonio's tone was persuasive. 'Sadie's too old for me.'

Snap. Aloud Mia said, 'I'm only sixteen. You're too old for me.'

'But you're so mature for your age,' Antonio persisted.

And you're so immature for yours, thought Mia.

'My dad's very over-protective. He'd go bananas.' Trapped behind the reception desk, she wondered why the phone couldn't come to her rescue and start ringing. 'Look, thanks for the offer, but I can't. You really should stay with Sadie.'

Antonio now looked like a baby seal about to be beaten to death with a club. 'I can't believe you're saying that.'

In all honesty, Mia couldn't either. But the time had come to backtrack furiously. 'You're perfect together. Everyone says so,' she lied.

'You think?'

'Definitely. God, Sadie's an amazing woman. In fact you're lucky to have her.'

Glancing to the left, Antonio blanched and began to sidle away. Mia followed the direction of his gaze and saw that the door to the ladies' cloakroom was open. Sadie was standing there, listening to every word.

'Right,' Antonio said hastily. 'Well, I've got a client waiting upstairs . . .'

Sadie watched him go, her face rigid. Turning, she eyed Mia stonily and gripped the handles of her Adidas bag so tightly her knuckles were white. 'I don't know what you think you're playing at,' she hissed through gritted teeth, 'but I've never been so humiliated in my life.'

Earlier, in the gym, Nancy had been fascinated by the sight of a plump, tousle-haired blonde in a pristine pale yellow tracksuit occupying the exercise bike next to hers. For forty minutes the blonde had sat there without exercising at all. Not a single revolution of the pedals, not a single calorie burned. Instead she had remained engrossed in a copy of

Heat and munched her way through two Wagon Wheels and a bar of Caramac. Looking up and catching Nancy glancing enviously at the half-eaten bar, she'd generously offered her a piece.

'Go on, have some. Best stuff in the world.'

'I haven't had a Caramac for years,' said Nancy. 'I didn't know they still made them.'

'If they ever stopped making Caramacs, life truly wouldn't be worth living. Bugger.' Having checked her watch, the blonde girl reluctantly closed her magazine and slid down from the unexercised bike. 'Speaking of life not being worth living, it's time for my class.'

Waving goodbye, Nancy watched her head – without discernible enthusiasm – for the aerobics studio. It was seven o'clock which meant the girl was booked into Sadie's advanced class.

No wonder she'd been conserving her energy.

Fifteen minutes later Nancy was at the bar ordering a coffee when she heard a strange wheezing sound like dusty bellows behind her.

'Oh God, my legs, my *lungs*,' panted the tousle-haired blonde. Grabbing a stool, she attempted to clamber onto it. An unlit cigarette dangled from her lips. 'That was the longest, most completely hideous thirty minutes of my life. Got a light?'

There was a box of Lazy B matches on the bar. Nancy struck one and held it to the girl's cigarette. 'Fifteen minutes, actually.'

'Bloody hell. It felt more like fifteen hours.' The girl ordered a large vodka and tonic from the barman and inhaled smoke right down to her toes. 'Never, *ever* again.' Holding out a trembling hand she said, 'I'm Tabitha, by the way.'

'Nancy.' Sympathetically Nancy shook her hand. 'First time?'

'First and last.' Tabitha grimaced. 'My darling boyfriend thought I needed to lose some weight so he bought me a year's membership for my birthday. Said a place called the Lazy B would suit me down to the ground.'

Now why did that sound familiar? Oh yes, it was just the kind of thing Jonathan would have said. Funny how she didn't miss him. Aloud Nancy said, 'Well, at least you can tell him you gave it a go.'

'Actually, my birthday was before Christmas. We've broken up since then. He was a bully, one of those controlling types.' Tabitha pulled a face. 'Otherwise known as a right bastard. I decided I deserved better than the kind of man who tells me how many calories there are in Christmas pudding.' She took another contented puff of her cigarette. 'But I knew the membership had cost a bomb so I thought I may as well come down here and check the place out. Bought this in Harvey Nichols this morning, specially.' Proudly she indicated the pale yellow tracksuit. 'I felt quite fit and healthy, just looking at myself in the mirror. The girls at work all wet themselves laughing when I told them what I was doing tonight. They thought it was the funniest thing ever. That's why I thought I'd show them, and booked myself into an advanced class. God, I'm such a durr-brain.'

'You don't have to do advanced,' said Nancy. 'Beginners is fine to start off with. Or just stick to the machines, like me. Then you can go at your own pace.'

'I think you saw my pace when we were on the exercise bikes,' Tabitha said wryly. 'To be honest, I can't see me getting into this fitness lark at all.'

'You never know.' Nancy's tone was encouraging. 'You might start to enjoy it.'

'I know what I'm like.' Stubbing out her cigarette, Tabitha glugged back her vodka and said, 'I bet I never come back here again. That's how these places make their money, isn't it? From the one-visit-wonders. Oh, I say, who is *that*? Does he work here?'

Tabitha's eyes had lit up. At the far end of the bar, Connor was pinning up next week's staff rota and joking with a crowd of squash-playing regulars.

Nancy's heart swallow-dived into her stomach. 'That's Connor. He owns the place.'

'Now that's my kind of man,' Tabitha said eagerly. 'Is he as nice as he looks?'

No, he's vile. 'Yes,' Nancy reluctantly admitted.

'Single?'

'Yes.'

'Hey, maybe this place isn't so bad after all.' Having finished her drink and been on the verge of leaving, Tabitha now settled herself back onto her stool and excitedly brushed cigarette ash from the front of her yellow tracksuit top. 'Do you know him to talk to? Could you introduce me? Shall we just go over and say hello? Oh God, do I look a mess?'

Dutifully surveying her, Nancy felt like one of the ugly sisters watching Cinderella walk off with Prince Charming. Now that she was no longer wheezing like an old pair of bellows, Tabitha was looking radiant, pink-cheeked from her recent exertions and glowing with anticipation at the thought of meeting Connor.

Forcing a smile, Nancy wondered if this officially made her a masochist. 'Don't worry. You look fine.'

Who knew, Tabitha might turn out to be just what Connor had been waiting for. Maybe she was just his type.

Chapter 43

It was Sunday afternoon. Carmen checked the oven where the fish pie was bubbling away under the grill. She'd made it herself, because it was one of Nick's favourite meals. Cod and prawns, layered with sliced potatoes, mushrooms, tomatoes and a rich cheese sauce. It had taken ages to prepare from scratch, but she didn't mind. Nick would love it.

As she wiped down the worktops, Carmen heard the front door open and bang shut downstairs, signalling Nick's return from the off-licence. Smiling to herself, she marvelled at the way her life had altered out of all recognition in the last couple of months. Last year she hadn't cooked a single meal for herself, because what would have been the point? It had been easier to exist on tins of soup, toast, cups of tea and biscuits. Every now and again she had ventured as far as a ready-meal. Cooking proper food had seemed like such a waste of time and effort, particularly when she wouldn't even have enjoyed eating it.

Oh yes, everything was certainly different now. Rinsing out the J-Cloth, Carmen proudly gave the chrome taps a quick polish and turned to greet Nick as he squeezed into the tiny kitchen.

'Valpolicella.' He waved the bottle at her triumphantly. 'I know it's red but it was on special offer. Three ninety-nine.'

'Red's fine,' Carmen assured him, because a special offer was a special offer. And even though he'd only been gone for ten minutes she gave him a hug to show how happy she was to have him back. 'Dinner's nearly ready.'

Nick's grey eyes crinkled at the corners. 'So, time for a quickie first? Or would you prefer a slow one afterwards?'

'You mean I have to choose? Tuh, you can tell you're not eighteen.'

He raised an eyebrow. 'Is that a challenge?'

'For you, obviously. Oh well, serves me right for getting involved with a man past his prime – oooh!' squealed Carmen as he grabbed her arms and began pulling her out of the kitchen.

'Right, clothes off. We'll see who's past their prime, shall we? Let me know if you can't keep up.' Bundling her through to the bedroom, Nick hauled her navy sweater over her head and pulled off his own sweatshirt.

'I should turn off the oven,' Carmen giggled as he tipped her onto the bed and romantically yanked down her jeans. 'The fish pie might burn.'

'Making feeble excuses already? Shame on you.' Stepping out of his own trousers, Nick tossed them dramatically to one side like a magician.

'What's that noise?' Carmen tilted her head.

'Oh dear, *more* excuses?' Tut-tutting, Nick shook his head. 'Getting desperate now. Don't tell me, let me guess – burglars have broken in, they're eating our dinner, drinking our—'

'No, I'm serious.' Sliding out from under him as he made a playful lunge towards her, Carmen said, 'I *can* hear something.'

He grinned. 'That's the sound of my heart beating.'

'Listen.' She pressed a finger to his lips and sat up. 'It's like someone taking a shower.'

Nick listened. 'Hygienic burglars?'

Leaping off the bed, Carmen raced across the bedroom in her bra, knickers and woolly socks.

'If there are burglars in your shower,' he called after her, 'you'll frighten the life out of them.'

'Oh oh *oh*,' shrieked Carmen, skidding to a halt at the entrance to the living room. Water was cascading down from the ceiling, drenching the carpet and furniture.

'Bloody hell,' exclaimed Nick, behind her.

'Stop it!' Carmen waved her arms helplessly at the cracked ceiling. 'How do we make it stop? Oh no, look at the walls! Look at my sofa!'

'Where's the stopcock?' Nick gazed wildly around, moving forward then grimacing as his bare feet sank into the sodden carpet. 'God, it's disgusting, like walking through a bog.'

Darting into the bathroom, Carmen seized a turquoise bath towel and wrapped it round herself. As she galloped downstairs, the door to her landlord's living room was flung open. Mr Sadler, an unedifying sight in his string vest with dark chest hairs poking through the holes and his stomach rolling over the waistband of his trousers, glared up at her.

'What the bloody hell have you been doing?' he roared. 'There's water coming through my ceiling!'

Incensed, Carmen shouted back, 'You think there's water coming through *your* ceiling? You should see it coming through *my* ceiling. The tank's burst up in the loft or something. Where's the stopcock?'

Mr Sadler let out the kind of disgusted groan that suggested it wasn't the first time this had happened. Carmen recalled the patchy stains on her living room ceiling – the ones she and Nick had so painstakingly painted over.

'Stopcock. Right,' he sighed, ambling into his flat. Really hoping that his state of undress didn't mean he'd been doing with his wife what she'd been about to do with Nick, Carmen followed him through to the kitchen and watched him turn off the stopcock in the cupboard under the sink.

'Now what?' demanded Carmen. 'What do I do about my living room?'

'Go and save what you can.' Straightening up with difficulty, Mr Sadler took his mobile out of his trouser pocket and began punching out a number. 'My brother's a plumber, I'll get him over here right away.'

Carmen said pointedly, 'Is he the one who fixed it last time?'

Mr Sadler grunted and reached back under the sink with his free hand, pulling out a box of household candles. 'Better take some of these too. I'll have to turn off the mains if we don't want to be electrocuted, and it'll be dark soon.'

Upstairs, Nick wrapped his arms round Carmen. 'It'll be OK. We'll get the place fixed up again, don't you worry.'

'Everything's ruined,' Carmen said sadly, as the drips fell steadily from the ceiling.

'It's only water. The carpet will dry out. I managed to save the TV.' Nick's tone was consoling. 'It's in the bedroom.'

'Mr Sadler's brother's on his way round to fix it. Probably with gaffer tape and Uhu.' Carmen pulled a face. 'We're not going to have electricity either. It's going to be pitch black and freezing in here by tea time.'

'Hey, don't worry.' Tenderly smoothing her damp spiky hair, Nick said, 'You can come and stay with me.' He gave the turquoise bath towel a playful tug. 'Better go and get dressed if you don't want Sadler's brother ogling you.'

'Bet you're glad you came over.' Carmen smiled ruefully. 'No heat, no light, no sex.'

'How can you even say that?' Nick narrowed his eyes lasciviously as she headed for the bedroom to retrieve her clothes. 'We still have home-made fish pie.'

By the time Carmen had finished dressing and had packed a holdall with spare clothes to take to Nick's flat, he had served up their meal. The sodden green carpet might resemble a swamp, but Nick had wiped down the tiny dining table and two chairs, decorated the table with every last one of Mr Sadler's candles and poured the Valpolicella into matching

244

glasses. He was now sitting at the table solemnly holding Carmen's purple and white striped umbrella over his head as water continued to drip-drip-drip from the ceiling.

'I love you.' Joining him, Carmen leaned over for a kiss.

'We'll have to share the umbrella. Love you too,' said Nick. 'Come on, eat up before it gets cold.'

Several minutes later there was a knock at the door.

'Plumber's here,' Mr Sadler bellowed as Carmen pushed back her chair and splashed across the carpet to let them in.

'Right, the hatch leading into the roof is in the living room,' Mr Sadler was telling the plumber. Turning to face Carmen he indicated that she should move out of the way to allow the ladder through. 'All right, love? Water stopped dripping now? My brother couldn't make it – he had tickets for the Arsenal match this afternoon – so I called a number out the Yellow Pages. Whoops, mind your back.'

Carmen looked at Joe James, behind him. Joe looked at Carmen, evidently confused. Time either stood still or sped by, she was too shocked to be able to tell which.

'Carmen,' said Joe.

'Well, well, what about that?' Mr Sadler nodded jovially. 'Know each other, do you?' Nudging Joe he added, 'Does that mean I get a discount?'

Carmen felt as if her head were full of the expanding insulating foam that got pumped into wall cavities. This was worse than Big Russ arriving at the shelter. She watched Joe haul his stepladder and tool case into the living room and plonk them down on the carpet. He stared at Nick, sitting surreally at the dining room table drinking red wine and holding the striped umbrella.

'I'm sorry,' said Joe, 'but I really don't get this. What is going on here?'

'Burst pipe, I imagine,' Nick said cheerfully. 'You're the plumber. You should know.'

Ignoring him, Joe turned to Carmen. 'You actually *live* here? What are you doing in a place like this?'

Numbly Carmen said, 'I just moved in a couple of weeks ago. Joe, could we chat privately for a—'

'Joe?' Nick picked up the name. 'Is this the ex-boyfriend you were telling me about?'

Joe's expression tightened. Defensively he said, 'What have you been telling people?'

Oh God, of all the plumbers in all the phone books . . .

'Look, *nothing*,' Carmen pleaded, 'but if we could just have a private word in the kitchen—'

'Don't expect to bill me for all this chit-chat,' grumbled Mr Sadler, checking his watch.

'This doesn't make sense.' Joe shook his head. 'What's happened to Fitzallen Square? Why aren't you there any more?'

Why can't you keep your big blabbering mouth *shut*, Carmen longed to flash back at him. Either that or take a swing at Joe with his ladder before stabbing him with her umbrella through the heart.

'Fitzallen Square?' Now it was Nick's turn to look perplexed. 'What were you doing in Fitzallen Square?'

'That was the last place she lived.' Joe shot him a look of disbelief.

'What?' Nick began to laugh. 'You didn't tell me about this! You mean you rented a room in one of those mansions? Or were you actually living with some mega-rich bloke?'

He was joking, but Carmen couldn't bring herself to smile.

'Hang on, who are *you*?' demanded Joe.

'I'm Carmen's boyfriend.' Nick remained calm. 'Why? D'you have a problem with that?'

Joe replied with a smirk, 'I reckon you're the one with the problem, mate, if you don't know where Carmen's been living up until now.'

'OK, stop it,' Carmen blurted out, horribly aware that even Mr Sadler was by this time agog. 'I'll *tell* Nick—'

'Why don't you let him tell me?' There was an edge to Nick's voice. 'He's clearly dying to.'

'So what happened?' Joe turned to Carmen. 'Did you sell it?'

Carmen said nothing.

'Sell what?' demanded Nick, putting down the umbrella.

'The house in Fitzallen Square.' Joe was by this time enjoying himself. 'Bloody great wedding cake of a place, five storeys high, pillars outside, the lot.'

Nick frowned. 'But whose house *is* it?'

'Hers, of course.' Returning his attention to Carmen, who was finding it increasingly hard to breathe, Joe said, 'Or have you rented it out to some Arab prince or something? I don't get it though. Why would you give up a place like that for a dump like this?'

Indignantly Mr Sadler said, 'Excuse *me*.'

'And forget to mention it to your new boyfriend,' Joe continued silkily, his eyes not leaving Carmen's chalk-white face.

Chapter 44

The room fell silent, apart from the steady drip of water falling from the ceiling. Finally Nick said in bewildered disbelief, 'You own a house in Fitzallen Square?'

'Yes.' Carmen nodded slowly. 'I do.'

'But how? How *can* you?'

'I . . . I . . .'

'She's loaded, mate. Got more money than the Bank of England.' Having realised that he'd put the cat well and truly amongst the pigeons, Joe said triumphantly, 'But she never told you. Funny, that. Then again, that's what these rich bitches are like, isn't it? Tight as two coats of paint. Probably terrified you might ask her to lend you a fiver.'

'And who was it,' Carmen shot back furiously, 'who made me feel like that? My God, you've got a nerve—'

'Is that true?' said Nick.

'What?' Carmen felt like a cornered animal. Everyone was looking at her.

'Is it true?'

'Of course it isn't true!'

'So why did you never tell me you were loaded?'

Oh *God*.

'Because . . . because it's not relevant,' stammered Carmen.

Behind her, she heard Joe's snort of derision.

'Because you didn't trust me?' Nick's expression was stony.

'No!'

'Then *why*?'

Floundering, Carmen babbled, 'I just . . . I just couldn't . . .'

'Fine.' Nick rose abruptly to his feet. 'Thanks for that. Bye.'

The door slammed shut behind him and he was gone.

'You *bastard*,' Carmen yelled at Joe.

'Am I? What, for telling the truth?' Joe shrugged, then broke into a broad, satisfied grin. 'Hey, I've just thought of something. If you'd lent me that twenty grand, I wouldn't still be working for this outfit.' Patting the company logo on his jacket he said, 'And your guilty secret would have been safe, because I wouldn't have been the one sent round here today.'

He was despicable. And Nick had every right to be upset with her. Unable to stand any more, Carmen raced out of the flat. Outside, it had begun to pour with rain. She caught up with Nick at the end of the street, tugging hard at the sleeve of his already sodden sweater when he didn't turn round.

'Nick, please, it isn't how it sounds. You have to listen to me.'

'Do I? I think you'll find it's exactly how it sounds.' Nick regarded her grimly, pushing his dripping wet hair back from his face. 'No wonder you've always kept so quiet about yourself. Where did the money come from?'

'My husband. I was married to Spike Todd.' Carmen's teeth were chattering with cold and fear. 'From Red Lizard,' she elaborated when Nick, whose favourite singers were Chas and Dave, looked blank. 'They're a rock band.'

'And now you aren't married any more. You divorced him,' said Nick, clearly none the wiser. 'But the settlement bagged you a house in Fitzallen Square. Handy, that.'

'I didn't divorce him. He died.' Part of Carmen marvelled that Nick genuinely didn't know. The other more shameful part wondered if the fact that she was a tragic young widow might work in her favour and earn her some much needed sympathy.

'When?' Nick wasn't looking remotely sympathetic.

'Three years ago.'

'How?'

'Drugs overdose.' Carmen blinked icy rain from her eyes. 'He was an addict.'

'Did you love him?'

'With all my heart.'

'How much is this house worth? The one in Fitzallen Square.'

He was interrogating her. Carmen knew how important it was to be honest now. 'I don't know. Six million, something like that.'

'Mortgage?'

'No.'

'And how much money d'you have besides that?

'I suppose . . . about the same again.' Carmen wondered if he'd expect her to produce bank statements. Maybe a tax return.

'And to think how great I thought you were when you gave that guy his train fare down to Cornwall last week.' Nick sounded disgusted. 'How stupid do you suppose that makes me feel?'

'Nick, I—'

'*Bloody* stupid, that's how much.' His mouth narrowed with anger. 'So this whole thing between you and me – I suppose it's all been some kind of sick joke.'

'No!' Horrified that he could even think that, Carmen took a step towards him but Nick moved smartly out of reach.

'OK, I'll ask you again. Why didn't you tell me?'

'I liked Joe. I trusted him.' Defiantly Carmen said, 'But I was wrong. He was stringing me along from the word go. All he cared about was getting his hands on my money.'

'And you thought I was the same.'

'I *didn't*.' Despairingly, Carmen willed him to understand.

'Right, so you thought I probably wasn't the same, but you weren't one hundred per cent sure,' said Nick.

'Well . . . kind of. I suppose so.' It wasn't perfect, but she didn't know how else to explain the fear Joe had instilled in her.

'You don't trust me. You think I'm a gold-digger.' Nick's fury was chilling.

'Oh please, I don't think that! I was *going* to tell you,' Carmen pleaded.

'No you weren't. You rented a flat in Battersea and let me help you decorate it.' His voice rising, Nick said, 'Annie went out and bought you a matching set of mugs as a house-warming present because I told her you didn't have any that weren't chipped. And guess what? *She* doesn't have six million in the bank. My God,' he retorted, 'I don't know how you can live with yourself.'

'I'm sorry.' Carmen had felt bad about that too. 'I'm sorry, but how could I have refused them?'

'Oh, I don't know,' Nick flashed back. 'Perhaps by telling her the truth? Confessing that you're a multimillionaire who doesn't actually need her lousy mugs? Explaining to her that when you aren't slumming it in a rented hovel in Battersea you live in a Chelsea mansion?' Something else occurred to him. 'Who else lives there? Or is it just you on your own?'

'Nancy,' said Carmen. 'And Rose, Nancy's mother. And Rennie, Spike's brother.' Honesty was one thing, but she couldn't bring herself to tell Nick that Rennie had disguised himself as a homeless person and come along to the shelter in order to quietly check him out.

249

'Nancy.' Nick's laugh was bitter. 'Your friend Nancy. Jesus, how do you manage to keep track of your lies? You've really taken me for an idiot, haven't you? Well, thank God I found out, that's all I can say.'

'*Wait*,' screamed Carmen as he began to stalk off. Chasing after him, half slipping on the wet pavement, she stumbled against his chest. 'Don't go, please don't go! I love you . . . we can go back to Fitzallen Square now, I'll show you the house—'

'Let go of me.' Less gently this time, Nick peeled her off him. 'You've known me for over a year and you still couldn't trust me enough to tell me the truth. I don't want to see you again,' he said icily, 'and I'm certainly not interested in your big fancy house.'

Leicester Square was awash with film fans undeterred by the grim weather. As Rennie and Karis made their way along the red carpet, flashbulbs popped and microphones were eagerly thrust out. Karis, who had begged Rennie to accompany her to the premiere, was having the time of her life posing for photographs in a hot-pink dress split to reveal skimpy silver knickers. Rennie, accosted by a journalist with a microphone, explained that yes, he was taking a few months off, no, he and Karis were just good friends and of course he was looking forward to seeing the film tonight, he wouldn't have missed it for the world.

Oh well, only two of those were lies. Karis was harmless enough but he wouldn't class her as a good friend. And the film was by all accounts a prize turkey. Still, at least he'd been telling the truth about taking time off.

'Rennie, this way.' Rejoining him, Karis intertwined her fingers with his so they could be photographed together for a gossip magazine. For such a small girl, she had a startlingly large set of teeth.

'Are you two an item?' another journalist asked hopefully.

'Just good friends.' Karis dimpled suggestively as she said it, implying with the aid of less than subtle body language that away from the spotlight they were actually at it like rabbits. Rennie wondered what on earth he was doing, preparing to watch a film he knew he didn't want to see, in the company of a girl he didn't particularly want to be with. If he were at home now, he could be watching Robert Donat in *Goodbye, Mr Chips*. Now that was a true classic. Instead, he was stuck out here in the freezing cold, being asked inane questions by inane people, and afterwards he'd be mentally blackmailed into saying nice things about ninety-five minutes of unadulterated—

'Switch it *off*,' hissed Karis.

'We're not in church.' Taking out his phone, Rennie answered it more to annoy Karis than for any other reason. The caller number wasn't one he recognised.

'Yes?'

'Um . . . right, is that . . . er, Rennie?'

'Who is this?' Rennie ignored Karis's frantic hand signals to end the call *this minute*.

'Right, well, I'm the landlord of the Queen's Head in Arnold Street. In Battersea.' Raising his voice to be heard above the babble of voices in the pub, the man said, 'I managed to get your number from a girl called Carmen.'

'And?' Faintly irritated, Rennie wondered what Carmen thought she was playing at, giving out his phone number to complete strangers. What was this bloke after, a signed photo?

'Rennie, put that bloody thing away.' Karis gave him a pointy-elbowed nudge. 'People are trying to *take our photograph* here.'

She said it as if it were on a par with splitting the atom.

'. . . lot to drink. So, um, maybe you should come and get her.'

What?

'Hang on, I missed that.' Batting away Karis's hand, Rennie frowned. 'Are you saying Carmen's there at the pub? Who's she got with her?'

'No one. That's why I'm calling you.'

'And she's been *drinking*?' Carmen had never been much of a drinker. Rennie wondered if this was a wind-up, someone's idea of a huge joke.

'Enough to float a battleship. And she's been buying rounds for everyone in the pub.' The landlord said wryly, 'I must be mad, I suppose, ringing you and asking you to take her away. But there you go. I reckon she needs to get home, sort herself out.'

'Let me have a word with her.' The landlord may have managed to get hold of his phone number but Rennie still found it hard to believe that this was really Carmen he was talking about.

'She won't come to the phone. She's up on the pool table right now, doing her Christina Aguilera impression.' He sighed. 'Again.'

'Carmen would never do that.'

'Hang on. Listen.'

Rennie listened as the landlord angled the phone – presumably – in the direction of the pool table. His blood ran cold as he heard a voice that was unmistakably Carmen's bellowing out, 'Because I'mmmm *beeeyooo-deefulll* . . .'

Shit.

'Rennie, what are you *playing* at?' Losing patience, Karis grabbed the sleeve of his jacket and tried to drag him forwards. 'The girl from *This Morning* is waiting to interview us! If we don't—'

'I'll be right there,' said Rennie.

'I should bloody well think so,' Karis huffed.

'Thanks, mate,' said the landlord.

Rennie ended the call and said, 'Right, I'm off.'

Karis stared at him as if he'd just slapped her round the face with a full nappy.

'You're *what*?'

'Leaving,' Rennie repeated. 'Sorry, it's an emergency. Have to go.'

'You mean, *now*?'

'No, next November. Of course I mean now.'

'But, but . . . we're at a premiere,' Karis wailed in disbelief. 'The girl from *This Morning* wants to talk to you about your shoes!'

Rennie glanced down at his green suede lace-ups. 'You can do it instead. Tell her they're size tens and quite similar to each other. I picked them up in a shopping mall in Baltimore. Forty dollars, bargain.'

'But what about me?' squealed Karis, beginning to panic. 'You're my partner! I can't go in and watch the film on my own!'

For a couple of seconds Rennie scanned the crowd of waving, cheering film fans lined up behind the metal barriers. Spotting a slightly gawky but presentable-looking young lad in his early twenties, he strode across and said cheerfully, 'Hi. Want to see the film?'

Aghast, Karis watched as Rennie, along with a couple of security staff, helped a gangly youth over the barrier and brought him over to where she was standing.

'This is Dave,' said Rennie, indicating that Karis should shake hands with the eager, bespectacled youth. 'He takes size ten too, isn't that a coincidence? Bought his shoes at Marks and Spencer, Marble Arch. He'd love to watch the film with you.'

'But . . . but . . .' Karis was gazing in horror at Dave's navy polyester jacket and perspiring upper lip.

'Sweetheart, you'll have a great time. Dave, take good care of her.' Giving Karis a hasty kiss on the cheek, Rennie said, 'Just think, this could be the start of a truly beautiful friendship.'

'Not between you and me, you rotten bastard,' Karis bellowed after him as he hurried off.

Chapter 45

Music was still blaring out as Rennie pushed his way into the Queen's Head in Battersea. Christina Aguilera had given way to Justin Timberlake on the karaoke machine. Over to the left, Carmen and a dreadlocked Wyclef Jean lookalike were arm in arm on top of the pool table, swaying recklessly from side to side as they sang along to 'Cry Me A River'.

Rennie walked over to the pool table. 'Carmen? Time to go home.'

'Cry me a ri-verrr,' Carmen wailed into her microphone, hideously off-key.

'Come on, sweetheart. That's enough now.'

'Heyyy! Rennie's here,' shouted Carmen, almost losing her balance and clinging to her singing partner for support. 'Three cheers for Rennie!'

'See what I mean?' said the pub landlord, materialising at Rennie's side. 'She's just bought another eight bottles of champagne.'

'Don't worry your pretty little head about it.' Carmen wagged her finger at the landlord. 'I can afford eight hundred bottles of champagne, OK? I've got *looooaaads* of money. Hey, Rennie, come on up here and sing with us, we're doing great!'

All around them, people were knocking back champagne from an assortment of wine glasses, tumblers and pint mugs. Some were swigging it straight from the bottle.

'Carmen. Let's go.' Rennie held out his hands.

'No. I'm *singing*.' Defiantly Carmen said, 'I'm fantastic.'

'Of course you are, but sometimes it's better to leave your audience wanting more.' Reaching up, he managed to prise the microphone from her hand and seize her by the wrist. 'Now just climb down onto this chair, good girl, and down again . . . that's it, excellent. OK, let's get out of here, shall we? I've got a car waiting outside.'

'You're no fun,' Carmen grumbled, stumbling against him. 'I only gave the landlord your number so you could come down here and join in. We've been having the best time, you know. I've made loads of new friends. Bye bye, everyone.' She waved and blew kisses at random, then twisted round to blow an extra big goodbye kiss at Wyclef Jean, still up on the pool table. 'See you all again soon . . . I'm going now . . . missing you already – whoops, who moved that door?'

Outside the pub, the cold night air hit Carmen like a brick. All the co-ordination went out of her and feeding her into the waiting car was like trying to fit an eel into a shoebox. With difficulty, Rennie persuaded her to stay on the back seat.

'I say, this is posh . . . it's years since I was in one of these.'

'Couldn't get a taxi.' In his hurry to rescue Carmen, Rennie had been forced to commandeer one of the stretch limos outside the cinema. The driver now turned and gave him a doubtful look.

'Not going to be sick, is she?'

'I'm never sick,' Carmen loftily proclaimed.

'Just take us to Fitzallen Square,' said Rennie.

'Oh look, all my friends have come out to say goodbye.' Carmen waved pointlessly through the blacked-out windows at the gaggle of regulars who had congregated on the pavement to gawp at the limo as if it were a spaceship. It clearly wasn't every day of the week that someone like Rennie Todd materialised in their little backstreet pub.

'What happened?' Rennie said bluntly as the limousine pulled away from the kerb.

Carmen wilted, rubbed her hands across her face and slumped back against the seat.

'A pipe burst. The flat got flooded.'

'And?'

Her eyes closed, Carmen said, 'Joe James arrived to fix it.'

'Ah.'

'Nick's gone. It's all over.' She took a deep shuddery breath. '*Again*.'

'Oh, sweetheart.'

'He hates me. And I don't blame him.'

'That's stupid,' Rennie declared.

'It's not stupid! I lied to Nick. I didn't trust him and I should have done. I knew he wasn't like Joe, but I carried on anyway and now I've lost him.'

Good, Rennie found himself thinking, and wondered why. Perhaps that was something he'd better not dwell on. Aloud he said, 'Did you explain why you did it?'

'He wasn't interested. As far as Nick's concerned, I thought he was a gold-digger.'

'Maybe when he's had time to think it through—'

'He's not going to change his mind.' Carmen raked her fingers through her hair and shook her head helplessly. 'It's over. He despises me. Of course he despises me, I did a terrible thing . . . he's the most honest, decent person in the world and I didn't *trust* him . . .'

If he was that honest and decent, thought Rennie, he'd surely understand why Carmen had done what she had.

'Do you want me to speak to him?'

'No point. Oops, head's gone spinny.' Swaying against him, Carmen mumbled, 'He wouldn't recognise you, you know, if you went to see him. He's never even heard of Red Lizard.'

Which only made him more of a dickhead as far as Rennie was concerned. The chauffeur turned into Fitzallen Square and he murmured, 'Never mind. Nearly home now.'

'Thanks for coming to fetch me.' Carmen leaned her head against his shoulder. 'I knew I was getting a bit drunk.'

'How much did you spend in the pub?'

'About seven hundred pounds. Lucky they took American Express.' Ruefully she said, 'You wouldn't believe how popular I was.'

'I'll bet.'

The limo pulled up outside the house. Rennie paid the driver and helped Carmen out of the back seat.

'Nancy and Rose are out. They're gone to the theatre.'

'I know. The pub landlord tried to ring them earlier, didn't get any reply. That's why I gave him your number.' Carmen looked at Rennie, evidently noticing for the first time that he was wearing a smart suit. 'You weren't doing anything special, were you?'

'Nothing special at all. Come on now, will your legs work? Let's get you inside.'

Rennie settled Carmen on the sofa with a duvet and a mug of strong black coffee before disappearing upstairs to change out of his suit. By the time he headed back to the living room in jeans and an old black T-shirt, he fully expected Carmen to be asleep.

Instead she was clutching the phone, gazing into space.

'I just rang Nick. He wasn't kidding when he said he didn't want to see me again.' Shifting over so that Rennie could sit down, Carmen said, 'He doesn't want me working at the shelter any more.'

Total dickhead.

'Tell him to get stuffed,' Rennie retorted. 'He can't stop you.'

'He's in charge. I'm only a volunteer. He says there are plenty of other charities I can work for.'

'What a tosser.'

'Oh God, what am I going to *do*?' Chucking the phone across the room, Carmen covered her face.

'Easy. Find someone who deserves you,' Rennie said bluntly. 'Because you can sure as hell do better than him.'

'Right. Silly me for asking.' Carmen raised her slanting dark eyebrows. 'And who exactly do you suggest this time? How about Prince William? He wouldn't let it bother him that I've got a few bob in the bank. Or Hugh Grant, maybe? Or . . . ooh, I know, *Hugh Hefner*.'

Or me.

Rennie didn't say it aloud. He kept this renegade suggestion to himself, firmly packed down somewhere deep inside his chest, in the place he had kept it hidden for the last two months. Since Christmas night, in fact, when he had realised for the first time the true extent of his feelings towards Carmen.

'What?' Carmen demanded irritably. 'Why are you looking at me like that?'

'Prince William's too young. Hugh Grant's too st-st-stuttery. Hugh Hefner wears too many dressing gowns.' Rennie shook his head. 'He's really not your type.'

'You're so critical.'

'I know you. I know you better than almost anyone else on this planet.' And I love you, Rennie silently added, because it was true. Now might not be the time to tell her, but he did.

'Oh God,' groaned Carmen, 'my life is such . . . crap. Whatever's going to happen to me?'

'Hey, you'll be fine.'

'Give me a hug.' She turned to him, craving reassurance and comfort, and Rennie told himself he could do this, he *could*. Even if he did feel like Cyrano de Bergerac.

With a smaller nose, naturally.

He put his arms round Carmen and she rested her head against his chest.

'Mmm. You smell nice,' she mumbled.

'Carbolic.' Rennie stroked her dark spiky hair and wondered what Carmen would do if he kissed her. Not that he could allow himself to do it.

'You know, you're a pretty good hugger.'

'Years of practice,' Rennie said lightly. This was killing him, just killing him. The timing couldn't be worse. All he could do was be patient, let her get this latest idiot out of her system, then let her know how he felt. And maybe use the time in between to prove that he had changed for the better.

Plus, a bit of celibacy probably wouldn't go amiss.

Drowsily Carmen said, 'Want to watch a film?'

'Fine. Any favourites?'

'You choose.'

Easing himself away, Rennie sorted through the pile of DVDs next to the TV. Having selected one, he sat back down and settled Carmen comfortably against him once more before pressing Play on the remote.

'*Brigadoon*.' The corners of her mouth lifted with amusement. 'You're such an old softy.'

'It's a brilliant film.'

Carmen, her eyelashes beginning to droop, mumbled, 'I'm quite sleepy now.'

'Go ahead. You can even snore if you like.'

'You're such a gentleman.'

I could be, thought Rennie as her eyelids fluttered shut. If you'd just give me the chance to prove it.

'Morning, sweetheart. How are you feeling?'

'Ancient.' Nancy pulled a face.

'You're in your prime,' Zac chided, reaching behind the workroom door and producing with a flourish a lavishly wrapped present awash with trailing silver ribbons and iridescent gauze. 'Ta-daaah. Happy birthday!'

'You really shouldn't have,' Nancy lied happily, tearing into the gauze and the lilac embossed paper. 'My God, you can tell you're gay. No straight man would ever bother to wrap like this.'

'Classic gay guy trick. Wrap fabulously and it makes up for a crap present.'

'Oops, you made a mistake,' said Nancy. 'You accidentally gave me a good one instead.' She separated the mounds of tissue to reveal a squashy, pyramid-shaped shoulder bag made from soft purply-blue leather striped with pink and green velvet and dotted with multi-coloured twisted leather butterflies. She gave Zac a hug, overwhelmed and secretly relieved that he hadn't presented her with one of his eccentric one-armed sweaters. 'In fact it's better than good, it's amazing. I don't know why you don't—'

'Stick to bags and give up the clothes?' Zac aimed a playful swipe at her head. 'Cheeky wench. I know how you feel about my collection.'

Yes, but I'm *right*, thought Nancy. The clothes Zac designed might be completely weird but his bags were divine with a quirky charm all of their own.

'Never mind. I love it. Thank you so much.' She kissed Zac on both cheeks. 'I don't even mind being ancient now. Are you still OK for tonight?'

Rennie had booked a table at the Tipsy Prawn in Mayfair, undoubtedly because it was a present he couldn't be expected to wrap.

'Try and stop me,' said Zac. 'I hear the waiters are out of this world.'

'Eight o'clock. Don't be late. Now, whose turn is it to make the coffee?'

'Yours.'

'But it's my birthday,' Nancy said smugly. 'I'm twenty-nine. Plus I'm too busy admiring my lovely new handbag.'

'I don't know.' Zac scratched his head in despair. 'One of us is the boss here. I just wish I could remember who.'

Chapter 46

The Tipsy Prawn, a riot of red and gold decor teamed with saucy waiters and chandeliers the size of dustbin lids, was already packed by eight o'clock. Nancy, greeting everyone as they arrived, wondered just how much of a masochist you had to be to welcome the object of your affections and his new girlfriend along to your own birthday party. Then she felt guilty, because Tabitha was great and she genuinely liked her. Plus, of course, they shared the same excellent taste in men. It was just her bad luck that Connor preferred Tabitha.

Anyway, she hadn't had much choice tonight. Rennie had invited Connor and Mia, and Mia had been the one to suggest that Connor brought Tabitha along too. Nancy knew that Mia was keen to encourage the budding relationship, both because she liked Tabitha and because it meant Connor wouldn't be tempted to drift back to Cyanide Sadie.

'Oh my God, let me see that,' Tabitha exclaimed. 'Where did you *get* that bag?'

'It's one of Zac's.' Nancy gave first Tabitha, then Connor, a kiss. 'You can shower him with praise when he gets here; he'll love that.'

'*Another* one? Rose, you're drinking like a fish tonight,' scolded Rennie.

'It's water, pet.'

'That's what you say. Looks more like neat gin to me. Now, are we ready to sit down?' Rennie was busy being in charge. 'Mia, you're over there. Carmen, you're next to me. What time's the stripper booked to arrive?'

'I hope you're joking,' said Nancy.

'Never presume, sweetheart. It's Brigadier Brough-Badman in a thong.'

Nancy swiped at Rennie with a napkin. 'Don't. Zac's still terrified you're going to say something to Marjorie.'

'As if I would. Soul of discretion, me. Bloody hell,' Rennie exclaimed, gazing past Nancy in disbelief. 'Who's Zac brought along with him? Don't tell me that's his new boyfriend.'

259

Nancy turned. The man with Zac was a couple of inches shorter than him and a couple of decades older. Amongst the trendily dressed diners and baroque decor he stood out as they wove their way between tables, in his brown speckled V-necked cardigan, white shirt, brown corduroys and polished brogues. His grey hair was cut short and neatly swept back from a face that was oddly familiar.

'You know,' said Rennie, mystified, 'Zac has the weirdest taste in men. And my God, what does *he* look like tonight? Is it some kind of kinky new thing, d'you suppose, to dress up like Percy Thrower?'

Nancy gave him a nudge because Zac's fine blond hair was tied back in a ponytail and he was wearing a moss-green sweater over a paler green shirt and plain dark trousers. She knew who the older man was. She just didn't know what he was doing here.

Clearly ill at ease, Zac approached her and said in a rush, 'Hi, Nance, sorry about this, I tried to reach you earlier but your phone was switched off. This is my father, William Parris. Dad, this is Nancy who works for me.'

'Zac's friend.' William nodded cheerfully, shaking Nancy's hand. 'I've heard all about you, love. Good to meet you at last. And many happy returns of the day.'

'Dad turned up unexpectedly this evening,' Zac went on hurriedly. 'Look, I know they won't be able to squeeze in another place, so we'll be off, but Dad just wanted to come and say hello before—'

'No problem.' Rennie indicated the waiter with whom he'd just had a word. 'All sorted, they can fit another chair round the table if we all breathe in. William, let me introduce you to everyone. I'm Rennie, this is Carmen and this is Rose . . .'

'God, I'm sorry,' whispered Zac as William was whisked away to meet the others. 'The doorbell went and there he was. No warning, nothing! He just announced he'd come to stay for a week. I mean, what could I do? And I certainly wasn't planning on bringing him along tonight—'

'It's fine,' Nancy said, because Zac was sounding panicky. And notably un-camp.

'But I'd written it on my kitchen calendar and he spotted it. As soon as Dad realised it was your birthday there was no stopping him, he *insisted* we—'

'Really, it doesn't matter a bit,' Nancy patiently repeated.

'But it *does*,' Zac blurted out, 'because what if someone *says* anything? You know, about *me* . . .'

'They won't. I'll tell Rennie,' Nancy promised, because this was clearly whom Zac was most bothered about.

'And it's not only that.' Zac gazed at her in anguish. 'I . . . er, well, I kind of let him think you're my, um . . .'

'He thinks I'm your girlfriend.' Belatedly realising what he was struggling to tell her, Nancy smothered the urge to laugh.

'I'm sorry. I told you I was a hopeless case.' Zac shook his head apologetically. 'And it's not a complete lie. I'm sure I'd fancy you if I was straight.'

Which was quite flattering in its own way.

'OK, don't panic. We'll get through this. You'd better sit by me. We'll put your dad next to Rose. And don't worry,' Nancy assured him. 'Everything's going to be fine.'

The waiter brought an extra chair and laid another place at the table. Nancy tried not to notice how happy Tabitha looked, next to Connor. The menus arrived, orders were taken and in his comfortable West Country drawl, Zac's father explained what had brought him to London.

'I had to get away from my next-door neighbour. Divorcee,' he explained with an economical shrug. 'Driving me mad, she is. You know how it is when you're not remotely interested in someone and they've got a bit of a crush on you? Well, that's what's gone and happened with Margaret.'

Inwardly wincing, Nancy avoided glancing across the table at Connor.

'What's she doing?' said Carmen.

'What isn't she doing, more like.' William pulled a rueful face. 'Let me tell you, I'm not getting a minute's peace. The blessed woman's knocking on my door at all hours, asking me to help her with this and that, bringing me food, inviting me along to the social club.'

'Maybe she's just being friendly,' Mia suggested.

'Hmm. I know what kind of friendship that one has in mind.' William gave Zac a back-me-up look. 'Am I right, son? Not backward in coming forward is Margaret. Rang my doorbell at ten o'clock last night in her negligee, begging me to go over and get a spider out of her bath.'

'Ah, the old spider in the bath trick,' Rennie said with a grin. 'Carmen's always trying that one on with me. Subtlety's never been her strong point either.'

'Rennie has delusions of desirability,' said Carmen. 'Ignore him.'

'Anyway, I'd just about had enough,' William went on. 'Margaret was putting pressure on me and not taking no for an answer. I needed to get away and I've never been to London before. So I just thought what the hell, let's go for it. And here I am.' He spread his hands happily. 'I've escaped. Come to visit my son for a week or two. And meet this lovely girlfriend of his in the flesh.'

This last pronouncement was greeted with something of a startled silence. Nancy took a big gulp of wine. Everyone was looking at her. After a pause, Rose said brightly, 'Well, it's lovely to meet you too, William. We'll have to make sure you enjoy yourself while you're here.'

'And I promise not to ask you to come and get spiders out of my bath,' said Rennie. 'Not in my negligee anyway.'

Tabitha leaned across, almost setting fire to Nancy's sleeve with her cigarette. 'I must say, you're a dark horse,' she exclaimed. 'I didn't even realise you and Zac were an item! To be honest, I thought he was—'

'God, sorry, I'm a clumsy oaf,' Connor exclaimed, having managed to knock his cutlery into Tabitha's lap.

'I hope I'm not going to be making things awkward for the two of you.' William turned to Nancy, concerned. 'I won't be in the way, will I?'

'Absolutely not.' Shaking her head vigorously, Nancy realised she was going to have to have a private word with Tabitha. 'We're taking things very slowly; you won't be in the way at all. Um, Tab, you couldn't come out to the ladies with me, could you? I need to borrow some mascara.'

'Hang on, let me just pull this fork out of my leg,' said Tabitha. 'Connor's just tried a spot of DIY liposuction. I think it's his way of telling me my thighs are too fat.'

Connor put his arm round Tabitha and planted a kiss on her cheek. 'There's nothing wrong with your thighs. Stop fishing for compliments.'

Tabitha was clearly overjoyed to be here with Connor. Mia was delighted Tabitha was here with Connor. And it was obvious that Connor was enjoying himself. Nancy, her stomach tightening, tried hard to be happy for them too. It wasn't easy, feeling like a wallflower at your own birthday dinner. She was so lucky to be here, surrounded by friends. Why on earth couldn't she get this stupid crush out of her system? Why did Connor have to be so nice and live next door?

'I only moved down here a few weeks ago myself,' Rose confided to William as their main courses arrived, 'so if you want showing around, I'd be happy to help. But only if you'd like me to,' she added hastily. 'I won't turn into a stalker, I promise.'

William's face softened. 'Of course you won't. I'd love a hand with the underground – can't make head nor tail of it at the moment. And I've heard all about you too. Zac tells me you're the best knitter he's ever had working for him.'

262

'Och, he's a lovely boy. You must be very proud of him, doing so marvellously, people from all over the world buying his clothes.'

'I am, I am.' William nodded. 'I mean, I know it's a funny job for a grown man, but Zac always had it in his head to be a designer, even from a lad. And who knows what'll happen now that he and Nancy have got together?'

Not a lot, thought Rose.

'You and I could end up as in-laws,' William went on with enthusiasm.

Hmm. Diplomatically Rose said, 'Well, maybe we shouldn't get too excited. As they said, it's still early days.'

'Yes, but wouldn't it be great?'

It would be astounding. Breaking into her monkfish *en croute*, Rose said, 'Now stop it. You know there's nothing more likely to put children off than parents frantically matchmaking. They have to make their own decisions.'

William leaned sideways and murmured, 'I know, but I've been waiting so long for something like this to happen. You see, Zac's never been exactly . . . well, he hasn't shown much sign before of getting himself settled down.'

Oh dear, thought Rose. Someone was going to have to tell him. It wasn't right that William didn't know.

Chapter 47

'Sorry about earlier,' Tabitha murmured in Zac's ear. 'Nancy told me in the loo. I spend my life putting my big feet in it. Now listen, this bag of hers is seriously fantastic. Can I ask how much it retails for?'

'Three fifty.' Zac didn't betray his surprise that someone who was got up like Tabitha should be interested in a bag that cost that much. Her dress sense might be abysmal, but women and bags were an unfathomable law unto themselves.

'Is that your best price?' Tabitha was gazing longingly at Nancy's bag.

'My God, you drive a hard bargain.' Zac smiled. 'OK, OK, three hundred.'

'Any colour I like?'

'Any colour you like.'

'Waiting time?'

'Two weeks,' said Zac.

'Excellent. My boss is going to love this.'

That explained it, then. The bag wasn't for Tabitha after all. To show how generous and broad-minded he was, Zac said untruthfully, 'I like your top.'

Tabitha looked smug. She was wearing a sleeveless pink and white striped rollneck sweater with sparkly bits in it. 'Vintage. I was over at my mum's last week and she was chucking a whole load of stuff out. This came from Marks and Spencer twenty-five years ago. Practically the time I was born! You'd never know it, would you?'

'Never,' Zac solemnly agreed. What had Nancy told him Tabitha did for a living? Financial journalist, that was it.

Well, that explained a lot.

Carmen was touched that Mia should be so indignant on her behalf, but it was a faintly bizarre experience being lectured to by a sixteen-year-old.

'Forget him,' Mia declared between mouthfuls of asparagus. 'Honestly, what a loser. You're way better off without someone like that, believe me.'

Mia evidently had never known a moment of self-doubt in her life. Humouring her, Carmen said, 'So what would you advise in future?'

'Well, the way I see it, you have a number of choices.' Putting down her knife and fork, Mia swished back her blond hair and with an air of importance began counting on her fingers. 'Next time you meet a man you like, you could just say, now look here, the thing is I'm really rather rich but because I've been mucked about in the past you have to understand that you won't be getting your sweaty paws on a single penny of my money because none of it is *ever* going to come your way.'

Sweaty paws. Attractive.

'Right.' Carmen nodded solemnly, envisaging herself announcing this to some open-mouthed potential suitor. 'Is that what you'd do?'

'Maybe, I'm not sure. Depends on the man.' Mia was entirely serious. 'Or you could do what you did with Nick and hope that the next man might be a bit more understanding than that wazzock when you tell him the truth.'

'I'm not going through that again,' Carmen said bluntly. 'Next?'

'OK, so maybe *having* all that money is the problem. In which case, have you ever thought of getting rid of it?'

The girl really was a case. 'Have a bonfire, you mean?'

'Nooo. Give it away to charity! All of it!' Spreading her hands in a gesture that signalled aren't-I-fantastic? Mia exclaimed, 'Then you'd be poor again and all your problems would be over!'

'That's the worst idea I've ever heard.' Carmen shook her head, struggling to keep a straight face because Mia was so young, *so* idealistic. 'One, I give plenty of money to charity, but there's such a thing as being too generous. Two, Spike earned that money, he worked his socks off for it and he'd go mental if I gave it away. And three, I don't want to be poor again. I'm sorry, I'm just not that unselfish.'

'Oh well, it was a long shot.' Mia shrugged. 'To be honest, I probably wouldn't want to do that either.'

'Any other ideas?'

'Find someone rich.'

Great. Back to Hugh Hefner.

'Rennie already had that idea,' said Carmen.

'Did he?' Mia speared a cherry tomato with her fork. 'Interesting.'

'Why is that interesting?'

'Well, Rennie's rich.'

Carmen choked on her drink. Spluttering and feeling hot, she said, 'What's *that* supposed to mean?'

'Nothing. I'm just saying.'

'Rennie's my brother-in-law.'

'So? It's not illegal. In fact it's surprisingly common,' Mia went on, warming to her cause. 'I mean, think about it. They have the same genes. If you like one brother enough to marry them, why wouldn't you like the other?'

Carmen took another gulp of wine. 'I do like Rennie. As a friend. But he isn't like Spike. They might share the same genes but if you didn't know they were brothers, you'd never guess. They're different in every way.'

'OK. But he's still rich.' Mia was implacable.

'So's Prince Philip, but it doesn't mean I fancy him.'

Rolling her eyes, Mia said, 'Excuse me. Rennie's a *teeny* bit better looking than Prince Philip. I mean, I know he's almost old enough to be my father, but even I can see he's a catch.'

Carmen couldn't quite believe they were having this conversation. Rennie would die laughing if he overheard what Mia was saying.

'It's not going to happen,' she repeated. 'He really isn't my type.'

'Why not?'

Oh, for heaven's sake. 'He just *isn't*, OK? Trust me.'

Mia said interestedly, 'Have you ever slept with him?'

'No!' Carmen gazed around wildly, wondering if anyone would notice if she gagged Mia with a napkin.

'Fine, calm down, only asking.' Carrying on unperturbed, Mia said, 'Ever thought about it?'

A napkin probably wouldn't be big enough. Maybe a tablecloth. '*No.*'

'What, never even wondered what it'd be like?'

'Of course I haven't!' lied Carmen, beginning to panic.

'No need to go red. It's only natural to *wonder* things. I mean, Rennie's got millions of fans. He's extra good-looking. They'd give anything to sleep with him—'

'And plenty of them have,' Carmen said bluntly, 'which could explain why the idea doesn't interest me.'

'Really? Gosh, now that *is* interesting.' Completely seriously Mia said, 'So who would you go for then, if you could choose? Cliff Richard?'

When dinner was over, everyone retreated to the bar downstairs to collapse into red velvet sofas, unfasten tight zips, and carry on drinking and

266

gossiping. Having checked that Tabitha was happily occupied chatting away to Mia and Nancy, Connor joined Rennie over at the bar and lit up a long overdue cigarette.

'Great evening,' said Connor, offering him a Marlboro and accepting a balloon glass of cognac. 'Thanks.'

'My pleasure.' Rennie's eyes glittered with amusement. 'Especially the look on Zac's face when Tabitha nearly outed him in front of his old man.'

'I thought Zac was going to wet himself. Poor Tab, she was mortified when she found out what she'd almost done.'

Rennie nodded over at Tabitha, with her tousled blond hair and merry face. 'So is this it then? Could she be the one?' It wasn't that he hankered after Tabitha himself, but the thought of couples being idyllically happy together had begun to stir envy in him in recent months.

'No,' said Connor.

'No? Really? I thought the two of you got on well.'

'We do. But she still isn't the one.' Shaking his head, Connor took a drag of his cigarette and exhaled a plume of smoke. 'OK, you want the truth? I've developed a system. It's called self-preservation. You see, Mia's desperate to see me settled down.' He pulled a face. 'And you know what my daughter's like when she gets an idea into her head. So what I do now is, I never let on when I really like someone, otherwise Mia just charges in like a rhino. It's mayhem. The best thing to do is head her off at the pass, just state categorically that whoever it is does nothing for you. That way, you nip her plans in the bud before she can destroy your life.'

Rennie grinned, only too easily able to imagine Mia in unstoppable matchmaking mode. 'She's a handful.'

'You're not kidding.' Connor spoke with feeling. 'Once, when she was ten, she asked me if I thought her form teacher was pretty. Miss Quinn, her name was. Well, the unfortunate woman had cross-eyes and a bit of a wart on her nose, but what can you do? I said I thought Miss Quinn was very pretty and didn't think any more of it. But that was enough for Mia. She wrote an essay about her daddy being in love with Miss Quinn and wanting to marry her so they could have lots of children together and live happily ever after in a big house by the sea. Bloody embarrassing parents' evening, let me tell you, being flirted with by Miss Quinn and her quivering wart. She kept telling me how much she loved the theatre, waiting for me to ask her out. Anyway,' Connor shuddered at the memory and stubbed out his cigarette, 'that was enough to scar me for life. Never again. Mia might be able to boss me around but there's no way she's going to interfere with my love life. She encouraged me to go out with Tabitha and I'm going along with that to keep her happy, but there's no future in it. If I really like someone, the last thing I'm going to do is let Mia get wind of – oh, hi!'

'Hi,' said Nancy, breathing fast as Connor spun round to face her. 'Sorry, I didn't mean to—'

'Pinch your bum?' said Rennie cheerfully. 'Nance, you have to stop doing that. It's harassment.'

'Interrupt.' Flustered, Nancy attempted to make sense of what she'd just overheard. If it meant what she thought it meant . . .

'Hey, no problem, Nancy can pinch my bum any time she likes.' Connor grinned, then glanced over at the sofas. 'Although Zac's father might wonder what's going on.'

'Not to mention Tabitha,' Rennie added with a wink.

'I didn't actually pinch anybody's bum,' said Nancy. 'I only came over to let you know Mia doesn't want ice in her Coke.'

Connor sighed. 'And there was me thinking I was irresistible.'

Nancy gazed at him, wondering why he always had to make it so hard to tell whether or not he was joking. Oh God, so did this mean his assertion to Mia that he didn't find her remotely attractive *hadn't* been true? Could he actually—

'Of course he's irresistible.' Appearing at Nancy's side, Tabitha gave her a cheery nudge. 'Didn't I tell you that the first moment I clapped eyes on him? I said, that'll do for me!'

'Flattery'll get you everywhere.' Connor slid his arm round her curvy waist.

'Ten out of ten, I awarded you. Of course, you've gone down to eight now.' Beaming up at him, Tabitha said, 'I've never known anyone take so long to order a round of drinks.'

'Ah well, there are some things you shouldn't hurry.' Connor's eyes crinkled at the corners. 'Take as long as possible, that's what I say, and make sure you get it right.' Puzzled, he lifted his head. 'What was that?'

Nancy looked as mystified as the rest of them, passionately grateful that nobody else seemed to have realised that she'd just squeaked like a mouse.

Chapter 48

Nick looked up as Rennie appeared in the kitchen doorway. 'Hi. Can I help you?'

Friendly and without a flicker of recognition.

'I'm Rennie Todd,' said Rennie, causing the thin redhead currently washing up at the sink to whip round and stare at him, open-mouthed in disbelief.

Nick's expression changed, grew less friendly. 'Carmen's brother-in-law. The big rock star.'

'Oh God, you're Rennie Todd,' gasped the skinny redhead. 'From Red Lizard.'

'I am,' Rennie agreed.

'Pat, just get on with the washing-up.' Nick's tone was curt. 'We're going through to the office.'

'Oh, but—'

'And we don't want to be disturbed.'

Once they were inside the office, Rennie said, 'This won't take long.'

Nick scowled. 'It certainly won't if you've come here to try and persuade me to change my mind. I suppose Carmen sent you, she's—'

'Yes, she sent me. And no, I haven't come here to try and change your mind. Far from it,' Rennie went on evenly. Deeply tempting though it was to tell Nick he'd made the biggest mistake of his life, he didn't want him thinking it through, realising that he might be right and promptly having a change of heart. The last thing he needed was Nick embarking on a campaign to win Carmen back. *Wanker.* Aloud he said, 'Anyway, never mind about that. Carmen's fine. Very well indeed. She asked me to come here because she has something for one of your clients.'

Nick's eyes narrowed. 'Who?'

'Harry. Carmen said he usually comes in around now for his lunch.'

'What's she got for him?'

Ignoring the question, Rennie said, 'Is he here?'

'Yes.'

'Good. I'll go and have a word with him.'

'I'll come with you, point him out.'

'No need.' Rennie, who remembered only too well what Harry looked like, said, 'I can manage.'

Harry was sitting in the tartan armchair at the far end of the room, away from the blaring television and a spirited debate about Premier Division football clubs. As before, he was buried in a book. When Rennie sat down beside him, he glanced up and – unlike Nick – recognised him.

But not in an overwhelmed, Pat-in-the-kitchen type of way.

'Hello,' said Harry.

'Hi. Rennie Todd.' As Rennie shook his hand, he saw that the book Harry had been reading was a yellowed, battered copy of Roget's Thesaurus. 'I'm a friend of Carmen's.'

Harry nodded slowly. 'She's a good girl. Everyone liked Carmen. Not working here any more, I understand. We'll miss her.'

'There's something she'd like you to have.' Rennie took a labelled key from the pocket of his leather jacket. 'She took a six-month lease on a flat in Battersea, but she won't be using it now. So it's yours if you want it. Otherwise it'll be standing empty.'

Harry's hand began to tremble as he took the key and looked at the address on the label. 'Why me?'

'Why anyone? Carmen thought you'd appreciate the peace and quiet. There's a word processor in the flat,' said Rennie, 'in case you feel like making a start on another book. You never know, things might turn out differently this time. No pressures. It's a decent little place. Furnished. Had a burst pipe recently, but everything's been dried out now and redecorated.'

There were tears in Harry's eyes. Aware that he and Rennie were being watched by everyone else in the room, he wiped his face with his sleeve.

'Tell her thank you. You don't know what this means to me.' Harry shook his hand. 'This is incredible.'

'No problem. Look, I'm going to go now.' Before he attracted too much more attention, Rennie rose to his feet. 'Good luck with the writing.'

Harry sat there for several seconds after Rennie had left, silently gazing at the key.

Nick came over and said, 'What was that all about, then?'

'Carmen's given me a flat for six months.' Harry's voice quivered with emotion. 'And a word processor. So that I can start writing again.'

Nick frowned. How on earth had Carmen found out about Harry's brief encounter with the world of publishing?

One thing was for sure, she certainly hadn't heard it from him.

*　　*　　*

'Crikey, it's Janice,' said Zac, startled and double-checking his watch. 'Hello, my darling, bit early for you, isn't it? I thought you didn't get out of bed before midday – whoaaah, whatever *happened* to you?'

Equally shocked, Nancy stared as Janice Hazzard removed her dark glasses to reveal dramatically blackened eyes and a bruised and swollen cheekbone. Only Doreen, unperturbed, leapt up from her basket and trotted across the shop to greet one of her favourite customers.

'You see, this is what's so heavenly about dogs,' Janice exclaimed, scooping Doreen up into her arms and letting the little dog lick her face. 'You can look a complete gargoyle and they still love you.'

'She loves you because you always give her chocolate buttons.' Bemused by Janice's chirpy manner, Zac peered more closely at her face. 'Did you have your eyes done? I can't see any stitches.'

'My darling, I was attacked! Mugged!' Janice tut-tutted. 'Honestly, you can tell you don't read the papers.'

'When? What happened? My God, sit down! Nancy, get her a coffee, run upstairs and get the brandy, the good stuff.'

'Will you stop fussing about me? I'm *fine*.' Janice flapped her bejewelled hands, wafting clouds of Eau Dynamisante. 'Calm down, for heaven's sake. I'm a tough old bird. Bloody hell, compared with all the crap I've had to put up with in my life from men, this was nothing.'

'You could have been killed,' Zac shouted, far more shaken than Janice.

'But I wasn't. What's more, I won.' Sitting down and crossing her legs, she looked triumphant. 'This *huge* bloke jumped me as I was heading up our front path, tried to grab my bag. Your bag,' she added, patting the turquoise and apricot suede and velvet shoulder bag on her lap. 'Well, what a cheek, I wasn't going to let him take *that*, was I? So we had a little wrestle.'

'Are you mad?' Zac bellowed in disbelief. 'You're lucky he didn't have a knife!'

'I love my bag. He wasn't having it,' Janice repeated. 'So anyway, that was when he punched me in the face, expecting me to go down like a skittle. Except what with all the practice I've had, getting battered by men, I didn't. And that was when I whacked him with my bag.'

'That bag?' Nancy said doubtfully. Suede? Velvet? Lined with silk?

'Ah, but what he didn't know was what I had in it.' Janice triumphantly recrossed her legs. 'Malcolm's always said I carry around everything bar the kitchen sink. That's why I like a bag that's nice and roomy.'

Zac said, 'What did you have in it?'

'Well, make-up case, obviously. Phone. Purse. Keys. Cigs, heavy lighter,

271

A-Z – you know, all the usual stuff. Then, happily, I happened to have nicked a really big glass ashtray from the restaurant my agent had taken me to at lunchtime.'

'That's a lot.' Zac nodded.

'Spare pair of shoes. Manolos, of course.'

'Ouch,' said Zac.

'And an alarm clock and a jar of olives,' Janice said happily. 'Oh, and a travel iron.'

'Jesus. So is he dead?'

'No, but he's completely ruined my lovely bay tree. Went flying backwards and squashed it flat. And he smashed the pot. Oh, thank you, darling.' Accepting a cup of coffee from Nancy, Janice went on, 'Anyway, I'd been yelling blue murder and my neighbours all came out to see what was going on. They sat on him until the police arrived. And that was it, he was arrested and carted off.' She rummaged busily in her bag, producing a newspaper. 'And I'm a heroine!'

'You've always been my heroine,' said Zac.

'That's not all. Lots of lovely publicity for you too, darling.' Smugly, Janice turned to page five.

Nancy and Zac gazed at the headline – Wallop! Brave Janice beats mugger – above a photograph of Janice and her black eyes, beaming triumphantly and brandishing her bag. To be honest, the bag had come out of it better than Janice. It was photogenic, the star of the show.

'Here we go, in the third column,' Janice pointed to the relevant paragraph. '"It's a Zac Parris bag, my pride and joy," said feisty Janice. "I wasn't going to let some big sweaty oik take it. Now I love it even more – from now on, a Zac Parris bag shall always be my weapon of choice."'

There was another photo showing the bag in close-up, and a further quote from Janice saying, 'Zac's wonderful bags are like me – they might look like a soft touch, but they certainly pack a punch!'

'You're a star.' Zac was delighted. 'This is fantastic. I owe you one – oh, you *bad* girl!'

Tired of waiting for her chocolate buttons, Doreen had leapt back onto Janice's lap, attempted to climb inside her bag, lost her balance and spilled coffee all over the newspaper spread out on the desk.

'I was going to frame that page,' Zac complained.

'Darling, I've got fifty more copies in the car. Anyway, it's not just that newspaper.' Janice preened. 'I'm in practically all of them, even the *Telegraph. And* I'm on Richard and Judy at five o'clock.'

'This is getting surreal.' Nancy, clearing away the uppermost coffee-stained pages, stopped and stared.

'I know! This week Richard and Judy, next week Parkinson! I mean, this could give my career just the boost it needs!'

'Actually, I meant this.' Nancy was gazing in disbelief at uncovered, un-coffee-stained page 26, part of the paper's fashion section. 'That's my . . . that's *my* bag.'

It was, there was no doubt about it. Under the heading Must-Have Bag of the Season was a photograph of her very own bag. 'Zac Parris, London's best-kept secret . . .' Nancy read aloud '. . . this fabulous custom-made bag sells for £299 and you get to choose your own colours. Just call 0207 blah blah or visit the website . . .'

'Copycats,' exclaimed Janice. 'But I was on page five, so I was first.'

'How did this happen?' Zac was bemused.

'I don't know, but this is the paper Tabitha works for.' Nancy took out her mobile, into which Tabitha's number was programmed.

Zac frowned. 'I thought you said she was a financial journalist.'

'I did. But Tabitha was the one who took that photo of my bag. When we were doing our make-up in the loos at the Tipsy Prawn, she pulled out a digital camera and . . . hi, it's me.'

'Hi, you.' Tabitha sounded as if she was grinning from ear to ear. 'I wondered how long it would take to hear from you this morning.'

'So it was you. You told the fashion editor at your paper about Zac's bag.'

'OK. Guilty confession time,' said Tabitha. 'I'm the fashion editor.'

Nancy inwardly digested this information. It was like Princess Anne admitting that she'd whipped off her kit and posed for *Playboy*.

The silence lengthened. Finally Tabitha said gaily, 'Poor you, plunged into shock. I know. Hardly the usual kind, am I? The thing is, you don't have to be a great artist to appreciate great art. Some people can't sing to save their lives but they still enjoy listening to music. And just because I don't choose to dress like a fashion victim doesn't mean I can't put together decent outfits for other people and write convincingly about next season's pin-striped bikinis.'

Dumbstruck, Nancy said, 'But . . . but you said you were a financial journalist.'

'Well, wouldn't you? It's embarrassing, doing this job! I mean, God, it's not as if a piece about padded shoulders is ever going to change the world. As soon as anyone finds out what I really do, they think I'm a complete airhead,' Tabitha protested, 'and I'm really not. I've got a first-class degree in economics, for crying out loud. I always wanted to work in financial journalism, but the paper offered me a start in this department and I just, well, kind of got stuck here.'

'Right,' Nancy said faintly. She looked down at the fashion editor's by-line. 'Who's Kate Harris?'

Except, of course, it was all coming back to her now. Tabitha's surname was Harris.

'Kate's my middle name. I was saving Tabitha for when I got a proper job in finance. Look, I'm sorry I fibbed to you, but I was desperate to impress Connor. I mean, fashion editors can be downright weird – lots of people think we're all barking mad – and I didn't want to put him off.'

Doing her best to sound concerned rather than hopeful, Nancy said, 'Do you think it would?'

'Oh, he knows now. I told him last night,' Tabitha rattled on happily. 'Now that he knows me, he's absolutely fine about it. Thank God!'

'Well, um . . . good.' Nancy tried hard to quash the twinge of disappointment. Ashamed of herself, she said hurriedly, 'What made you choose Zac's bag?'

'It's a great bag! Everyone in the office loves it! Besides, it's my way of thanking you.'

'For what?' said Nancy, although she'd already guessed.

'You introduced me to Connor. I *owe* you,' Tabitha exclaimed. 'Crikey, you did me a *huge* favour! I thought it would be nice to do one in return. Cheerfully she went on, 'After this, Zac's bound to give you a bonus!'

The phone on the desk began to ring. Zac, snatching it up, said, 'Hello, Zac Parris. Yes, it is. Oh, right. Great!' Waggling his eyebrows excitedly at Nancy and Janice, he listened some more and said, '*How* many? Hang on, let me just grab a pen . . .'

Chapter 49

Rose felt like an old hand, showing Zac's father the sights of London. Having hopped off the bus at Trafalgar Square, she and William made their way down to the Thames and began walking across the Hungerford Bridge. Ahead of them on the other side of the river, the Millennium Wheel glinted white in the sunshine. William's face fell when he saw it.

'What rotten luck. Not working.'

Rose, who had thought the same thing the first time she'd caught sight of the wheel, felt wonderfully superior. 'It is. Look, it's just moving really slowly. You expected to see it whizz round, didn't you? Like a ferris wheel.'

'I'm just an innocent country bumpkin.' William's eyes fanned into creases at the corners. 'I'll never be a smart city slicker like you.'

Rose experienced a warm glow in her stomach, not because of the compliment but because it was so nice to be in the company of such a gently humorous, genuinely nice man.

'More often than not, smart city slicker types don't have any manners. They just elbow you in the ribs and shove you out of the way. You have lovely manners,' said Rose. 'And you grow all your own vegetables. How many city slickers can say they do that?'

'How many city slickers can knit?' countered William.

'Heaven forbid.' Rose smiled, picturing an all-important board meeting with everyone in their smart suits sitting around a polished table, furiously knitting away as they discussed unit trusts or whatever it was that people at important board meetings discussed.

'And how many have ever sneaked out of their fancy offices in the middle of the day to ride the Millennium Wheel?' said William.

'Well, to be fair some of them may have done that.'

William raised his bag. 'With homemade ham and pickle sandwiches and a thermos of tea?'

'Probably not,' Rose agreed.

'There, you see, they don't know what they're missing.' Linking his arm companionably through Rose's, William said with satisfaction, 'Country bumpkins win over city slickers every time.'

Four hours later they made their way home, William having gallantly insisted on escorting Rose back to her door even though it was out of his way. As they meandered through the gardens of Fitzallen Square, enjoying the emergent signs of spring and breathing in the smell of damp earth and greenery, footsteps on gravel sounded ahead of them.

Next moment Brigadier Brough-Badham rounded the path, hesitating when he saw who he was about to pass. Something in his expression changed, the habitual grimness giving way to uncertainty verging on panic.

As they drew closer he slowed his pace. Above the collar of his white shirt a blotchy flush materialised and his Adam's apple bobbed up and down like a stuck table tennis ball. Mesmerised, Rose watched it bob.

Finally Brigadier Brough-Badham nodded in acknowledgement, cleared his throat and said, 'Good afternoon . . . ah, Rose.' Bob, bob, bob-bob went the Adam's apple. 'And . . . er, how are you today?'

Rose was speechless. If she'd been wearing heels she would have toppled off them. Fighting the urge to laugh she nodded carefully and said politely, 'Good afternoon, um, Geoffrey. I'm very well, thank you.'

Heavens, it was like something out of *Pride and Prejudice*.

'Well, good. Very good.'

'And you, Geoffrey? Are you well?'

The Brigadier cleared his throat again. 'Yes, yes, very well thank you. Marjorie and I are both extremely, um, well.'

'I'm very pleased to hear it.' Rose smiled. 'Hasn't it been a beautiful day?'

Bob-bob, bob-bob went the Brigadier's Adam's apple, like a tiny dinghy cast helplessly adrift in a wild ocean. 'Very nice, yes, very nice day indeed. Well, better be getting on . . . off to the newsagent to pick up Marjorie's magazine.'

'Enjoy the rest of your afternoon,' Rose said pleasantly.

'Friend of yours?' said William when the Brigadier was out of earshot.

'Next-door neighbour.'

'Good to get along with your neighbours. Well, within reason.' William's tone was rueful. 'At least he doesn't want to get you into bed like mine does.'

'No danger of that,' Rose said with amusement. 'I wouldn't imagine I'm the Brigadier's type.'

'Then again, did you see the way his Adam's apple was going up and

276

down? You never know,' William gave her a nudge, 'you may have more of an effect on him than you think.'

'Either that,' Rose said lightly, 'or his shirt collar's too tight.'

Rennie had a plan and it was about to be put into action. He'd waited long enough; now he had made up his mind to act. Rose had gone out for the evening with William. Thanks to the recent surge in demand for Zac's handbags, Nancy was working overtime at the shop frantically processing orders and wasn't expecting to be home before midnight. The timing couldn't be more perfect. Carmen was upstairs in the bath. Any minute now she'd come down and be hugely impressed to find him preparing dinner.

Well, taking the just-delivered pizzas out of their boxes. And opening a decent bottle of wine.

Hearing the faint creak of her footsteps on the stairs, Rennie felt his throat constrict and his heart begin to quicken. Ridiculous; he'd never even experienced stage fright, let alone been nervous at the prospect of declaring how he felt about a woman to her face.

Except, come to think of it, he never had. Had never needed to do that. They'd always made their own feelings so absolutely clear, it hadn't been necessary.

And what if Carmen didn't feel the same way? What if she turned him down flat, or burst out laughing? Or screamed in horror and locked herself in the bathroom? Oh *shit*.

'My God, I'm having a hallucination.' Having padded barefoot into the kitchen, Carmen stopped dead in her tracks. 'This can't be happening. What are you trying to do, give me a heart attack?'

She was right. It was without doubt a startling sight. Out of sheer blind panic, and without even realising what he was doing, Rennie had grabbed the J-Cloth and a bottle of spray kitchen cleaner and was frenziedly scrubbing the worktop.

'I was just . . .' he forced himself to stop scrubbing, but clung on to the cloth and spray for security, 'um, cleaning up.'

Carmen narrowed her eyes suspiciously. 'Why? What did you spill?'

'Nothing! Just crumbs. All done now. Right.' Pulling himself together – Jesus, how could one small female with wet spiky hair terrify him more than a stadium packed with screaming fans? – Rennie said, 'Take the wine through to the living room. I'll bring the pizzas.'

'Stop!' shouted Carmen as he chucked the J-Cloth into the sink and reached for the plates.

Rennie froze. 'What?'

'Kitchen spray, you idiot! You have to wash your hands after using that stuff or the pizza will taste of bleach. And probably poison us.' Tut-tutting, Carmen said, 'Honestly, you are *such* a hopeless case.'

Which, Rennie felt as she disappeared with the wine and he washed his hands, wasn't the most promising of starts.

Carmen's choice of TV viewing didn't improve matters. Having gener-ously allowed her to decide what they watched, Rennie was soon regret-ting it. Much as he loved *EastEnders*, you couldn't call it conducive to seduction at the best of times. And tonight's, needless to say, was an extra shouty, extra extra angst-ridden episode.

'Hit him!' Carmen bellowed at the screen. 'Go on, really wallop him – he deserves it, the bastard. Yay, and again!'

Rennie looked at her, stretched across the sofa with her legs resting on his lap. Five feet two inches tall, luminous dark eyes, expressive eyebrows and a complexion like Snow White. She was wearing white flannel pyjama bottoms and a pink and white polka-dotted strappy top that would have looked sexy if she hadn't added a hideous chunky Starsky-type cardigan in shades of virulent purple and elephant-grey.

Dammit, she still looked sexy. Even if she was currently yelling at the TV like a deranged wrestling fan.

At long last the end credits rolled and Rennie shifted Carmen's legs off his lap. 'OK, film next. I've got a great—'

'Oh no you don't.' Carmen grabbed his arm as he made to get up. 'Hold your horses, Mr Bossy. I think you're forgetting something here.'

'What?'

'It's not your turn. You chose *Brigadoon* the other night, remember. Tonight I get to choose.'

'But I've already—'

'I know you have.' Carmen rolled her eyes. 'But we're not watching it, whatever it is, OK? Because the world doesn't always revolve around you. For once we're watching what *I* want to watch.'

'Which is?' Rennie's heart sank; he'd lined up *Brief Encounter* specially for tonight. An all-time classic. All that erotically charged suppressed emotion – what could be more conducive to his cause?

'Ta-daaa.' Having rolled onto her side and groped under the sofa, Carmen resurfaced with a DVD in her hand and a look of triumph on her face. 'Mia lent it to me. I haven't seen it for years. We can join in all the songs, do the dances – now you can't say this isn't a brilliant choice!'

Bloody can, thought Rennie, because *The Rocky Horror Show* might be a cult classic but it wasn't what you'd call romantic.

278

Then again, a fight now wasn't likely to help.

'Wouldn't you prefer to watch *Brief Encounter*?' He gave it one last desperate shot.

'Hmm, let me think,' said Carmen, clambering off the sofa and heading happily over to the DVD player. 'Does everyone do the Timewarp in *Brief Encounter*? Do the men wear stockings and suspenders? Does *Brief Encounter* have Meatloaf on a motorbike in it? Excuse me, but I don't believe it does. So how about . . . *no*?'

Steam trains, stiff upper lips and men in unfeasibly high-waisted forties-style suits lost out to bawdy double-entendres and transvestites in make-up and unfeasibly high heels. Having completely geared himself up to the fact that Tonight would be The Night, Rennie was now feeling like a pressure cooker left on an increasingly high heat. This wasn't fair. How could everything be going so wrong? He'd even planned – more or less – what he would say to start the ball rolling, but it simply wasn't possible when a bunch of pouting, pelvis-gyrating transsexuals from Transylvania were leering at you from the TV screen.

One hundred minutes, that was how long it lasted. Back in position on the sofa with her legs draped comfortably over Rennie's and her plate of pizza resting in her lap, Carmen jiggled her feet, wiggled her toes and sang raucously along while Rennie counted down the minutes to the end of the film. They'd started watching at ten past eight. Allowing for one bathroom break and one fetch-and-open-another-bottle-of-wine break, normal service would be resumed at around ten o'clock. Since Rose was expected home at eleven and he'd prefer to say what he had to say to Carmen without an audience, this meant he had a window of opportunity of an hour at most in which to say it.

Oh God, he'd never felt like this before.

Twenty minutes of the film left.

Ten minutes.

Three minutes to go . . .

'See? Didn't I tell you it was great?' Carmen demanded when the film ended. Reaching for her glass of wine, she spilled a bit on Rennie's denim-clad thigh. 'Whoops, sorry. Lucky it's only white. There now, you can't tell me you didn't enjoy that.'

Only Carmen could mean the film and not the fact that she was rubbing at the damp patch on his jeans with a tissue.

OK, no more shilly-shallying about. Down to business. Reaching for the remote, Rennie pointed it at the screen.

'Oh no, don't turn it off.' Carmen let out a wail of protest. 'We're watching *Willy Wonka and the Chocolate Factory* next.'

'For crying out loud, what's the matter with you?' Rennie raised his eyebrows in despair. 'You're a girl. Girls are supposed to like soppy romantic films. *Four Weddings, Sleepless in Seattle*, that kind of stuff. *Willy Wonka* isn't romantic.'

Carmen grinned. 'You don't know that. He might be. Ask Mrs Wonka.'

Wrong, wrong, all going horribly wrong. And he hadn't even started yet. Rennie heaved a sigh.

'What's the matter?' Tilting her head to one side, Carmen said incredulously, 'Do *you* want to watch *Sleepless in Seattle*?'

'Yes. No. It's too late now. I'm just saying it might have been . . . oh God.'

'*What?*' Carmen was by this time thoroughly confused.

'Helpful.'

'Helpful *how*?'

He had to do it now, had to.

'OK, there's something I need to say to you. About how I . . . um, the way things have . . . well, it's just that . . .'

'Rennie, you're making no sense.'

Rennie closed his eyes. He was making no sense and time was running out. Terrific.

Actually, keeping his eyes closed was helping a bit.

'Right. The thing is, we've always got on really well. I've always liked you. But things have changed now. Since I've been back . . .'

'You don't like me any more?'

'No, it's not that.' Rennie shook his head.

'Your eyes are shut.' Carmen sounded worried. 'Open them,' she ordered.

'I can't.'

'Rennie, you're scaring me. Tell me what's wrong.'

Rennie took a deep breath, wondering if she could hear his heart thudding against his chest. 'I love you.'

Silence.

Followed by more silence.

At least he hadn't had his face slapped.

Chapter 50

'Say something, for God's sake,' Rennie murmured when he could stand it no longer.

'I can't.' Carmen's voice was strained and distant.

When he finally opened his eyes, he saw that she was shaking her head.

'Sorry,' said Rennie. 'Bit of a shock.'

'You don't love me.'

'I do. Oh, I do. I've known it for weeks. Maybe long before that,' he admitted, 'but I never really allowed myself to think it because you weren't over Spike. You were so off limits, it wasn't an option. But you're over him now, and I realised what was happening when you started seeing Joe. I hated it. I was so bloody jealous. Then when that ended and you got together with Nick, I was even more jealous.' Rennie was astonished to discover that now he'd started, he couldn't stop; the words were tumbling out. 'Because I knew you deserved so much better than him, and I wanted you to realise I was right, and—'

'You thought you were better than Nick? That I deserved *you*?' Carmen began to tremble. 'Rennie, don't you see? You're not better. You're a hundred times worse!'

Stung, Rennie said, 'How can I be worse? We know everything about each other. The money thing isn't an issue. I make you laugh. You can't tell me I'm not better looking than that scruffy, gangly human scarecrow.'

'Like you just said, we know everything about each other. I know everything about *you*.' Carmen's dark eyes glistened as she met his gaze. 'And yes of course you're good-looking and funny and successful and rich, but you're also the last person any sane woman would risk getting involved with. Because all you do is sleep with them, leave them and break their hearts.'

'But that's because I didn't love them.' Rennie shook his head, willing her to believe him. 'Everything's different now. I wouldn't do that to you because I *do* love you.'

A single tear slid down Carmen's cheek. 'Rennie, that's not true. You *think* you wouldn't do it, but you would. Sooner or later it would happen.'

'It wouldn't because I've changed. I'm tired of all that old stuff,' Rennie insisted. 'I don't need it any more. How often do I go out now? Hardly ever, because I'm just not interested. Girls ring me and I don't return their calls. I get invited to clubs and I don't go. I stay here instead because I'd rather be with you. I've never felt that way about anyone before, but I do now.'

'People don't change just like that.' Miserably Carmen shook her head. 'You can't just wave a magic wand.'

For the first time, Rennie glimpsed a chink of light. She wasn't telling him she couldn't stand him, that the sight of him made her skin crawl. If the only stumbling block was her fear that he was incapable of changing his old ways, all he had to do was persuade her that he could.

'Warren Beatty led a pretty colourful life.' He nodded at Carmen. 'Then he married and had kids.'

'Oh please. That's *one* person.'

'Paul McCartney. Look how he changed after meeting Linda.'

'Fine.' Carmen raised her eyebrows. 'Any more?'

'Um . . .' Damn, he couldn't think of any more.

'Oh dear,' Carmen sighed. 'Just those two then. I think that says it all, don't you?'

'Rennie Todd,' Rennie blurted out, daring at last to stroke her face.

'Stop it.' She turned her head away.

'I love you,' he repeated more bravely, sensing that she was weakening.

'We can't do this,' Carmen mumbled.

'Does that mean you'd like to?'

'It means we're not going to.'

'But you don't hate me?'

'Of course I don't hate you.'

Well, this was progress. She didn't hate him and she hadn't slapped his hand away from her face. Gaining in confidence Rennie said, 'So you like me a little bit?'

Carmen was quivering. 'This isn't fair. How much I like you doesn't come into it. It's still not going to happen.'

Rennie's other hand moved to the back of her head, his fingers trailing through her just-washed hair. She smelled gorgeous. She was terrified. Well, that was OK. He could gain her trust. Carmen felt the same way and that was good enough for him. He felt as elated as if he'd just climbed Everest.

282

'*It* isn't going to happen,' he said, 'if that's what's scaring you. I've told you how I feel about you, and that's enough for now. This isn't about sex, believe me. We have the rest of our lives for all that. No hurry, no hurry at all. I can wait. You're in charge. The rest is up to you.'

Carmen lifted her head, gazed at him. She was torn, that much was evident. In a voice barely above a whisper she said, 'What would Spike think?'

The nerves had lessened. Baby steps, baby steps. His mouth mere inches from hers, Rennie said, 'He'd think I was a damn sight better bet than those last two losers you got yourself involved with.'

'Oh God, I don't know.' Shaking her head, Carmen said, 'At the restaurant the other night, Mia asked me if I'd ever considered you.'

'For a flaky sixteen-year-old, that girl talks a lot of sense.' Rennie paused. 'And have you?'

No reply.

Which was, of course, exactly the reply he wanted to hear.

'Right.' Breathing in the smell of her shampoo, Rennie inwardly marvelled at his self-control. 'We're stopping now. You can relax, I'm not planning to seduce you. Just take what I've said on board and don't automatically think of me as the devil. Give me a chance, OK? Don't write me off. I might not be as much of a nightmare as you think.'

Carmen met his gaze. 'Really?'

Rennie couldn't tell whether she was querying his remark about stopping now or the one about not being a nightmare. To be on the safe side he smiled and said, 'Really. We're going to crack open the Pringles and watch *Willy Wonka*. Just relax and enjoy the film, OK? I'm not even going to try and kiss you.'

A spark of disappointment flickered in Carmen's eyes. Defiantly she said, 'Well, good.'

Rennie waited, idly stroking the side of her neck. 'Unless you want me to.'

Another spark, this time of relief.

'Why would I?' Carmen's tone was challenging with an undertone – a very faint undertone – of flirtatiousness.

'Well, it might be the sensible thing to do. Just to make sure we're compatible.'

Carmen nodded thoughtfully. 'That does make sense. You might not know how to do it properly.'

'Exactly. Could have been doing it wrong all these years. Better find out then.' Rennie's green eyes glittered with amusement. 'Tell me if I have.'

Carmen closed the gap between them, her mouth seeking his. For the first time in his life Rennie experienced the sheer pleasure of a kiss in its own right, rather than as a prelude to sex. A warm, exhilarating sensation like electricity flooded his body. His mouth and Carmen's fitted together just perfectly.

So this was what he'd been missing out on all these years. If he was honest, he'd never really seen the point of mouth-to-mouth combat before.

But now he knew. This was what kissing was *for*. Even more extraordinarily, his natural reaction at this point would have been to slide his hand beneath the chunky Starsky cardigan in order to reach the strip of exposed flesh between Carmen's polka-dotted crop top and the waistband of her pyjamas, *but he wasn't doing it*. Possibly the hideousness of the cardigan was acting as a kind of contraceptive device. Then again, he knew that he couldn't afford to make a mistake. This was his chance to impress Carmen and he mustn't, *mustn't* blow it.

'Right.' Having made the effort to pull away, Rennie was delighted to see the look of disappointment on her face. 'You put the DVD in. I'll fetch the Pringles.'

Flushed and bright-eyed, Carmen attempted to smooth down her hair. 'OK.'

'Coffee? Or more wine?'

'Um . . . coffee, thanks.'

Heading for the kitchen, Rennie paused in the doorway. His heart turned over with love at the sight of Carmen on the sofa, still flustered and making ineffectual attempts to tie a double knot in the belt of the Starsky cardigan.

'By the way,' he said lightly. 'How was I?'

Carmen smiled over at him. 'So-so.'

'Fine. More practice, that's what I need.' Rennie felt ridiculously happy at the prospect. 'Don't worry, I'll get the hang of it in the end.'

As he waited for the kettle to boil, Rennie thought his heart would burst. Carmen was in the living room wanting him to kiss her again. And he wasn't going to. If it killed him, he was going to prove to her that he could wait.

Seconds later the kettle clicked off and the front doorbell simultaneously rang. Clutching a tube of paprika Pringles, Rennie went to answer it. Rose was home early, another excellent reason why he and Carmen shouldn't have stayed glued together necking like teenagers on the sofa.

It wasn't Rose. Rennie found himself staring at a bespectacled tabloid journalist whom he vaguely recognised, having seen him before at various music awards ceremonies.

'Rennie, hi, how are you?' the journalist said matily. 'Eric Carson, remember?'

For a bizarre split second Rennie wondered if the man was here to ask him for details of his relationship with Carmen. Hastily pulling himself together he said, 'What's this about, Eric?'

'Brrr, chilly out here.' Eric stamped his feet as if he were in the Arctic.

'Excuse me if I don't invite you in,' said Rennie. 'I'm busy.'

'Of course you are.' Eric glanced at the Pringles tube. 'And I won't hold you up, I promise.' Behind his spectacles his eyes gleamed. 'I just wondered how you're feeling about the news that you're about to become a father.'

'Who is it?' said Carmen, when Rennie dived into the living room to grab his mobile phone. The mobile phone he'd deliberately switched off two hours earlier so that his all-important evening with Carmen wouldn't be interrupted by irritating, unimportant calls.

'No one.' Switching the phone on, Rennie saw the messages stacked up. Abruptly he left the room, returned to the front door. Felt sick when he saw the spark of schadenfreude in Eric's beady eyes.

Bluntly, Rennie said, 'Who is it?'

'Biba Keyes.' Eric licked his lips. 'Remember her?'

Biba Keyes. Oh yes, he remembered. New York, last summer. Biba had appeared backstage after a concert, introduced herself as a fellow Brit and invited him along to a party. With her waist-length blond hair, flawless figure and saucy sense of humour, he hadn't needed much persuasion. She had done a bit of Page 3 modelling, Rennie subsequently discovered, a spot of acting and a lot of turning up wherever the paparazzi were most likely to be, dressed in improbably skimpy outfits. As she'd cheerfully confessed at the time, it beat working for a living.

They'd spent a weekend together. Beneath the airhead exterior, Biba Keyes had actually possessed a quick brain and a refreshingly down-to-earth attitude. She was twenty-two years old and life was what you made it. An added attraction as far as Rennie was concerned had been her acceptance that their fling was just that, a bit of fun to be enjoyed before they headed their separate ways. Unlike so many girls, she hadn't told him she loved him and begun to fantasise that they might have a future together.

The other added attraction, needless to say, had been her proficiency and boundless enthusiasm in bed.

Jesus.

'She's saying it's mine?' Rennie forced himself to breathe slowly. 'How pregnant is she?'

'Eight months.'

New York. Count back. Fuck.

'You'd think she might have mentioned it before now.'

Eric shrugged. 'According to Biba, she's tried. Phoned you, left messages and texts, but you never bothered to reply.'

Rennie's blood ran cold. Was this true? Sometimes he deleted texts and voicemail messages without reading them if they were from girls he had no interest in seeing again. But Biba wasn't stupid; if she'd wanted to contact him, she could have done so via his agent or manager.

'So might we be hearing wedding bells in the near future?' Eric's tone was deliberately provocative.

'No comment.' Thinking how nice it would be to punch him down the steps, Rennie made a move to close the front door.

'She's calling you the love of her life,' Eric shouted as the door slammed shut.

Wrong, thought Rennie. The love of his life was sitting twenty feet away, wondering what was keeping him out here.

And he suspected she wasn't going to take it well when she found out.

Chapter 51

Carmen didn't cry or yell or throw heavy objects at Rennie. What would be the point? He was Rennie Todd, always had been. It was a wonder this hadn't happened before.

If anything, she should be glad it *had* happened, serving as a salutary reminder of how Rennie led his life. Finding out now was almost unbearable, but finding out in six months' time, when she would have been that much more deeply involved with him, would be infinitely worse.

'She means nothing to me!' Rennie was raking his fingers through his hair, scarcely able to believe this was happening. 'The baby might not even be mine!'

'But you slept with her,' Carmen said wearily.

'Well, yes, but—'

'What about safe sex? Didn't it even occur to you that something like this could happen?'

'Of course it did. We used condoms. It can't be my child, she's just—'

'Rennie, condoms can fail.' Exasperated, Carmen banged her fist against the arm of the sofa. 'This girl is pregnant and she says it's yours.'

'But it doesn't have to change things between *us*,' he pleaded.

'It does.' Carmen couldn't look at him. 'It already has. Because this is what you're like. You sleep with girls like other people eat biscuits, just because they're there.'

'But that was eight months ago.' Rennie's voice rose. 'I wouldn't do it now! *I love you.*'

'Sorry.' As she shook her head, Carmen heard a key turn in the front door. 'It would never work, Rennie. I was stupid to even think it might.'

'Coooeee,' Rose called out, signalling her return home and appearing moments later in the living-room doorway. Her eyes bright, she beamed at them. 'Had a lovely evening. You two?'

Carmen rose to her feet. 'You can tell her,' she said to Rennie. 'I'm going to bed.'

*   *   *

The double-page spread in the newspaper that had broken the story featured three photographs of Biba Keyes. The first was a reprint of an old Page 3 photo, the second a casual snap of her and Rennie carousing at the party they had attended in New York on the night they met. The third and largest was a demurely posed portrait of Biba, eight months pregnant and with her long blond hair tied back in a plait, tenderly cradling her vast bump whilst gazing with wistful eyes into the lens of the camera.

Rennie had already left the house for an emergency meeting with his manager and agent. Carmen, who had barely slept, wondered if this was Spike's way of letting her know how stupid she'd been to even contemplate getting involved with someone as wildly unsuitable as his brother.

Biba Keyes had confided some pretty salacious details of her torrid, albeit brief, affair with Rennie. 'We couldn't get enough of each other,' Carmen read, hunched over the paper and feeling sick. 'He has the best body I've ever seen. And he seemed to like mine too! But it wasn't just the sex, although that was mind-blowing enough. We really connected as people. I knew Rennie cared deeply for me. He promised we'd see each other again and I believed him, but he cruelly went back on his word. I was devastated. When he told me he loved me, I thought he meant it. Still, now that I'm having his baby, I hope Rennie will reconsider. I know we could have a fantastic life together. He's the only man I've ever really loved and I know I could make him happy. I've even given up drinking and going out to parties for the sake of our baby, that's how seriously I'm taking my responsibilities. You're more likely to see me in Mothercare these days than the latest trendy clubs.'

Nancy put a cup of tea on the kitchen table in front of Carmen and gave her shoulder a squeeze. 'I've got to get to work. Will you be OK?'

'Oh, I'll live. *Again*. Third time unlucky and all that.' Having swallowed a mouthful of hot tea, Carmen said drily, 'I'm really getting the hang of it now.'

'And I'm not far behind you. Catching up fast.' Nancy pulled a face. 'Fine pair we are.'

Carmen managed to smile, because Nancy was besotted with Connor and Connor was seeing Tabitha, and Nancy – thanks to the bonus Zac had given her – was beholden to Tabitha to the tune of, so far, twenty-three thousand handbags, with more orders pouring in by the day. It was actually funny in a tragic kind of way.

'Go to work. I'll be fine, really.'

Nancy gazed one last time at the photograph of Biba in her white Lycra top and hip-hugging pink jeans, displaying her distended belly with pride. 'It might not be Rennie's baby. We've only got her word for it.'

'It doesn't matter whether it is or not,' said Carmen. 'It's been a wake-up call for me. I must have been mad to even think we could be happy together.'

The letterbox clattered, signalling the arrival of the post. Nancy brought the handful of letters into the kitchen and left for work. Sorting dispiritedly through them, Carmen left the ones that were obviously bills and opened a cream, manila envelope franked with the logo of Pariah Records, the company Red Lizard had been signed to prior to Spike's death. Fans sometimes still wrote to her (and sometimes, more worryingly, to Spike) and the record company forwarded the letters every couple of weeks.

But this wasn't a fan letter. Feeling hot and ashamed, Carmen read the opening lines.

Dear Carmen,

You obviously didn't remember me, but I eventually remembered why you seemed so familiar the other week when we met at the shelter. I told you I would! My name is Russell Taylor, but I was always known as Big Russ when I worked as a roadie for Red Lizard. Ring any bells now? Maybe not, we were only the crew shifting equipment in the background, after all. But I wanted to write and let you know that I *did* know you. My wife Josie, God rest her soul, was always very fond of you too. We both thought you were a lovely girl, and maybe the fact that you are now working in a shelter proves this.

Carmen stopped and took a deep breath. She had pretended not to remember Big Russ for her own selfish ends. She'd betrayed him, refused to acknowledge him. What a Judas. She wasn't nice at all.

Anyway, the other reason for this letter is to say thank you for what you did. You'll be glad to hear I caught the train from Paddington (this time!) and made it down to Penzance in one piece. My brother gave me a bit of an earful when I rang him from the station, but eventually came to pick me up.

The other good news is that I have realised you were right. All I've been doing is making my life harder to bear. I haven't had a drink since leaving London and have been to daily AA meetings since then. I know it's early days but I really think I can do this, thanks to you being so kind to me and making me see sense. When I get a job down here, I'll send back the money you gave me and that's a promise, but maybe you could give me your address otherwise those thieving bastards at Pariah Records might not bother to pass it on.

Well, that's about it. Spike was a good lad and I know you must miss him a lot. Are you still in touch with Rennie these days? Always up to mischief, that boy, but he had a big heart. I hope you are getting on with your own life. You deserve to be happy.

Thanks again for everything.

All the best, Big Russ.

Carmen finished reading and put the letter down on the kitchen table. Burying her face in her hands, she burst into tears.

How could Doreen be gone?

Mia, her heart beginning to race, double-checked that the gate leading into Fitzallen Square's garden was still shut. This made no sense; a dog didn't simply vanish into thin air. Doreen couldn't have been beamed up by aliens. She had to be here somewhere.

Bloody hell, she'd only offered to give Doreen her afternoon walk out of the goodness her heart because Zac and Nancy were still rushed off their feet at the shop. If anything happened to the little dog, Zac would have her guts for garters.

Her guts, not Doreen's.

'Doreen!' Fear drove her voice up a couple of octaves. Dropping into a crouching run – dimly aware that she now looked like Groucho Marx – Mia began peering under bushes. She prayed that Doreen was playing an ill-timed game of hide and seek. 'Doreen, this isn't funny, come back here this minute! *Doreeeen . . .'*

'Oh my God, where is she? What have you done with her?' The moment Zac saw the look of anguish on Mia's face he knew something terrible had happened. The dressmaking shears clattered from his fingers and three metres of chartreuse duchesse satin slithered to the floor. 'What's happened to Doreen?'

Mia blurted out, 'I'm so sorry,' and stood there gasping for breath, evidently having raced all the way back to the shop.

Feeling himself go white, Zac said through numb lips, 'Is . . . is she d-dead?'

'She just disappeared.' Mia spread her arms helplessly, at a loss to explain. 'We were in the square, I let her off her lead for a run-about, she trotted off behind that kind of clump of bushes next to the ash trees, and the next thing I knew, she'd gone!'

'You left the gate open.'

'I didn't leave the gate open! I closed it!' Mia's lower lip began to wobble. 'And I looked for her and looked for her, because I thought maybe she was hiding from me or had fallen down a rabbit hole, or had a heart attack or something, but she wasn't *anywhere*. Then I . . .'

'Then you what?' Zac demanded as she faltered.

'Oh God, it's probably nothing, but I checked outside the gardens and at the far end – you know, the corner by Amber Road – I found clumps of fresh mud on top of the railings, like you'd get if someone had climbed over them. But that's stupid, because who would want to take Doreen? I mean, I know she's a sweet little thing and all, but nobody would actually set out to steal her.' Mia's voice faded away as she saw the look of utter disbelief on Zac's face. Quivering, she pleaded, 'Well, they wouldn't, would they? It's not as if she's valuable.'

Nancy arrived back from a five-minute trip to the post office to find the shop in uproar. Zac was pacing around the workroom yelling into the phone and Mia was sitting on a spindly pink and silver chair sobbing noisily. There was a spilled cup of coffee on the floor, and over in the corner the fax machine was churning out fresh orders for handbags from the hottest designer in town.

'Well, you're a big help. Thanks for nothing!' bellowed Zac, slamming down the phone.

'What's happened?' The hairs on the back of Nancy's neck prickled in alarm.

'Doreen's been kidnapped.' Zac was shaking. 'Some bastard's taken her and the police say they can't do anything because we didn't see them do it. A missing dog is presumed to have strayed. Oh God, I can't believe this is *happening*.'

Nancy went to put her arms round Mia, who was in a terrible state.

291

'No, don't.' Mia pulled away, distraught. 'I can't bear it.' Bursting into even noisier sobs she wailed, 'It's all my fault.'

Zac's mobile phone rang an hour later. He snatched it up.

'Yeah, hi, have you lost your dog?'

The tag that dangled from Doreen's collar was engraved with her name and Zac's number. Despite his misgivings, Zac's hopes rose. 'Yes, yes I have! You've found her?'

'Yeah. Wandering across the King's Road. Nearly got mown down before I rescued her,' said the youngish-sounding male voice. 'Is her name really Doreen?'

Tears sprang into Zac's eyes. 'It is.'

'Funny name for a dog.'

'Is she OK?'

'Hey, calm down, she's just fine and dandy. So you'd like her back then, would you?'

'I can come and get her,' Zac blurted out. 'Where are you? I'll come now.'

'Whoa, hold your horses.' The caller sounded amused. 'Steady on there. Before that happens, I wondered if you'd considered a reward at all.'

Zac's heart sank. 'Sorry?'

'You know, mate. To show us how grateful you are to be getting your dog back. Just as a token of appreciation, kind of thing. Unless you're not really bothered about seeing Doreen again.'

Zac said flatly, 'How much?'

'Five grand.'

'*What?*'

'Fine.' The caller's tone was dismissive. 'Suit yourself.'

The line went dead.

'Oh God.' Sinking into a chair, Zac clutched his forehead and moaned, 'I've killed her.'

Nancy grabbed the phone, dialled 1471, scribbled down the number and pressed 3. The phone was picked up on the fifteenth ring.

'Hey, don't be a cheapskate,' the same male caller chided as Zac snatched the phone back from Nancy. 'Five grand isn't that much, is it? Compared with a furry little paw through the post.'

'I'll pay it.' Zac was so agitated he could barely speak.

'Good, good. That's what we like to hear. Now, I'll give you a ring later to fix a time and a place. Used notes please, in a Boots carrier bag. And if you're thinking of contacting the police, well, I wouldn't do that if I were you. Not a good idea if you want to see little Doreen again.' He chuckled. 'Woof woof.'

'Right.' Zac nodded, feeling sick at the thought of Doreen at the mercy of this lunatic.

'Okey dokey. Bye for now. I'll let you tootle off down to the bank,' the man said cheerfully. 'Pick up that cash!'

Chapter 52

Zac closed the shop. Nancy walked Mia home. Since Mia was inconsolable, Nancy took her into number sixty-two, despatched Rennie to make coffee and phoned Connor at the Lazy B.

By the time Zac arrived at six o'clock, everyone was gathered at the house.

'I still think you should call the police.' Rose was worried.

'No.' Vehemently Zac shook his head. 'I won't risk it. Too much could go wrong.'

'But they could trace the number the man was calling from.'

'Phone box on the King's Road,' Zac said bitterly. 'I kept ringing back and eventually someone answered. They told me.'

'But—'

'And I went over there to double-check.' With a trace of impatience Zac added, 'Kidnappers don't generally call you from their own phones.' Then he saw the expression on Rose's face and raised his hands. 'Sorry, Rose, I didn't mean to snap. I just want Doreen back safe and well. And we're not calling the police.'

'Probably too busy giving out parking tickets,' said Rennie. 'Did you get the cash?'

Nodding, Zac patted the inside pocket of his jacket.

'What a bastard.' Connor shook his head in disgust.

'Plural,' said Zac. 'He said we and us. I'm pretty sure there's two of them.'

Rennie raised an eyebrow at Connor. Connor nodded briefly.

'Just a thought,' said Rennie, 'but there's more than two of us.'

The kidnapper phoned at eleven o'clock. Everyone in the room fell silent as Zac answered it.

'Hey,' drawled the voice, 'did you think I wasn't going to ring?'

'I've got the money.' Zac's hand might be trembling but his voice was steady.

'Then we're ready to rock and roll, my friend!'

'Is Doreen all right?'

'She's just dandy, can't wait to see you again. So long as you don't try anything stupid.'

'I just want my dog back.'

'And you'll be welcome to her. She pissed on my shoe earlier. Had to give her a bit of a kicking for that.' The man chuckled. 'I mean, it's not nice, is it? We're in another call box, by the way, in case you were wondering. Not the same one as before.'

'Where d'you want to meet?' Zac managed to remain outwardly calm.

'Hey, don't flatter yourself. This isn't a dating agency, you know. I don't want to meet you. I just want my financial reward.'

Zac gritted his teeth. 'Right.'

'OK, here we go. The place where Doreen went missing. Fitzallen Square. Put the bag of money in the rubbish bin next to the bench. Then go and wait in Tindall Road, OK? Someone'll be along to pick up the cash. When they've checked it out, made sure it's all there, you'll get your dog back.'

'How do I know that?'

'You don't. That's the beauty of it,' Doreen's abductor said smugly. 'You just have to cross your fingers and hope for the best. Good game, eh? Now, pop along and drop that dosh into the bin, there's a good chap. Woof, woof!'

It was eleven thirty. The Boots bag containing the money was in the waste bin. Zac was waiting two streets away in Tindall Road. Nancy, wearing a black fleece and jeans, lay on her front between two dense bushes in the square and wondered if her racing heart was audible to Rennie, lying ten feet to her left. Further away, ranged around the enclosed garden and similarly concealed by foliage and darkness, lurked Connor, Mia and Carmen.

So far there hadn't been any sign of Doreen's abductors. A blade of grass tickled Nancy's chin and she hoped they wouldn't have to stay out here all night. Good job she wasn't bursting for the loo or—

Shit, footsteps.

Nancy held her breath as the gate creaked open on its hinges. The footsteps grew nearer, approaching the bench. The next moment a lighter briefly flared, illuminating the features of the man holding it, and she saw that it was Brigadier Brough-Badham. Returning from a night out, he was sitting on the bench enjoying a cigar before heading home to his wife.

'Hey. Brigadier.' Rennie's voice, low and urgent, cut through the blackness. 'No questions. Over here.'

Nancy flinched, expecting their neighbour to leap to his feet barking, 'What? Who's that? What's going on?' But by some miracle – presumably thanks to his military training – the Brigadier rose and moved towards Rennie. It was his turn to flinch when he saw who had called his name.

'Just leave, OK?' Rennie murmured. 'Doreen was abducted. The ransom money's in the bin. Zac wouldn't risk getting the police involved.'

Remaining commendably calm, the Brigadier glanced around the square. When he was satisfied he wasn't being observed he murmured back, 'What time did they say?'

'They didn't. But it should be soon.'

'Right.' The Brigadier extinguished the just-lit cigar beneath the toe of his highly polished brogue and lowered himself to the ground alongside Rennie. Nancy prayed Rennie wouldn't choose this moment to make any Kiss Me Hardy type jokes.

Or to whisper cheerfully that he was dying for a fag.

They heard the faint whirring noise less than ten minutes later, of bicycle tyres on the road beyond the railings. Then the gate creaking again and the bicycle being ridden into the gardens. Her mouth dry, Nancy watched from the shadows as a figure in a hooded jacket plucked the Boots bag from the bin, briefly shone a torch into it then stuffed the bag inside his jacket and headed back to the gate. Pausing to listen and peer up and down the road, he took out a mobile and said, 'Yeah, got it,' before cycling off.

Nancy could have wept. Thirty minutes of lying in cold damp undergrowth, all for nothing. And where was Doreen anyway?

Then she heard a sharp intake of breath from either Rennie or the Brigadier and realised that they could see something happening at the far end of the square. Leaping to her feet a split second after them, Nancy realised that their first cyclist had slowed, a second had appeared from the direction of Merivale Street, and that the rider of the second bike was hanging something from one of the railings. Then they all heard a roar of fury, a series of shouts and the metallic clatter of bicycles hitting the ground as Carmen, Mia and Connor leapt over the railings and launched themselves at the two abductors. Tearing after Rennie and the Brigadier, her throat burning and adrenaline surging through her body, Nancy saw one of the two manage to twist free. Unable to reach his bike, he turned and began to race up the road on foot, heading towards their end of the square. Abruptly changing direction, Rennie and the Brigadier veered towards the gate. The man attempted to dart away but Rennie was too fast for him. The next minute he was on the ground swearing and wriggling like an eel whilst the Brigadier efficiently twisted his arms behind his back and Rennie, brushing mud from his jeans, phoned the police.

Zac appeared from the direction of Tindall Road, out of breath and terrified. 'I heard all the shouting. You actually got them! Where's Doreen?'

Oh God, where *was* Doreen? Nancy turned and looked back to where Carmen and Connor had finally managed to bring the first abductor under control on the pavement next to the abandoned bikes. Mia, walking up the road away from them, was carrying something inside her zipped-up jacket. Nancy's heart began to thud with fear when she saw that Mia was crying.

The front door of number sixty-two burst open and Rose and William – forbidden from joining the stake-out – came rushing down the steps.

'I've got this if they need tying up.' William brandished what looked like Rose's washing line.

'Is Doreen all right?' cried Rose.

'Doreen,' Zac croaked, breaking into a run. 'Is she dead? *Doreen . . .*'

Mia carefully unzipped her navy jacket. 'She's not dead. She's OK. Just shaken.'

Zac let out a sob of relief and took Doreen into his arms. As the little dog snuffled and clung to him, her tail began to wag, slowly at first, then gathering speed. Burying his face in her fur, Zac kissed the top of her head and Nancy, watching the reunion from a distance, felt a lump form in her throat.

'They hung her from the railings in a bag.' Tears were still pouring down Mia's cheeks. 'She was just dangling there. I saw her little eyes looking up at me . . . oh God, the look on her face when she saw—'

A roar of fury from further down the road caused Nancy to jump. Connor, cursing loudly and still hanging on to his abductor, gazed helplessly as a flurry of banknotes escaped from the unfastened carrier bag and swirled like autumn leaves up into the air. 'If anybody wants to come and give us a hand,' he shouted, 'there's some money that needs to be caught.'

The police arrived a couple of minutes later. Most of the escaped banknotes were retrieved, although eighty pounds' worth was last seen making an exultant bid for freedom down Merivale Street. The abductors, who turned out to be teenagers rather than men, were arrested and carted off to the Brompton police station in Lucan Place.

Zac went with them to make his statement, reluctantly handing Doreen over to the care of Nancy and promising to be back as soon as possible. Aware of his father's gaze upon them, he had planted a fervent kiss on Nancy's mouth. When she glanced over Zac's shoulder and saw Connor grinning broadly, Nancy flicked a quick V sign at him and waited a discreet length of time before wiping her hand across the place where the kiss had landed.

'Right,' Rennie announced, rubbing his cold hands. 'I think we've earned ourselves a drink. Last one to down a large Scotch is a cissy.'

Mia said brightly, 'Even me?'

'Well, I'll be off.' The Brigadier gestured awkwardly as Rennie led the way up the steps to number sixty-two.

Rennie turned to look at him. 'We're celebrating getting Doreen back. You could stay for one drink, surely?'

'Well . . .'

'Come on, pet . . . er, Geoffrey,' Rose urged kindly. 'Bring Marjorie with you if you like.'

'Marjorie's away until tomorrow. Visiting an old schoolfriend in Kent.'

'Then just bring yourself,' said Rennie. 'You know, we couldn't have managed without you tonight. You did a fine job.'

The Brigadier's Adam's apple bobbed with embarrassment. At last he said stiffly, 'Well, I suppose one drink can't hurt.'

'Great. I'll be on my very best behaviour.' Ushering him in through the front door, Rennie said cheerfully, 'And I promise not to bite the heads off any bats.'

One drink turned to several. Exhausted by her ordeal but clearly relieved to be back among friends, Doreen wolfed down half a tin of Marks and Spencer steak casserole and seven Maltesers before curling up and falling asleep in the living room on William's lap. Much to their astonishment, Rennie and the Brigadier discovered a shared passion for Second World War films and military museums. Rose, meanwhile, was in her element rustling up bacon sandwiches and a huge bowl of cheese fondue.

Nancy, halfway down her third glass of wine, did her best to look nonchalant when Connor wandered into the kitchen with Mia in tow. So long as she didn't blurt out *I love you* at the top of her voice, she should be all right.

'I used to do that when my aunties came to visit,' Connor told her with a grin.

So big, so handsome, *so Tabitha's*.

'Do what?'

He mimed being given a noisy kiss, then grimacing and wiping his mouth with his hand.

'I know.' Nancy shook her head. 'I'm ashamed of myself. Just couldn't help it.'

'It's a reflex.' Connor's tone was consoling. 'If you don't want someone to kiss you but they go ahead and do it anyway, you have to wipe it off.'

'Eamonn O'Hara tried to kiss me once, on a school trip,' said Mia. 'I wiped it away. Then I punched him so hard he landed on Shona Murphy's sandwiches.'

'Nancy didn't really want to do that to Zac,' Connor said patiently.

'Poor Zac. I don't suppose he enjoyed it much either,' said Nancy, to be fair. 'He probably wiped his mouth too, when we weren't looking.'

'If Johnny Depp kissed me, I wouldn't wipe my mouth.' Mia beamed. 'Not for weeks.'

'You might if he dribbled.'

'He wouldn't. Johnny would never do that.'

'Ah, but you don't know,' said Nancy. 'He could be the slobberiest kisser on the planet, but nobody's ever told him so he just doesn't realise.'

'You know, I always thought I liked you.' Mia looked wounded. 'But I don't any more. That's a terrible thing to say about the love of my life.'

'Sweetheart, take these through.' Having assembled another pile of bacon sandwiches, Rose pushed the plate into Mia's hands. 'Before that greedy father of yours guzzles the lot.'

'Rose, do you think Johnny Depp's a slobbery kisser?' said Mia.

'Oh pet, of course he isn't. He's always been perfectly lovely when he's kissed me.'

Chapter 53

Doreen was in the middle of a dream. Mia hoped it was a happy one. Sitting down carefully next to William on the sofa in the living room, she watched Doreen's paws twitch and her eyelids flicker, for all the world as if she was chasing rabbits.

Or was that just Irish dogs? Could a London one, born and bred in the city, dream of chasing something it had probably never seen in its life? Maybe urban dogs dreamed of chasing taxis or traffic wardens, or just old discarded burger wrappers as they blew down the street.

It was one of those things you'd never know.

Oh thank God Doreen was still alive.

William, careful not to disturb Doreen while he ate a bacon sandwich, said comfortably, 'Don't blame yourself, love. It wasn't your fault.'

Forcing herself to get a grip, Mia thought how nice he was.

'You and Rose seem to be getting along well.'

'We are,' William agreed. 'Well, who wouldn't get on with a lady like that? What you see is what you get with Rose.'

Mia nodded. This was true, more or less. Apart from the fact that Rose knew something he didn't know.

Quite a big something actually.

The beginnings of an idea began to unfurl inside Mia's head. It was so unfair that Nancy and Zac should have to pretend to be a couple purely for William's benefit. In fact, more than that, it was ridiculous.

Taking a sip of her drink, she said, 'Can I ask you a question?'

William shrugged and swallowed a mouthful of sandwich. 'So long as it isn't about quantum physics.'

'Do you think my dad seems like a kind of . . . forgiving person?'

'Forgiving? In what way?'

'OK,' said Mia. 'There's something I really should tell him, but I can't because I'm scared he'll hate me for it.'

William, watching Doreen's ears twitch, said easily, 'I can't believe that. Fathers don't think that way. What kind of something?'

Exactly the question Mia had wanted him to ask. This was going perfectly to plan. Fiddling with the stem of her glass, she said, 'I can't tell you. It's . . . difficult.'

'Well, are you a mass murderer?'

'No.'

William tilted his head to one side. 'Worse than that?'

'No. At least, I don't think so.' Mia paused. 'Dad might.'

'It's hard for me to judge if I don't know what it is that's worrying you.'

'OK.' Taking a deep breath, Mia said, 'I'm gay.'

William gazed steadily at her. Doreen opened one eye then closed it again as he stroked her head.

Finally he said, 'Well, that's not so terrible, is it? I've only met Connor a couple of times but I can't imagine he'd refuse to speak to you again. You're his daughter, his own flesh and blood. He loves you. He just wants you to be happy.'

Mia took another swig from her glass. 'You think?'

'Definitely,' said William.

'Oh. Good. Well, thanks.'

'Don't mention it, love.'

'Actually, I was lying,' said Mia. 'I'm not gay.'

William looked at her. 'No?'

'No.'

'Why did you say it, then?'

'Because Zac is.'

William said nothing. He carried on stroking Doreen's head. Then he exhaled slowly, stirring the hairs on her silky ears.

'But you already knew that,' Mia said finally. 'Didn't you.'

'I didn't. Not for sure.' Shaking his head, William said, 'But I suspected he was. He never told me, though. Never dropped any hints, never said anything. Which made things difficult. I mean, it wasn't something that ever came up in conversation. We just aren't that kind of family. And it wasn't up to me to force the issue. How could I ever ask Zac if he was gay? What if he wasn't? He'd never have forgiven me.'

'So you just left it,' said Mia.

'I just left it.' William nodded. 'I figured if Zac wanted me to know, he'd tell me. If he didn't want me to know, he wouldn't. And maybe he wasn't gay after all, in which case all the more reason not to say anything.' He frowned slightly. 'Does Nancy know?'

'Everyone knows,' said Mia.

'So there's nothing going on between them?'

'Nothing. It was all for show. To be honest, I had high hopes for Nancy and my dad, but she isn't his type. I've done my best.' Mia gestured ruefully in the direction of the noisy kitchen. 'But this lot are hopeless. Everyone's destined to be just good friends.'

'Rose did mention that you were a bit of a meddler.'

'I don't meddle. I just try and help out.'

'Was Zac really afraid to tell me because he thought I'd hate him?'

'I don't know. But that's why people generally hide that kind of thing from their parents, isn't it? I just think it's better to get it out in the open,' Mia said simply. 'Then everyone can relax.'

'You what?' Dazed, Zac stared at Nancy, who had opened the front door.

'Your dad knows you're gay. He'd pretty much guessed anyway.'

'H-how does he know?'

'Mia told him.'

'Jesus, did she get drunk again?'

'No. She just thought it was time you came clean. It's all right,' said Nancy. 'You don't have to worry.' Her mouth twitching, she added, 'You won't have to kiss me any more either.'

'It wasn't very nice, was it? Sorry about that.' Anxiously Zac said, 'Are you sure Dad's OK?'

Nancy pulled him into the hall. 'Why don't you go and see for yourself? He's in the sitting room with Doreen.'

Bracing himself, Zac went to meet his father. As he entered the sitting room, Doreen leapt down from William's lap and launched herself joyfully at Zac. Picking her up and cuddling her, Zac wordlessly met his father's gaze.

'It's fine, son. You don't have to say anything.' Rising to his feet, William made his way across the room to Zac.

'Dad, I'm sorry.'

'Nothing to apologise for.' Slightly awkwardly – they'd never been a demonstrative family – William rested his roughened hand on Zac's shoulder. 'I'm as proud of you today as I was the day you were born. No one could have asked for a better son.'

Zac's eyes filled with tears as the weight of keeping his secret all these years fell away. 'I've had a good dad.'

Evidently terrified that Zac might be about to hug him, William gave his shoulder a series of jerky pats, while Doreen licked Zac's face.

'Come on then, son. It's been quite a day. Let's go through to the kitchen, shall we? I reckon we could both do with another drink.'

Rennie stood in the kitchen and silently re-read the copy of the press release faxed through by his agent.

Biba Keyes had been rushed to hospital last night in excruciating pain and had undergone an emergency caesarean. The baby, born five weeks prematurely, was a healthy boy – name yet to be announced. Biba was currently exhausted and recovering from the trauma of surgery but delighted by the safe arrival of her beautiful son.

A boy.

Biba had a son.

Did *he*?

'All right, pet? You've gone pale.' Rose, busy making a plum crumble, looked anxious. 'Bad news?'

How could the birth of a child be bad news? His emotions scarily mixed, Rennie offered the fax to Rose, who held up her sticky hands.

'I'm all messy. You'll have to hold it, pet.'

Rennie's hand shook as she read the press release. Rose's expression changed and she said, 'Oh, sweetheart, and they didn't even ring you. Well, I suppose it all happened too fast. Thank goodness they're both OK.' Wiping her hands on a cloth and pushing the bowl of crumble away, Rose said tentatively, 'Am I allowed to say congratulations?'

'I don't know. It feels a bit weird.' The phone in Rennie's jeans pocket burst into life.

'Well, you'll be going to visit them.'

Would he?

'For Christ's sake don't visit them,' his agent announced without preamble. 'Don't go near the place. I've been in touch with the lawyers and they're arranging the DNA test.'

'She says it's mine.' Rennie watched Rose untie her floury pink apron and slip out of the kitchen.

'Ha,' his agent snorted. 'And her dad's Elvis. Innocent until proven guilty, remember. Just make sure you keep away from her and the kid.'

Rennie hung up. His agent had three ex-wives and five children he seldom saw but paid a fortune to support.

At this moment, his own son could be lying in a hospital cot less than two miles away.

Rose reappeared clutching something small wrapped in turquoise tissue.

303

'Here, pet, I made it last week. I don't know if you'd like to take it with you when you visit.'

Rennie took the small parcel and unwrapped the crackling tissue paper. How typical of Rose to have thought of doing such a thing. The hand-knitted jacket was tiny, white and immaculate. Extraordinarily, the sight of it almost brought tears to his eyes.

Worried, Rose said, 'If you think it's too old fashioned—'

'It's not.' Rennie bent to kiss her on the cheek. 'It's perfect.'

'What's perfect?' Carmen, yawning and running her fingers through her spiky hair, wandered into the kitchen. Since giving up her work at the hostel she had taken to sleeping late.

Rennie, his stomach churning, said briefly, 'The baby was born last night.'

'Oh.' Carmen turned away, headed over to the kettle. 'Does it look like you?'

'They just sent a fax,' Rose explained. 'We don't know yet.'

'Well. How exciting.' Reaching for a cup and a tea bag, Carmen sloshed in boiling water. Her shoulders stiff and her tone brittle, she said, 'You're a dad.'

'I might be,' said Rennie quietly.

Carmen shrugged, still not looking at him. 'Call me old fashioned, but don't you think it might be an idea to find out?'

'I'm here to see Biba Keyes,' Rennie told the receptionist. 'Can you tell me which room she's in?'

Of course he'd had to come to the hospital. How could he stay away?

'Just one moment please.' The receptionist picked up the phone and murmured into it.

Three minutes later, the faint smell of hospitals was replaced by a blast of Obsession as a blonde girl tapped Rennie on the shoulder. Heavily made-up and less pretty than Biba, wearing a glittery yellow boob tube with spray-on jeans and yellow stilettos, she eyed him up and down before breaking into a slow smile.

'So, you bothered to turn up.'

Rennie disliked her at once. 'I'd have been here last night if I'd known what was happening.'

'I'm Jodie, Biba's sister. You can't see them now. Biba's knackered and the baby's asleep.'

'I'll wait,' said Rennie. Good grief, how could anyone wear that much perfume?

'No, you don't understand. Biba doesn't want to see you. She feels very let down by the way you've treated her. It's, like, she needs time to work through the pain of your heartless rejection, after everything you meant to each other.'

Rennie wondered if Jodie always spoke tabloid, or just saved it for special occasions.

'Do I get to see the baby, then?'

Jodie painstakingly adjusted her sizeable breasts inside the confines of their yellow Lycra cage. Then she shook her head.

'Biba says she needs some quality time alone with her precious son, in order to come to terms with the pain of your heartless rejection.'

'You already said that.' Rennie tried not to breathe in the overpowering smell of Obsession.

'Yeah, but it's like a kind of grief she needs to work through,' Jodie parroted. 'Becoming a single parent is, like, *so* not what Biba wanted.'

'Five minutes, OK?' If the child was his son, Rennie couldn't bear the thought of not seeing him.

Jodie shook her head again, clearly enjoying her new-found power.

'Nope.'

'Please. Just *two* minutes.'

Without warning Jodie reached out and shoved him violently away from her. Staggering backwards on her high heels she yelled, 'Security! Get this man out of here! HELP!'

Rennie sighed. Perfect.

Chapter 54

The temperature wasn't exactly tropical – it was only the end of March, after all – but at least the sun was out and doing its best to cast some warmth on the proceedings. And when you were sitting naked on one of the brass lions in Trafalgar Square – well, let's face it, every little bit of warmth helped.

At least it wasn't snowing.

Ignoring the laughter of the pointing, camera-clicking tourists who had congregated around the lion, Mia proudly shook back her hair and watched the two policemen as they headed across the road towards her.

'Right. Down you come, miss,' the burlier of the pair called up to her.

'Sorry, I can't do that.'

'You've had your bit of fun. Are these your clothes?' Reaching for the neat pile at the base of the statue, the skinny one said, 'Just climb down and put them on, there's a good girl.'

Mia smiled. 'Yes, those are my clothes. And this,' she held up a small tube, 'is my Superglue.'

The two policemen looked at each other. The skinny one took out his walkie-talkie. The burly one said, 'Is this a joke?'

'Not a joke at all.' With her free hand, Mia indicated the banner stuck to the side of the lion. 'I'm protesting on behalf of the animals who have to endure appalling conditions while they're being transported from one country to another prior to slaughter. They're crammed in together so tightly they can't move, they aren't given enough water, they—'

'I meant have you really Superglued yourself to that lion,' the burly policeman said wearily.

'Oh yes.' Mia beamed down at him. Having chosen a fairly ladylike side-saddle pose, she had sparingly dabbed the glue onto her bottom, the palm of her left hand and the inner edge of her right knee.

'You're going to be in trouble,' the skinny policeman pronounced. 'We'll have to arrest you, love.'

'I know *that*.' Honestly, did they think she was completely thick?

'Lewd and offensive behaviour,' said Skinny.

'Breach of the peace,' sighed Burly.

'Criminal damage to the lion,' said Skinny.

'Fine,' Mia said cheerfully, 'but you'll have to unstick me first.'

After an hour-long workout in the gym, Nancy was puce in the face and sweating profusely. Back in the changing room, more than ready for a long cool shower, it wasn't until she unzipped her sports bag that she discovered the top had snapped open on her shampoo bottle, leaking shampoo all over her towel. Lovely.

As she made her way through to reception to pick up a fresh towel – yuk, Cyanide Sadie was there behind the desk checking bookings – the door to Connor's office crashed open. Connor, standing in the doorway, bellowed, 'My God, what have I done to deserve this?'

He looked as if he should have steam shooting out of his ears. Zena, the new part-time receptionist, said apprehensively, 'What's wrong? Did I make a mistake?'

Raking his tousled hair, Connor said, 'I wish. The only mistake around here is the one I made when I said Mia could move to London. I've just had a call from Trudy Mulholland. One of our members,' he explained, because Zena was looking blank. 'She thought she should let me know that while she was stuck in traffic going round Trafalgar Square, she happened to notice my daughter sitting on top of one of the lions.'

'Oh,' Zena said anxiously. 'Is that not allowed?'

'She didn't have any clothes on!' roared Connor.

Sadie smirked.

'She had some kind of banner with her,' Connor went on. 'And there were police there, and paramedics, not to mention a crowd of people *gawping* at her.'

'That girl's always been an attention-seeker,' Sadie murmured.

'I'll have to get over there.' Patting his pockets, searching for his keys and cigarettes, Connor said, 'God only knows what she thinks she's playing at.'

'I don't have a class until six,' said Sadie. 'Want me to go with you?'

He looked at her blankly. 'You hate Mia. How would that help?'

Sadie shrugged, her magenta curls bouncing around her shoulders. 'I didn't say it would help. I just thought it'd be a laugh.'

Having lit a cigarette, Connor turned to Nancy.

'Will you come along?'

Perspiration was drying on Nancy's face, tightening her skin like a face mask. Her droopy T-shirt and baggy jogging trousers stuck damply to her body. With no make-up and her hair tied back she felt clammy and disgusting and undoubtedly looked worse. A shower would take *five minutes*—

'Please?' said Connor agitatedly, jangling his keys. 'She might listen to you.'

Sadie snorted with derision. 'That girl doesn't listen to anyone. She's out of control.'

Longing to slap her, Nancy moved towards Connor. 'Come on, let's go.'

The Bentley was perilously abandoned down a side street on double yellows. Racing across the main road and up onto Trafalgar Square, Nancy panted, 'I thought they'd have got her down by now.'

'I don't believe this. She's got a bigger audience than Posh Spice. MIA!' Connor yelled over the heads of the massed onlookers. 'What the bloody hell do you think you're doing? Get down from there THIS MINUTE.'

'Hi, Dad.' Spotting him, Mia waved excitedly. 'Fancy seeing you here!'

'Oh *God*.' Connor winced and turned away.

'What?' said Nancy.

'She's my daughter. She's stark naked. I can't look at her.' Grabbing Nancy's arm, he said urgently, 'You tell her to get down.'

'She can't get down,' sighed a burly policeman. 'She's Superglued herself to the lion.'

'I'm going to emigrate.' Connor groaned and clapped his hands over his eyes.

'Is she your daughter, sir?'

'No. I've never seen her before in my life.'

'I know how you feel, sir.' Burly nodded sympathetically. 'I've a teenager myself. Nightmare.'

Gesturing without looking, Connor cried, 'Can't you at least cover her up?'

'We've tried, sir, with blankets. But she keeps ripping them off. One of the paramedics is going to try and fix up a screen. How old is your daughter, sir, may I ask?'

'Sixteen,' Connor said heavily. 'How are they going to get her unglued?'

'Some kind of solvent.' Burly pulled a face. 'But it's going to take a while.'

'Will it hurt?'

308

'She'll be pretty sore afterwards.'

'Good,' said Connor.

It had been Nancy's idea to drape the banner – announcing that Animals Have Feelings Too! – around Mia's body.

'Your dad's embarrassed,' she told Mia. 'This way you won't be naked but you'll still get the message across.'

'Is he mad at me?'

'It's his job to be mad.' Nancy smiled as she tied the ends of the banner – a white sheet daubed with red emulsion paint – over Mia's shoulder. 'He'll get over it. In a few years.'

'Ouch.' Mia winced as the paramedic with the solvent-soaked gauze swabs attempted to peel her skin prematurely from the bronze back of the lion.

'Right, that won't slip.' Double-checking the knot was secure, Nancy said with relief, 'I'm getting down now.'

'I know. It's higher up here than you think, isn't it? Thanks for coming along with Dad, by the way.' Breaking into a grin, Mia eyed the hideous jogging bottoms and crumpled T-shirt. 'Especially at such short notice.'

'At least I'm wearing clothes,' said Nancy. 'Anyway, thank your lucky stars. If I'd said no, he'd have brought Sadie instead.'

It took another ninety minutes to free Mia, by which time she'd been interviewed by three journalists, offered a deal to pose for a top shelf magazine and witnessed her father threatening to punch the guy who'd made the offer.

Pocketing a parking ticket and escaping being clamped by the skin of his teeth, Connor drove with Nancy to Charing Cross police station in Agar Street where Mia, now under arrest, had been taken.

They loitered outside the building and Connor smoked yet another cigarette. He saw that Nancy, drinking coffee from a polystyrene cup, was looking tired.

Connor, overcome with guilt, said, 'Look, you don't have to stay if you don't want to.'

Nancy pulled a face, her hand going up to her tied-back hair.

'Is that your way of telling me I'm too embarrassing to be seen with in public?'

'After Mia's one-woman show this afternoon,' Connor said fervently, 'I can promise you, I'm beyond embarrassment.' A split second later, realising his unintentional gaffe, he waved his arms. 'Oh hell, I didn't mean you *are* embarrassing. You look fine, honestly. Very . . . natural.'

From the expression on Nancy's face he sensed that this was wrong too. Bugger, why did he always manage to mess things up when he was with her?

'I'm a mess.' Nancy fiddled self-consciously with her fringe. 'Still, never mind. Anyway, I really don't mind waiting. Mia shouldn't be long now.'

'I owe you one.' Eager to make amends, Connor said, 'Tell you what, why don't I treat you to dinner tonight, to make up for all this? How does that sound?'

There was an odd look in Nancy's eyes, one he was completely unable to read. Finally she said, 'It sounds as if you've forgotten you're seeing Tabitha tonight.'

Bugger, he had too. Having left a message with Tabitha's answering service earlier, letting her know what was happening, Connor reached automatically for his mobile. 'Look, Tab won't mind. I'll just give her a ring and—'

'The three of us can go out together?' said Nancy.

What? That wasn't what he'd meant at all. Connor opened his mouth to say so, then abruptly closed it again. Nancy wasn't remotely interested in him and the thought of the two of them having dinner together was, quite clearly, a chore. Plus, she thought he was trying to chat her up – which he *was*, of course – and resented the fact that he was being unfair to Tabitha. Friendly, cheerful Tabitha whom she had introduced to him in the first place.

'Of course,' Connor feigned delight in a last-ditch effort to redeem himself. 'Fine! Great idea.'

Nancy shook her head. 'No thanks.'

'Oh. Why not?'

'You don't have to do that.' She shivered and took another gulp of coffee.

'But I'd like to,' Connor protested.

'Really, you don't need to thank me.' Nancy sounded either upset or irritated, he couldn't tell which. 'Anyway, I'm busy tonight.' Balancing her coffee on a window ledge, she rubbed her arms.

'Here, put this on.' Removing his black suede jacket, Connor draped it round her shoulders. Standing in front of her, holding the lapels, he watched Nancy avoid his gaze.

His phone chose that moment to start ringing. Nancy fished the mobile from the pocket of his jacket and handed it over.

'Hi, it's me,' sang Tabitha. 'I've just got your message! How's Mia?'

'Unglued at last. We're at the station now.'

'Don't worry, I hear Holloway's fab these days, better than any five-star hotel! Joking,' Tabitha said brightly. 'She'll be fine. Crikey, at least she had the body for it. Wouldn't catch me cavorting naked in public! So, are we still on for tonight?'

Connor raised his eyebrows enquiringly and mouthed *Sure?* at Nancy, who was close enough to hear every word.

Shaking her head, Nancy turned and walked over to the waste bin to dispose of her empty polystyrene cup. As he watched her, Mia emerged from the police station fully clothed and minus her banner. Spotting Nancy, Mia raced over and flung her arms round her.

'Hello?' Tabitha sounded concerned. 'Are you still there?'

'Yes, great. I'll pick you up at eight thirty. I'd better go now,' said Connor. 'Mia's just come out.'

'No problem, we're busy here too,' Tabitha said cheerily. 'See you later. And give Mia my love.'

'They dropped the charges.' Mia was triumphant. 'Let me off with a caution.'

Relieved, Connor eyed the raw patch on the palm of her hand and said, 'They probably thought you'd suffered enough punishment.'

'Ha, that's nothing. You should see the ones on my—'

'Thanks very much,' Connor swiftly interjected, 'but I'd rather not.'

'Were you scared?' Nancy indicated the police station behind them. 'When they were questioning you there?'

'Nooo.' Mia looked scornful, then broke into a tiny grin and said, 'Well, maybe just a bit.'

Reaching for his car keys, Connor said, 'Serve you right.'

'But I did it for a reason. I had a point to make and I made it.' Mia's silver-grey eyes shone with pride. 'And I tell you something, if I have to do it again I will.'

'Let *me* tell *you* something.' The note of paternal warning in Connor's voice prompted Mia and Nancy to exchange amused glances. 'You're my daughter, you're sixteen years old and you *bloody well will not*.'

Chapter 55

Rose was sitting on her favourite bench in the square when she saw Marjorie Brough-Badham hurrying towards her. Putting down her knitting and shielding her eyes from the sun, she saw that Marjorie was carrying an armful of glossy magazines.

'Marjorie, how nice to see you,' said Rose. 'You're looking . . . well.' If a bit wild-eyed, to be honest.

'I saw you out here. Had to come and tell you.' Straight-shouldered as ever, Marjorie abruptly sat down next to Rose and said, 'You'll never guess.'

The magazines weren't magazines, Rose realised. They were upmarket travel brochures.

'Um . . . you're off on holiday?'

'No! Well, yes,' Marjorie flapped her hand impatiently at the brochures, signalling their unimportance in the great scheme of things, 'but that's not it. You can't imagine what's happened.'

Was she supposed to try? A trifle despairingly, Rose said, 'What is it?'

'Geoffrey's mother died yesterday.'

'Oh, I'm so sorry.' Heavens, it was hard to imagine Geoffrey *having* a mother. 'Is he dreadfully upset?'

Marjorie barked with laughter, then abruptly covered her mouth. 'It's certainly had an effect on him. The matron from the nursing home rang yesterday morning to let him know that Alice had died in her sleep. Passed away peacefully, the best way to go and all that. Well, she was ninety-four, so it was hardly unexpected. Bit of a battleaxe, to be frank. Always ruled her family with a rod of iron. Used to call Margaret Thatcher a wet blanket.'

Carefully Rose said, 'I see.'

'We were having breakfast together at the time. When the matron phoned,' Marjorie gabbled on, her fingers agitatedly rolling a corner of one of the travel brochures. 'Not the kind of having-breakfast-together you see on TV. Geoffrey was reading his *Telegraph* in silence. I was

312

sitting there wondering what it must be like to feel happy. Anyway, he took the call, spoke to the matron, then told me his mother was dead. After that he left the room for twenty minutes. When he returned he sat back down at the breakfast table, poured himself a fresh cup of coffee and asked me to pass him the marmalade.'

'Right.' Rose wondered where on earth this was going.

'So by then his toast was stone cold of course – he *hates* it when his toast is cold – but he buttered it anyway and spread it with marmalade. And I said, "Are you all right, Geoffrey?" and he looked across the table at me and said, "Yes thank you, absolutely fine. I'm a homosexual."'

Rose dropped her knitting. 'Oh good grief. Just like that? Oh *Marjorie* . . .'

'I know, I know! Can you believe it? I couldn't move. I said, "What are you talking about?" and Geoffrey said, "I'm sorry, but it's true." So I said, "You can't tell me that when your mother has just died," and he said, "Marjorie, I can tell you that *because* my mother has just died."'

'You poor thing,' breathed Rose, recalling the moment last week after Doreen's abduction when Zac and William had walked into the kitchen together, Zac's guilty secret from his father no longer a secret. Fear and alarm had initially flickered across the Brigadier's granite features; Rose had glimpsed them there before he had rapidly composed himself.

Maybe Zac's happy outcome had prompted him to try for one of his own.

'And that was when it all came out,' Marjorie continued. 'Geoffrey told me everything.'

Everything? Heavens above.

'And I can hardly believe I'm saying this, but I actually ended up feeling sorry for him. And relieved.' Marjorie nodded vehemently, her eyes abruptly brimming with tears. 'Yes, *relieved*. Because I realised it meant I hadn't done anything wrong, and I can't tell you what a weight off my mind that was! You see, it's not that I've been an undesirable wife all these years. Geoffrey simply wasn't able to, well, desire me because I was the wrong sex. Oh, look at me, blubbing again when there's absolutely no need. I know I'm probably still in a state of shock, but I woke up this morning feeling happy! You wouldn't believe how much talking Geoffrey and I did yesterday . . . heavens, more talking than we've done in our whole marriage! He apologised for being so buttoned-up all these years. Basically, he's just been incredibly unhappy, feeling he can never be himself. Poor man, all that shame and guilt takes its toll. And I was never remotely sympathetic because I didn't know *why* he'd distanced himself from me . . . Anyway, that's all behind us now. Last night Geoffrey offered me a divorce . . . damn and blast, where did I put that hankie?' She fumbled clumsily in her skirt pocket.

Rose handed her a clean tissue. 'Is that what you're going to do?'

'No, not yet. Maybe not at all.' Shaking her head and noisily blowing her nose, Marjorie said, 'We've decided to leave it for now. We're used to each other, you see. As companions at least. It'll take a while to become accustomed to living alone, so we're putting this house on the market and buying two more, but we shall share them. A villa in Menorca, we thought. And a cottage in North Wales. That way, sometimes we'll be together and sometimes we won't.' She paused, dabbing at her long nose with the tissue. 'Does that sound silly?'

Rose said warmly, 'It sounds like an excellent idea.'

'So that's something to look forward to. And in the meantime I've decided to take a cruise. I've always wanted to try it, but Geoffrey was never keen on cruising. So I'm going to go alone!'

Clearly, Marjorie's wasn't aware that cruising had other connotations. Rose tactfully didn't mention it.

'I can't believe I'm sitting here telling you this.' Like a brief shower, Marjorie's tears had passed and she was looking cheerful again. 'My husband's a homosexual and I'm actually happy about it, because now at last everything makes sense!'

'That's wonderful. Er, does he know you're over here?' Rose couldn't help glancing across at the glinting windows of number sixty-four, wondering if the Brigadier was aware that he was being publicly outed.

'He's gone to Hampshire to organise the funeral. Sounds frightful, but I'm rather glad Alice died now. Poor Geoffrey, he could never have done it while she was alive. Men are funny creatures, aren't they?' Pausing to think about it, Marjorie said brightly, 'Mind you, I suppose if I was a lesbian my mother would have been cross with me too.'

Biba's tabloid of choice had been running with the story for the last six days and Rennie was beginning to know how it felt to be a pantomime villain. When he ventured out, women of all ages narrowed their eyes at him in disgust and muttered sneering insults under their breath. One or two had even hissed.

Maybe he should get a T-shirt with *It's not mine* printed across the front.

As he climbed out of the car in leafy Fulham, Rennie looked up at the second-floor apartment and saw Jodie at the window gazing impassively down at him. Following their last encounter at the hospital, the paper had reported that he had caused mayhem in the reception area, turning up and loudly demanding to see Biba and the baby before having to be ejected by security guards. Biba had reportedly been in floods of tears and deeply shaken by the incident.

God, no wonder everyone despised him. If he passed himself in the street he'd hiss too.

'I'd like to see Biba. Alone,' Rennie said pointedly when Jodie answered the door.

'Suit yourself.' Jodie showed him through to the living room and left them to it.

Biba, far prettier without make-up and wearing a simple emerald-green velour tracksuit, was sitting on the cream leather couch with her feet up on the sleek chrome and glass coffee table, painstakingly applying clear varnish to her toenails. Looking up at Rennie she waggled her fingers and said, 'Hi, babes. All right?'

'I'm not the father.' Rennie had come straight from his lawyer's office. He held out his copy of the official result of the DNA test.

'I know. My agent just rang. Sorry, babes.' Biba carefully fastened the lid on the nail varnish bottle and gave him a sympathetic smile. 'Are you disappointed?'

Since there really wasn't any answer to that, Rennie said, 'You knew it wasn't me. You knew all along.'

Biba pushed back her long ash-blond hair, careful not to get her fingers tangled in the knots attaching the extensions to her scalp.

'Rennie, don't be cross. You know how this business works, right? If you can sell a story, you sell it. You'd be mad not to. Look at it from my point of view. I'm a single mother with a baby to support. Now, do I take some crappy little office job for five quid an hour and work my fingers to the bone to earn enough money to buy a pram? Or do I go to the papers for twenty grand and let *Hi!* magazine into my lovely home for another thirty?'

Rennie repeated, 'But I'm not the father.'

'You slept with me. You could have been.' Biba shrugged, blithely unconcerned. 'Don't worry, I'll put out a press release announcing it wasn't you. Oh, come on, babes, it's over now. You're off the hook. Don't be grumpy.'

She was right, Rennie realised. There was absolutely no point in losing his temper because Biba genuinely didn't feel she'd done anything wrong. This was, effectively, how she earned her living.

The babes thing was getting on his nerves though – she hadn't called him that when they'd been together in New York. He'd never have slept with her if she had.

Biba said cheerfully, 'Want to see him, then?'

Did he? Rennie nodded. For some reason he really did want to see this child who had, through no fault of its own, caused him such trouble.

Keeping her wet toes splayed, Biba carefully hauled herself upright and led the way through to the nursery. The baby lay in his ornately carved cot, asleep, with his chubby hands curled above his head.

'Isn't he gorgeous?' This time Biba spoke with genuine pride. 'I just love him to bits. Oops . . .'

At the sound of her voice the baby's eyes had snapped open. As he regarded them in silence for several seconds, Rennie found himself, ridiculously, searching for some hint of a resemblance between this week-old infant and himself. How would he feel if this child had been his? How must it feel to have a child with someone he actually loved?

'Want to hold him?' Biba offered. 'Just for a few seconds, before he starts screaming the place down.'

Rennie lifted the baby out of the cot and held him in his arms. His heart swelled with emotion; it really was incredible, the ability babies had to make you feel—

'Ha, you big softie, you're crying!' crowed Biba.

'I am not.' Cursing himself, Rennie blinked furiously.

'You wuss! Wait till I tell Jodie!'

Great, something to really look forward to.

'You made me think I was a father,' Rennie told Biba. 'And I'm not.'

'Oh, cheer up, I thought you'd be thrilled to be off the hook.' Surveying him with amusement, Biba said, 'Tell you what, I'll be getting him christened in a few months. You can be godfather if you like.'

'No thanks.' As the baby opened his mouth to yell out in protest about the lack of food, Rennie passed him over to Biba. 'He's a pretty good weight, isn't he? Doesn't look premature.'

Biba, her eyes dancing with mischief, said, 'Now if you were selling your story to the paper, which would sound more exciting to you? Mother in labour rushed to hospital for emergency life-saving op? Or, mother turns up carrying suitcase, ready for pre-booked caesarean?' She shrugged. 'Go on, pick one. Your choice.'

Of course. Why hadn't that occurred to him before?

Anyway, it was all over now. Deciding he was relieved, Rennie said, 'Did Josie give you the parcel I brought to the hospital?'

'That funny little cardigan-type thing?' Biba wrinkled her nose. 'Was that meant to be some kind of joke?'

'Didn't it fit?' Rennie thought of the amount of work that had gone into the outfit.

'I've no idea, we didn't put it on him! Only the best designer gear for this one, thanks very much.' Patting her son's duck-egg blue romper suit, Biba said with pride, 'Try Versace, if you want to buy him something else. Or Baby Dior.'

Rennie turned to leave. At the door, he paused.

'What's his name?'

'Come on, you think I'm going to tell you that now?' Biba flashed him a triumphant smile. 'Can't let the cat out of the bag yet, can we, babes?' This time, thankfully, the *babes* was directed at her son. 'You'll have to wait and read all about it,' she told Rennie, 'in next week's *Hi!'*

Rennie shook his head; he no longer had the energy to be angry. It was his own fault for tangling with a girl like Biba in the first place. He had no one to blame but himself.

'Rennie? Can we still be friends?'

He looked over at Biba posing with her son beside the cot, supremely aware of the touching tableau they made. 'I don't think so. After all, we never were.'

She kissed the baby's dark downy head, then hoisted him up to her shoulder.

'Oh well, never mind. But you do understand why I did it, don't you? Going to the papers is money for old rope. I needed the money, so I gave them the rope.'

'You certainly did that,' Rennie agreed.

'But it's over now,' Biba said chirpily. 'No harm done, babes. You can just carry on being you, having a ball and breaking hearts . . .'

No harm done. For a moment he was almost tempted to tell her just how much harm had been done. And that the only heart to have been broken was his own.

But what would be the point of that?

'Bye,' said Rennie.

317

Chapter 56

'He's miserable. He's been an idiot and he knows it. Dammit, he's making *my* life a misery,' Annie declared. 'He's no fun any more. In fact I'll tell you how bad it's got. Who's the grumpiest, stroppiest, most irritable man you've ever met in your life?'

That was easy. 'Grumpy Gus,' Carmen said promptly. Grumpy Gus, a frequent visitor to the shelter, was a foul-mouthed curmudgeon of truly heroic proportions.

'Correct. Ten points to you. And last week even *he* told Nick to cheer up.'

'Really?' Carmen looked sceptical.

'Well, not really. His actual words were, "For fuck's sake, you miserable bastard, get a fucking grip on yourself and cheer the fuck up."'

'That sounds more like it.'

Annie grew serious. 'But it's not funny, Carmen. Nick really is regretting what he did. He misses you terribly. That's why I had to see you today. I thought you might want to know.'

Carmen laced her fingers tightly round her cup of coffee. Hearing from Annie out of the blue after all these weeks had come as both a shock and a relief. Terrified that Annie despised her as much as Nick did, Carmen had been deeply touched by her former workmate's response.

'You twit,' Annie had chortled down the phone. Not many people could chortle, but Annie could. 'Of course I don't hate you!'

'But you bought me those mugs for the flat . . .'

'So?' Annie had retorted in disbelief. 'I like buying presents for my friends. Look, meet me in Luigi's at six o'clock. And if it makes you feel any better, you can pay for the coffee and doughnuts.'

Now, ensconced with Annie in the steamy cafe a couple of streets away from the shelter, Carmen's stomach tightened as she wondered if she did want to know how much Nick was regretting what he'd done.

Except she did, of course she did. He'd made a mistake, he missed her terribly. She was vindicated.

'So?' said Annie, licking sugar from her fingers and greedily eyeing her second toffee doughnut.

'So what?'

'Don't give me that! Do you miss him too?'

Carmen's heart began to gallop. She and Nick had been so happy together. Of course she'd missed him. And then the thing had happened with Rennie – the thing that had first begun to make itself felt on Christmas night, if she was honest – and that had remained uppermost in her mind. But she and Rennie had no future together, she knew that. And no two men could be more different than Rennie and Nick. Which had to mean something, surely?

'He was the one who ended it,' said Carmen.

'You were such a great couple.' Annie pushed up the baggy sleeve of her pink sweater. 'Look, it's twenty past six. Nick will be leaving work in ten minutes. How about if I give him a ring?'

'And say what?' Carmen began to scent a set-up.

'That we're here, you berk!' Delving into her bag, Annie eagerly whipped out her phone. 'That you'd like to see him again, and if he wants to drop by you could have a chat about . . . you know, stuff.'

'Does he know you're meeting me?'

'You're joking.' Vigorously Annie shook her head. 'He'd have killed me. Anyway, you might not have wanted to see him and then he'd have been even grumpier.'

Picturing Nick with his dear familiar face, scruffy hair and lamentable taste in clothes, Carmen realised how much she did want to see him again. He was kind, caring and the most genuinely selfless man she'd ever known. And he would never deliberately hurt her.

She shook her head at Annie. 'You know what? You're shameless.'

'So is that a yes?'

Her stomach contracting with anticipation, Carmen said, 'Go on then.'

So this was how it felt to be stood up. Having packed Annie off home forty minutes earlier because some reconciliations were definitely better carried out without an interested audience, Carmen had ordered a fresh coffee and waited. And waited.

When Annie had spoken to him on the phone Nick had agreed to join them at Luigi's. Clearly he'd had no intention of doing so.

It was almost seven o'clock. Nick wasn't coming and that was that. Wondering if anyone in London had a more disastrous love life than she did – the words, *what love life?* sprang to mind – Carmen said her good-byes to Luigi and his son and left the cafe.

The way things were going, Luigi's effusive garlicky kisses and rib-crushing embrace were the nearest she was going to get to love for quite a while.

It was a warm evening. When she emerged from the stuffy tube station, Carmen took off her navy sweatshirt and tied it round her hips. From a newsagents she bought an *Evening Standard* and a Cornetto.

Five minutes later, rounding the corner into Fitzallen Square, the Cornetto slid from her hand and hit the pavement. Ahead of her, scarcely recognisable with his hair short but otherwise deeply familiar in his old green jumper and dilapidated jeans, stood Nick.

'My God.' Carmen's hand flew to her mouth. She heard herself stupidly say, 'You're here.'

'I know.' Nick's smile was crooked, tentative. 'Amazing, isn't it?'

'I waited for you in the cafe.'

'Sorry. I wanted us to talk properly. I couldn't do it in Luigi's, in front of bossy Annie.' With a self-conscious gesture he reached up to rub the back of his head. Close to, Carmen saw that it was actually a pretty terrible haircut.

'I sent Annie away. She wouldn't even have been there. I thought you'd stood me up.'

'I was nervous. And I wanted to impress you.' Ruefully Nick tugged at a stray asymmetric tuft of hair. 'Should have gone to a proper barber, I guess.'

'Who did it?'

'Albert.'

'Albert the chess Grand Master?' Carmen struggled to keep a straight face.

'We were in the middle of a game when Annie rang. I happened to mention I'd be seeing you after work. That was when Albert asked me if I wanted to look my best and told me he used to be a hairdresser.'

'And you believed him, obviously.'

'He said he'd trained with Vidal Sassoon. Started talking about the parties him and Vidal used to go to with Twiggy and Mary Quant. They're real people,' Nick added defensively. 'Even I've heard of them.'

'So you let Albert cut your hair,' said Carmen.

Nick nodded bashfully. 'With the kitchen scissors.'

'I hope you didn't give him a tip.'

'Oh God, is it really that terrible?'

'Hey, it's only a haircut. Hair grows back. Or you could shave it all off.' Carmen realised she was babbling out of sheer nerves. This was

320

ridiculous, why were they standing here talking about hair? Taking a deep breath she gestured towards number sixty-two and said, 'That's where I live. Are you coming in?'

'I rang the doorbell ten minutes ago. Your brother-in-law answered the door.' The expression on Nick's face indicated that he hadn't received the warmest of welcomes. 'Could we talk out here instead?'

Feeling nervous, Carmen led the way across the road and into the garden square. When they'd reached the wooden seat and sat down she said, 'Talk about what?'

'Me being the world's biggest idiot.' Nick heaved a sigh, twisting an elastic band round his wrist and avoiding Carmen's gaze. 'Me realising that I should never have said those things to you. Me having to listen to Annie going on and on about how unfair I'd been, and knowing she was right.' Bowing his head he went on awkwardly, 'Me missing you more than I'd imagined possible.'

'Have you?' A lump sprang into Carmen's throat.

'Me wondering if you've missed me,' Nick continued. Round and round went the elastic band on his bony wrist.

Carmen nodded. 'Of course I've missed you.'

'Could you ever forgive me, d'you think? For behaving like a prize prat?'

'Oh, I think so.' Managing a smile, she said, 'Do you think you could forgive me for being filthy rich?'

Finally looking at her, Nick reached for her hand.

'I wish you weren't, but I suppose I can tolerate it.' He gave Carmen's fingers a squeeze. 'As long as it stays your money. If we're going to give things another go, you have to get your lawyer to draw up some kind of document for me to sign, stating that I never want a penny of it.'

'You berk,' Carmen said happily. 'I know you'd never do anything like that.'

'But I want to sign something anyway. Nobody's ever going to accuse me of being a gold-digger.' Nick was pale but determined. 'So d'you think we have a chance?' he said tentatively. 'Can we start again?'

How many times had she dreamed of him saying this? And now it was actually happening. Throwing her arms round him, Carmen whispered, 'Oh Nick . . .'

Rennie felt as though he'd been knifed in the stomach. Watching from his bedroom window, he experienced a surge of pain so acute it was almost physical, combined with more boiling jealousy than he'd known he possessed. That was it, then. He had lost. And Nick had won, not because he had the looks and the money, but because he was a genuinely decent, easy-going, *thoroughly nice bloke.*

When Nick had rung the doorbell earlier asking for Carmen, Rennie had been tempted to punch him.

Now he really wished he had.

Feeling sick, Rennie's fingers gripped the window ledge. Over in the square Nick and Carmen were still clutching each other, talking together, no doubt planning their shared future. He watched Nick in his manky green sweater stroking Carmen's arm as she spoke, then drawing her against him once more. Unable to bear it a moment longer, Rennie swore and abruptly turned away. This was his punishment for having lived the life he had. Worst of all, he knew that for Carmen's sake he would have to pretend to be pleased for her when she waltzed into the house with Nick and announced that the two of them were back together.

Well, maybe he could manage that for a couple of minutes but there was no way he was going to be cracking open the champagne and sitting around toasting their future happiness.

His jaw tightening, Rennie decided he'd go out. Congratulate them, then apologise and say he had to be somewhere. Then he'd shoot off and leave them to it.

What he might be leaving them *to* didn't bear thinking about.

Chapter 57

After a long shower Rennie returned to his room and pulled on a clean white shirt and faded jeans. He hadn't shaved – his hands hadn't been steady enough to risk it – but he splashed on some aftershave anyway in the vain hope that it might make him feel better.

Checking out of the window, he saw that the square was now empty. Having dimly heard the front door opening and closing while he'd been in the shower, this meant that Carmen and Nick were here in the house.

Rennie ran his fingers through his wet hair and grimly surveyed his reflection in the mirror. Here he was, the so-called rock star with everything. And how much good had it done him?

Right now he'd never felt colder and emptier in his life.

You lost, he won, sang an irritating voice in his head as he made his way downstairs. You lost, he won, you—

'Shit!'

The sound of Carmen's cry of anguish caused Rennie to halt abruptly at the foot of the staircase. Would it be too much to hope that she'd just accidentally trapped Nick's willy in his trouser zip? So painfully and irretrievably that there was nothing the surgeons could do but amputate? Oh yes, that would do very nicely indeed.

The curse had come from the living room. Much as he had no desire to view another man's trapped willy, Rennie moved towards the closed living-room door. Maybe he could call the ambulance.

Innocently he said, 'Everything all right in there?'

He heard frantic scuffling, then Carmen yelling out in alarm, 'Rennie! Don't come in!'

Rennie pictured Nick, his teeth gritted with pain as he struggled to free his willy from the mercilessly sharp teeth of the zip. Or maybe Carmen was hurriedly making herself decent.

'Fuck, *fuck*,' he heard Carmen gasp as a clattering sound ensued.

'What's wrong? Carmen, are you OK?'

'Oh, *I'm* OK.' Carmen sounded out of breath and panicky. Could

323

Nick's unfortunate accident be causing him to gush litres of blood all over the pale carpet?

'Want me to fetch the first aid tin?' Rennie offered, beginning to enjoy the fantasy of his rival in love losing his most prized possession.

Except he wasn't his rival in love, was he? Nick had won.

'Not the first aid tin,' Carmen yelled. 'Fetch the Cif. And that squirty carpet cleaner stuff. And lots of J-Cloths and kitchen roll. And stay outside,' she added distractedly. 'Just leave them by the door.'

Gallons of blood then. Excellent. Having located everything Carmen needed, Rennie returned from the kitchen and pushed open the living-room door. Well, if Nick was dead she wasn't going to be able to shift the body on her own, was she?

'Can't you *ever* do anything I tell you?' Carmen let out a wail of despair. 'I *said* don't come in.'

She was on her knees in front of the TV, surrounded by a slew of videos and DVDs in and out of their cases, a snowstorm of damp scrunched-up tissues and a brown stain spreading across the carpet. An empty coffee cup lay on its side, coffee was dripping from the DVD player and there were wet patches on the knees of her jeans.

There was no Nick in the room, either dead or alive, mutilated or intact. Carmen was on her own, looking harassed and caught out.

'What happened?' Rennie was referring to the absence of Nick.

'For crying out loud, what does it look like? I tripped over the sodding mains lead from the stupid DVD player and lost my balance and spilled my *buggering* cup of coffee.' Carmen's cheeks were hectically flushed, her tone defiant. 'It's gone into the DVD player and all over your precious videos and DVDs and I'll replace them, OK? But I'm warning you, if you start shouting at me for wrecking your collection I shall have to kill you, because I'm not in the mood for being shouted at.'

Rennie watched her frantically shaking coffee out of his video of *The Asphalt Jungle*, before wiping it with a handful of tissues. Crouching down next to her, he silently inspected the damage. The DVDs would be fine but the videos were all coffee-logged and beyond saving. *Scaramouche,* with Stewart Granger. Garbo's *Ninotchka*. The Marx Brothers' *Night at the Opera*. He picked up his favourite Humphrey Bogart video, *To Have and Have Not*, and lukewarm coffee seeped out onto the sleeve of his white shirt.

'I'm sorry,' said Carmen.

'Where's Nick?'

'Gone.'

Rennie's throat tightened. 'Why?'

'Because he has.' Reaching for a J-Cloth and the aerosol can of foam carpet cleaner, Carmen turned her attention to the carpet.

'What was he doing here?'

'Saying sorry. Asking if we could get back together again.'

'And?' said Rennie.

'I said no, we couldn't.'

Yes, yes, yes.

Carefully he said, 'I was watching the two of you out in the square.'

'Well, that figures.' Still squirting mountains of foam and energetically scrubbing away, Carmen kept her head down. 'Allowing people their privacy never has been your strong point.'

Rennie ignored this. 'Why did you say no?'

'Because it would never work.'

Evenly he said, 'Still the money thing?'

'No. Because I don't love him.'

'I thought you did.'

'So did I. At first. But . . . well, as it turns out, I don't.'

'Why not?'

'God, you're nosy.' Leaning back on her heels, Carmen watched as Rennie reached for her right arm and firmly prised the J-Cloth from her hand. 'What are you doing?'

'I was watching from the window,' Rennie repeated. 'You were in his arms.'

'It was nice to be asked. Nick's a great person.' Carmen's eyes were bright. 'I hugged him and thanked him, then I turned him down. If you must know, he was quite upset. You really shouldn't spy on people,' she added defiantly. 'It's rude.'

'So you changed your mind about Nick.' Rennie had no intention of giving up now. 'Does that mean you may have changed your mind about anyone else?'

'Give me back that cloth. If I don't scrub this stain out—'

'Carmen, just tell me.'

'We'll need a whole new carpet.'

'Sod the carpet,' said Rennie.

'Ha, that's easy for you to say! This cost thousands!'

'Sod the carpet and stop changing the subject.' Rennie gazed intently at Carmen. 'Why don't you tell me what's really going on here?'

Carmen felt the adrenaline zinging like sparklers through her body. As if bloody Rennie hadn't already guessed. Recklessly she said, 'Fine. OK. If that's what you want, I will.'

The diamond stud in Rennie's ear glittered as he nodded. 'I do want.'

Bastard, he was going to make her say it.

'Right.' Carmen took a deep breath. 'Well, I realised I didn't love Nick because he could never make me feel like . . . I knew somebody else could make me feel. Even though the other person is a completely hopeless case and the last person in the world anyone with any sense should get involved with.'

'I see.' Rennie nodded again. 'Tricky situation. How does this other person – the completely hopeless one – feel about you?'

'God knows. He told me he loved me.' Carmen heard her voice begin to shake. 'But he's such a smooth-talking bastard, you can't believe a word he says. So it's probably just one of those lines he uses on girls to get whatever he wants.'

Rennie said, 'On the other hand, he could really mean it.'

'I hope so.' Carmen risked a smile. 'For his sake.'

'Or you'd punish him severely. Do something completely terrible,' Rennie pointed out, 'like destroy his entire video collection.'

'I really am sorry about that.'

'So you should be. I'm deeply traumatised.' Doing his best to look traumatised, Rennie reached for his sodden copy of *The Great Escape*. 'In fact, I shall probably need months of professional counselling.'

'I'll do that, it'll be cheaper. Are you going to shut up now,' said Carmen, 'and kiss me?'

He broke into a grin. 'You're the one who started all this. I'd say it was up to you to make the first move.'

Pushing aside the scattered DVDs and videos, Carmen shuffled on her knees through the white drift of carpet cleaning foam until she reached Rennie. She had loved Spike so much, but his descent into drugs had been hard to bear, a millstone round both their necks. It was a problem she would never have with Rennie, who had never touched drugs. Furthermore, she was sure Spike would approve of them getting together.

When Rennie put his arms round her, she breathed in the scent of his aftershave and felt the warmth of his body against hers. Sometimes these things happened and you just had to learn to go with them. No matter how much she'd fought against it, she had no control over her feelings for Rennie. Like it or not, for better or for worse, he was the one she loved and couldn't live without.

As his mouth closed over hers, Carmen realised that this was all she wanted. It was like coming home.

* * *

'Nancy, come home. *Please.*'

Nancy gazed at the bouquet on the kitchen table – a rainbow of lilies, roses, long pointy blue foxgloves, glossy exotic leaves, curly twig things and, her all-time favourite, stupendously gaudy sunflowers. It was a vast arrangement, almost as big as the table itself. Of course whenever this happened in films – woman receives bouquet from man she no longer likes – the woman in question invariably dumped it in the nearest bin.

But Nancy couldn't bring herself to do that. It wasn't the flowers' fault that they'd come from Jonathan. They were far too gorgeous to throw away. Besides, even if she'd wanted to, this lot wouldn't fit into any normal-sized bin.

'Nancy? Are you still there?'

'Of course I'm still here. And this is where I'm staying.' As she spoke, Nancy idly turned over the card containing her unfaithful husband's grovelling, over-the-top apologies. 'Jonathan, I'm happy here. I'm not coming back. Our marriage is over and we're getting a divorce.'

'But it doesn't *have* to be over.' Jonathan's tone was warm, comforting. 'Look, I know I hurt you and I did a really stupid thing, but I've *learned* from that. You don't know how much I've missed you, sweetheart. We had a great marriage. After this, we can make it an even better one. If you want kids, fine. We'll have as many as you like.'

Nancy hid a smile. Oh, she wanted children all right. But not with Jonathan.

Aloud she said, 'How about a dog?'

Jonathan, who loathed dogs with a passion, said immediately, 'Of course you can have a dog.'

'Great. And a cat?'

'OK, and a cat.'

'And a giraffe?'

'Wh— ha ha ha. Very good.' Jonathan chuckled. 'OK, sweetheart, maybe not a giraffe. But anything else, within reason.' His voice softened, became cajoling. 'I just want to make up for all the hurt I caused, is that so terrible? I want you to be *happy.*'

Out of curiosity, Nancy said, 'What did you do with the sit-on lawnmower?'

'Nothing! It's right here.' Jonathan sounded excited. 'Waiting for you!'

Maybe that was why he was so keen to have her back, because the grass needed cutting. 'Jonathan, about these flowers.'

Eagerly he said, 'Do you like them?'

'Well, yes, of course I *like*—'

'I knew you would! And I told them to put sunflowers in, because I know they're your favourites. Remember the time—'

'Jonathan,' Nancy blurted out before he could get completely carried away, 'you can't seriously expect me to come back to you just because you've sent me a bunch of flowers!'

'It wasn't a bunch.' Hurt, he said, 'It was a bouquet. It cost two hundred pounds!'

'Good. I'm glad.'

'But I didn't mind spending that much,' Jonathan protested, 'because you're worth it.'

Nancy marvelled at his optimism. 'And you think that's what's needed to make me change my mind about divorcing you? Two hundred pounds' worth of flowers?'

'Sweetheart, listen to me, I'll do whatever it takes. I'll come down to London and beg you on my knees if that's what you want.' Sounding increasingly desperate, Jonathan shouted, 'Nancy, I love you, I'll do anything—'

'Really, you don't have to bother.' Smiling to herself, Nancy began hunting in the utility room for vases. 'I'm not going to change my mind, Jonathan. So I promise you, there's no point.'

Chapter 58

Mia had never been in love. Without worrying about it in the slightest, she had always vaguely assumed that there must be something a bit wrong with her, that maybe she was missing some vital gene in that department. She was almost seventeen, after all. The other girls at school had spent all their time mooning over boys, flirting and giggling at every opportunity, endlessly discussing with their friends what clothes and shoes to wear on their dates then sobbing helplessly in the toilets when their relationships broke up.

It had all seemed such a criminal waste of time as far as Mia was concerned, when there were so many more interesting things these girls could have been doing with their time. The allure of boys was a mystery and no mistake; it seemed such an endless cycle with no point to it at all. Mia was actually glad she was immune.

Until, arriving back from Ireland on Friday morning, she pushed through the smoked glass doors of the Lazy B and clapped eyes on, well, a *vision*.

No, really. That was how it felt. And there were butterflies swooping around in her chest who clearly thought so too.

Unversed in the way these scenarios were usually played out, it didn't occur to Mia to pause in the doorway, catch her breath and surreptitiously survey this vision from a safe distance. Instead she strode up to the reception desk – *her* desk – and said eagerly, 'Hi there.'

The vision grinned at her. He had dark curly hair cut close to his head, sparkling denim-blue eyes and endearingly crooked white teeth. There was a pale scar bisecting his left eyebrow, he was tanned and fit-looking and his fingernails were short and clean. All of a sudden Mia realised that these were the very attributes she'd been subconsciously searching for in a man her whole life.

'Hi. How can I help you?'

'Well, you can tell me your name for a start.' He wasn't too tall either, five foot ten or so, just the right height.

'Sorry. It's Gerry.' Reaching across the desk, Gerry took her hand and solemnly shook it. 'I should have a name badge, but I only started here yesterday,'

You could tell a lot by a handshake and his was perfect.

'I'm Mia.' Mia realised that she was still clutching his hand, even though the shaking part was over. Reluctantly she let go before she kissed it.

'Mia. Hey, you're the receptionist.' Gerry nodded in recognition, his eyes lighting up. 'Great to meet you. I thought you weren't due back until Monday.'

Five days in Ireland had been more than enough for Mia. 'I wasn't, but my mother was doing my head in, so I caught an earlier flight. And I knew there wouldn't be anyone at home so I came straight here. Is my dad around?'

God, you are gorgeous.

'Gone out to a meeting. He should be back by three. It really is great to meet you.' Gerry surveyed her with undisguised pleasure.

'I know, I'm fantastic, aren't I?' Sliding her heavy rucksack off her shoulders and thudding it down onto the counter, Mia said, 'So is this Dad's way of letting me know I've been sacked?'

'Don't worry.' Gerry's smile broadened, revealing even more teeth. 'I'm really a lifeguard, but there was no one free to cover reception today so I'm helping out.'

Lifeguard, eh? Better and better. Lovely broad shoulders and lots of experience in mouth-to-mouth techniques.

'In that case I'll just sit here and watch.' Happily the reception area was quiet. Darting round to his side of the desk, Mia grabbed a high stool and began unzipping her rucksack. 'How old are you, by the way?'

'Fifty-three.'

'Excellent. D'you dye your hair then? Or is that a toupée?'

'I'm seventeen.' Gerry grinned.

'Girlfriend?'

'No. Do you always ask so many personal questions?'

'Only when I want to know the answers. And in case you're wondering, I don't have a boyfriend,' Mia went on happily. 'So that's great news, isn't it? How come you're so brown anyway, d'you use a sunbed?' As she said it she felt the butterflies in her stomach pause for a moment, awaiting Gerry's reply. Could she really bring herself to adore a boy who used a sunbed?

'My parents run a bar in Tenerife. I've been working out there all winter. Only came back to England three days ago. I'm staying with my sister. What's *that*?' Gerry picked up the muslin-wrapped parcel she'd just pulled from her rucksack.

'Soda bread.' He didn't use a sunbed. Yay, he was still perfect. Untying the ends of the muslin cloth and tearing off a chunk of the bread, Mia said, 'Try it. Homemade. I've some cheese in here too – Cashel Blue, lovely stuff. And a gorgeous piece of Cahil Porter.' Triumphantly she produced two smaller packages and began unwrapping them. 'Cahil Porter's made with Guinness, you know. It's completely out of this world.'

'Should we be doing this?' Gerry looked concerned. 'I mean, all this food out here on the desk?'

'Ah, don't worry, there's plenty for everyone.' Breaking off a piece of the marbled Cahil Porter, Mia reached over and popped it into his mouth. 'There now, are you in heaven?'

'I'm in heaven.' Gerry nodded in agreement. Having swallowed the cheese, he looked at her. 'I've never met anyone like you before.'

The butterflies in Mia's stomach got busier, their wings whirring like helicopter blades. Oh God, was she doing it all wrong?

'Is that a good or a bad thing?'

He grinned. 'I'd call it a brilliant thing.'

Phew. Reassured that she wasn't making a complete hash of this flirting malarkey, Mia rummaged once more in her rucksack and brought out a bundle of lumpy socks. Emptying the eggs out of the socks, she said eagerly, 'Do you like duck eggs?'

'Love them.'

'Hot chilli sauce? The hottest chilli sauce ever?'

'Scotch Bonnet? My favourite.'

Mia almost toppled off her stool with excitement. 'Dolly Parton?'

'Who?' Gerry's face fell. 'You mean do I like her music? No, I don't. I can't stand all that waily, twangy stuff.'

They gazed at each other in dismay. Mia's heart sank; this was terrible news.

Leaning towards her, Gerry clutched her hand. 'But if it means that much to you, I could give it another try.'

'Oh yes, of course you can!' Brightening, Mia exclaimed, 'I'll lend you all my CDs!' Overcome with excitement she threw her arms round Gerry's neck and kissed him – *mwah!* – full on the mouth. 'We'll keep playing them over and over again until you change your—'

'*Aaarrgh,* I don't *believe* this!' bellowed a furious voice above them. 'I just do not bloody believe it!'

Tearing her gaze away from Gerry, Mia saw Sadie Sylvester with a face like thunder. As Sadie began stomping down the steel spiral staircase, Gerry muttered worriedly, 'Oh shit.'

He was new, this was only his second day here. Refusing to let him back away, Mia said reassuringly, 'Hey, don't let Cyanide Sadie worry you, nobody takes any notice of that old witch.'

'*You*, let go of him,' Sadie barked at Mia, her magenta ringlets quivering with disdain. Turning her attention to Gerry she said icily, 'And you, are you completely out of your mind? I *told* you not to have anything to do with this girl.'

'Excuse me?' Outraged, Mia shot back, 'How dare you tell him that! You don't own this club! My God, you have a nerve—'

'Sshh, save your breath,' said Gerry. 'She never listens to other people anyway.'

Oh hell. Gazing from Gerry to Sadie and back again, Mia cottoned on at last. 'She's your sister.'

'Cyanide Sadie.' Gerry's mouth began to twitch. 'You didn't tell me they called you that.'

'They don't.' Pointing a scarlet fingernail at Mia, Sadie spat, '*She* does. And if anyone's poisonous around here, let me tell you, it's *her*.'

'It's midday.' Having checked her watch and the timetable on the desk, Mia said coolly, 'Don't you have a class you should be taking?'

Without another word, Sadie turned and stomped back up the staircase.

'Well.' Mia collapsed onto her stool. 'I can't believe you're Sadie's brother. This is terrible news.'

'Why is it terrible?' Looking alarmed, Gerry said, 'Has it put you off me?'

'Not a bit. But hasn't it put you off me?'

'Hey. Annoying my sister has always been my favourite hobby. She doesn't scare me.' His denim-blue eyes alight with mischief, he reached out and touched Mia's face. 'How about you?'

How about her? She thought they were a match made in heaven!

'Ah well, I've always enjoyed a good fight.' Tearing a chunk of crusty, hand-baked soda bread from the loaf and drizzling it with hotter-than-fire chilli sauce, Mia lovingly offered it to her own real-life vision. 'The more we annoy Sadie, the happier I'll be.'

Chapter 59

The time had come, as it invariably did, to call a halt on a relationship that wasn't going anywhere. Connor sighed as he made his way across town to Tabitha's flat. He hated this bit, the telling-them-it-was-all-over bit, but he could no longer put it off. The other day Tabitha had rung to invite him to meet her parents this coming weekend. They were lovely people, she'd eagerly assured him, it wouldn't be a chore and they were *so* looking forward to meeting him.

Connor was sure he would have liked Tabitha's parents, but what would be the point of meeting them? They would be mentally sizing him up as a potential son-in-law and that wasn't fair, on either them or Tabitha. He had made an excuse, followed by another excuse when she had said brightly, 'Well then, how about the weekend after next?'

Tabitha was a great girl. He didn't want to hurt her or string her along. So here he was, about to do the deed as gently as possible.

God, he hoped she wouldn't cry.

'Sweetheart, you're early!' Excited to see him, Tabitha gave him a hug and pulled him into the flat. 'Now don't be cross, I know I said I was cooking tonight, but something's come up and I just haven't had time so we're going to be ordering in a pizza instead.'

'That's fine.' Connor hadn't wanted Tabitha to cook in the first place, but she had gone all Nigella on him and insisted. Finishing with someone over a pizza would be far easier than doing it during the course of some dinner it may have taken her hours to cook.

'Let's have a drink. We need to talk. God, everything's happened so fast.' Hurrying him through to the comfortably cluttered living room, Tabitha sloshed red wine into two glasses. All the better to throw at a man when he chucks you, thought Connor, watching her take out a cigarette. She was wearing a green striped shirt and a figure-hugging pink woollen skirt, and her handbag and jacket were dumped on the blue checked sofa, indicating that she hadn't long arrived home from work.

'So what's all this about then?' Connor pulled a lighter from his trouser pocket and lit her cigarette.

Tabitha exhaled a long stream of smoke. 'I've been offered a new job.'

'Hey, great.'

'In financial journalism.'

'Tab, that's fantastic news!' He was genuinely pleased for her.

Taking a hefty gulp of wine, Tabitha said, 'In New York.'

Connor almost shouted, 'That's *brilliant*,' but sensed it wouldn't be appropriate. Over the rim of her wine glass, Tabitha was eyeing him intently.

Aloud he said, 'Well . . . that's a surprise.'

'I know. And I'm flattered, of course I am. It's always nice to be wanted. But I don't know whether to accept.'

'I see.' Carefully, Connor said, 'And why's that?'

'Well, I was rather hoping you'd guess. It's a pretty good job,' said Tabitha, 'but it's still only a job. How would you feel if I went to New York?'

'Well, I'd . . . um, I don't really . . .'

'Because if you'd rather I turned it down and stayed here,' Tabitha went on hurriedly, 'I would. You know, if you thought we had something worth hanging on to, I'd turn them down in a flash.'

There was a kind of hopeful yearning in her eyes, but it was tinged with sadness.

'Tab,' Connor said gently, 'you're a great girl and I think a lot of you, but you mustn't turn down an opportunity like that on my account.'

There was a long silence, then Tabitha heaved a sigh and said, 'Bugger. How did I know you were going to say that?'

'Sweetheart, it's not you. It's me.'

Tabitha rolled her eyes. 'How did I know you were going to say *that*?'

'I hope we'll always be friends,' Connor struggled on.

'*And* that.'

'You deserve better than me,' said Connor.

'And *that*!' By this time half laughing, half crying, Tabitha picked up her packet of cigarettes and pretended to throw them at him. 'OK, don't say any more, I get the message.' She wiped her eyes and raised her glass. 'Let's have a toast, shall we? To my dazzling new job and my dazzling new life. And to the fact that the next time I hear some man churning out those clichéd old lines, he'll be saying them to me in an American accent.'

They smiled at each other and clinked glasses. Overcome with relief, Connor gave Tabitha a hug, then they settled down together on the sofa.

'You didn't even tell me you were applying for jobs in New York.'

'It wasn't that planned. A friend of mine went over there last year. She emailed me a couple of days ago, to tell me her latest boyfriend had dumped her. I emailed back and told her that mine was about to chuck me. I'd kind of guessed,' Tabitha explained drily in response to the look on Connor's face, 'when you made all those excuses not to meet my parents. Anyway, I jokingly asked Kate if there were any jobs going on her paper. Ten minutes later she rang me from work and told me there was. The next thing I knew, she'd put me on to the editor of the financial section whose assistant had just handed in his notice. We had a long chat – his name's Duane, can you believe it? – and he said he'd need to see some of my work. So yesterday I sat down and wrote three completely brilliant pieces – if I say so myself – about mutual funds, futures and annuities. At midnight I sent them off to him. Then this afternoon he rang back to offer me the job!'

'It's the opportunity of a lifetime. You couldn't turn that down,' said Connor.

'No.' Her smile rueful, Tabitha said, 'But I would have.'

Connor reached for the bottle of wine and topped up her glass. 'Trust me, you'll have the time of your life. And end up meeting someone who really deserves you.'

'How about you, then?' Tabitha eased off her pink high-heeled shoes and tucked her feet under her. Tilting her head to one side, she said, 'Who deserves you?'

Connor pulled a face. 'God only knows. Who'd want an old wreck like me?'

'Don't be flippant. Honestly, typical man. Any mention of emotions and you panic.' Taking a sip of wine, Tabitha said, 'Come on, you can tell me. Who do you like?'

Connor immediately began to panic. As if he was going to tell her *that*. Banishing all thoughts of Nancy firmly from his mind, he said, 'Well, Michelle Pfeiffer's not bad. If you want to put in a good word.'

'See? You're doing it again.'

'Or that Penny Thingummy who reads the news on GMTV. Sparkly eyes,' said Connor. 'And a naughty smile. I like her.'

'How about Nancy?'

'What?' A breezeblock landed with a thud on Connor's chest. Had he just said Nancy's name aloud instead of thinking it? And why was Tabitha looking at him like that?

'You heard.'

'I don't know what you mean.' The breezeblock was pressing ever more heavily on his lungs. Was this how it felt to have a heart attack?

'Oh, come on, Connor, why don't you just admit it? Because I know,' said Tabitha. 'I *saw* you.'

'Saw me where? Saw me when? Doing what?' He'd felt like this once before, upon being caught stealing apples from the local priest's garden. He'd denied it, despite the fact that apples were bulging from the pockets of his grey school trousers. For thieving *and* having the shameless gall to lie about it, the priest had walloped him so hard he hadn't been able to sit down for a week.

Except he'd been eight years old then. At least Tabitha wasn't likely to give him a walloping.

'Your face.' Lighting another cigarette and taking fast, jerky puffs, Tabitha said, 'You should see yourself. OK, remember me ringing you from work after Mia glued herself to that lion?'

Rather than risk actually saying anything, Connor nodded.

'Well, I wasn't at work. As soon as I got your message I jumped into a cab and came down to Trafalgar Square, but you'd already left by then, so I guessed I'd find you at the police station. And I did,' Tabitha went on, her expression rueful. 'When I turned up, there you were. Outside the station with Nancy. I watched the two of you together from across the road. That's where I was when I phoned you.' Puffing faster than ever on her cigarette, she said, 'That's when I knew, really. Well, you'd have to be blind not to know. It was so obvious.'

Connor exhaled slowly. Tabitha sounded resigned rather than angry. 'Was it?'

'Oh yes.' Her smile was crooked. 'Well, I clung on for a bit, you know. Tried to pretend it hadn't happened. Deep down though, you know when you're beaten, don't you? But what I don't understand is why the two of you never got together in the first place. I mean, what was to stop it happening before I came along?'

Oh well, if Tabitha could be blunt, so could he.

'It hasn't happened because Nancy doesn't want it to happen,' Connor admitted. Now that it was finally out in the open, he felt a rush of relief. 'I'm crazy about her, but she just isn't interested. I asked her out more than once and she said no every time. So you see, I do know how it feels not to have your feelings returned. And there's nothing I can do about it.' Resignedly he said, 'I suppose I'm just not Nancy's type.'

Two dimples appeared in Tabitha's cheeks. 'You berk.'

'I know. God, talk about embarrassing. To think you could tell, just from watching from across the street.' Closing his eyes, Connor sighed. 'She must be laughing her head off. I can't believe I was so obvious.'

'You complete and utter berk,' Tabitha repeated, patting his knee and starting to laugh. 'You really don't get it, do you? When I was watching the two of you, it wasn't just you who was being obvious.'

'What?' Connor's eyes shot open in disbelief.

'You should have seen the way Nancy was looking at you when you weren't watching. I'm serious,' Tabitha insisted, stubbing out her cigarette. 'This was absolutely a two-way thing. I know what I saw that day, and I don't know why she turned you down before. But trust me, you are one hundred per cent *most definitely* Nancy's type.'

Chapter 60

A letter had been pushed through the letterbox. Nancy, arriving home from work, bent to pick it up and carried it through to the kitchen. The house was empty. Rennie had whisked Carmen down to Nice for a couple of days and Rose was spending the weekend with William at his home in Weston-super-Mare. Nancy dumped her bag on the kitchen table, filled the kettle at the sink then messily tore open the envelope with her name on it.

Her name but no address, indicating that the letter had been hand-delivered.

Except it wasn't a letter, it was an invitation. As the kettle behind her came to the boil, Nancy gazed at the thick white card and felt the first stirrings of annoyance. Bloody hell, this was all she needed.

'Dear Nancy,' said the invitation. 'You are cordially invited to a picnic in Fitzallen Square on Friday at six o'clock. No need to RSVP. Just be there, please.'

It wasn't signed, but it didn't need to be. And it was already two minutes past six. Irritated, Nancy slapped the invitation down and stormed through to the sitting room. Bloody Jonathan, up to his stupid tricks again. *Why* couldn't he accept that she wasn't going back to him? She'd told him not to come down to London but that was Jonathan for you, he'd never been able to admit defeat.

There was no sign of him outside in the darkening square but Nancy knew he'd be there waiting for her, somewhere out of sight behind the clump of trees and bushes to the left of the wooden bench. She had, in effect, belittled his attempt to woo her with two hundred pounds' worth of flowers, so now he was going that bit further, upping the stakes, making a more extravagant gesture that would no doubt include vintage champagne, smoked salmon and, knowing Jonathan, crystal glasses and fine china plates.

God, what an idiot he was. Checking her watch – ten past six – Nancy wondered what Jonathan would do if she simply ignored the invitation. How long would he stay out there, waiting for her to turn up?

That was one possibility. The other was to march over there right now and tell him in no uncertain terms that he was wasting his time. Which to do? Which to go for? Raking her fingers agitatedly through her hair, Nancy realised she couldn't bear the thought of Jonathan sitting out there all evening with his ridiculous picnic, waiting for her. She had to get rid of him now. Once he was gone, she could get on with having a bath and washing her hair in peace.

Dusk was falling as Nancy crossed the road and clicked open the gate. Reaching the wooden bench she turned left and saw the picnic area exactly where she'd known it would be. There were ballons tied to the lower branches of the trees in the mini-glade and candles flickering in glass holders, and a green and red tartan rug had been laid out on the grass.

No vintage champagne, no smoked salmon and no glittering crystal. No Jonathan either.

Instead there was a cake.

Moving towards the rug, Nancy heard a rustling of leaves and saw Connor step out from behind the cluster of trees.

Evenly he said, 'You're late.'

Adrenaline zapped through every fibre of her body. Nancy, her mouth dry and her brain a whirl of confusion, really wished she hadn't stormed out of the house without first combing her hair and repairing her end-of-a-long-day-at-work make-up.

'You didn't sign the invitation. I thought it was from Jonathan.'

A flicker of apprehension crossed Connor's face. 'Were you hoping it was from him?'

'In a way.' Nancy couldn't begin to figure out what was going on. 'But only so I could march over here and tell him to fuck off back to Scotland.'

Connor almost smiled, and she realized it was probably the first time he'd heard her say fuck.

'Well, that's good. The reason I didn't sign the invitation was in case I lost my nerve and ran away. Then you wouldn't have known it had come from me.'

Lost his nerve? Connor was always so utterly laid back and relaxed it was impossible to think of him as being nervous. Yet he *was* looking ill at ease, his hands shoved into the front pockets of his jeans, his hair more rumpled and his eyebrows somehow less . . . assured than normal. And he was scuffing the ground with the toes of his Timberland boots like a teenager. Her heart banging against her ribcage, Nancy said, 'Where's

339

Tabitha?' and wondered if at any moment Tabitha would leap out from behind the bushes shrieking, 'Here I am! *Surprise!*'

Connor shrugged awkwardly and said, 'It's over. Tab's fine. She's going to live in New York. This was kind of her idea, actually.' He indicated the picnic. 'All this.'

Horror and shame seized Nancy by the throat. Had Tabitha finished with Connor and somehow managed to persuade him, against his will, to make some form of clumsy play for her instead? *Out of pity?* Oh God, oh God.

'Look, there's no need,' Nancy blurted out, her skin crawling with embarrassment as she backed away from the picnic, the candles, the cake. 'I don't know what Tab's trying to do here, but—'

'Ah shit, I've got this all wrong again.' His Irish accent becoming more pronounced, Connor shook his head in despair and said urgently, 'Wait, you can't go, it isn't what you're thinking at all, I'm just making a complete balls-up as usual. Listen to me,' he pleaded, taking a couple of steps towards Nancy. 'It's not what Tab's trying to do here, it's what *I'm* trying to do. It's just that according to Tab I did it all wrong last time so this time she gave me some advice on how to make it go a bit better.'

Nancy began to tremble. 'I don't know what you're talking about.'

'All this.' Gesturing helplessly at the balloons, the rug, the candles flickering in their holders, Connor said, 'She knows how much I like you, but I told her you weren't interested in me because when I asked you out before you said no. Tab said I had to make more of an effort, do something . . . you know, romantic. So that's what I'm doing, but to be honest it's not really working out all that well. I've never tried anything like this before. Tab said it would be great, but now that you're here to see it, I feel a bit stupid.'

OK, breathe, just try and breathe normally. Feeling light-headed, Nancy said, 'I heard you telling Mia I wasn't your type. In your office at the club. You sounded pretty certain then.'

'Oh God.' Connor slammed his hand against his forehead. 'I just told her that to stop her sticking her oar in! You know what Mia's like. I wanted to do it by myself, without my bossy daughter scaring you witless with her high-pressure sales pitch.'

For the first time Nancy smiled, thinking of all the trouble Mia had unwittingly caused.

'So that was it,' Connor went on. 'I thought I had no chance at all. Until Tabitha told me otherwise.'

That wiped the smile off Nancy's face. Appalled, she cried, '*What? How did Tabitha know?*'

'Just did. Saw us together outside Charing Cross police station,' Connor shrugged, 'and that was it. According to Tab it was blindingly obvious. One of those girl things, I suppose. Anyway, that was why I took her advice with this whole making-an-effort malarkey.' Scratching his head and pulling a face he said, 'Which just goes to show how bloody daft I am.'

Nancy felt her heart swelling to beachball proportions. 'I don't think you're bloody daft.'

Connor looked hopeful. 'You don't?'

'You made me a cake. I think that's the most romantic thing anyone's ever done for me.' Unable to hold back any longer, Nancy closed the distance between them and threw her arms round Connor. Her hair was uncombed, her lipstick was worn off and she looked a fright but it didn't matter. She kissed him anyway.

Oh yes, this was definitely, wonderfully, gloriously romantic.

Connor eventually pulled away. For several seconds he gazed down at her without speaking.

'What?' said Nancy.

'Just waiting to see if you wipe your mouth.'

Breaking into a broad smile, Nancy kissed him again for good measure before dragging him over to the rug. 'We've got to try this cake. I haven't even seen it properly yet. I can't believe you actually made it yourself.'

It was obvious that Connor had. No self-respecting shop would ever sell a cake as badly decorated as this.

'It's harder than it looks to ice a cake.' Connor's tone was defensive.

Nancy surveyed the lumpy white icing, thickly slapped on all over and studded with Maltesers and fruit pastilles for that elegant finishing touch. The cake itself was round, six inches in diameter and decorated with a red satin ribbon like a gaudy bride-to-be's garter. Struggling to keep a straight face, she said, 'What kind of sponge is it?'

'Oh, you know.' Connor shrugged modestly. 'The usual kind.'

He'd actually made her a cake. Picturing him getting into a flap in his kitchen, inexpertly weighing out flour and cracking eggs, Nancy's heart swooped with love. Since he'd forgotten to bring a knife along, she flipped open the Swiss Army penknife on her keyring.

'No, don't cut it!' shouted Connor.

'Don't be daft, we've got to see what it tastes like – *oh*.'

Taking the penknife from Nancy, Connor drew her to him once more.

341

'OK, that's my cover well and truly blown. I'm rubbish at cakes. But I do have other talents, I promise.'

Thank goodness for that.

'Don't worry, I'm still impressed.' Feeling she could afford to be magnanimous, Nancy said, 'You remembered that I like Maltesers.'

'I did.'

'And fruit pastilles.'

'Those too.' Connor looked pleased with himself.

Reaching up to kiss him, Nancy said happily, 'And no one's ever decorated a bath sponge for me before.'